T0354851

Three Sisters

DAPHANIE CAROL TAYLOR

authorHOUSE®

AuthorHouse™ UK
1663 Liberty Drive
Bloomington, IN 47403 USA
www.authorhouse.co.uk
Phone: 0800.197.4150

Published by AuthorHouse 05/19/2017

ISBN: 978-1-5246-7725-1 (sc)
ISBN: 978-1-5246-7724-4 (e)

Library of Congress Control Number: 2017901273

Print information available on the last page.

Any people depicted in stock imagery provided by Thinkstock are models, and such images are being used for illustrative purposes only. Certain stock imagery © Thinkstock.

This book is printed on acid-free paper.

CHAPTER ONE

Three sisters – Evelyne, the eldest; Ruth, the middle sister; and Joanne, the youngest – lived with their parents, John and Jane Kershaw, in St John's Wood, a leafy suburb of London. Their father, an industrialist, owned an engineering company which had been handed down from two generations. John Kershaw, the third generation, was proud of its history as a forerunner in the industry. Times were now changing in England after the Second World War – "the war to end all wars," said the government of the day. It had made the John Kershaw family very wealthy.

Evelyne and Ruth, the two oldest girls, had an idyllic upbringing and could pursue all their ambitions. The family fortune enabled them to attend the same private school for girls their mother had attended years earlier. Eve shone at the school and ended up being head girl. Though John was proud of all his daughters, Eve was his favourite. Ruth, for her part, was very sociable and enrolled in all sorts of outer-school activities, mainly because they got her beyond the school grounds. She never aspired to head girl. Both girls did well in their academics, and university was the next step to achieving their aspirations. They were eighteen months apart in age, and they were extremely close.

When Joanne came along and was old enough, she wanted to attend the local girl's grammar school in Oxford with her friends. Her mother wouldn't hear of it. She was adamant that Joanne, like Eve and Ruth, would go to Hadlington Girls School. Joanne protested, but to no avail. From day one, she was anti-public school and became a thorough nuisance to her teachers. The headmistress was dismayed that Joanne was not like her mother or her older sisters.

Jane Kershaw encouraged her daughters to reach their full potential, follow their dreams, and become as independent as possible, much to the dismay of their father. He thought his girls should be at home, preparing to marry the right men – and, of course, into the right families. Jane, however, saw that times were changing. People, including women, wanted more freedom to do whatever they wanted, within reason. This was even more so in Joanne's era.

Despite her unhappiness regarding her parents' choice of schools, Joanne did knuckle down to her studies. She was a very talented artist, like her mother. Jane wasn't surprised at all by this. John told his daughter, "One day I can see you following in your mother's footsteps."

Joanne just smiled at him and muttered under her breath, "No chance."

Much to everyone's surprise, Joanne succeeded in her academics, which meant she could go to university. Her mother was shocked at the results. The head was astonished as well. She shook her head at Jane and admitted, "I don't know how she managed to achieve the grades she needed. It's totally beyond me." Jane was just relieved. At least now John wouldn't keep going on about Joanne and what a waste of money it was sending her to Hadlington.

While Evelyne and Ruth enjoyed every minute of their debutante experience, Joanne of course rebelled and swore she would never follow that route. She had more freedom than her sisters ever had in their teenage years. After all, it was the sixties. Joanne – Jo to her friends – shared a flat with five others while at college in London, studying art and design. When it was rag week, everyone was involved with wild parties, drinking, smoking, and kicking against the establishment of the day. The younger generation wanted change, and the sooner the better.

Jane despaired of Joanne, and John threatened to stop her generous allowance. None of that made a difference to Jo. Evelyne, being the eldest, tried to persuade Joanne to do her studies first and then let her hair down. Ruth, however, was too preoccupied with her own career to worry about Joanne now.

Despite everyone's doubts, Joanne managed to get her art-and-design degree. The family was delighted.

* * *

At the height of summer, the family – except for Eve and Ruth – headed off to their villa in Tuscany. Jane looked forward to spending her summer there, as she adored Tuscany. It was one of the few pleasures that really belonged to her and only her. The memories she had of summers gone by warmed her heart and made her smile.

In Jane's day, the only thing her father had wanted was to marry her off into the right family. She really hadn't been in love with John Kershaw. On the contrary – she was deeply in love with a fellow artist called Peter Richards and really wanted to marry him. He was a tall and handsome man, the kind every woman dreamed about. She begged her parents to let her marry Peter, pleading that she didn't want to marry John Kershaw. But they paid no attention. To them, it was a matter of self-esteem and social standing in the village.

Her father told her, "He comes from a good family. He will be a good husband, and you'll want for nothing."

Jane continued to plead with her father, but it was of no use. She still harboured resentment at having to marry into the Kershaw family. Oh, it was true she'd never wanted for anything, but Jane was never really madly in love with John. He was no knight in shining armour, whisking her off to utopia.

Joanne loathed being in Tuscany. She wanted to be in London, where it was all happening. Over the years, there were about six families in the area from England who owned or rented a villa for the summer. Most of the kids had grown up and no longer came to Tuscany. Only four of them were left. Marjorie Winters and Elizabeth Ashurst were Jane's best pals from Hadlington, and they kept in touch with the Kershaws on a regular basis. In fact, they all lived very close to each other in London and quite often socialised there.

Joanne and her pals Maggie Winters and Racheal Ashurst formed a gang and ventured out of the village into territories unknown. Everyone pointed at Joanne as the gang leader. They caused considerable havoc around the villages. They were caught drinking on more than one occasion. Maggie and Racheal smoked pot – though, to her credit, Jo warned the pair about how dangerous it was. Tommy, Racheal's twin, agreed with Joanne. Peter, Maggie's brother, didn't show any interest in what his sister got up to.

When Jo's father arrived, he was met with all sorts of tales about his daughter and what she and the others had been up to. Her mother was most distressed because she couldn't control her. Joanne's father gave her an ultimatum: "Start behaving, or when you return to England, I will cut off your allowance. Do I make myself clear?" Joanne just nodded and sheepishly crept out of the room.

Her mother just looked at her with a face that said it all. But Jane wondered at times about Jo. She wasn't at all like her sisters, and that sometimes bothered her. Jane had had Joanne in her late thirties, which sometimes brought a tinge of guilt.

When the gang came for Jo the next day, she told them everything that had gone on. They promised to be careful for the duration of their holiday. That didn't mean they were angels. It was merely a case of out of sight, out of mind.

* * *

Soon, the holiday was over. With no more college for Jo, she had to think about getting a job. She had one or two ideas of what she wanted to do. If anything, she was cleverer than her sisters. She hardly did any revision all the time she was at college; it came easy to her.

Joanne begged her father to let her rent one of his properties in the Soho area. Allowing this was something he'd regret for a long time after. It was the swinging sixties, and Jo wanted to be in the thick of it. She was in her element. Jo met up with her sisters every so often and stayed over at their shared flat in Sloane Court.

Evelyne was worried about Jo's lifestyle. She feared nothing good would come of it. Ruth, however, was too preoccupied with her own studies to worry about Jo. She had obtained her doctor's degree and was working at Guy's Hospital. She had two more years to become a fully qualified doctor in paediatrics. Jo thought the world of her sisters, but she felt Ruth was always distant. Ruth had to work very hard to get into med school and didn't want any distractions. She needed to concentrate on her career.

* * *

It was nearing Christmas. The family planned its usual get-together for two or three days, depending on calendars and workloads. Jo wasn't too keen about going, but Evelyne persuaded her to come and spend time with the family. Jo agreed but added, "If something better comes up, Eve, I might stay here."

However, Jo did go down to see the family, taking a chap with her. Mosie – no one knew why they called him that – worked in a laboratory near Letchworth. Where Jo dug him up, God only knows.

Jo's parents were mortified when they saw him. He had long, scruffy, shoulder-length hair. His denim jeans had holes in them, and he looked as though he hadn't washed for weeks. Their other guests were embarrassed. Jo's father took her aside. "What the hell are you playing at, bringing him here?"

Jo interrupted her father. "He is called Mosie."

"I don't care what the bloody hell he is called. Get rid of him!"

Jo looked at him and said, "If he goes, then I go."

Her father stared right back at her and said, "Then go, and don't bring him here again."

So, without leave or goodbye, Jo stormed out of the house vowing she would never return, no matter what. Mosie put his arm around her and said, "Come on – I know a place we can go to crash out for a couple of days and get pissed."

They set off in Jo's Mini to go somewhere near Bletchley to Mosie's friends, It only took an hour's drive. When they arrived, the party was already swinging.

This would be the most disastrous and significant decision in Jo's life – one it would take her years to escape from.

John Kershaw went back to join his other guests and apologise to them.

"No need to apologise, John. We are in the same boat as you," replied another father in the group. "Don't know what's got into these kids these days."

Another said, "I blame the government. It's too darn soft. We should have kept the national service. The army would have sorted these layabouts out. It's a free-for-all these days."

Soon dinner was ready, and the guests trotted into the dining room. Jane asked John about Joanne. "Later, Jane. Not now," he replied.

Dinner was cordial. Eve and Ruth were dying to know what Father had said to Jo, but they knew it wasn't the right time or place to ask.

Charles Winters asked Ruth how she was enjoying working at Guy's. Ruth said she was loving every minute of it and was looking forward to finishing her course in paediatrics, which would take another two years.

"Blimey, that long? No wonder doctors get paid handsomely!" he said, and everyone laughed.

Robert Ashurst then asked Eve about her job in the city and whether she was enjoying it. "Fine, Mr Ashurst. As you know, I qualified as a lawyer two years ago, and I still have one more year left to become a fully fledged lawyer, so I know how Ruth's feeling. It seems endless."

"You do company law, don't you?" asked Mr Ashurst.

Eve replied, "Yes. I thought it would be more interesting for me, and it may be helpful to Father one day, who knows."

Jane said, "That's enough of our family. Now tell us about yours. Is Maggie getting along all right at Cambridge?"

Marjorie Winters winced and looked at her husband.

Charles Winters answered, "It's Margret's last year, and she still hasn't a clue what she wants to do – just like your Joanne, defiant and wilful. We can't do a thing with her. Her head is full of the swinging sixties. She gets up to all sorts, and we hardly see her."

Winters carried on, "Now Peter is a totally different kettle of fish – very studious, loves what he is doing, and has no time for any of that nonsense. He wants to be a civil engineer."

Jane then asked, "What about you, Robert? How are your two doing?"

Robert started to tell them that for now, things seemed fine, although Racheal was a handful at times. "We hardly see her. It's all this women's lib we keep hearing about. I bet if we cut her allowance off, she would come running home soon enough. They just have six months to do. Tommy wants to be a journalist; he fancies travelling around the world with his job, so who knows. We are keeping our fingers crossed. With all this smoking pot and 'Peace man' ..." Robert put his two fingers up as a gesture, and everyone thought it was very funny. It lightened the conversation.

When dinner was finished, the men went into the games room and the ladies into the lounge to play bridge. Time was getting on. The maid came in with coffee and liqueurs, and eventually the men joined them, drinking mainly whisky.

Soon, it was time for their guests to leave. "Our place next year, John," said Robert Ashurst. John Kershaw nodded in agreement.

"Don't forget the New Year with us, Jane," said Marjorie Winters.

Jane replied, "Looking forward to it, Marjorie."

It was well past midnight. The family all had another nightcap and wished each other goodnight. Eve and Ruth went upstairs, chattering all the way. They pecked each other on the cheek and then went into their respective bedrooms, probably to ponder on what had gone on. Eve was in a more pensive mood. She was hoping Joanne hadn't done anything stupid.

Chapter Two

Ruth was also in a thoughtful mood. She was worried about her forthcoming exams early next year in May, to be precise. If everything went to plan, she would be a step closer to becoming a paediatrician. She had really enjoyed herself being with the family and didn't realise how much she had missed her parents. It was good to get away, relax, and chill out. She was looking forward to having a few more days with her parents – hopefully being waited on hand and foot, and being spoiled rotten.

When John and Jane retired, all they could talk about was Joanne. John told Jane everything that had happened – every single detail. Jane was deeply upset about what she had learned. After all, Jo was the one who was really close to her, or so she had thought. It hurt to think the girl could just walk out on her family like she did, without goodbye or leave.

I'll never forgive her for what she did tonight and the embarrassment she caused, thought Jane. She was very upset indeed, especially when she thought of the sacrifice she made in giving birth to Jo.

The next morning, Jane tried to dismiss the happenings of the day before and focus on enjoying her time with her other two daughters. After all, it was supposed to be a joyous time. The girls indeed enjoyed their stay at the Harrows. Finally, it was time to leave. Kisses and goodbyes were in order.

* * *

It was now well into the new year. Spring was just around the corner. Eve was caught up with a company takeover. It was a very complex case, to say the least. Eve was part of a team, all of whom were concerned about the case. They had to leave no stone unturned.

The company involved in the takeover had assets scattered all over the place, so they had to be very careful as to the true value of the takeover for their clients. It meant they had to dot every *I* and cross every *T* till they were satisfied that the deal was worth it to their clients and that there were no other assets hidden away in an offshore bank somewhere.

Eve liaised very closely with the client's accountants and the lawyers representing the other company involved. One of them was called Matthew Emerson. Matt, unknown to Eve, was also cheesed off with the case. Eve was wishing she hadn't taken the case on, but she couldn't just walk away; her reputation was on the line. She just knew she had to see it through for the sake of her client, even if it meant they would walk away from the deal, which could cost thousands in fees.

The company that wanted to buy her client's company was only interested in the building and land, or so it seemed to Eve. The company's representatives were evasive about its true assets. Eve was very suspicious about it all. She thought the price on offer was well under the market value.

Eve, along with a fellow lawyer, arranged a meeting with Matt and his associates to discuss the case, which they agreed to do. They discussed the case from each other's perspective, not divulging any information about their clients but trying to find a solution. Matt was also weary of his client and its reputation on dealing with other companies in buyouts. In fact, he thought they were brokers looking for established companies that would fit the bill for prospective buyers either to keep as a profit-making business or, in so many cases, strip for assets, especially if the company was sitting on potentially prime building land. He was fed up with his clients and their cloak-and-dagger tactics. He couldn't get a straight answer from them.

Eve was uneasy hearing about this, and it confirmed that her suspicions were correct. She was now sorry she had involved Matt and his associate. Eve told him, "I think we'll call it a day." She was concerned about putting herself and her work colleague in any sort of jeopardy with the case. Meeting up with Matt and his associate hadn't been the best idea. It was a monumental error in judgement, not letting her employers know what she intended to do.

By the time Eve reached home, her head was spinning. When she entered the flat, Ruth was in situ. She had finished her final examination paper and was hoping that she had done enough to see her through.

"Boy, am I glad to see you," said Ruth. "I want to let my hair down tonight and paint the town."

Eve looked at her and said, "I'm really sorry, Ruth. Perhaps we can let our hair down tomorrow instead. I'm bushed."

Ruth was disappointed but understood.

* * *

The next day was Saturday. They set off to go into town, reaching Carnaby Street first. It was crowded with fashionable shops, and all the bars were packed out. They entered a bistro, managed to find a table, sat down, and talked for ages. They wondered what Jo was up to. Ruth was now able to focus on Jo's goings-on. She also was worried.

They did some window-shopping and laughed at some of the outrageous fashion designs. Nearly every shop in Carnaby Street was playing extremely loud music. It took them all their time to hear themselves speak or to hear one another. The place was buzzing. There was a certain atmosphere in that part of London.

They decided to go to Oxford Street. To them, it was a more genteel way to shop. Even these fashionable shops, however, were changing to a more modern style.

The sisters had a super weekend together. Ruth was totally relaxed – well, almost – till her results came through. Since she was now on leave, she thought of going to the Harrows for a couple of weeks or so. The Harrows was their parents' country home in Ditton Thames.

"Do you fancy coming down with me, Eve?" asked Ruth.

"I only wish I could, Ruth. I need a break. It's hectic now at work. We are working on a very complex takeover bid, and it's giving everyone a headache."

Ruth was sorry to hear this. "Another time, perhaps." Eve just nodded at her.

They caught a taxi to the Savoy for afternoon tea. Upon arrival, they were greeted by James, the commissionaire.

"Nice to see you, Lady Eve, Lady Ruth." He touched his hat. They both acknowledged him and giggled as they entered and walked towards the lounge, where they ordered drinks. When the waiter arrived, he said the drinks were from the gentleman sitting over there. They both looked, and to their astonishment, it was their mother and father. They immediately went over to join their parents.

"Congratulation, Father, on your knighthood!" said Eve. "Sorry I couldn't make the ceremony."

"That goes for me too, Dad. We are very proud of you," Ruth said.

He just beamed at them both.

Ruth then looked at her mother and said, "Do we have to call you Lady Mum now?" They all laughed.

Eve said, "We know what you mean. It's daunting when someone calls me 'Lady Evelyne.'"

"That goes for me, too," said Ruth. "It somehow doesn't fit well with Dr Ruth Kershaw." Everyone laughed.

Their mother said, "I wish everyone we know personally would just call us John and Jane like they used to. It irritates me when my best friends call me Lady Jane."

"You'll get used to it, Mother. You must do," said Eve.

Sir John added, "Here, here," and they all chuckled.

They spent a lovely afternoon. Everyone who knew John Kershaw kept coming to congratulate him on his knighthood. No one mentioned Jo. Well, at least the girls never mentioned her. They didn't want to spoil their parents' day.

Soon it came time to leave.

"It's about time you two came down and stayed for the weekend," their mother said.

Ruth said, "Well, as a matter of fact, I was planning to come down in a couple of days."

Her mother was delighted. She missed her girls very much. "Will we see you too, Evelyne?"

"Sorry, Mother, I have a very nasty case on now regarding a takeover. There is something fishy about it, and it is difficult to get proper answers."

"If there's anything I can do, Evelyne, get in touch," said her father.

"I will," Eve replied.

"It was nice to see Mum and Dad," said Ruth as they headed back to their flat. Eve agreed. They hailed a taxi to Slone Court, entered the flat, kicked off their shoes, and relaxed, each in her own thoughts – Ruth about her graduation day, which wasn't that far away (presuming she had done enough in her finals), and Eve about the case that was causing her all sorts of headaches. The client wanted to finalise the deal one way or another. It had gone on long enough for his liking. Eve still had this nagging feeling that things were not quite right. After an hour or so, Eve decided to retire for the night, leaving Ruth deep in thought.

* * *

It was now graduation day for Ruth. Her mother was fussing around. Eve and her father thought it amusing. Upon arrival, they had been invited by the chancellor's office to have lunch along with other dignitaries. Ruth, of course, couldn't attend. The chancellor greeted Sir John and Lady Jane Kershaw warmly. Sir John knew quite a few people, mainly politicians and academics. Eve didn't have a clue, nor did her mum, but Jane was loving it. She felt like royalty.

After lunch, they all made their way to the main hall for the presentation. The first to be presented were the graduates who had achieved honours with their degrees. Ruth Kershaw received her doctor's degree at last. Sir John and Lady Jane were delighted, and so was Eve. After all, Ruth had worked so hard. It had taken four years of her life, plus another three years, but now she would be known as Dr Ruth Kershaw, paediatrician. She was at the bottom of the ladder, so to speak, next to her mentors, but Ruth relished every minute of the accolades she received.

The day soon went into evening. By this time, Sir John was tired, and so too was Lady Jane. They excused themselves from the celebrations. Eve and Ruth decided to stay a while longer. Luckily, Sir John had booked into a hotel for the night.

Ruth and Eve partied nearly all night. By this time, everyone was drunk. Most of them were so relieved that it was finally over – no more tutorials and not a university in sight. They had all had enough and just wanted to let their hair down.

A couple of students came over to Ruth and said they were off to another party. "Do you and your friend fancy coming?" one asked.

Ruth looked at Eve and said, "Why not?" So off they went to another house party somewhere in the back and beyond.

Eve was beginning to sober up. She was very anxious, Ruth was now falling asleep. Eve tried to wake her, but it was no use – she was well gone. Eve noticed a sign which said Baldock. "Can you let us out here?" asked Eve. "Ruth isn't feeling too well."

The van stopped, and out they got. By this time, it was six in the morning. It felt cold even though it was late July. Eve tried to get her bearings, and then she heard a car. She saw that it was a taxi and waved it down.

"Can you take us to Cambridge?" asked Eve.

"I'm finishing now. I can drop you off at Stevenage if you want – it's on my way home."

Eve jumped at the chance. She too was feeling tired. By the time they arrived at the Roebuck Inn, it was seven o'clock.

The night manager came into view. Eve asked the manager if he had any rooms, and he said there was only one – a double room. Eve didn't hesitate. "That will do," she told him.

After the necessary paperwork, someone took them to the room. It was adequate; that's all you could say. Ruth, by this time, had started to focus. "Where are we?"

"You might well ask," said Eve.

Ruth could tell Eve was not pleased. Ruth was trying to recollect what had happened. It started to unfold in her mind.

"I'm so sorry, Eve," said Ruth.

Eve just ignored her sister. All Eve wanted to do was sleep. She put a "do not disturb" sign on the door and then got into bed. Ruth sheepishly followed. It wasn't too long before they fell fast asleep.

Ruth woke up first. She looked for the time and managed to find her watch, and then she proceeded to the bathroom. Her head was banging. She was well and truly hung-over, and she vowed never again. When she had finished, she looked at her watch and saw that it was three in the afternoon. Good heavens!

She went to Eve and said, "Wake up, Eve. Come on, sleepyhead. Time to get going."

Eve just groaned and tried to ignore her sister.

"Evie, get up! It's past three in the afternoon."

A little alarm bell started to ring in Eve's ear. "What!" she exclaimed and grabbed for her watch. After an hour, they went to see the receptionist about trains to London. The receptionist gave Eve a timetable. The trains were reduced on Sundays, but luckily there was one due at five in the evening to Euston Station.

"That'll do," she said. By this time, it was half past four. "Can you order a taxi to the station, please?" asked Eve. The taxi arrived within five minutes and took them to Stevenage station.

CHAPTER THREE

Meanwhile, Jo had found a job working in a fashion designer's shop in a top London house. She loved working there, but her employers were not too happy with the way she conducted herself in front of clients. They warned Jo on several occasions to dress and behave in a manner appropriate to the surroundings she worked in. What she did in her own time was her business.

The owners loved her work, but to put it bluntly, Jo had to conform to the strict rules of conduct the company had laid down. Of course, she paid no attention to the warnings she was given. Eventually, her employers lost patience with her and gave her a month's salary to leave.

Jo left with a few choice expletives along the way, much to the owners' disgust. They would have been more disgusted with Jo had they known she had a title. As it was, they threatened to have her thrown out if she didn't leave quietly. They did not want the clients to hear what was going on. After all, they had their reputation to think about.

The manager turned to her boss and said, "Such talent going to waste."

The boss agreed, but it was a great relief that Jo had left.

* * *

Jo went immediately to a place she knew where her so-called mates would be, and she decided to paint the town. Her drinking went on all night. The next morning, she had no idea where she was. She fumbled about, falling over bodies, and managed to pull the blanket that was over the window so she could look for her clothes.

A voice said, "Going already? Come on, let's do an encore."

Jo was horrified. She didn't even know who the lad was. She just took one look at him and said, "Piss off, you moron."

He laughed. "You didn't say that last night. Come on, let me show you a good time."

Jo just scampered out of the room. She tiptoed downstairs, stepping over bodies, and managed to get out of the building.

It took Jo a long time to get into her head what she had done. She was most concerned about any repercussions there might be. Once she got outside, she noticed that it was an empty office block which was up for sale. They had all been squatting in the property.

She went to look for her car. Fortunately for Jo, she hadn't been robbed at the squat, which was a great relief. Eventually, she found the car. It had a parking ticket stuck on it, which she just tossed on the floor. After about an hour, some additional expletives, and a hair of the hound, she decided to go and see Evie at her flat, hoping her sister would be there.

Eve and Ruth were just having breakfast when the doorbell rang. Eve looked puzzled and then had a sudden panic, hoping it wasn't that Matt Emerson. She cautiously opened the door, and suddenly Jo brushed past her.

"Gee, that smells good! I'm starving!" Jo exclaimed.

Eve could smell the booze on her and the cigarette smoke. Eve was not amused, and neither was Ruth. "Not before you get cleaned up. You know where the bathroom is," Eve said in a tone that Jo knew only too well.

An hour later, Jo came in looking more like herself. Eve had prepared bacon and eggs plus toast for Jo, who ate as though she hadn't eaten in days.

"Where the hell have you been? You look dreadful," said Ruth.

Jo looked at them both and said, "I've just been sacked," and she came out with some more expletives.

Eve was really cross with her. "Jo, no swearing, do you hear me? You weren't brought up to live like this. Pull yourself together. A girl with your standing should be showing an example, and with your talent you will always find work if you knuckle down to it."

Jo just looked at them both, and the penny dropped. *Gosh, you are duplicates of my parents. I'm an individual. I do what I want,* Jo said to herself.

Ruth asked Jo, "What do you intend to do now?"

"Not sure yet. I might go back home, or I might go to St Albans. I have some friends there. Also, Maggie Winters is there. I can crash out with her."

Eve changed the conversation. "Ruth's now Dr Kershaw, paediatrician."

Jo knew Ruth had worked hard to become a doctor. "I'm truly happy for you, Ruth. You deserve it after all the studying you've had to do."

Ruth was taken by surprise. "Thanks, Jo. That's one of the nicest things you have ever said to me."

Eve then said, "I have to go to work in an hour. You can stay here if you want."

Jo replied, "Thanks for offering, but I need to get my head around a few things first. I will write and let you know where I am staying." With that, she hugged her sisters and left.

Ruth looked Eve and said, "I didn't like the look of her. She has gotten so thin, and the drinking won't help any. Dad and Mum have spoiled her rotten. It's this generation gap we keep being told about. Mark my words, no good will come of it. She will either grow out of it and settle down or go into self-destruction mode."

Eve just nodded and then said to Ruth, "Not too sure what time I'll be home tonight. It's this case I'm working on."

"Not to worry, Eve," said Ruth. "I may drive down to the Harrows. I'll leave a note if I do."

They hugged each other, and Eve left for work.

* * *

By the time she arrived, everyone was in a tiswas. "What's happening?" Eve asked.

"Matt Emerson has been on the telephone and has given our client an ultimatum."

When Eve heard this, she went straight to Mr Hunter's office. She knocked and entered. Sitting there were her two bosses and their client. They looked at her. "Yes, what is it?" said Mr Owen, one of the senior partners.

"Can I have a word before you make any decision?" she asked.

They looked at one another. "Well, get on with it," said Mr Hunter.

Eve thought, *Well, here goes*, and set off telling them what she had discovered in her investigations into the takeover bid. "It turns out that the company you are dealing with is a type of company known as asset strippers," she began. "Their sole purpose is to look at companies at risk with a view to buying them out and undervaluing the property and assets." Eve carried on to say, "Then they either sit on the company or sell it off to interested parties. If the factory has prime building land and is freehold, it could be worth millions to the asset stripers or speculators. It can of course backfire on them if they end up with no takers, as they usually end up borrowing the money and then repay the loan back to the bank."

Mr Hunter just sat there speechless. He was annoyed with Eve. There was a fat profit for him and his partner, Mr Owen, if the deal went through.

The client couldn't believe what he had just heard. He blurted out, "My company isn't in any financial difficulty at all. It has its money worries like other businesses like ours. We have been through difficult times this year. But I would say that we are on a sound footing, so I don't quite understand why they have got in touch with us."

Eve suggested, "Then you must have some asset that attracted them to make the offer."

Mr Hunter gathered his thoughts and said, "What would you do, Miss Kershaw?"

"I would show them the door and say something like, 'After careful consideration, your offer is well below market value, so the board have decided to decline.'"

The three men looked at one another. Mr Hunter said, "Well, thank you, Miss Kershaw," and proceeded to open the door for her. Inside he was raging, for he knew the property was undervalued, but they had clients lining up for a share after the deal was concluded.

Eve felt chuffed. She entered her office where the rest of the team were. Everyone looked at her, waiting for her to say something. Eve said nothing. She just sat down and carried on with her job. People just stared at each other. One shrugged his shoulders as if to say, *I've got work to do too*, and made his way to his desk. The others soon followed. The office was buzzing again, like a busy lawyers' office does, from the minions on the ground floor to their superiors or bosses on the upper floors.

For the rest of the day, Eve kept herself busy. She was really exhausted but also relieved. She thought that Mr Hunter would let her know of the outcome, but it never happened, to Eve's disappointment. She simply knuckled down again to the job in hand.

* * *

Ruth arrived at the Harrows. Her mother was overjoyed to see her, especially now that Ruth was Dr Ruth Kershaw, paediatrician.

"Did you have a good journey down?" her mother asked.

"Yes, fine, no holdups, thank God," was Ruth's reply. Then she said, "I plan to stay a couple of weeks, if that's OK with you and Dad."

"Of course! You can stay as long as you want. This is your home!" Ruth got up and pecked her on the cheek.

Daisy the maid came in. "Hello, Lady Ruth, nice to see you."

Ruth looked at Daisy and said, "No need to call me Lady Ruth, Daisy. Ruth is just fine."

Her mother butted in with, "Unless we have company, that is." Daisy just smiled at Ruth.

Daisy then brought a tray of sandwiches that Cook had made, which Ruth was grateful for. By this time, it was edging towards four in the afternoon. Her mother asked about Evelyne. Ruth told her that Eve was fine but had a difficult case to finish. Otherwise, she would have come down too. "We saw Joanne a couple of days ago," she added.

Ruth was about to tell her mother how Jo looked when suddenly her mother yelled, "Don't speak to me about Joanne at the moment! I am not in the least concerned with what she's up to. I'm still annoyed with her letting us down like she did at Christmas."

There was an uneasy silence. Ruth said, "I think I'll go up and freshen up." Her mother just nodded to her.

Ruth couldn't get out of the room quick enough. *Wow*, she said to herself, *wait till Eve hears about this*. Ruth was really mystified at her mother's outburst. After all, everyone knew Jo was no more a rebel than Maggie Winters or Racheal Ashurst. They were all just as bad as each other, listening to the gossip that goes around. Ruth thought it funny that the boys never seemed to misbehave – or was it they were just cleverer than the girls in what they got up to?

Lady Jane was upset about her outburst in front of Ruth. Truth was, deep down she was unhappy. On the surface, everything in the garden was rosy. But Sir John was a bully if anyone got in his way, especially in business circles. Unknown to his family, he had secrets, and if they came out, it would ruin him, the family, and their status. Jane, for her part, was completely unaware of his misdemeanours. She only knew that she was in love with someone else and would always be in love with him.

Her mind drifted back to the past. The man's name was Angelo Giuseppe. They would meet up when she was on vacation in Tuscany. He owned the artist studio there, or his father did. It was in the local village only a couple of kilometres away from the villa.

Jane frequently visited the studio to sell her landscapes when she needed the cash. She had opened up a private bank account in Siena in her maiden name for a rainy day and called it her getaway money, but it never felt like the right time. Then one fateful day whilst in

London, she learned that she was pregnant again. She was numb to the core. The family doctor was elated for her, but all she could think about was getting rid of it.

The doctor said, "Wait while John hears of this. He will be thrilled to bits." This jolted Jane back into reality that she had to keep the baby, and she put all thoughts of Angelo on hold. Of course, John was indeed delighted, and so too were the girls. They wanted another sister. Their father, of course, wanted a son.

John told his two girls. "We must look after Mummy now, so you two must be very good, do you hear me?" They both nodded. Eve and Ruth were not at all naughty. They were always quiet and well behaved, except when they were squabbling over each other's toys, like any other child would do at their age.

Jane managed to take some time off to go to Tuscany. Unfortunately for her, she had to take the girls with her, which meant less freedom, but somehow she managed to get away for a couple of hours on the pretext that she was painting. Jane told Angelo about the baby, and he wanted her stay with him. Jane was torn now by guilt and also by duty to stay with her husband.

Angelo was upset about this. Like all Italians, he was irritable and very emotional. He just kept pacing up and down, muttering to himself. Jane tried to calm him down. He brushed her aside with such force that she fell to the ground, and then he ran off. Tears were falling down Jane's face. She now had a void in her life that she had never felt before.

Somehow Jane had to steel herself away from all thoughts of Angelo for the sake of her family and try to forget about him. It took her a very long time to get over him, if she ever did. With the passage of time, the guilt and feeling for Angelo diminished. The family still went over to Tuscany, and Jane got on with her life as if nothing had happened. She often wondered what had happened to Angelo, as the studio shop was now owned or rented by someone else.

Jane was jolted out of her thoughts when Ruth came in. Ruth looked at her mother and said, "You look pensive, Mother. Is everything all right?"

Her mother replied, "Yes. I was just thinking it wasn't that long ago when you used to try to sit on my knee when Evelyne was on my knee, and the times I had to try to wrestle with both of you." Jane laughed, and so did Ruth. "Now what would you like to do tomorrow? Do you fancy shopping in Oxford? We can make a day of it, and even stop over if you wish."

"That sounds like a great idea, Mother," replied Ruth.

CHAPTER FOUR

Eve arrived at work and was immediately summoned to Mr Hunter's office. Eve knocked on the door. "Come in," Hunter said.

She entered, and when he said, "Sit down, Miss Kershaw, this won't take long," a lump came to Eve's throat.

Hunter carried on, "Our client was most impressed with the job you did. I won't beat about the bush. Mr Owen and I think your talents are wasted here. We are only a very small firm compared with other firms, so reluctantly, we have agreed to let you go with severance pay of course and an excellent reference."

Eve was stunned. In fact, she was speechless. She just stared, half-believing what she had just heard.

Mr Hunter then handed Eve a brown envelope. He shook her hand and wished her all the best. She looked at him, said nothing, and walked out the door.

Eve composed herself, went to her office, collected her belongings, emptied her desk, and walked out the door, never saying a word to anyone. Then, when she got home, she collapsed in a chair and just sobbed her heart out. She felt utterly alone, with no way of knowing that she had stumbled onto one of Hunter and Owen's shady dealings.

After an hour or so, Eve got herself organised. She rang her father to tell him what had gone on. He was shocked to hear it.

"I'll be around in an hour, Eve."

"No need. I'm OK," said Eve.

"I'll be around in an hour," her father answered, then put the phone down. "Miss Johnson," he said, "cancel all my appointments for this afternoon, will you?"

His secretary just nodded at him.

Sir John rang Jane up. Daisy answered. "Sir John here. Can you put Lady Jane on?"

"I'm afraid Lady Jane is out with Ruth, in Oxford I think," was Daisy's reply.

"Never mind. Tell her to ring me at home tonight. It's important."

"I will," replied Daisy.

* * *

It was now lunchtime, Eve decided to change and then wait for her father. It wasn't too long before he arrived. Eve opened the door, and when she saw her father, she started to cry again. He put his arm around her to comfort her.

"I'm sorry. I'm being stupid, I know, but it hurts – after all the hard work I put into the case."

Sir John was furious with Hunter and Owen. He vowed he would get to the bottom of it, if only for his daughter's sake. "Come, get your coat," he said. "I'm taking you to lunch." He added, "I need to have a chat with you about something I have been pondering for some time. Now seems to be the right time."

Eve grabbed her coat and handbag and went with her father for lunch. He took her to the Ritz, one of Sir John's favourite restaurants. They entered and proceeded to the dining area.

Chris was attending to the clients today. He greeted them warmly. "Sir John, Lady Eve, how nice to see you both. It's been some time."

Sir John just nodded. Henry showed them to their table and then went over to the waiter who would be waiting on them. Eve and Sir John didn't notice, as they were too preoccupied with what had gone on.

The waiter came over, gave them a menu, and then went to serve another client. The wine waiter arrived, and Sir John told him, "A bottle of your best claret."

"Certainly, sir," the waiter answered.

They both looked at the menu. Eve wasn't feeling that hungry.

"You have to eat, Evelyne," her father said. "You can't let the bastards beat you."

Eve was most surprised at what she had heard. She had never heard a father swear before – well, not that sort of language. *Gosh, he is upset as much as I am*, she said to herself.

The waiter came over. "Are you ready to order, sir?"

"Yes," replied Sir John.

They each ordered what they had chosen, and then the wine waiter arrived. "Shall I pour, sir?"

"No, I can manage, thank you." Sir John poured the wine out for his daughter.

"That's enough," she said.

"Drink it," said her father.

Eve just nodded. "What did you want discuss with me?" she asked.

"After lunch," her father replied.

When the meal was over, Sir John told Eve what he had in mind. Eve listened intently as he explained to her his reason for asking Eve to have lunch. He detailed everything to her and then said, "Think about it and let me know as soon as you can. Then I can set my stall out."

Eve was in shock. *Two in one day is just too much for anyone to take in*, she said to herself. By this time, it was mid-afternoon.

"What will you do now?" her father asked.

"I'm thinking of going to the Harrows and then over to Tuscany with Mother. I am utterly exhausted, if truth be known. The case has really drained me."

"That's a terrific idea," her father said. "I may even spend the weekend with you all before you leave. Then you can let me know one way or the other."

"Why not join us at the villa if you can get away?" asked Eve.

Her father didn't answer her, and Eve wondered why, but she never pursued it.

They left the Ritz and said goodbye to each other. Eve felt much easier after seeing her father. When she got home, she immediately rang her mother. Daisy answered, and Eve said, "Hi Daisy, Eve here. Is mother there?"

"I'm sorry, Lady Eve, your mother is in Oxford with Ruth. They will not be back till sometime tomorrow."

"I see. Well, I'm coming down tomorrow, Daisy. If Mother rings, let her know, will you?"

"Of course, Lady Eve."

Eve decided to have a leisurely bath and prepare everything for the trip home. Eventually, she settled down to watch some TV, but her mind was racing. She couldn't settle.

She emptied her briefcase, looked at her notes, and decided to burn them. Then suddenly, for some reason, she decided to keep her notes just in case, so she put them into her safe. She then opened the envelope that had been given to her at the office. It contained generous severance pay, but that didn't make Eve feel any better about how they had treated her. However, she made her mind up to put it all behind her and learn from her experience.

* * *

Her father, however, was angry and perturbed over how his daughter had been treated. After all, Evelyne was his favourite. He always thought she was the most like him. He decided he would keep a close eye on the activities of these so-called lawyers.

Sir John tried again to reach Jane. Daisy picked up the phone. "Is Lady Jane there now, Daisy?"

"I'm afraid not. She has rung to say she and Ruth are staying overnight and will be home sometime tomorrow."

"Do you know what hotel they are staying at?" asked Sir John.

Daisy said she didn't know, and he hung up the phone.

Sir John then decided to go to his club, Boodles. He rang for a taxi. Boodles was a gentlemen's club only. Upon his arrival, he was greeted by the doorman, who said, "Good evening, Sir John."

Sir John acknowledged him and proceeded to the lounge. He glanced around and saw Sir Henry Maxwell, an eminent judge. "Can I have a word, Henry?" Sir John asked.

The judge looked up. "Good heavens, John Kershaw! Or should I call you Sir John? It's been a while since you've been in here."

Sir John sat down, and a waiter came up to them. "Drinks, sir?"

Sir John replied, "Whisky and soda. What are you drinking, Henry?"

The judge replied, "Brandy and soda."

"Right you are, sir," said the waiter. He left and returned after about five minutes with the drinks. John asked the waiter to put it on his tab. The waiter nodded and gave him a chit to sign.

"Now what is it, John?" asked the judge. "I can call you John, can't I? All this Sir business – a bit ridiculous, if you ask me."

John just laughed. "I wish everyone who knew me well enough would call me John, especially my friends. I think they are embarrassed and don't quite know how to address me."

He then started to tell the judge everything Eve had told him. The judge listened and waited till John had finished, and then he said, "Leave it with me, John. I'll see what I can do and let you know."

"I would be very grateful to you, Henry – or should I say, Sir Henry?" They both grinned at each other.

"Think nothing of it, my boy," said the judge.

John then ordered two more drinks. The conversation after that was cordial. Soon it was eleven o'clock. Sir John bid the judge goodnight and hailed a taxi to St John's Wood.

When Sir John reached home, he immediately went into his study and rang a telephone number. He waited a while. The person he was ringing was out and had an answering machine. Sir John said, "Max, couple of jobs for you. Meet up at the usual time and place."

* * *

Eve was up early and buzzing with excitement now. The thought of spending a few days at home, then on to Tuscany, was just the pick-me-up she needed. Like her mother, she just loved Tuscany. It was so peaceful where the villa was; it was another world.

She drove down to the Harrows. By the time she arrived, her mother and Ruth were there to greet her.

"You poor thing, Eve!" said Jane. "Father has told me all about it. Well, it will be their loss, you mark my words."

Eve smiled at her mother. She really just wanted to forget the whole episode. Ruth came up to her and gently embraced her; they exchanged looks rather than words.

Changing the subject, Eve said, "What did you two get up to in Oxford?"

Mother and daughter looked at one another and grinned, and then Jane said, "Nothing, really. We just had a girlie two days away. It was wonderful."

Eve then said, "I must say, I'm looking forward to Tuscany."

Her mother interrupted her. "You and me both," said Jane, "only I shall be staying a couple of months like I used to. I'd gotten out of the habit lately. I do so much enjoy painting. It's so therapeutic for me. I can completely unwind and go into myself."

Eve just looked at Ruth with a wry smile on her face. Only their mother knew what she meant. Jane changed the subject and said, "Your father is coming down Friday, so that'll be nice for us all to be together."

Ruth said, "That's enough talk for now. You must be exhausted after the drive down. Shall I order tea?"

Eve said, "Yes."

Ruth went to ask Daisy to make them tea. Jane said she was lying down for an hour or so and asked Daisy to bring tea up to her room. Daisy just nodded. When Daisy arrived in the lounge with tea for the sisters, Ruth poured. She was itching to tell Eve what had happened when she mentioned Joanne to her mother.

Eve listened to what Ruth had to say. Eve too couldn't understand why their mother reacted like she did. It made no sense to them. They surmised all sorts of things, and then Eve said, "I need to freshen up" and retired to her bedroom. Ruth was still trying to find a solution to her mother's outburst, to no avail.

* * *

The next couple of days were idyllic. Eve and Ruth just lazed around, chatted, and giggled.

"What are you two up to?" their mother asked.

They both said, at once, "Nothing." For that, they got one of their mother's looks, and they burst out laughing again. Jane just shrugged her shoulders and muttered, "Girls these days don't know they're born," then she tutted again as she walked out the door. Eve did notice her mother had changed and wondered if it centred around Joanne.

Sir John arrived. Ruth thought her father looked tired and not his usual self, but she dismissed it as being due to the journey. He embraced Jane and Ruth, and then he looked for Eve. "She's in her room now," said Ruth. "I'm sure she'll be down shortly."

Indeed, it wasn't too long before Eve entered and greeted her father warmly. They looked at one another briefly, but nothing was said. The night went well enough. They had a lovely meal at the Royal, as everyone called it. People kept themselves to themselves, just acknowledging the Kershaws as they arrived in the dining room, with Sir John nodding back. The girls were oblivious to this. To them, it was wonderful to spend time with their parents, although, due to work commitments, it happened very rarely these days.

They were getting on fine when Ruth mentioned to her father that she and Eve had seen Joanne. Jane glared at her daughter. "I thought I told you we are not at all interested in what Joanne gets up to these days," she said.

Sir John interrupted her. "God, Jane, I'm interested in what my daughter is getting up to even if you are not!"

There was a deadly silence. Then Eve said, "Perhaps now is not the time."

Her father looked at Eve and decided to let it go. There was an awkwardness for about two or three minutes, and then Eve said, "Well, thank you both for a lovely evening. It's good for us all to be together. We should do this more often."

Her father said, "I'll drink to that," and they raised their glasses. When they reached home, their mother and father wished them goodnight and retired. Though the two girls didn't know it, their parents were having the fiercest row.

Eve turned around to Ruth and said, "What on earth did you do that for when Mother asked you not to mention Joanne in front of her? You know, Ruth, Mother must have been very upset when Jo chose to leave instead of staying. After all, she idolised Joanne."

Ruth just looked at Eve, blurted out, "I don't know," and started to cry. Eve put her arm around her sister. "Come on, bed for us too."

* * *

The next morning, when Eve entered the dining room, the smell of bacon and eggs enticed her to eat. The fact was, she was hungry. Even though she'd had a three-course meal at the Royal Oak, truth was Eve had barely eaten anything since being dismissed. Now she had put that episode all behind her and was looking forward to a completely new role.

"Good morning, Eve. Did you sleep well?" asked her father.

Eve replied that she had slept very well.

Daisy came in and said, "Morning, Lady Eve. Full English?"

"Oh, yes, please," was Eve's reply.

When Daisy left the room, her father said, "We need to have a chat later, Eve. I know your mother has no plans this morning, so that might be a good time to have the chat."

Eve just smiled and said, "Fine."

The door opened, and it was Ruth. "Morning everyone," she said in greeting. Eve and her father acknowledged her. "Where's Mother?" asked Ruth.

"Having a lie-in," said their father. Then he asked Ruth what plans she had for the morning.

"Nothing planned, Father. I am just going to relax and read and be thoroughly lazy." They all laughed.

Daisy came in with breakfast for the two girls. After breakfast, Eve went into the conservatory to read the morning papers, while Ruth went back upstairs to read. Their father said he had to make a few telephone calls and went into his study. Eve really didn't hear him; she was too absorbed reading the paper.

Suddenly, she was interrupted by her mother. "Where is everyone, Eve?"

"Ruth is in her bedroom reading, I think," Eve answered. "Father is in the study."

"I thought we might go to the St Albans today and have afternoon tea," suggested Jane.

Eve answered, "If it's all right with you, Mother, I would just like to unwind today. Perhaps tomorrow. But Ruth may go."

Disappointed as her mother was, she understood perfectly and agreed that Sunday would be better.

* * *

Both Ruth and Eve lazed around nearly all day. Finally, their father appeared and said, "Ruth, would you mind? I need to have a word with Eve."

Ruth went out to look for her mother to apologise. She found Jane in the garden pruning the roses. Ruth took a deep breath and thought, *Here goes.* She moved towards her mother. "I'm sorry about last night, Mum. I thought you were joking about Joanne in the heat of the moment."

Her mother turned to her and said, "Ruth, I'm sorry too, but I meant every single word I said, so we'll leave it at that, shall we?"

Ruth just nodded, put her arms around her mother, and hugged her. Of all her three daughters, Jane thought that Ruth was the most loving one and the most sensitive one. She knew her daughter would become a great doctor one day.

* * *

Meanwhile, Eve and her father had a talk in his study.

"I've had word with Judge Henry Maxwell," said Sir John. "Thought you might be interested to know that the Law Society have had a number of complaints about the law firm Hunter and Owen. They are being investigated on certain cases they have been involved in."

Eve was all ears.

"It seems that they are in cahoots with another company which deals in asset stripping," Sir John continued. "It is not illegal to deal with other parties, but they have to be open and honest about their association. If Hunter and Owen have not exactly been truthful about the facts and the true value of the properties involved to their clients, then of course, it leaves a question mark." (Of course, Sir John should have mentioned his own involvement with the company Williams and Thomson Asset Strippers over the years, but he didn't.)

Eve was relieved to hear this. It meant that she had done everything above board. But she was also worried about Mathew Emerson, who had put the boot in. Eve's thoughts were interrupted by her father.

"Now, Eve, have you thought about what I asked you, about joining the company and working alongside me?"

Eve answered, "I have and would love to, but you will have to be patient with me. It isn't really my field."

Sir John got hold of Eve. "Of course I will guide you. You will make a fine chairman one day. I have no doubt about that." He then pecked her on the cheek. "Come on. Let's tell your mother and Ruth."

Before they went into the garden, Sir John said, "Just a minute, Eve." He returned to the house, and a couple of minutes later he returned. When they found Jane and Ruth, he said, "Jane, I have an announcement to make. Eve is joining the company and will be working alongside me. It'll mean I will have more time to spend with you and the girls."

Jane wasn't too pleased about John being able to spend more time with her, but she was delighted for Eve's sake, and so was Ruth.

"Don't forget, John. Eve is spending a month with me at the villa."

"I haven't forgotten," he assured her.

Daisy suddenly appeared with a bottle of champers. "Good, Daisy. Place it there, will you?" said Sir John.

The champagne poured, they all raised their glasses: "To Eve!" Her mother kissed her and said, "I'm so happy for you, Eve!"

Ruth hugged her sister and said, "Balls to Hunter and Owen." It took Eve by surprise.

* * *

Soon it was time for Ruth to leave. She had loved every minute of it, but now she had to start her new role as a paediatrician at Guy's Hospital. Although she hated leaving Mum and Dad and Eve, there was another path for Ruth to follow now and make a name for herself in the job she loved. Goodbyes were said, and Ruth set off for London.

Eve shouted, "Write if you can at the villa!"

Ruth just smiled and waved. Her head was now full of expectations.

* * *

The next couple of days felt strange to Eve. She was used to seeing Ruth at some stage of the day, whether she was on nights or days or on shifts. It was quiet without her. Eve had a certain melancholy about it.

Her father came in and said, "I'm off tomorrow, Eve. I'm sure you'll enjoy the villa with your mother. She is really excited about it. See you on the tenth, bright and early."

Eve kissed her father. "Thanks for everything. I won't let you down."

He smiled as if to say, *I know you won't.*

Her mother entered and asked, "What are you two whispering about?"

"Nothing," said Eve. Her father was bemused at her reply.

CHAPTER FIVE

Lady Jane and Eve were having a lovely holiday. They would take themselves off to little villages that brought back childhood memories for Eve. One day, her mother said that she wanted to sell some paintings at a studio she knew in Siena, and would Eve like to come. Eve wasn't all that bothered and said, "If it's OK with you, I'm happy to stay here."

It was music to Lady Jane's ears. "That's settled," she said. "I'll go tomorrow. I think I'll go to my room and freshen up."

"I'll make supper," Eve said and kissed her mother gently on the cheek.

Later that evening, Jane told Eve, "That was a lovely meal. You'll make someone a good wife someday. I am hoping sooner than later. I'm looking forward to grandchildren. After all, your father I aren't getting any younger."

Eve replied, "I've got to meet someone yet, Mother. Give me a chance. All I've done is study. That goes for Ruth too. You shouldn't have pushed us to have careers and stand on our own two feet if you wanted grandchildren."

Eve laughed, and then she noticed a stack of paintings. "Are these the ones you want to sell?" Her mother nodded at her. Eve looked at them and said, "You are so talented. I can see where Joanne gets it from." Then she realised what she had said and waited for a tirade of abuse. Instead, her mother ignored her.

Eve then said, "I'd love to buy one of these if I could, Mother."

Jane replied, "You'll do no such thing. Choose one. It's yours."

Eve was delighted and chose a beautiful sunset scene. Her mother looked at it, and a tear trickled down her face. "What is it, Mother?" she asked.

"Nothing. It just brings back memories of a bygone time, that's all."

Eve said, "You're such a romantic. I can see were Ruth gets it from." They both laughed out loud.

Next morning, Jane had already left, leaving a note to say she would probably stay overnight if it got too late and not to worry. Eve looked at her painting again. It was really beautiful. In a way, she felt a tinge of sorrow for her mother. Jane was really very talented and perhaps could have gone a long way in another era.

Eve idled the morning away and decided to go into the local village for lunch. She told Maria to take the rest of the day off, which Maria protested about. It took Eve all her time to persuade her.

Eve got the hired car out and set off to the village. It was a precarious drive to say the least. No one took any notice of road signs at all. It was all downhill, with narrow roads and a deep ravine on one side. People would overtake on a bend or when a car was approaching the other way. Eve was a nervous wreck by the time she reached the village. She needed a drink as she sat at the café, just watching the world go by. She was totally unaware she was being watched.

Finally, Eve ordered lunch. Most of the villagers recognised her and nodded at her or smiled. Of course, she hadn't a clue who they were.

After about an hour, she meandered around the local shops, and then she spotted the art gallery and studio. She made her way over, looked into the window, and thought she recognised a couple of her mother s paintings. She decided to enter the studio.

A young man came to her. "Señorita, can I help you?" he asked in pidgin English. She tried to ask him about the two paintings in the window, but he just shrugged his shoulders. Then an older man came in from the back of the studio. His English was only slightly better.

"Can I help you?" he asked.

Eve said, "Yes, I was wondering about the two paintings in your window."

He replied, "They are not for sale."

Eve was taken aback. "Who painted them?" Eve asked him.

He murmured something which Eve didn't catch, and he then left to go back into the room he came from.

Well, I never! What a funny how-to-do. Wait till Mother hears about this! Eve said to herself as she left the shop. She peered through the window trying to see the signature on the picture, but it was faded. Eve never noticed the villagers watching her. After all, they all knew about Angelo and the affair with the Englishwoman. Gossip was rife at the time.

* * *

Meanwhile, Jane had managed to sell all her paintings. It was getting late, and she decided to stay over in Siena for the night. She didn't fancy travelling home, as it was late evening. After booking into the hotel, she asked the receptionist if she could use the telephone. He nodded and handed her the phone. She rang Eve.

It rang for ages. Jane was about to put the receiver down when Eve said hello. She was out of breath.

"Mother here, darling. I have decided to stay overnight. Back tomorrow afternoon. Will let you know what time to pick me up at the station," her mother said quickly and hung up.

Eve so much wanted to tell her mother about the paintings she saw in the art studio and was disappointed. Eve had thought she and her mother would be going to places like Florence, for instance, and popping into Siena together, and possibly visiting Anzio or even Pisa. She decided to write to Ruth and her father and opened a bottle of wine, and then she went into her bedroom. The sun was just about ebbing away. She settled down to read her book, and it wasn't too long before she fell asleep.

* * *

The next morning, Eve was awakened by the telephone ringing. By the time she got downstairs, it had stopped. Eve went into the kitchen and made coffee for herself. The phone rang again, and she rushed to pick it up.

"Hello, Mother," she said.

A voice responded, "It's not Mother, it's Mathew Emerson. Can we meet up? I was really surprised to see you in the village yesterday."

Eve was taken aback, and then in a different tone she said, "Tell me why we should meet. You put me in a terrible position when you told my bosses that we had met regarding the case."

Matt replied, "Hold on there. I never mentioned that we had met – and for your information, I ended up losing my job."

Eve was shocked to hear this. "If it's any consolation to you, so did I."

There was a momentary silence, and then Matt Emerson said, "Well, someone has it in for both of us. Anyhow, are we meeting up or not!"

Eve hesitated and then agreed. "I have to pick my mother up at the station sometime this morning. Will this evening do?" asked Eve.

Matt said OK. Eve gave him the address of the villa and then asked Matt how he had managed to get the telephone number.

"That's easy. Your sister Ruth gave it to me when I called at your flat to see you. Till tonight then," he said and put the phone down.

Eve went back into the kitchen to make breakfast. The phone rang again, and she picked it up.

"Mother here. Eve, I will arrive about two o'clock. OK. See you then."

Eve couldn't wait to meet her mother. She had plenty to talk about – the art studio was one and Matt Emerson the other. She was intrigued by it all.

To pass the time, she wandered about the garden. It was a beautiful garden.

"Good morning, Eve."

She turned around. It was Pepe the gardener. Eve replied in broken Italian, "Morning, Pepe. The garden looks wonderful. It's a credit to you."

Pepe just tipped his cap and carried on with what he was doing.

Maria arrived. "Morning, Miss Eve."

Eve said good morning to her.

Maria asked Eve if she would be in for lunch. Eve replied no and said, "I'm meeting Mother at the station, but we will be here for dinner."

Eve looked at her watch. It was now eleven o'clock. She decided to get herself ready and go into town sooner, hoping she would bump into Matt Emerson. So off she went again, driving cautiously as she did. The other drivers put the fear of God in her, the young lads whistling and doffing their caps as they passed her. *Silly sods, imbeciles*, Eve said to herself. *They'll kill somebody one day driving like they do.*

Soon she approached a bend. Someone was waving her down, and she wondered what for. Then she could see that there had been an horrific crash between a wagon and a car. A man came to her talking Italian, too quick for Eve to understand. Eve tried to make him understand, and then she brushed him aside to see what she could do. She said, "English – does anyone speak English?"

A little boy tugged at her skirt and said he knew a little.

It turned out that they wanted her to report the accident to the police and get a doctor, which she agreed to do. It was unnerving for Eve seeing the accident. She drove even slower. When she reached the village, she headed for the police station.

Having done what she promised, she left. It was now getting on for one o'clock. *I need a drink*, Eve thought. As she sat there, who should come into view but Matt Emerson with an elderly lady. Matt had spotted her. He went over to Eve and said, "This is getting a habit."

Eve explained what had gone on. Matt ordered two coffees and introduced his grandmother to her. He then told her why he was in Italy. "My grandfather passed away, and I attended the funeral on behalf of my parents and aunts, who couldn't make it because of work commitments."

"Look," said Eve, "why don't you come to the villa and have dinner with us and meet my mother? Bring your grandma if you wish."

He said he would be delighted to have dinner with them.

"About seven then," said Eve. Then she left to pick her mother up at the station. The train was on time for once. Her mother saw Eve and waved, and then they greeted one another. Eve then said, "Wait till we get home. I've loads to tell you."

Her mother said, "I hope you've met someone."

Eve just smiled and said to herself, *Maybe.*

All plans changed when they arrived at the villa, however. Maria was waiting for them, and she came running.

"What is it, Maria?" Jane asked.

Maria hesitated. "You must ring home. Important."

Lady Kershaw was numb. She knew her husband wasn't too well. She immediately went into the lounge to ring home.

Daisy answered and said, "Terrible news. I'll put you onto Sir John."

CHAPTER SIX

"Is that you, Jane?" said John. "Bad news, I'm afraid."

Jane felt faint. *My God, it's Joanne*, she was saying to herself.

Sir John interrupted her thoughts to say, "There has been an horrendous car crash, with four killed and two badly injured. Apparently, they had all been to the Glastonbury festival travelling back to Harpenden, all smashed out of their minds with drugs and booze. They even found a couple of empty whisky bottles near the car, the police said. However, why I'm ringing you, Joanne is one of the badly injured, along with another girl."

Lady Jane nearly fell over and had to sit down.

Sir John carried on. "Are you still there, Jane?"

She said in a shocked voice, "Yes."

He carried on again. "There is more." Jane listened intently. "This is really bad news, Jane. Maggie, and Racheal, along with a couple of lads, were the ones killed outright. The Winters and Ashursts are devastated. I think you had better come home immediately."

Lady Jane gathered her thoughts and asked, "How badly is Joanne injured?"

He answered, "Joanne will need to stay in hospital for quite some time, the doctors have said."

Jane didn't want to go home. This was her time. She said, "Is there any reason why I should come home just yet, John? I can't do anything if Joanne is in hospital."

Sir John was furious with her. "I cannot believe you have said that, Jane. Just remember, she is your daughter. You have a duty of care. Besides, what would the Winters and the Ashursts think if you stayed over in Italy?"

"We'll catch the soonest flight back," said Lady Jane. Immediately, the phone went dead.

She knew John was annoyed with her, but she had been so much hoping to meet Angelo again, if he was still around. She was obsessed with him. All she wanted do was to find him again and hope that they could rekindle something they once had.

Her thoughts were interrupted by Eve asking her what had gone on. Jane explained to Eve what had happened and that they were to leave as soon as possible.

"Oh crumbs, I've invited Matthew Emerson and his grandmother for dinner tonight. I don't know how to get hold of him," Eve said.

Her mother looked at her. "Well, they can still come. I'll have a word with Maria about dinner."

Eve pecked her mum on the cheek and then said, "Do you think we would be selfish to stay on a day or so?"

"No, I don't. Besides, from what your father said about Joanne, she is not in any danger. We will leave Friday morning. You know how Italians are. They don't rush about for anything. Now tell me about this chap you've met."

Eve said, "First of all, I must tell you that while I was in the local village the day you were in Siena, I came across an art studio and wandered over to look at the paintings on display in the window. I felt sure that a couple of the paintings were your work and decided to go in and enquire about them. A young boy came to me; he spoke little English, and my Italian is not that great. A man appeared, and when I mentioned the paintings, he abruptly said they were not for sale and went back into another room. I was flabbergasted to say the least."

Her mother gasped at hearing this. Could Angelo be back at the studio after all this time? She was in a world of her own. Her thoughts were interrupted again by Eve. "I'm sorry, Eve. Carry on."

"That's it," said Eve. "I arrived back at the villa, and the telephone started to ring. I thought it was you, but it was Matt Emerson. He was the one working on the case with me." She told her mother that somehow she blamed him for getting her dismissed, but it turned out he also lost his job, and that she had met him in the village "while I was waiting to pick you up at the station. He had come over for a family funeral."

Lady Jane was so pleased. Of all her children, she always thought Eve would make the perfect wife for someone. She was hoping this one would be her knight in shining armour, but there was tinge of sadness that she would not be able to see Angelo before she returned home. Eve's story rekindled her love for him and made her very uneasy.

It was precisely seven o'clock when the doorbell rang. Eve went to greet their guests, and found Matt there on his own. "Grandmother couldn't make it. She is still in mourning," he said.

"I'm sorry. I should have been more thoughtful." Eve showed him into the lounge.

"This is my mother, Jane."

Matt shook Jane's hand. "Pleased to meet you," he said warmly.

"Likewise" was her mother's reply.

The night flowed on very amicably. Matt had a great sense of humour, which Lady Jane appreciated. It didn't matter to her that he was a commoner; she could see Eve was besotted with him. What her father would think was another matter.

All too soon, it was time for Matt to leave. Eve went with him to the door, and he kissed her gently on the cheek. "Can I see you again?" he asked.

Eve said, "We have to leave on Friday. Family business, I'm afraid. I hope we can meet up back in London. You have my telephone number; no doubt Ruth gave you that as well."

He just smiled and then said, "Nothing sinister. I just wanted to see you, that's all."

Eve smiled at him.

* * *

Meanwhile, Sir John telephoned Ruth to tell her about Joanne's accident. Ruth said she would come as soon as she could. Her diary

42

was full, and she had to rearrange appointments. Ruth was relying on her team to carry on while she was away. She arranged to meet her father in a couple of days at the hospital.

Joanne had been moved to a private room at the request of Sir John, as the newspapers were having a field day over the society girl's tragic accident. There was a lot of speculation going around as to what had happened. The inquest had not opened yet; they needed statements from Jo and the other girl.

Ruth and her father went into the hospital the back way, as photographers were outside the main entrance hoping to catch a glimpse of Sir John and his family entering the building. When they reached Joanne's room, Ruth took one look at her and was shocked at the extent of her injuries. Even though some were superficial, it wasn't a pretty sight. Ruth had just started to read Joanne's charts when a nurse came in.

"Excuse me," said the nurse. "These notes are for the doctors only and are private."

Ruth just looked at her. "Why put them at the bottom of the bed if you don't want anyone to look at them?" she said to the nurse, who didn't answer Ruth.

The door opened. It was the consultant with about half a dozen doctors. He immediately recognised Sir John and shook his hand. Sir John introduced Ruth. "This is my daughter, Dr Ruth Kershaw, paediatrician." He glared at the nurse.

The consultant shook hands with Ruth and then, turning around to the nurse, said, "That'll be all for now, Nurse Mills." She left the room.

"Now Sir John …"

"Please, call me John. We are on a level footing here, aren't we."

The consultant then started to tell them that after exhaustive tests and X-rays, it was his opinion that that Joanne would be all right after physiotherapy. He also mentioned that she had the liver of a thirty-year-old man and, in his opinion, needed help in fighting her addiction. Sir John nodded in agreement.

"We don't know yet if your daughter will remember anything," the consultant told him. "We will just have to wait and see. Her injuries are superficial to some extent. Both her legs were trapped in the vehicle, which has caused considerable damage to one leg especially. We have kept her sedated for the time being and will see how it goes."

After they had left, Ruth looked at her father and said, "I think I'll try to have a word with one of her doctors. Back in a jiffy." Ruth went to the nursing station, introduced herself, and asked if there was a doctor free to discuss Joanne Kershaw with her. The ward sister said, "Certainly, Dr Kershaw." She then went away, and suddenly a doctor appeared.

"Hi, I'm Dr Robert Waddell. I'm in orthopaedics and one of the consultants when my boss is not available. How can I help you?"

Ruth introduced herself to Dr Waddell and asked if she could discuss Joanne's medical notes with him. He nodded. They discussed Joanne's condition in detail for some time, and then Ruth said, "Well, thank you very much. That answers some of my questions." She shook his hand, returned to her father, and said, "Nothing we can do now, Dad. We might as well go home." With that, they slipped out the back.

Over dinner that night, Ruth discussed her conversation with Dr Waddell. Ruth noticed that her father wasn't all that attentive. "What's troubling you, Father?"

He started to tell her that nearly every time he visited Joanne, there was another girl there with a little girl about three or four years of age. "The girl doesn't say anything when she sees me – she just gets up and goes out the door. The little girl looks back at me with big doleful eyes. I can't stop thinking how much she looks like Joanne at her age."

"Have you asked the staff?" asked Ruth.

He answered, "They have never seen her but said they will keep an eye out for her."

After dinner, her father went into his study. He had other things on his mind. Ruth sorted herself out and had a shower. When Ruth arrived downstairs, she rang the hospital to speak to one of her team to see if everything was running smoothly. Ruth then went into the lounge.

She was suddenly interrupted by voices. She went into the hallway and saw that it was her mother and Eve. She greeted them fondly.

"Where's Father?" Jane asked.

"In his study," Eve replied.

Sir John was not at all pleased to see Jane. "How could you be so heartless about Joanne? I couldn't believe you could be so self-centred. It nauseates me."

Jane just looked at him with tears in her eyes and left the room. She immediately went upstairs and cried her heart out. Truth be known, the marriage was a sham. To the outside world, it was a marriage made in heaven, but due to Lady Jane's indiscretion, shall we say, the marriage was so wafer-thin it could break down quite easily.

Sir John had found out years earlier about the affair with Angelo. The gossip was rife in the village. He gave her an ultimatum, one that she couldn't refuse. He only relented when it was the summer holidays. Then he would go over for a month or spend weekends there for the sake of the girls.

Ruth chatted with Eve, telling her everything about Joanne – and about their dad having an intuition about the little girl being Joanne's daughter.

"Wow," Eve replied. "Well, I have news for you." Eve filled her in on all that had gone on with Mother and the paintings in the artist studio, and her meeting up with Matt Emerson. "I owe you a favour," she concluded.

Ruth interrupted her. "What for?"

Eve carried on, "For giving Matt the telephone number." Ruth laughed.

Their father entered the room, and Eve embraced him. He went to the drinks cabinet, asking, "Drink, anyone?" They both said yes.

Eve said, "I'll just nip up and change."

A while later when Eve returned, she was surprised not to see Mother. "Is Mother not joining us?" asked Eve.

Her father replied, "I think the shock is just too much for her, and with the journey also, we may not see her till tomorrow." Their father then excused himself and went back into the study. The girls thought nothing of it. They sat and chatted, going through all the scenarios that could have caused the car accident. One thing was for sure, they were all on drugs – with one exception, which was Joanne. There were no drugs found on her at all, which surprised them.

They also discussed the young girl. Eve said, "We may well see her tomorrow when we visit in the morning instead of the evening."

Their father came back into the lounge. He asked Eve if she was looking forward to working with him. Eve said she was, and then she told him about meeting Matt Emerson in the village with his grandmother. She mentioned that he also had been dismissed by his law firm, and they were both mystified as to why they had both been sacked. Eve carried on and said she had arranged to see him again but with all that had gone on, she had to leave in a hurry. She was hoping to meet up again with him sometime soon.

Her father smiled. *Perhaps there is a silver lining after all,* he said to himself. Although he wasn't too pleased about Matt working for the other law firm. That could prove to be a bit awkward.

* * *

The next day, their father had set off for London. He decided to let the women take over the visiting of Joanne, particularly their mother. She couldn't very well say no to the girls, or it would put her on a spot.

When their mother arrived downstairs, Eve and Ruth where already there. Ruth said, "Morning, sleepyhead."

Her mother just glared at her.

"How are you feeling? Father said you were in shock and upset over Joanne," Ruth tried again.

Her mother just nodded and said nothing.

"We are thinking of going this morning, if you feel up to it," said Ruth.

Their mother declined and said, "Perhaps in another day or so. Your father said she is sedated at the moment."

The girls thought no more about it.

* * *

It was midmorning when they arrived at the hospital. The reporters where still hovering around. Ruth and Eve went into the hospital the back way and proceeded to Joanne's room. Upon entering, they saw a girl sitting there. She got up immediately to go.

Ruth closed the door. Eve then said, "Who might you be? One of Joanne's friends?"

The girl answered, "Yes."

Eve then looked at the little girl and said, "What's your name?"

The little girl replied, "Lucy."

Eve then asked her, "Lucy What?"

Before the child could answer, the girl said, "I think we shall go now." The girl refused to give them her name. Eve and Ruth looked at one another, and then Eve took control.

"Are you wanting Lucy to be with her mother?" she asked.

The girl didn't answer.

Eve then asked her, "Do you want to leave Lucy here with us? She will be safe with us. We are Joanne's sisters."

The girl looked shocked and then said, "Here, take the kid, and tell her mother she owes me big time. I want fifty quid when she's out of here."

Eve went into her purse. "No need to wait. Here you are," and gave her the fifty pounds. The girl hightailed it out the door.

The little girl started to cry. Ruth picked her up, and the child tried to fight her. Eve got hold of Lucy and sat her down and tried to explain that they were her aunties Eve and Ruth, her mummy's sisters. The little girl seemed to understand.

Eve then said, "You have a grandma and granddad too, Lucy." At the sound of *grandma* and *granddad*, Lucy's eyes lit up.

With all the commotion going on, there was some movement by Joanne. Ruth immediately rang for a doctor. They were ushered out of the room by a nurse and told to wait in the corridor. Eve held Lucy.

After about ten minutes, the doctor came out. "She is stable now. We needed to sedate her again to rest her body." Ruth understood.

Eve turned to Lucy and asked, "Would you like to come with us till Mummy's better?" Lucy nodded, so off they went back to the Harrows.

The little girl was taking everything in. Ruth thought she was a bright spark for her age, or perhaps it was her upbringing having to stand on her own two feet from an early age and perhaps what she saw around her. "You may be right, Ruth," said Eve.

Eventually they arrived home. It was decided that Eve should break the news to their mother that she was indeed a grandmother. Eve went upstairs and knocked on the bedroom door.

Her mother said, "Yes."

"Can I come in, Mother?" Eve entered. She could see her mother was upset.

"Joanne is going to be OK, Mother. Ruth has had a word with the doctors."

"I do hope so," her mother said.

"We have another shock for you," said Eve.

"What is it this time? Don't tell me you're pregnant."

"Oh, nothing as tragic as that!" replied Eve. They both managed to raise a smile.

"Well, what is it?"

"Come downstairs and see for yourself," said Eve.

Eventually, Jane arrived downstairs. "Where is everyone, Eve?" she asked.

Eve replied, "In the kitchen."

Jane proceeded to the kitchen and immediately saw the little girl.

Ruth said, "Mum, this is Lucy. She is your granddaughter."

Jane froze. She was speechless. Ruth started to repeat herself, but Jane stopped her. "I heard you the first time, Ruth."

Jane looked at the little girl with the melancholy eyes and thought, *My God, she is the spitting image of Joanne at her age.* She turned around and went towards the lounge. Eve and Ruth just looked at one another in total disbelief at what had just happened.

"Maybe Mother's still in shock with what's gone on with Joanne and now this," wondered Ruth.

Eve then said, "I don't know. Something is going on here. Father has seemed distant towards Mother lately," said Ruth.

Daisy came in and asked, "Can I get you anything?"

"Tea please, in the lounge," said Eve.

They made their way to the lounge with Lucy. Their mother was on the phone. They all sat down and waited while she finished. Jane turned around to see the three of them just staring at her.

"That was Marjorie Winters on the phone, telling me of the arrangements for Maggie. I hope you two can make it."

"How does she seem?" asked Eve.

Her mother replied, "OK, I guess. It was a short conversation and awkward for me, with Joanne still being alive. I must ring Elizabeth Ashurst up now, if you will excuse me."

Eve said, "We will be in the conservatory." Their mother just nodded in a vacant sort of way.

Finally, Jane went to the conservatory. She spoke to Lucy. "Do you know who I am?"

Lucy nodded,

"Who am I?" asked Jane.

Lucy didn't answer her.

Ruth said, "Leave it to me, Mother." Ruth then said to Lucy, "Has Mummy told you about her mummy and daddy?"

Lucy nodded again.

"Do you know me and Eve?"

Lucy replied, "Yes. You are mummy's sisters."

"Lucy, you speak well. How old are you?"

Lucy replied, "I am nearly six."

"Well, you speak very well for a five-year-old," replied Ruth.

"Would you like some biscuits and hot chocolate?" asked her Auntie Eve. She nodded again. Eve thought she looked sad for her age.

Eve went to fetch some biscuits and hot chocolate. Ruth carried on, "Well, this is your grandmother."

The little girl thought for a second or two, then smiled. She went over, put her tiny arms around Jane, and said, "Grandma."

Jane was full of emotion by this time. *If Lucy is really my granddaughter*, she thought, *I will make sure I do not make the same mistakes as I did with her mother*, she said to herself. Jane was fighting back the tears. It was a very moving moment for both Eve and Ruth to witness. They too were emotional, and then it was smiles all around.

Eve said, "I think I will have a lie-down. I'm exhausted." As Eve left them, she turned around and saw that Jane had Lucy on her knee. Eve had never seen her mother so happy.

CHAPTER SEVEN

Sir John was in conversation with Sir James Walker, chief of police in Hertfordshire. He had asked to be kept informed of the outcome of the police investigation into the car crash.

"Leave it with me, Sir John," replied Sir James. "I'll keep in touch."

Sir John decided to ring home – to see how Joanne was doing, and to see if there was any improvement. Daisy answered.

"Sir John here, Daisy. Put Lady Jane on, will you?"

Daisy went into the lounge. "Sir John is on the telephone."

Lady Jane immediately went to the phone, and then she hesitated. She wasn't too sure what sort of response she would get. *Well, here goes*, she said to herself. "Hello, John."

Sir John asked Jane – not in an abrupt way but in an enquiring way – about Joanne. She answered, "She is improving, John, thank goodness. There was slight movement today, but the doctors want to keep her sedated for a while longer."

Thank God, he said to himself. To Jane, he said, "Just to let you know, I will be down in a couple of days."

"John," she began, "I have something to tell you. It's important."

"It can wait till you see me. I have to go into a meeting now."

The phone went dead. The mystery man had been in touch with Sir John, and they had arranged to meet up.

Jane repeated to herself the vow that she would not make the same mistake again regarding her granddaughter, Lucy.

Ruth interrupted her thoughts. "Was that Father on the phone?"

Her mother replied, "Yes. He wanted to know how Joanne was doing. I never got a chance to tell him about Lucy. He had an important meeting to attend to," her mother said wistfully.

"That's a shame," said Ruth.

Her mother asked Ruth if she wanted to take Lucy out for an ice cream or something – perhaps the local park. Ruth immediately said yes and carried on. "I'll let Eve know."

So off they all went to the local village to find an ice cream parlour or an ice cream van, whichever came first. They drove for quite some time, and then they noticed a sign saying "Village Fair." It was on all week.

Their mother said, "This will do nicely." So they parked up and went towards the village green to see what was on offer. To their joy, they saw that there were rides for children.

They spent about an hour or so. Lucy was in her element, smiling and laughing. It did the little girl a power of good. At this moment in time, no one knew what this little girl at nearly six had endured with an alcoholic mother.

Ruth promised herself that she would watch over Lucy's well-being and hoped to give her a happy and loving environment.

"Come on, Ruth you're daydreaming! We've shouted to you twice!" said Eve in a jocular way. Ruth just smiled. They climbed back into the car.

"Where to now?" their mother asked.

"Afternoon tea would be nice. Let's go nearer home. There's Betsy's Tea Room. They have scrumptious homemade cakes," said Eve, getting all excited.

Jane smiled and thought to herself, *Just like old times. Perhaps this is just what the family needs. It might be a blessing in disguise for us all, who knows.*

It had been a lovely day. Lucy had enjoyed herself. Even the grownups were like little children again. It brought back happy memories for the two sisters and their mother.

It wasn't too long before they reached home. Lady Kershaw was exhausted by this time and went to lie down. Ruth and Eve decided to take Lucy to see her mummy. Lucy was reticent at times, but took everything in.

When they arrived at the hospital, to their surprise, the reporters and photographers were no longer pitched outside hovering for pictures. *Thank the Lord for that*, Ruth said to herself.

They entered the main door and were stopped by a porter, who said in an abrupt voice, "No children allowed."

Eve and Ruth just brushed past him and proceeded to Joanne's room. He was furious and followed them, and then he realised that they were heading for the private rooms and made his way back. Eve and Ruth were unaware of him following them, but Lucy noticed.

They entered the room and saw that nurses were attending to Joanne. Ruth said, "We'll wait outside." The nurses smiled at them but said nothing.

After ten minutes or so, the family was allowed into the room. There was little sign on the outside that Joanne was improving. Ruth looked at the notes and was pleased at what she read. Joanne's pulse rate had improved and also her temperature had reduced somewhat. Small signs they might be, but significant to the medical profession.

Ruth went to discuss Joanne's progress with the doctor on duty and ask what they had in mind for the forthcoming week in regards to keeping Joanne under sedation. After an hour, they returned home.

Their mother was in the lounge. "How is she?" Jane asked.

Ruth said that Joanne was doing fine and there were signs of improvement, small as they might be. *Thank you, God*, said Lady Jane to herself.

Daisy came in and announced, "Dinner's ready." They all trooped into the dining room.

Jane noticed that Ruth was pensive. "What is it, Ruth?" her mother asked.

"Where will Lucy sleep?"

Her mother answered, "Daisy and I have moved one of the single beds into the main bedroom for now, so she can sleep with me and your father – for the time being anyway – till she gets used to us."

The house did have four bedrooms, but one was completely full of unwanted or unused things. Their mother carried Lucy upstairs with little effort. Eve was amazed; she herself had struggled with Lucy.

"Did you see that, Ruth? She carried her upstairs, no trouble."

"I guess she's used to it. It probably never leaves you," replied Ruth.

* * *

Their father arrived a couple of days later and was shocked to learn he was a grandfather. It was hard for him to take it in. He needed time to absorb it all. He could see, though, that Jane and the two girls were delighted.

Jane left the room, and a while later she entered with Lucy. "Here she is, John. Meet your granddaughter."

Sir John looked at Lucy, and his heart melted. Such emotion came over him. He had never experienced anything like it before. He was fighting to hold it all together.

Jane went over to her husband, put her arm around him, and said, "I'm so sorry. It was very thoughtless of me. It will never happen again, I promise you. Family first."

John caught hold of her hand and squeezed it, as if to say all was forgiven.

Cook came in to say dinner was ready.

"Can you give us a few minutes, Mrs Brown?"

"Certainly," Mrs Brown replied. They all chatted for a while longer, and then Lady Jane said, "Shall we dine now?"

They made their way into the dining room. Lady Jane went into the kitchen to ask Mrs Brown to serve dinner. Sir John was quite impressed with Lucy; her manners were impeccable. He said to Lucy, "Your mummy has taught you good, Lucy." Lucy just beamed at him with the most beautiful smile.

She'll break someone's heart one day, thought Sir John.

* * *

Weeks passed into months. The coroner's report on the road crash was accidental death due to dangerous driving whilst under the influence of alcohol and drugs. The press had a field day. Sir John and Lady Jane tried to support their four friends as much as possible, but there was always that guilty feeling that Joanne had survived and their children didn't.

The last time they all met up was at the Masonic Ball. That's when things came to a head. All the bottling up inside Elizabeth Ashurst came to the surface, and she came out with a tirade of abuse to Charles Winters, blaming him for all their woes. Charles just stared her out and said nothing. He didn't even look at Marjorie – to Marjorie's surprise. She was waiting for fireworks from Charles, but it never happened.

Then Elizabeth turned on Lady Jane and Sir John, saying that it was their Joanne's fault for leading her daughter astray. Jane was dumbstruck at first, and then she felt the urge to say something. "Joanne might have been drunk, Elizabeth, but she wasn't driving the bloody car, was she? It was your daughter, and for your information, Joanne had no sign whatsoever of any drugs in her body." She turned to her husband and said, "Come on, John. We don't have to listen to this."

As they went to leave, Lady Jane turned around to Elizabeth Ashurst once more and said, "Don't you think, Lizzie, that John and I feel guilty about what has happened and the fact Joanne survived while Maggie and Racheal didn't? We have felt the burden of that on our shoulders too," and then she walked away. As soon as they entered the car, Jane burst into tears. She was inconsolable. John just put his arm around her and said, "I have never been as proud of you as I am tonight." He held her as tight as he could.

It took some time for Lady Jane to get over the falling out. After all, they had been friends for years. Marjorie Winters still kept in touch with Lady Jane, and they sometimes had lunch together. But they never mentioned Elizabeth for fear of raking up the past. Marjorie and her husband, Charles, knew their daughter's failings. They had tried everything to get her off drugs, even spending a small fortune on dry-out clinics, but all to no avail. To be honest, it was a relief to them both when she unfortunately died.

Joanne, meanwhile, was improving day by day. Lady Jane had managed to get Lucy into the village school. She thought it might help her to interact with other children, and it paid off. Lucy became more confident and very chatty. She was now a six-year-old child again.

* * *

Excitement filled the air as once again Eve and Ruth were to spend the weekend at the Harrows. Their mother was overjoyed. She loved seeing her daughters and catching up on the gossip in London circles – not that Eve or Ruth were all that interested.

Lucy was helping Cook to make some buns and cakes for the occasion. She too was excited. There was more flour on her face and the floor – in fact, it was all over the place. Cook laughed and said, "Here, let me finish that, Lucy. You can lick the bowl," which was every child's dream, to lick the leftovers.

Sir John arrived home first. He had decided to leave the office early. He greeted Jane and then looked for Lucy.

"Your granddaughter's in the kitchen helping cook," said Lady Jane, smiling as she said it. Having Lucy had somehow helped to heal the rift that was beginning to destroy them. Although Lady Jane had not completely forgotten about Angelo, her thoughts for the moment were fixed on her family and, of course, Lucy.

Daisy brought tea into the lounge. After she had left, Lady Jane mentioned that the hospital had rung to say that in their opinion, Joanne was fit enough to leave, but she would need physio and counselling for her alcohol addiction. "The doctor wanted to know if Joanne would be coming to stay with us to convalesce. He said he thought it might help having her family around her."

Sir John asked, "And what does Joanne think about coming here?"

"I don't know. The doctor put the phone down before I could ask him anything."

Sir John pondered and then said, "I think we should go up tonight to see her after dinner and find out what Joanne wants to do. After all, Jane, it is her life to live any way she chooses, even though we don't approve of her lifestyle. There is one thing for sure: I will not be supporting her financially. I have made sure that she cannot get hold of her trust fund, so she will have very limited resources to spend on alcohol. She will definitely have to find work of some description. It's her choice. From now on, she will have to stand on her own two feet.

"What about Lucy, John?" asked Lady Jane.

It was a great worry for Sir John also. Lucy had come on by leaps and bounds since staying with them.

Jane especially was upset at the thought of losing Lucy. She asked, "John, is there any way we can keep Lucy? Make her a ward of the court or something? I don't really know. I'm clutching at straws here. But if I know Joanne at all, she will definitely not want to leave her daughter here with us," Jane said in an emphatic voice.

Sir John replied, "I have taken some steps towards this scenario and had a word with Sir Henry Maxwell, an eminent judge. He is considering options for us. He pointed out to me that attitudes were changing towards women, with all this women's lib stuff, which doesn't help our situation. I'll keep in touch with you when I have something concrete."

They decided, rightly or wrongly, not to mention anything to Lucy.

* * *

By the time the girls arrived, it was past seven. Lady Jane came to greet them. "You poor things. You must be exhausted."

"We are. There was a car crash on the main highway. It took ages to get through," said Ruth.

"Look, girls, we have to go and see Joanne. Cook has left you some sandwiches, and the cakes are what Lucy has made for you."

Eve smiled. "Is Lucy still up?"

"Yes, she wanted to see you both before she went upstairs. Would you mind awfully, Eve, doing the honours?"

Eve was delighted. "Not at all, Mother. Give our love to Joanne."

"We will." Sir John came into view, and he embraced his daughters. "Sorry we have to dash off."

Ruth looked at Eve and said, "That's a bit melodramatic, don't you think?"

Eve nodded. They entered the lounge, and Lucy came running up to them. She put her arms around them, and Eve was choked.

Ruth just smiled and said, "My, you have grown since we last saw you." Lucy just smiled.

Eve went upstairs to freshen up and change. After a while, she came into the lounge. Lucy had fallen asleep. Ruth said, "I'll take her up, common sleepyhead."

Lucy's eyes opened momentarily and then closed again. While Ruth took the child upstairs, Eve went into the dining room, which had been set for them.

"Gosh, I'm hungry," said Ruth when she returned.

Eve said, "Wine?"

Ruth nodded. They talked nearly all night about work and the men in their lives. Joanne was discussed at some length. They wondered about their mother and father, taking off just like that, especially as they had come down to spend time with them.

Eve then said, "I'm bushed, Ruth. I think I'll go up."

"I won't be too long myself," replied Ruth.

* * *

Meanwhile, Joanne's parents were having a heated discussion with their daughter. She didn't want go back to the Harrows with them. In fact, she didn't want to see them ever again. She just wanted to get on with her life. She wasn't concerned about her drinking habit; she believed she could control it.

"Where will you go?" asked her father in an aggressive tone.

Lady Jane knew only too well how angry John could get, but she had never seen anything like this before. He was really angry.

Suddenly he said, "Come on, Jane, we're not wasting a minute on her any longer." He then turned around and said, "As far as we are concerned, you are no longer our daughter."

They both left the room. "You go to the car, Jane," said Sir John. "I need to speak to a doctor if one is on duty."

Jane proceeded to the car, tears falling down her face. She couldn't cope with all this vehement behaviour around her, and she couldn't understand why Joanne hated them like this. The girl had wanted for nothing.

Sir John paced up and down. Finally, a nurse came to him. "Telephone call for you, sir."

He went to pick the phone up. "Mr Philip Grahame here, your daughter's consultant," the voice on the other end said. "I believe you wanted to speak to me?"

Sir John was taken by surprise and then answered him. "Would it be possible to meet up with you tomorrow or as soon as possible to speak to you about my daughter Joanne? It is imperative that I have a word."

"I'll have to check my dairy," said the doctor. "Give me your telephone number; I'll ring in the morning."

Sir John thanked him for his courtesy and understanding at interrupting him in his personal time. He gave the consultant his number.

When Sir John reached the car, he could see Jane had been crying. He turned to her and said, "Jane, she is a closed book as far as I am concerned." They drove home in silence, each lost in thought, both trying to find a solution as to why.

CHAPTER EIGHT

Eventually they arrived home, emotionally drained. No one was around. Sir John poured them each a large whisky, kissed Jane on the cheek, and went into his study. Lady Jane just sat there in a fog. She finished the drink, poured herself another, and retired upstairs.

The next day, when Lady Jane woke, she had splitting headache. It took her a while to focus, and then it all came flooding back. *What a night*, she said to herself.

She went into the bathroom looking for a couple of aspirin and then lay down on the bed. When she woke again, it had turned ten o'clock. Lady Jane's headache had gone, at least. She gathered her thoughts and dressed, and then proceeded downstairs and into the kitchen.

"Just tea and toast for me, Mrs Brown. I'll be in the lounge." She peeked into the dining room, and there was no sign of anyone.

Daisy came in, and Lady Jane asked, "Where is everyone?"

Daisy answered, "Eve and Ruth have taken Lucy to the park to feed the ducks."

After breakfast, Lady Jane wandered into the study, expecting to find John there. To her surprise, he wasn't there. She shouted for Daisy, "Where's Sir John gone?"

Daisy said, "I'm sorry, Lady Jane, he left a note for you. I forgot." Lady Jane just took the envelope off her and said nothing. The note read:

Jane, meeting up with Joanne's consultant this morning. Need to get my head around a few things. Going back to London; have arranged to meet up with Sir Henry Maxwell this evening at the club. Will telephone when I have anything positive to tell you. I think you had better tell the girls what has gone on. Ruth might also do some digging around for us as far as Lucy is concerned. Ask Eve if she knows anyone in family law. It might be helpful to know.

An hour passed, then suddenly the peace and quiet was no more. The girls had returned, and they were all giggling and laughing. They went into the lounge, and they could see their mother was pensive.

Eve said, "Whatever's the matter, Mother?"

Her mother replied, "Not now. I'll speak to you both later." Then she changed the subject. "Did you enjoy the park, Lucy?"

Lucy nodded with excitement.

"Were there a lot of ducks?"

Lucy replied, "Geese as well, and I had an ice cream." Her little face was beaming from ear to ear. Lady Jane looked at her granddaughter and said to herself, *If only she knew what might be in store for her.*

Eve went up to her room. She wanted to catch Matt Emerson before he went out. The phone rang for ages, and she was about to put the receiver down when a breathless voice said, "Matt here."

"Hi," said Eve. "I just wanted to hear your voice."

"Missing me already?" he asked.

"Don't you do anything stupid tonight," she replied. "I don't want to be bailing you out on Monday morning."

Matt just laughed. "Everything OK at your end?"

Eve answered, "I don't know. Something is afoot. Father and Mother are both on the offensive again. It will be something to do with Joanne, you mark my words. Anyhow, I think we may know tonight. Watch this space. Have a good night, and remember, nothing stupid."

Matt said, "I'll behave, and I love you."

Eve replied, "Love you too." She put the phone down and wished she was there with Matt, for they had indeed become an item. Both wanted to leave the rat race to live in Italy, but both knew that it would never happen. Still, they could dream, couldn't they?

Eve was waiting for Matt to propose to her. She knew her biological clock was ticking down, and she wanted children so much.

It was funny that although Ruth was a paediatrician, she didn't seem interested in marriage or children. She was ambitious, of course; she enjoyed men's company and had a string of suitors after her. But she has only one faithful buddy, and that was Jed. They were soul mates, and he would do just about anything for Ruthie (as he called her). He seemed besotted with her.

After dinner, Eve and Ruth cleared away. It was Mrs Brown's and Daisy's night off on Saturdays. They also had an afternoon off during the week. Lady Jane had said it was only right for them to have some personal time to themselves with their families.

It wasn't too long before the girls came back into the lounge.

"Drink, anyone?" asked their mother.

"I'll have a sherry," said Eve.

"Whisky and ginger," said Ruth.

Their mother poured herself a large scotch and looked at her girls. Then she started to tell them everything that had gone on – including Joanne calling them all the names under the sun and swearing she wouldn't live with them if they were the last people on the earth. She mentioned that their father had cut off all financial support for Joanne and frozen her trust fund.

"Your father's gone back to London to see Judge Maxwell about the legal implications regarding Lucy," Lady Jane continued. "Your father has also had a word with Joanne's consultant at the hospital, which I don't know the outcome of yet. I am and hoping your father will ring later if he can."

Eve and Ruth just stared at one another, trying to take it all in. Eve offered to help and said, "If there is anything I can do, Mother, from a professional point of view, don't hesitate to ask."

Jane just smiled at them both, and then the tears began to fall again. She sobbed and then said, "After all we have done for her, how can she treat us like this?"

The girls tried to comfort her, but without success.

"I think I'll go upstairs," Jane said, pouring herself another large whisky.

When she was gone, Ruth turned to Eve. "Well, what do you think?"

Eve replied, "I don't know what to think, but I know one thing: if there is a battle for Lucy, Joanne will win, unless they can prove her incapable of looking after Lucy properly. It could turn out to be very nasty indeed. The press would have a field day, especially the gutter press."

Ruth felt inadequate in dealing with family matters. She said to Eve, "I'll try to find out about her medical condition if I can – what the emotional stress of the car accident may have caused, plus the fact that she is an alcoholic and her liver is shot, which could reduce her life expectancy considerably unless she stops drinking. That's really all I can do at the moment."

"I'll have a chat with Matt when I get back, see what he thinks. He may know someone who can help us," said Eve.

Ruth got up and poured herself and Eve another drink. "How's it going with you two?" she asked.

Eve answered, "Fine, I guess. Just waiting for him to pop the question."

"Why don't you ask him?"

Eve stared at her sister. "Because that is not the way it's done, Ruth."

Ruth could see that Eve was annoyed with her. "Sorry, Eve. You do what's best for you, I suppose."

Eve then said, "I think it is bedtime, don't you?"

Ruth just nodded.

* * *

The next morning, Eve was later than usual for breakfast. Ruth had already eaten, and Lady Jane was still having breakfast looking at the newspaper.

Eve asked if she had any news. "Not at the moment, Eve. I'm sure your father will ring when he has something positive." Her mother carried on reading the paper.

Eve said, "Just tea and toast for me, Daisy, thank you." She was not in the best frame of mind. It had unsettled her, what Ruth had said. She made up her mind that she would have it out with Matt Emerson about getting married. Did he want the commitment of marriage or not? If he didn't, there was no point in carrying on the way they had been.

Eve's thoughts were interrupted by Ruth. "Eve, I am really sorry about last night. I don't know what got into me."

Eve said, "I do. Too many whiskys." She smiled.

It was a leisurely morning, as Eve and Ruth would be leaving for London about three in the afternoon. They had to prepare for Monday morning and do some research on certain criteria regarding a court hearing that might never happen. Their mother was playing the piano; it was her way of relaxing. When they went into the music room, as they called it (it was really what they call a snug room), it just about fitted the piano and a large armchair plus a very small cupboard for Mother's music. *She is a competent pianist*, thought Eve. *I could listen to her playing all day.*

Lucy was in the corner drawing and looking very content with life. Eve became anxious as to how this would all affect Lucy. The child must be protected no matter what.

Suddenly, Lady Jane realised Eve and Ruth were there and stopped playing the piano.

"Carry on, Mother, it was beautiful!" said Eve.

"No, that's enough for now. I just like to practise now and again. What time are you thinking of leaving?"

"A little after three, I should think. We both have things to do before work in the morning."

Her mother kissed them and said, "I'm sure your father will keep you both informed."

It soon reached three o'clock. "Are you ready, Eve?" asked Ruth. Eve replied, "Yes."

There were goodbyes all around. The girls really didn't like leaving their mother, but they had jobs to go back to. They deliberately didn't look back, as they were both emotional. The stay had drained them. They felt exhausted and just wanted to get back to some sort of normality.

It took a couple of hours to reach home. It always took a little longer to get back to London because of the heavy traffic. Ruth dropped Eve off at Holland Park, where she was now living with Matt.

Ruth headed for her flat in Sloane Court. When she entered, she could hear noises coming from the bedroom. Ruth was wary, since Jed was away on business.

She opened the bedroom door, and what she saw shocked her to revulsion. There was Jed with a young lad having sex with him. He was too much involved in his sexual activity to notice Ruth.

"What the! Bloody hell!" Ruth said in a rage that engulfed her. "Get out, get out, you effin' bastard!" she cried, throwing all sorts of things at him. She picked his clothes up and the lad's and threw them outside the door.

Jed was too shocked to do anything. He quickly went out with the lad to retrieve his clothes. As he did, Ruth slammed the door in his face. He banged and banged on the door. When the neighbours came out to see what was going on and saw Jed half naked. they assumed it was a lovers' row. By this time, the lad had scarpered, taking Jed's wallet with him, which Jed was unaware of. Jed was raging. "I'll get even with your effin' family one day if it's the last thing I do! I too have friends!" he cried.

Ruth was extremely upset. After all that had gone on at the Harrows, she was exhausted with the tension, and now this. Ruth had more or less kept him for the last two years. He had always been work-shy, but Ruth ignored it, as he made her laugh. She thought they were soul mates. She couldn't get her head around what she had seen.

She set about getting Jed's clothes together and putting them in a black bin bag. Then she set about cleaning the bedroom from top to bottom. The sheets were thrown away. The mattress was put out for the refuse collectors. The revulsion of it all made her sick to her teeth. Ruth went into the other bedroom and cried herself to sleep.

Meanwhile, Eve nearly fell in the door when she saw Matt. She burst out crying. It had all been too much for her. She was sobbing her heart out. Matt just stared at her and tried to comfort her.

After about ten minutes, Eve composed herself and told Matt everything that had gone on. He listened to her every word and then put his arms around her. "Come on," he said. "What you need is a nice stiff drink."

An hour later, Eve decided to have a shower. She was feeling much better now. Matt was a tower of strength for Eve, and she was glad she had someone to talk to. She felt safe with him, and it was comforting.

* * *

The next day, Sir John received a call from the hospital to say that his daughter had signed herself out and had left no forwarding address. Sir John was surprised by this but also relieved. It meant they could get their house in order regarding Lucy. He telephoned his wife immediately about the news. Lady Jane was pleased, and said, "Tell the girls, will you, John?"

"I will," he said, and then he said goodbye.

CHAPTER NINE

Some time went by, and nothing happened regarding Joanne and her daughter, Lucy. Sir John thought it had died a death. Nonetheless, he had done his homework, and the girls also came up with some ideas, just in case it was ever needed. They were as prepared as they could be, just in case a writ was issued.

Matt had passed on to Sir John the name of Richard Holden, a solicitor who only dealt in family law. Holden suggested that they apply for legal guardianship right away, until Lucy was twenty-one. On Holden's advice, Sir John started an application for guardianship.

In the meantime, Charles Winters was getting tired of Elizabeth Ashurst's accusations regarding the death of Racheal. He protested vehemently, to no avail. Marjorie was also becoming more suspicious of the rumours being wantonly brandished around. She too started to ask Charles if there was any proof that he had in a hand in the accident.

A heated argument took place.

"For God's sake, woman! Do you really think I would kill my own daughter? What would I gain from that?" He was very angry.

Marjorie carried on. She knew only too well how Charles could be if people got in his way. He and John Kershaw were two peas out of the same pod. She let it drop, but it unnerved Marjorie.

Marjorie decided to visit Elizabeth to ask her why she thought Charles was involved in the car accident. Upon her arrival, there was a lot of commotion going on. She ventured nearer and asked a neighbour, "What's going on?"

The neighbour replied that Robert has committed suicide. He had never gotten over the loss of Racheal. "I feel sorry for Tommy," said the neighbour. "He'll be one to pick the pieces up. Elizabeth is incapable."

Marjorie was so upset about this, she high-tailed it back home and never said a word to Charles. Even though she was upset, she got herself organised, went to her friends, and played bridge all afternoon.

"You are not your usual self, Marjorie. Are you all right?" asked her bridge partner.

Marjorie replied, "I'm fine. I didn't sleep very well last night, and my bridge is telling me that."

Everyone laughed – except Marjorie, of course.

* * *

Five years had gone by with no word from Joanne whatsoever. It was as though she had vanished from the face of the earth.

So it was a surprise when she turned up one day at Eve's house in Holland Park. She hovered outside for some time, hoping to catch a glimpse of her sister. She watched her mother leave, and then she said to herself. *Here goes*. Mustering her courage, she ventured towards the door and was about to ring when the door opened. It was Ruth.

"What the hell are you doing here?" Ruth yelled.

Joanne replied, "Well, Eve has some drawings of mine that I asked her to look after for me. I need them back now, urgently."

Ruth replied, "You're lucky. You have just missed Mother."

Joanne never said a word.

"You know Eve is getting married," said Ruth.

"Yes, I read the papers, Ruth." Joanne carried on, "I know I have put my mum and dad through hell and back. I know they will never forgive me, but I need a favour."

"What's that?" asked Ruth.

Again Joanne hesitated, and then she carried on. "I have been clear of alcohol for nearly five years, and I have the chance to do something with my life. I've met this chap called Buzz – well, that's what everyone calls him. He is an American. He has been on twelve-month visa, which is running out. He wants me to go with him to America; New York, to be precise. I have told him everything, Ruth, about my past and Lucy living with Mum and Dad. I have been totally honest with him, and he still wants me to go with him to America."

"So what's stopping you?" asked Ruth,

Joanne replied, "Money, Ruth. I have no visible means of support if I go to America. I was hoping Eve could have a word with Father on my behalf, to let me have some of my trust fund – and of course, my drawings, which I left with Eve at your place. Hopefully they will help me to get a job in New York."

Ruth was taken aback. "What about Lucy?"

Joanne started to cry. "It hurts like hell that I have lost Lucy, but one day I will redeem myself. For now, I know Mum and Dad will look after her and give her every opportunity that I can't give her right now. I made a vow to myself, Ruth, that I would get myself sorted out, which I have done. Therapy helped a lot. They made me realise that it wasn't just about me, it was about family and family duty."

Ruth said, "Eve will be too busy, Joanne. I'll give Father a ring when we get to my place."

Joanne was hesitant but finally agreed to let Ruth have a word with their father. Ruth took Joanne to her place, which of course was not Sloane Court but another apartment.

Joanne suddenly started to panic. "It's no use, Ruth. Father won't want to know me after what I put them through."

Ruth replied, "Nonsense." She telephoned their father.

Sir John answered the phone. Jo could hear a heated argument going on. She was about to leave when Ruth said, "Come on."

"Where to?" asked Jo.

"To see Father."

Jo groaned.

"It will be OK, Jo, trust me," Ruth assured her.

After a lot of deliberating, Sir John finally agreed to give Joanne the money she needed, but he wanted one thing in exchange.

"What's that?" asked Jo.

"You will never seek custody of Lucy while we are alive." Jo thought about it long and hard, and although it pained her, she agreed.

"I will get my solicitor to draw up the necessary paperwork tomorrow. When you have signed it, I will release all of your trust fund to you. Spend it wisely, Joanne. There will be no more."

Joanne made an effort to kiss him, but thought wisely about not doing so. Finally, she just said thank you. Her father told her to meet him at the office at eleven the next morning.

Ruth kissed her father and whispered, "Thank you. Eve will be so proud of you." They both left.

"Do you want to stay overnight with me, Jo?"

Jo nodded and then said, "Can we ring Eve for my drawings?"

"Sure," replied Ruth.

Ruth rung Eve. She explained everything to Eve, and Eve then said, "Can I have a word with Jo?"

Jo came to the phone, and Eve said, "Don't let Lucy and the family down, Jo. There will be no second chance."

Jo just answered, "I know."

Eve added, "Jo, we are so proud of you. Keep it up."

Jo smiled to herself.

* * *

The next day, Jo went to see her father. With trepidation, she entered the office, asked for Sir John, and waited and waited. Jo was getting restless, and then a girl said, "You can go up now. Someone will be there to meet you." It was all very formal, which Jo had not anticipated.

Upon her arrival on the first floor, a girl was indeed waiting for her. It turned out that this was Sir John's private secretary. "This way, Joanne," the secretary said and smiled at her.

Joanne felt a little easier. She entered the room and saw Father in conversation with another chap. "Sit down, Joanne," he said. "I won't be a minute."

Suddenly, he turned to Jo. "Sign this, Joanne," he said.

She read it. The document said that Joanne was in full agreement for her daughter to remain with her parents until such time as they no longer could take care of her. Lucy would then be the responsibility of Lady Eve Kershaw, soon to become Eve Emerson, their eldest daughter.

Jo smiled to herself. She duly signed the papers – a copy for her and one for her father. The lawyer witnessed her signature. Sir John then handed Joanne a significant cheque and her drawings.

"Don't squander it, Joanne. There will be no more."

Joanne just acknowledged him and walked out the door with tears falling down her face.

Sir John rung Lady Jane. "It's done, Jane."

"Thank goodness for that. How did she look, John?"

"Remarkably well. She looked as though she is on the right track, Jane."

Thank God for that, thought Jane.

* * *

The wedding went without a hitch. Eve didn't want a big social marriage, so they only invited a few close friends from both sides of the family. Matt's family came from a place called Mumbles, on the Gower Peninsula. It was a lovely place to relax and unwind. Eve loved to spend weekends there. For Matt, it was a place made in heaven. He only wished he could live there, but work was hard to find, and London had more opportunity for him.

His mother and father were overjoyed with the wedding. They were awed by it at first, but they found Sir John and Lady Jane were very amenable when in their company. They said to Matt's parents, "We just want to be normal and be known as John and Jane, Eve's parents."

A week later, Jane was in a pensive mood when Sir John entered the room. *Now what?* he thought. Jane turned to him and said, "Do you think Ruth will ever marry? She seemed really fond of this Jed chap, talked about him all the time, but now she dismisses him out of hand."

Sir John laughed. "Don't tell me you want another wedding? No thank you, one's enough for me!"

Jane just smiled at him and said, "I'm thinking we should take Lucy to the villa for the summer holidays. Ben Johnson – Lucy's special friend, as she calls him – will be there. He lives in the next village to us at Giggs Hill Green. Lucy says Ben is her blood brother."

Sir John just smiled to himself and said, "I don't see why not. You don't usually ask me. Why now?"

"I thought you might be able to get away yourself for a few weeks," she replied.

Sir John looked surprised at her. "I'll see what I can do," was his reply.

When Grandma told Lucy about the trip, she was so excited about spending her summer holiday at the villa for six whole weeks.

* * *

As soon as they arrived at the villa, Lucy went to look for her friends who were already there – especially Benjamin. Everyone called him Ben except his mother, of course. He and Lucy were blood brothers and had made a pact to stay friends forever no matter what. Of course, childhood dreams don't always come true … or do they?

The kids had a lovely time. It was so peaceful. Lady Jane asked Ben's mother if she would keep an eye on Lucy while she went off to paint. "No problem, Lady Jane."

"Oh, please call me Jane. No formalities here."

"Well, if you're sure," said Ben's mum.

"That's settled then," said Lady Jane. She shouted for Lucy and told her that Mrs Johnson would be keeping an eye on her while Grandma went off to paint.

"All right, Grandma," Lucy said and then ran off to play with the others.

Jane Kershaw came across a lovely spot that was ideal for a landscape. She was in her element and in another world.

Suddenly, she saw a figure walking towards her. She just stared in disbelief. *No, it couldn't possibly be. Is it?* she said to herself.

The figure came closer and closer. *Oh, my God, it is.* It was Angelo. Her heart leapt as it had never leapt before. All her feelings came to the fore, as he came closer and closer, his eyes transfixed on her. His eyes said it all.

He gathered pace, grabbed hold of her, and embraced her like a man possessed. Jane responded passionately. Then it happened – they made love with no concern for the consequences whatsoever. The passion was just too great. It was ecstasy.

As the passion subsided, they lay beside each other taking in the experience they had shared together. They were one again – well, for the time being, anyhow. Their passion had blinded them to reality.

They lay there for ages, just looking and smiling at one another. Then suddenly, Jane made a move to get up. He grabbed her; he didn't want to let her go. She insisted. The significance of what had just happened was beginning to sink in. What had she done?

Jane tried in vain to get away from Angelo, but the emotion was too great and once more got the better of her. She lay there just gazing into his eyes, seeing the burning passion he had for her. Suddenly, she made herself steel away from him. She had to go for the sake of her family, and she was ashamed of herself for letting her emotions get the better of her once more.

She couldn't deny the truth that she was still madly in love with Angelo, even after all the years that had passed by. The passion had been reignited. It was the same as before, and it frightened her. She ran off, dropping most of her paint brushes, and jumped in the car. He just stared at her, not moving. She couldn't turn around to look at him, for she knew there was a lot at stake. The guilt she felt would haunt her for a very long time, and the consequences of it all were still to come.

Lady Jane composed herself and went to pick Lucy up. She really didn't say too much to Mrs Johnson except "Thank you." She hurried home to the villa, closed the door, and gave a sigh of relief.

"What is it, Grandma?" asked Lucy.

"Nothing, darling. I'm just tired. Shall we go sightseeing tomorrow? We can take Ben with us if you wish."

Lucy put an arm around her and kissed her. "I love you, Grandma," she said. Lady Jane became emotional. "Don't cry, Grandma," said Lucy with a worried look on her face.

Lady Jane pulled herself together. "I'll go and have a shower, Lucy," she said, hoping she could wash the guilt away.

The next day, as promised, Lady Jane took Lucy and Ben away for a couple of days. They started off in Siena, going into the museums and art galleries. Lucy was fascinated, but Ben was fed up. Later on, they caught a train to Rome.

This is more like it, thought Ben. They went to the Coliseum, the Roman baths, Trevi fountain, and the Spanish steps.

"That's enough for today. Grandma's tired," said Lady Jane. She hailed a taxi to the Hotel la Meridienne. The taxi driver acknowledged her. They all jumped in, and after about ten minutes they arrived. A porter came for their luggage. They were travelling light – Lucy and Ben only had rucksacks, and Lady Jane just had hand luggage.

The porter took their bags away and placed them in the bedroom. Lady Jane went to the receptionist and said, *"Vedera Signora"* in almost perfect Italian. She said she had booked a family room with a suite.

"Your name, Signora?"

Suddenly, a voice said, "Signora, Signora, you are so welcome."

Lady Jane's eyes lit up. "Please, no fuss."

"Excuse, I understand," the manager said. He took her up to the room, opened the door, and gave her the key. When they entered, there were gardenias all over the place. The fragrance filled the air.

The children were tired and hungry. They each ordered what they wanted from room service. A while later, the waiter arrived. The food smelled good.

"Dig in," said Lady Jane, and the children demolished their food in no time at all. She ordered them ice cream. She was still on her first course. She opened a bottle of white wine to go with her dinner.

There was a knock on the door. Lucy opened it, and the waiter came in with ice cream sundaes. Lucy and Ben just goggled at them. They were huge.

Lady Jane smiled to herself. *They'll remember this day for a very long time*, she thought. The next time she looked, they were both fast asleep, fully clothed. She placed the duvet over them, and then she got herself ready to retire. Her thoughts swiftly diminished as she fell into a deep sleep.

Suddenly, she was awakened by noise and screaming. It took her some time to focus, and then she saw Lucy and Ben having a pillow fight.

"What on earth?" she yelled. They stopped dead in their tracks. "Must you be so noisy at this time of morning?"

Lucy said, "But Grandma, it's past nine o'clock."

"What?" Jane exclaimed. She jumped out of bed and went into the bathroom. When she had finished dressing, she rang for room service to order breakfast.

Lucy asked, "What shall we do today, Grandma?"

"Would you like to visit Vatican City?"

Ben chirped in, "Yes, please." Ben was about eighteen months older than Lucy, and it showed at times. He always seemed more mature somehow.

Lady Jane rang down to reception to arrange a visit to St Peter's Basilica. The receptionist said she would see what she could do. An hour passed and no word.

Lady Jane said, "Perhaps we should have booked earlier. We can always visit there again." She could see the children were disappointed.

They went down to reception, and Lady Jane went over to ask, "Any luck?"

The receptionist mentioned that Lady Jane should have booked prior to their visit. She was sorry, but Lady Jane understood perfectly.

Lady Jane said to the children, "No joy, I'm afraid. What would you like to do next?"

Ben asked if they still go to the Vatican and wander around outside, which is what they did. After a couple of hours, Lucy was fed up. "Can we go back, Grandma?" she asked.

"Yes, of course we can go back home," said Jane.

After a late lunch, they made their way home. It took about an hour or so to reach the village. It was a tiring journey, especially in summer. The heat could be unbearable at times. She looked at Lucy and then Ben. They looked exhausted.

* * *

By the time they reached the villa, a storm was brewing. Lady Jane and Lucy just made it into the villa before the rains came. Jane went to look for the oil lamps and to check the generator just in case. Lucy was cold and tired. Her grandma lit the log fire as the storm raged. The lightning was deafening at times, echoing in the hillside.

The storm stopped as quickly as it came, freshening up the night air. Lucy had fallen asleep. "Come on, sleepyhead, bed for you," said Jane.

That night, Lady Jane had a restless sleep. All she could think about was Angelo. He had a spell over her; she was smitten by him. He was just the opposite of John. Was this what pulled her towards him? His carefree approach to life exhilarated her.

John was loving in his way and a lovely family man, but he was not at all adventurous. He would no more think about making love in the open air than fly to the moon. It would just be beyond his comprehension. It took her quite some time to fall into a deep sleep.

The next thing Jane heard was, "Wake up, wake up, Grandma!" It was Lucy.

Jane's eyes opened, and she had to try very hard to focus. She groaned, "What time is it?"

Lucy answered, "Ten o'clock, Grandma."

Jane groaned again as if to say, *Go away and let me sleep.*

Lucy jumped on the bed. "Come on, Grandma, I'm hungry."

With great effort, Jane hauled herself out of bed, sat upright, and then sat on the edge of the bed. With another huge effort, she made her way to the bathroom. To Lucy, she said, "Be down shortly. Lucy, you set the table."

CHAPTER TEN

Eve and Matt spent their honeymoon at Mumbles on the Gower. They had rented a lovely holiday home at Langland Bay. There were three bays all in close proximity to one another. Matt's mother and father lived not too far away in Newton. Matt loved coming back to Wales; it brought back all sorts of childhood memories for him.

Soon it was time for them to return to the rat race. For Eve, it wasn't all that bad; working for her father gave her some flexibility. Matt, on the other hand, loathed his job. Eve convinced Matt to study for his law degree, which he hadn't pursued at the time. He'd had enough of all the studying and wanted to earn some money. He had been conscious that his parents were still supporting him, and the opportunity for him to return and finish his law studies and obtain his law degree never presented itself again,

Matt had settled for a lesser role in law, being a post-graduate. If he could obtain his degree in law now, however, it would prove to be a huge advantage to him and open more prospects.

* * *

When they reached home, Eve picked up the mail and looked through it. She came across one from America. It was from Joanne, and it read:

Hi Eve,

Sorry we missed each other when I was in London. Good luck on your marriage. Just to let you know, I got my drawings. Thank you. Managing to keep off the booze. Have set up in New York – what a fascinating and vibrant city it is. Everything is done at high speed. Living with a guy called Buzz – don't ask! Working in the rag trade over here, taking everything in, hopefully so I'll be able to sell my designs one day. Tell Mum and Dad that I do love them and realise what I put them through. I know they will look after Lucy. I only hope one day Lucy will forgive me.

If Lucy ever asks about me, Eve, will you tell her I love her dearly, and if she wants to write to me she can.

Love Jo

Well I never! thought Eve. She was upset and yet pleased that everything seemed to be going OK for Jo.

Eve was interrupted by Matt. "Anything for me?"

Eve replied, "Yes, a couple."

She then went upstairs to change. They still had a couple of days left before starting work. She rang Ruth and left a message. She tried home only to find Mother was in Tuscany. She then rang her father.

"Eve! Lovely to hear from you. Had a nice honeymoon, have we?" her father said in a questioning way. Eve just smiled to herself. "I shall have to call you Lady Kershaw Emerson from now on," he added. They both laughed.

"See you Monday," Eve said and put the receiver down.

Ruth received the message and rang Eve. They arranged to have lunch at Annabel's. Matt made an excuse that he didn't want to sit with two women; to him, one was enough. He arranged to meet the lads for a few beers.

Eve said, "Make sure it is a *few* beers, Matt."

He just smiled at her with his boyish grin, and then said, "Bye then, see you later."

When Eve arrived at Annabel's, Ruth was already waiting. They embraced one another and entered, and from that point, they never stopped talking.

Ruth said, "I have something to tell you. I know you won't say anything to anyone."

Eve was on her guard, "What is it? Ruth, you look worried."

"I was worried to death, but all the tests have come back negative."

Eve was troubled but listened to what Ruth had to say. It shocked her to the core. "The bastard!" said Eve.

Ruth laughed, "I thought of something worse than that. That's why I left Sloane Court and looked for another apartment. I couldn't bear to live in our flat after that. However, I do have some good news ..." but before Ruth could tell Eve, Eve produced the letter from Jo. After reading it, Ruth looked at Eve and said, "That's encouraging. I do hope she can make something of herself now."

"So do I," replied Eve.

It turned out that Ruth had been offered a post at Ormond Children's Hospital as a consultant, to work alongside colleagues in the paediatrics department. Ruth was delighted. All the hard work she had done had finally paid off. To be recognised by her peers was something that really pleased her.

Eve said, "This calls for a celebration," and she ordered a bottle wine. "Are Father and Mother aware of your promotion?" Eve asked.

Ruth replied, "Not just yet. You are the first to know."

They chatted for some time, each outlining her plans. Eve then ventured onto a more serious topic – for her, at least. "Do you think, Ruth, that I am too old for children?"

Ruth looked startled. It took her a while to respond. Finally she said, "I don't see why not. Many women have children nearing their forties. Some conceive after forty. I can refer you to someone, if you're concerned."

Eve smiled at her sister and then said, "We'll see how it goes."

It was now getting quite late, so they made their way home, promising to keep in touch more often.

* * *

The next day, Sir John decided to take three weeks off from the office and travel over to Tuscany to meet up with Jane – but, more importantly, Lucy. He telephoned Eve to let her know his plans and ask her to keep things ticking over; in any emergency, she was to get in touch with him.

"I have so much to tell you, Father," said Eve.

Sir John replied, "I'll pop around tonight. You can make dinner for me, and then we can have a chat."

Matt entered the room. "Who was on the phone?" he asked.

Eve replied, "It was Father. He's coming over for dinner tonight. By the way, what time did you crawl into the house?"

Matt replied, "I wasn't that late. You must have retired early. I tiptoed around so I wouldn't wake you."

Eve smiled to herself and then said, "A likely story."

* * *

Later that evening, Sir John arrived and met up with Eve and Matt. After a brief chat about their honeymoon, Eve asked her father, "Has Ruth rung?"

"Indeed! Wonderful news, isn't it? Your mother will be overjoyed."

"Did Ruth mention the letter?"

Her father interrupted her. "What letter?"

Eve began to tell him. "I received a letter from Joanne, saying she has settled in New York and has managed to secure a job in the rag trade, whatever that implies. She keeps knocking on doors with her designs and one day hopes to have her own designer brand. She has been booze-free for well over five years now, I think. Finally, Father, she said she regrets everything she has done to hurt you both and hopes that one day you'll forgive her."

Sir John never said a word about the letter. "What's for dinner? I'm starving!" was the only thing he said.

During dinner, Matt said, "So, you're off to Tuscany."

"Yes. I am going to surprise Jane and Lucy," Sir John said.

"What a lovely idea!" said Eve.

They chatted about all sorts of things – including the company and the financial prospects for the forthcoming year. Matt mentioned that he was thinking about finishing his law degree.

Matt produced a bottle of matured whisky. "Here you are, Dad. A present from us."

Sir John looked as pleased as punch. "Thank you very much. I shall think of you two when I drink it."

"Not all at once, I hope," said Eve.

It was now time for goodbyes. "Let us know when you arrive," said Eve. "Love to Mother and Lucy from us both."

Her father embraced her, shook hands with Matt, and made his way to a waiting taxi. When he reached home, he rang Max. "I will be away for three weeks. Is everything in order?" A voice said yes and to meet in the usual place tomorrow.

CHAPTER ELEVEN

Back in New York, Jo was finding the rag trade very tiring, with little or no reward for the hard work involved. Had it not been for her trust money, she probably would have jacked it in, but something inside gave her self-belief that she could overcome her demons and the obstacles placed in front of her – one being waiting for a green card, which she didn't apply for right away. That's why she was working in a sweatshop, but at the same time taking everything in to learn the trade. There was more to it than she had bargained for, including the long hours. At night, she would collapse on the sofa, more often than not falling asleep until the dreaded alarm clock went off at six thirty in the morning.

After several months and numerous phone calls, her green card was finally granted, much to Jo's relief. It meant that now she could look for work in any fashion or designers' factory shop. Buzz, by this time, had flown the coop.

Jo was on her own, and in a way, she was glad to get rid of him. She decided to look for another flat nearer the city. This particular day, whilst travelling to work on the subway, she noticed an advert in one of the daily newspapers a women was reading. She tried to glance at it, nearly straining her neck, but to no avail. When she reached her station, Jo reluctantly alighted. The woman also got off at the same time and proceeded to walk out of the subway onto the main street. To Jo's amazement, the woman dumped the newspaper in a trash can, and Jo immediately retrieved it. Finally reaching work, Joanne went straight to her locker to peruse the paper. She spotted the advert, which read:

> Wanted: an experienced seamstress in an up-and-coming fashion house

The ad included a telephone number and address.

Jo wasted no time. She hurriedly went back to her flat, telephoned the fashion house, and asked about the advert. She had a long chat with a woman at the other end of the line. The woman said, "We have quite a lot of applicants, but if you can make it in the next hour, I'll fit you in for an interview." Jo thanked the women and wasted no time in sorting herself out.

When Jo arrived on Ninth Street, she entered the building, climbed up the steep stairway, opened the door on the left, and entered. There were half a dozen girls sitting there patiently. *Blimey*, she thought to herself.

Jo waited and waited, getting more and more agitated by the minute. Then, at last, she was called into an office by a young girl. Jo saw a woman in her mid-fifties sitting there. The woman introduced herself with, "My name is Suzanne Emmott. I started the business in 1950, and it has grown and grown. I am always looking for young talent." She looked up at Jo and smiled to herself. Jo looked quizzingly back at her.

Suzanne Emmott began her interview. "Sit down, Joanne, or is it Jo? Sorry, you've been waiting a long time. I have looked at your application. You don't seem to have had much experience as a seamstress. What made you apply for the position?"

Jo answered the questions truthfully and tried to fill in her background, including the dreadful accident and her drinking problem, which was well behind her now. "So you see, I do not have that much experience, really. I just want a starting point so I can show off my designs."

"Joanne," said the woman, "we will let you know as soon as possible. Thank you for being honest." They shook hands.

It was about three weeks before Jo received a letter. She opened it with trepidation. It read:

Dear Joanne,

We thank you for your application regarding the vacancy for a seamstress. Unfortunately, we feel that this is not the job for you. However, we would like to invite you for second interview next Monday at 11 a.m. to discuss a possible vacancy in another department. Please bring whatever drawings you may have with you. If you are still interested, please ring to confirm.

Yours faithfully.

Suzanne Emmott

This gave Jo the impetus she needed to look for alternative accommodation in the Brooklyn area, which was closer to Ninth Street. If the interview didn't work out, she would carry on looking.

Monday couldn't come soon enough. She got all her drawings and sketches together and thought about what to wear. Jo always had style, like her sisters and mother.

* * *

Monday morning finally arrived. Jo was up with the larks making sure that everything was in place. This was her big chance, and she wanted to make a good impression. She caught the subway to Ninth Street and arrived at the fashion house with five minutes to spare. Upon entering, she proceeded up the stairway and entered a room. She spoke to the receptionist and gave her the letter. The receptionist said, "Just a moment, Joanne."

Eventually, she returned. "This way, Joanne," she said.

Jo followed her. They stopped, the receptionist knocked on a door, and a voice said 'Enter.'" The girl opened the door for Joanne.

Suzanne Emmott greeted Jo and said, "Before we begin the interview, I need to know a few more details off you. Joanne, I notice you gave your address here in New York. Can I ask what part of England you lived in?"

Jo looked stunned. She really didn't want to talk about her family.

"Can I ask why?" said Jo.

Suanne Emmott replied, "Of course you can," and carried on, "I noticed that you put down Hadlington Girls School then on to London School of Art on your application."

"That's correct," replied Jo.

"Did you live in London?" asked Suzanne Emmott.

By this time, Jo was very wary of the questions and where they were leading. She looked at Suzanne Emmott in an interrogating sort of way, which didn't go unnoticed by her potential employer.

"I think you need an explanation, Joanne. I too went to Hadlington Girls School, and you remind me so much of one of my school friends a little younger than me. Her name was Jane Ashton."

Joanne again just stared at her. Finally she uttered, "That's my mother's maiden name. My father is John Kershaw. I have two older sisters called Eve and Ruth." They both said the names together, to Jo's astonishment.

Suzanne then asked how her mother and father were.

"To be honest," Jo replied, "I think they are OK. I'm in the doghouse with them, as you no doubt know."

"Tell me, do they still live in that lovely house called the Harrows?"

"Yes. I was brought up there, in fact," replied Jo.

"I did read that your father had been knighted for contribution to industry."

Jo replied, "Yes, he has."

Suzanne Emmott then said, "Joanne, unless I am mistaken, that makes you Lady Joanne."

Jo blushed and said, "I really don't talk about it."

Suzanne said, "Just a minute" and ordered more coffee. Then she carried on. "I read that Eve got married recently, and Ruth is a doctor, I believe."

Joanne was amazed. "How do you know all this?"

Suzanne smiled, "I get the *Tatler*."

Joanne just looked at her.

The interview itself took well over an hour. Joanne was introduced to Kate Taylor, who was Suzanne's head fashion designer. Suzanne asked Jo to show Kate the drawings and any sketches she had done. Kate never said a word.

Finally, Suzanne Emmott said, "Would you mind, Joanne, popping back this afternoon about two o'clock?"

Jo was as nervous as a kitten. She just played with her lunch, clock-watching. The time was ticking away ever so slowly.

Finally, it got to one forty-five. Jo headed to the fashion house. All at once, she was tempted to buy cigarettes. She chastised herself: *Don't be a bloody fool after all this time.* She entered the fashion house and went to the reception desk. The girl smiled. "They are waiting for you. Go straight up."

Jo nodded and proceeded to Suzanne Emmott's office. She knocked. "Enter," a voice said. She opened the door not knowing what to expect. Her heart was beating so fast.

Suzanne looked at Jo and said, "Sit down, Jo." She then said, "I will give you six months' probation, and we will take it from there. You can start tomorrow, 8 a.m. sharp. Report to the front office and ask for Kate Taylor." She carried on about salary and then said, "Bring your green card with you."

Jo just nodded. Deep down, she was elated.

"Don't let me down, Jo," Suzanne concluded. "There is a lot of talent out there who would love to be in your shoes right now." Jo just shook her hand and left the premises.

Jo decided to have a good look around to get her bearings. What she saw was the frontage of the fashion house, named, "Suzanne, Fashion Designer." It looked high-class indeed. This warmed Jo immensely. She was really chuffed and vowed to make the most of the opportunity.

Jo moved into a new apartment. It had two bedrooms and a large kitchen, plus a lounge and an exceptionally large bathroom. It wasn't too far from the city and quite near the subway. For once, Joanne was very happy.

* * *

On her first day of work, Jo was raring to go. She arrived early and was annoyed with herself. *They'll think I'm too eager.*

About fifteen minutes passed before Jo's manager, Kate Taylor, arrived. She shook Jo's hand, and after formal introductions, Jo followed Kate to another department. When they entered, there were half a dozen girls and one boy working on projects. Kate explained that each person had his or her own clientele who would give details as to what they were looking for, or what they had in mind. The designer would then have to come up with some drawings and outlines based on what the clientele had detailed. At that stage, the customer would either decline or give the go-ahead.

"You are responsible for the costings and materials that you use in your finished product," said Kate. Jo took it all in.

Kate then said, "We have lined a client up for you who you will work with, but under my supervision. If you feel overwhelmed or need advice, I am always available. Just take your time and listen to what they have to say. Jo, write it all down if you are not sure. Ask the client to repeat what they have said. Some people use a Dictaphone, others a small tape recorder. It is solely to protect you if any problem arises."

Kate concluded with, "You need to keep in touch with your client constantly." Then she added, "Please, Joanne, if you are not sure, come to me, no matter how busy I am. OK?"

Joanne nodded.

"Now let me introduce you to the girls and Darrel."

Once the introductions were out of the way, Joanne was shown to her desk and drawing board. "Your client will not be here till Friday," Kate said, "so you can just watch and observe. It will help you to see how things are done. We all wish you a sincere welcome and hope you will enjoy working for the company," Kate said.

CHAPTER TWELVE

Sir John and Lady Jane were having a lovely time at the villa. When John had finished his business calls, which was a daily routine, they would spend as much time as they could together. Somehow, Lucy seemed to have brought them closer. For Jane, all thoughts of Angelo were a distant memory – for the time being, at least. She still felt ashamed for what she had done, succumbing to Angelo's passionate attentions again. She hoped it would never come back to haunt her. Even though she was deeply in love with Angelo, she knew it could never be – even though her marriage was non-existent as far as intimacy was concerned.

Sir John broke her thoughts and mentioned that Jo had sent a letter to Eve. He relayed to his wife what Jo had said. Although Lady Jane had said she never wanted to hear about Jo again, that anger had now subsided. She was pleased that Jo had finally pulled herself out of the hellhole she was in. She had always been very close to Joanne, her youngest, and Jo's drawing and imagination matched Jane's. She was also overjoyed to hear of Ruth's promotion and now going to work in Omer od Children's Hospital for poorly children. It had a great reputation for treating poor children.

One day, whilst in the garden at the villa talking to the gardener, she watched a figure coming forward towards the villa, and her heart missed a beat. *Oh please, God, no.* She turned to go back inside.

Angelo shouted, "Jane! Jane!" She pretended not to hear him.

Just then, John appeared. *Who can this be?* he thought to himself and went to meet the man. Angelo was stunned to see him. He was motionless.

"Can I help you?" said Sir John.

Angelo replied, "Does Signora Jane live here?"

Jane came out, and he doffed his cap. "Scusa, Signora," he said in pidgin English, thrusting some paintbrushes towards Jane. "Are these yours?" Of course he knew they were.

He smiled at her, and Jane's heart began to melt again. *Stop it, Jane. Control yourself,* she said to herself. Then, in Italian, she said, "Yes, they are mine. Where did you find them? I have been looking for them."

Angelo replied, "Someone brought them to my studio. He found them while out walking with his family."

Jane replied, "I see. Well, thank you very much. I really do appreciate it. Would you like a cool drink? It's a long walk to the villa. You must be very thirsty in this heat."

Angelo excused himself and went on his way. As they watched him go back down to the village, Sir John said, "How did he know they were your brushes?"

Jane replied, "Because they have my name on them," and she showed Sir John. "Eve bought them for me one Christmas. She thought it was a novel idea."

"Being as you mentioned a drink, let's get out of this bloody heat," said Sir John.

Jane pondered for a while and said to herself, *I hope he didn't suspect anything.* She was interrupted by Lucy and Ben. "Good heavens, you look exhausted!" she cried. "Come on, you two, and sit in the lounge. It is cooler there. I'll bring you some lemonade." They both giggled.

Jane noticed Sir John looking pensive and asked what he was thinking about or what was troubling him.

He retorted, "You know damn well what's bothering me – this Angelo chap coming to the villa."

Jane looked at him, not knowing what to do or say. She could feel herself getting heated. "I didn't know this Angelo was coming here," she said.

Sir John looked at her. "I hear rumours, Jane, in the village about this Angelo. They say he is a gigolo who looks for wealthy English and American women on their own. If I hear any rumours about you and him, Jane, it's over. I gave you the benefit of the doubt last time and ignored what the villagers were saying about you, but not this time. If there is any truth at all in the rumours this time, trust me, the marriage is over. No second chance."

Jane protested, but it fell on deaf ears. The row disturbed Lucy and Ben. When they came into the conservatory, Sir John looked at Lucy and said, "How would you and Ben like to come to the village?"

They both jumped up and down with excitement. "Please!" said Lucy. She looked at her Grandma. "You too, Grandma."

Sir John said, "No, Lucy, just us."

Lucy could see that her grandma was upset and gave Jane a wistful smile. Then she left with her granddad.

Jane was keeping it together, but once they were gone, her heart broke. She sobbed and sobbed. She couldn't stand it anymore. She decided to bide her time, and then she would definitely leave Sir John and sod the consequences.

She went for a shower and thought about what John had said to her about Angelo being a gigolo. It hurt her. She started to have doubts. After all, she had given him money to help him in establish his art studio. *Did he really love me, or was it the money? How many more women has he had?* Jane now felt betrayed and embarrassed about it all, especially if it was true.

Meanwhile, Sir John took Lucy and Ben to the ice cream parlour. "You two stay here and do not leave. I have an errand to do. Lucy, wait for me. Do you hear me?"

Lucy just looked at him and nodded.

He left them and headed for the art studio. When he entered, Angelo came from the back. Sir John spoke in Italian to him. "I want to buy those two painting you have in your window."

Angelo replied, "They are not for sale."

Sir John said to him in a threatening voice, "Oh, I think they are for sale!"

Angelo looked at him and could see the anger in Sir John's face. Immediately he said, "Take them."

When Sir John had the paintings in his possession, he went straight into the back, caught hold of Angelo by the scruff of the neck, and gave the man the biggest hiding of his life. Angelo just played dead.

"Stay away from my wife, you gigolo, do you hear me, or you'll regret it," warned Sir John.

Angelo never said a word. He was cowering by this time.

Sir John stormed out of the studio and went to pick up Lucy and Ben, who were waiting patiently for him. He gestured for them to come over to him. He then took them to a sweet and chocolate shop. Lucy thought it was her lucky day; she was in paradise.

* * *

By the time Lucy and her granddad arrived home, there was a note saying that Lady Jane was going to Siena for a few days to sort things out. Sir John was now even more furious with her. *Playing games, are we? Well, two can play at that.*

He turned to Lucy and said, "I have to go home in a few days, Lucy. Would you like to come home with me and stay with Aunt Eve, or wait for Grandma? She has gone away for a few days."

Lucy looked at her granddad and said, "What about Ben and my friends?"

"You'll have time to say goodbye to them. Ben only lives in the next village, doesn't he?"

Lucy looked at her granddad and replied yes.

Sir John went into the kitchen. Jane had left them something to eat. He wasn't hungry, but Lucy was. After Lucy had eaten, it was getting late, so she went up to have a shower and change for bed. Sir John went up later, tucked her in, and read her a story. It didn't take long for Lucy to fall asleep. He looked at her and thought how much she was like her mother. He kissed her gently on the cheek and then closed her door.

Sir John then set about going over the paperwork Max had managed to procure from Williams and Thomson Asset Strippers and from Hunter and Owen solicitors (*not for long*, Sir John said to himself). After Sir John was satisfied that all the documents he had signed were in his possession, he poured himself a drink and sat and pondered for a while. He got up, went to the car, brought out the paintings, and burnt them along with all the paperwork that Max had given him.

* * *

The following day, Lucy woke up and went running into Grandma's bedroom, only to find that the bed had not been slept in. Then she remembered her granddad. She opened his bedroom door only to find no one there. Lucy ran down the stairs in a panic.

"Stop!" she heard. "Steady on, Lucy! You'll fall."

It was Granddad, to her relief. They had breakfast, and Lucy chatted all the way through. Sir John hadn't realised how much he had missed, living in London. Lucy was growing up fast.

Some time later, Sir John was startled by a noise. It was Jane, and she looked dreadful. He was glad that Lucy had left the room. He just stared at her, waiting for her to speak first.

Jane hesitated and then said, "If you want a divorce, then you can have one. I can't live this way any longer."

Sir John said, "You're not going anywhere until we sort this whole bloody mess out, and I'll decide if we divorce or not. Do I make myself clear?"

Jane started to cry. "I'm lonely when you are in London. I miss the girls terribly, and most of all, I miss Joanne."

Sir John looked stunned and said, "After all she has done and put us through?"

Jane answered, "Yes, but she is still our daughter and Lucy's mother."

"We'll talk tomorrow," said Sir John, and he walked into the garden. Jane just sat there in a dilemma.

When Lucy spotted her grandmother sitting there, she was elated. She ran and flung her arms around Jane and cried, "I thought you had left me and Granddad!"

Lady Jane was gobsmacked. She realised that Lucy was indeed growing up fast. Sir John was coming back from the garden and heard every word.

The rest of the day was spent preparing to leave and securing the villa. Sir John checked the generator and essential equipment, just in case an emergency arose. Pepe would deal with it while they were away.

* * *

The next morning, Lucy trundled into Grandma's room. Her face lit up when she saw that her grandmother was still there. Lady Jane and Lucy came downstairs together for breakfast. Sir John said, "Our flight is this afternoon."

Jane didn't say a word, except, "I'll get breakfast ready."

After breakfast, Sir John said, "I will contact my solicitors and sort things out. In the meantime, we carry on as before." Sir John then went into the conservatory. He was not in a forgiving mood.

Although Lady Jane was in turmoil, she didn't let it show to Lucy. Yet Lucy could sense that things were not right. She said, "Are you all right, Grandma?"

Jane looked at her and said, "Yes, I'm OK. I wanted to stay a while longer, that's all. But you have something to look forward to: going back to school." Lucy just smiled.

A few hours later, they arrived at Heathrow. Sir John said, "We will stay at St John's Wood for a few days till we sort things out." Again Jane never uttered a word. Lucy had never been to the London house. She was excited about it. All sorts of pictures came into her mind.

When they arrived, Mrs Brown was waiting for them. Sir John thanked her for staying on.

"Think nothing of it, Sir John," she said, and then she noticed Lady Jane and Lucy. "Nice to see you, Lady Jane. It's been a long time."

Lady Jane just smiled at her. Mrs Brown had left them a cold buffet, which they were grateful for, as they were feeling hungry and jaded. Lady Jane took the cases upstairs and showed Lucy to her bedroom. It was more spacious than the one at the Harrows, and it had a lovely double bed, which Lucy bounced on.

Later, with Lucy safely tucked up in bed, Lady Jane went back downstairs.

"Don't wait up. I might sleep at the club tonight," Sir John said.

Jane was grateful for that. She decided to ring Eve, but the phone just kept ringing, to her disappointment. Next she tried Ruth. Eventually a voice said, "Yes, who is it?"

"It's Mother, Ruth."

"How nice to hear from you! When are you coming home? I have something to discuss with Father."

"As a matter of fact, Ruth, we are already here in London. We are staying at the house for a few days."

"That's great news. I have a couple of days off, so I'll come over tomorrow to see you. Will Dad be there?"

"Not too sure, Ruth. Best ring in the morning. He is at his club now, and he might stay over. Have you seen anything of Eve?"

Ruth went quiet, and Lady Jane sensed something was wrong. "What is it, Ruth?"

"You would be better speaking to Eve. Nothing serious, Mother. Have to go now. See you tomorrow."

Lady Jane was even more perturbed now by what Ruth had said. She decided to try Eve again, but the phone just rang and rang with no answer. She rang Ruth again, and when Ruth answered, she said, "I can't get hold of Eve. Where can she be? It's past eleven o'clock. I can't go around to see what's happening. I can't leave Lucy with your father at the club."

Ruth just wanted to crash out. "OK," she said. "I'll go around. I have a key. I will let you know."

* * *

Eventually, Ruth reached Holland Park. She made her way to the house and saw that the lights were still on. Ruth knocked, but there was no answer. She knocked again, and still no answer. Ruth then entered, and she noticed the table lamp had been knocked over. She cautiously entered the lounge and was startled to find Eve on the floor and blood everywhere. She immediately knew what happened and telephoned for an ambulance. Ruth then went over to examine her sister.

The ambulance soon arrived. "Can you take her to Royal London?" Ruth asked.

The ambulance men looked at her.

"It's OK," Ruth assured them. "I'm a doctor, and they are expecting you. Can I come with you?"

Again, they both looked at one another. Finally, one said, "Well, it's really against the rules, but hop in."

Ruth secured the house and then rode with the ambulance. When they arrived at the accident and emergency department, Eve was rushed inside. Two doctors were waiting for them. Ruth explained what had happened, and Eve was rushed to theatre. A couple of hours later, one of the doctors came to Ruth. "You were right. She has miscarried."

Ruth told him who her father was and that he was coming right over. Sir John arrived before too long, and the doctor took him and Ruth to a private room. He told them, "I need to speak to her husband."

Ruth explained that Matt was with his parents in Wales. "We will get in touch with him."

The doctor then said, "Tell him to ring sometime tomorrow after eleven o'clock."

Sir John and Ruth went back to St John's Wood. When they arrived, Lady Jane was still up. John looked at Jane, and Ruth noticed the chill in the atmosphere. *God, not again. This is becoming a regular habit*, she thought to herself.

Sir John said to Lady Jane, "Eve has had a miscarriage." Jane just started to sob. Ruth went over to comfort her mother.

"It's just one thing after another, Ruth," Jane sobbed. "I can't cope anymore."

Ruth took charge. She made her parents and herself a coffee and poured them all a whisky. She looked at the time: it was three in the morning. Ruth contemplated and decided to ring Matt later. She then turned to her parents and said, "I think we should go to Eve's and clean up the mess as much as we can before Matt gets home."

Jane looked at Ruth and said, "Do you mean me?"

Ruth was annoyed. "Yes, I do mean you, Mother."

Sir John said in a stern voice, "That's what mothers do, isn't it?" in a sarcastic way.

"What about Lucy?

"I'll see to Lucy," Sir John replied.

Ruth called for a taxi. It didn't long for one to arrive. As they entered, Jane was apprehensive at what she might see. She hesitated and then said, "Is it a mess, Ruth? I'm not too good at cleaning."

Ruth couldn't believe what she had just heard. "Of course it's a bloody mess, Mother!"

They entered the lounge, and Jane felt nauseous right away. Ruth looked at her mother and said to herself, *You're a waste of space.*

Ruth set about cleaning the best way she could. By the time she had finished, dawn was approaching. Ruth went up to the bathroom and showered, looked for a change of clothing in Eve's wardrobe, and managed to find something suitable to wear. Then she went back downstairs to her mother, who had fallen asleep at the table. Ruth decided not to wake her.

In a way, Ruth felt sorry for her mother. She realised that her dad could be difficult at times and had a nasty temper, and she often wondered if Mother had someone else. Both she and Eve had noticed a change in her when she came back from Tuscany, but her mother said nothing.

Ruth made herself tea and toast. The smell stirred Jane. She opened her eyes, having to focus on where she was, and then it all came flooding back to her. She immediately looked around and saw Ruth.

"I'm sorry, Ruth," she said. "I have had a terrible few days. I'm exhausted."

Ruth didn't chastise her mother. She could see Jane was in a state.

After an hour, Ruth decided to ring Matt up. It was now five thirty in the morning. The phone rang and rang, and then suddenly a voice said, "Hello?" in a Welsh accent.

"Is Matt there? It's Ruth."

"Do you know what time it is!" the not-too-friendly voice said.

Ruth was furious. "Do you think I would ring now if it wasn't an emergency?" she yelled down the telephone.

There was no response. At last Matt answered the phone. "Hi, Ruth. What's up?"

"It's Eve." Ruth paused. "Matt, Eve has miscarried and is in London Royal."

"Oh my God!" Matt cried. "I will be there as soon as I can."

Ruth asked her mother to stay at Eve's and wait for Matt. Jane really didn't want to stay; she was still overwhelmed with everything that had gone on. She just wanted to get back to the Harrows, which was her bolthole and retreat. But Ruth was sensing that things were not quite right with her mum and dad, and she wanted to return to St John's Wood alone.

When she got there, Mrs Benson answered the door and said, "Lady Ruth, so nice to see you. Sir John is in the study."

Ruth acknowledged her and went to the study. Her father was on the phone. He beckoned her to sit down, which she did.

Sir John put the phone down and turned to Ruth. "Had a word with the senior gynaecologist at the Royal and asked him to arrange a private room for Eve, so we can visit without any prying eyes. I expressed to him the utmost need for privacy."

Ruth just nodded and thought how money talks.

Sir John interrupted her thoughts by saying, "Where is your mother?"

"Still at Eve's, waiting for Matt to arrive," Ruth answered. She saw her opportunity and said to herself, *Well, here goes.*

"Dad, are you going to tell me what the hell is going on with you and Mum?"

He looked at her surprised. "Does it show that much?" Sir John said.

"You could cut the atmosphere with a knife between you both. And this isn't the first time I've noticed," Ruth replied.

Sir John then had to explain what had gone on. Of course, it was no surprise to Ruth – nor would it be to Eve. Ruth then asked her father what they planned to do. He answered, "I have made an appointment with my solicitor to see about a divorce. We'll take it from there."

That was something Ruth was not expecting. She couldn't wait for Eve to know – when, of course, her sister was up to it.

Ruth rang work to have a word with Dr Richard Evans. She explained the situation to him.

"Have you thought about what we discussed?" he asked.

Ruth replied, "I haven't now with so much going on. I will definitely give you an answer within the next week or so."

"OK, Ruth, but don't leave it too long. They are waiting for an answer."

"I won't." Ruth put the phone down.

She went into the lounge, where Lucy sat in a corner drawing. Ruth wondered if Lucy had any idea what was going on with her grandparents.

"Can I look at your pictures?" Ruth asked her niece. She was impressed by Lucy's work.

"Where's Grandma?" Lucy asked. "I miss her."

"Grandma is at Auntie Eve's waiting for Uncle Matt to arrive, and Granddad has had to go to work, so you are stuck with me."

Lucy just smiled and said, "I'm hungry."

They went into the kitchen. "Mrs Brown, Lucy is hungry," said Ruth. Lucy looked at Mrs Brown with appealing eyes.

"I don't think we have that much in," said Mrs Brown. "I wasn't expecting Sir John to be home so soon. I'll see what I can muster."

The telephone started to ring, and Ruth picked it up.

"Matt here, Ruth."

Ruth was relieved. "Has Mum filled you in?"

"In a spasmodic way. Is she OK, your mother? She seems distant."

"We have been up most of the night, Matt. It's been a terrible shock for us all, and Mum is not getting any younger. Order her a taxi, will you, to St John's Wood?"

"Will do. I'm off to the hospital now. I have rung the hospital, and Eve has had a quiet night, so that's something, I suppose. See you later."

Ruth turned to Lucy and said, "Grandma's coming home now, Lucy, but I think she will need to rest."

Lucy was busy eating her sandwiches and just nodded.

When Matt arrived at the hospital and went to reception, a nurse came to him. "This way, Mr Emerson."

He followed her, and it seemed ages before they reached Eve's room. He noticed it was in the private area of the hospital. Before he entered the room, a doctor came out and shook Matt's hand. He explained what had gone on and that they had to perform a hysterectomy, which meant Eve would not be able to have any children.

"Can I see her?" he asked.

The doctor said, "She is sedated now, but of course can see her if you wish." Matt entered the room and was shocked to see Eve motionless. He was full of emotion. They had both dreamed of having kids.

CHAPTER THIRTEEN

It had been a dreadful few days. Ruth was tired out. The emotion had finally gotten to her. When she arrived home, she just crumbled and sobbed uncontrollably. She cried herself to sleep.

By the time Ruth woke, it was well into the afternoon. *Good heavens!* she said to herself. She gathered her thoughts, went into the kitchen, and made coffee and a bite to eat. She sat for a while, her mind turned to the proposition that her boss had offered her. She needed to have a word with her dad sooner rather than later. She rang him at the office.

"Hi, Ruth. What is it?"

Ruth asked, "Are you free tomorrow sometime or this evening at your place?"

Sir John thought for a moment and then said, "Come over for dinner at seven o'clock tonight. See you then. Have to go now, Ruth."

She wandered into the lounge and decided to ring Matt.

"Hello. Matt here."

"Hi, Matt. It's Ruth. How's it going?"

"Eve is OK. She is very upset about losing the baby. I haven't told her what the doctors have said about not being able to have any children. I just don't know how to tell her. I look at her and fall soft. It hurts so much, Ruth."

"I know, Matt. It can't be easy. Can I give you some advice, Matt?"

"Anything, Ruth."

"Let the doctors tell her. Just be there to pick up the pieces."

Next, Ruth rang her mother.

"Lady Jane speaking."

"Hi, Mum. You sound much better."

"I am, Ruth. I must apologise for my behaviour at Eve's. I am deeply ashamed of myself."

"Think nothing of it. We were all in shock. Anyhow, I'm ringing to say I'm coming over tonight for dinner. I need to discuss a couple of things with Dad."

"I know. Your father has rung me. Why don't you stay here for a couple of days and rest up here rather than be on your own."

Ruth thought about it. "OK, I will," replied Ruth.

Ruth went to have a shower. The phone started to ring again. *What now?* she said to herself. She answered it.

"Ruth, Robert Waddell here. Just learnt about your sister. How is she?"

Ruth was taken aback. "Eve's doing fine, Robert. Thanks for asking."

Robert then said, "It's two-pronged, really. I have heard on the grapevine that you may be going into the private sector. Any truth in it?"

Ruth was now paying attention. "I haven't made my mind up yet," she answered.

"Look, can we meet up? I would like to discuss something with you before you decide."

This put Ruth into a dilemma. She hated not knowing what to do. She said, "Are you free tomorrow?"

He replied, "Yes."

Ruth made arrangements for him to come to her parents' house at ten thirty in the morning, which he agreed to do.

Well, that's put the cat amongst the pigeons, she thought to herself. At the same time, she was intrigued.

* * *

The evening went very pleasantly indeed. Whatever her parents' differences were, they seemed to have resolved them – or shelved them for one night, at least. *Who knows?* thought Ruth. When it was time for her to have a word with her father, they went into his study.

Her father asked her about this Jed fellow, and did she intend settling down with him? Ruth answered, "About Jed, Dad." Ruth told him everything. "That's why I moved out of Sloane Court. I couldn't live in the flat any longer. I needed to find somewhere else. Every time I entered the flat, I would see him standing there naked. It nauseated me."

Sir John was raging inside. "What's this fellow called?"

"Jed Butler," replied Ruth. Sir John was incensed because he had an idea who this Jed Butler might be.

Ruth could see her father was agitated. "Leave it, Dad. I have something more important to discuss with you. I have been offered a post in the private sector. My boss has put my name forward. I am seriously thinking about it, Dad. It would mean having more time to myself."

"So why ask me?" her father asked,

"The practice want me to stump up £50,000 pounds."

Sir John whistled. "Where is the practice?"

"Harley Street," Ruth replied. "The name is Hopwood Private Clinic."

Sir John jotted it all down. "Leave it with me. I'll see what I can find out."

Ruth then mentioned that Robert Waddell, a colleague at work, had asked her to hold fire on making her decision until he could have a word with her. "You may remember him from when Joanne was in hospital. He was one of the consultants."

Sir John said, "You have a word with this Robert fellow and see what he wants to say, and we'll take it from there."

Ruth felt much easier now having told her father.

He then asked, "Does Mother know about this chap Jed Butler?"

"Good God, no! And that's the way I want it," Ruth said in an emphatic voice.

* * *

The next day at ten thirty, Robert Waddell arrived. Mrs Benson showed him into the lounge. He noticed Ruth and smiled, and then he saw that she was with an older woman and a young girl.

Ruth gestured towards Lady Jane and said, "This is my mother."

"Please to meet you. Robert, isn't it?"

He acknowledged her. "And who is this?" he asked.

"My name is Lucy."

Everyone laughed. Lady Jane rang Mrs Benson. "Coffee, please, Mrs Benson." Then to Lucy she said, "Come on. We will go into the study."

Robert Waddell just sat there. "Blimey, Ruth. I knew you came from a wealthy family, but not this wealthy."

Ruth laughed and said, "I never see any wealth, Robert."

Mrs Benson came in with coffee, and Ruth said thank you.

Lady Jane entered the room and said, "Robert, you're welcome to stay for lunch."

Robert hesitated.

Ruth said in a commanding voice, "Yes, Mother. Robert will stay for lunch."

"That's settled then." Lady Jane went back to the study.

Ruth was beginning to like Robert Waddell. There was something about him. He reminded her of her father in a funny sort of way. They just looked at one another for some time in silence, and for some reason there was no awkwardness at all. It became apparent that Robert's concern about her leaving for private practice had to do with them no longer working together. Though he couldn't quite come out and say it, he wanted to keep seeing her every day.

Mrs Benson interrupted them. "Lunch is ready, Lady Ruth."

Ruth just smiled. Robert looked in amazement. "What's this 'Lady Ruth' stuff?" he asked.

Ruth was embarrassed. "Oh, it's nothing. It's just formalities and decorum, really. My father is Sir John Kershaw, that's all."

Robert said, "Wow."

"Please, Robert, no fuss. We are a normal family ... if any family can be normal, that is."

They both laughed. Ruth led Robert to the dining room for lunch. Lucy had already eaten and was in her bedroom, doing what girls do at her age. Robert stayed most of the afternoon. Lady Jane liked him. She was hoping he would be the one for Ruth.

Finally, Robert said, "I have to go now."

Ruth walked him to the door.

"Can I see you again?" he asked.

Ruth immediately said, "Yes, but not here."

Ruth gave Robert her Chelsea address and telephone number. He gently kissed her on the cheek and then left. Ruth went back into the lounge.

"What a nice fellow he is, Ruth."

Ruth looked at her mother. "Don't you go planning any weddings for me, Mother, do you hear?"

Her mother said, "Who, me?"

Ruth saw Robert quite a few times that week. She told him that she had declined the offer to join the private clinic and put it to Dr Evans that she was happy with the job she had.

"How did he take it?"

"He wasn't too pleased," Ruth replied. She added, "I'm back on duty tomorrow, so I'll see you when I see you."

Robert grabbed hold of her. "Don't leave it too long," he said in a loving way. It took Ruth by surprise. She just smiled at him and said nothing.

* * *

When Ruth returned to work, the hospital was rife with gossip.

"What's all the commotion?" asked Ruth.

"Dr Richard Evans has resigned," said one of her work colleagues.

Ruth was shocked to hear this. Another colleague came up to Ruth and asked, "What's all this I hear about you and Robert Waddell?"

Ruth looked stunned. "Why? What are they saying?" she asked.

The doctor replied, "That you and he are an item. You have been seen about town together."

"Well, I'm damned," Ruth said.

"You know, Ruth, there's nothing sacred in this place. You are now the envy of all the nursing fraternity in the whole hospital."

They both laughed.

"Come on. Let's get to work," said Ruth. The morning went very quickly. It was as though Ruth had never been away.

"By the way, Ruth, how is your sister doing?" asked another colleague.

Ruth replied, "Eve's doing very well, thank you."

* * *

Eve was out of hospital now. She had been depressed for weeks. Ruth advised Eve to go to a therapist to help her through her trauma, and Eve took the advice.

A year passed before Eve showed any signs of improvement. Lucy helped Eve a lot when she was not at school. She would talk all day to Eve, mainly about school and how she and Ben Johnson were blood brothers, and one day she would marry him. Eve just smiled to herself. Lucy reminded her of Joanne even more so now that she was getting older.

Lucy also told Eve that one day she would be famous for her drawings. Eve asked her, "What sort of drawings?" thinking they might be fashion drawings like her mother. Lucy got her drawings out and showed them to Eve. "My word, Lucy, these are incredible!"

Lucy replied, "I know."

Eve just stared at the girl and thought how confident she was.

Lady Jane came in and said, "Come on, Lucy, time to go." Lucy kissed Eve and waved goodbye.

When Matt arrived home from work, he asked, "How's your day gone?"

"You've just missed Mum and Lucy. She has exhausted me."

"Who, your mother or Lucy?"

Eve smiled. "Lucy, silly!"

Matt smiled and then said, "I've got some good news, Eve. I have been accepted at Oxford to gain my law degree."

Eve was overjoyed. It was the boost she needed. This would mean they would be able to work together.

"If I can help in any way, Matt, you will ask, won't you?"

Matt was so pleased to hear this. It showed that Eve was now beginning to look forward again for the first time since her miscarriage.

After another month, Eve was ready to return to work, which delighted the whole family, her father especially. He tried not to burden her with too much work to begin with, but gradually, Eve got into the daily grind of meetings.

Sir John would give Jane daily reports on Eve's progress. Jane was toying with the idea of going down to the Harrows. It would soon be the start of the summer term for Lucy, and she knew how much Lucy enjoyed it down there. To be honest, Jane was missing the peace and quiet of country life.

Jane ventured to tell John what she had in mind and asked him what he thought about it.

"Leave it with me a couple of days, Jane," he said. "I don't want to put too much on Eve right now."

Jane just said, "Fine." She was resigned to the fact that nothing would ever be the same again.

CHAPTER FOURTEEN

Jane lived in situ now with Sir John at the London house. Lucy was now at university. If they went down to the Harrows, Sir John would accompany Jane. She had shot her bolt, and the leash was beginning to tighten even more.

Nothing happened about the divorce on the advice of his solicitor, who said it would be too costly for Sir John. The solicitor advised him to split up his assets between his children. "As it stands right now, you would be thumped heavily by corporation tax and income tax. Have a word with your accountants and then get back to me."

Sir John took the solicitor's advice and put nearly all his assets in his daughters' names, including Joanne and granddaughter Lucy. He left absolutely nothing to Jane except his pension fund and a small annuity to be paid yearly.

* * *

It was a week before Lucy's summer holidays from uni. Sir John rang Lady Jane and told her, "We'll go over to Bath to pick up Lucy tomorrow and then go down to the Harrows. Can you let Daisy know and Mollie?"

Jane was over the moon. Even though John would be there, he spent more time in his study than with her these days. She and Lucy would be able to trot off and do their own thing.

Lady Jane rang Daisy to say they would arrive in a couple of days or so and would let her know precisely when. "Will you organise everything?" she asked.

After speaking with Daisy, she rang Ruth and left a message, and then Eve. With all that in order, Lady Jane set about getting everything ready. She made up a couple of flasks and took a couple of blankets. *I think that's all,* she said to herself.

Sir John arrived home and went up to change, and then he spoke to Mrs Brown. He gave her an envelope, which didn't go unnoticed by Jane. "Ready," said Sir John, and then they set off for Bath.

The journey was uneventful. Jane was in her own thoughts, thinking about seeing Lucy again. There was no chit-chat, not even a comment when a driver cut in front of them. Sir John would usually come out with very abusive language. Jane was feeling uncomfortable and wishing the journey would end.

Traffic was heavy; it took nearly two hours to get to Bath. Sir John had booked them into the Gainsborough, where they were greeted by a porter. "Evening, sir," he said and proceeded to carry their bags and cases.

The receptionists stood there waiting for them. "Good evening, Sir John, Lady Jane. Nice to see you back. It's been a long time. Here are your keys. Usual suite." Sir John just nodded. Jane smiled and said thank you.

* * *

Jane had a lovely couple of days. She pampered herself, and the spa was invigorating. She had a massage every day and just wound down. She was feeling refreshed and now getting excited about seeing Lucy. It had been arranged to pick Lucy up early, as Sir John had to check into the office before they set off to Ditton Thames. He was still worried about Eve.

They arrived at the campus, went straight to the dormitory, and asked for Lucy. Ten minutes later, she arrived with the house prefect.

Jane was ecstatic. Lucy was beaming; she was so happy to see them. Sir John helped to carry her things.

"Good God, Lucy, so much!"

Lucy just grinned at her granddad. She had missed her grandparents so much. "Come on," she said. "Let's get going. Plenty of time to catch up."

Sir John wanted to miss the heavy traffic if he could. Jane and Lucy chattered all the way. It didn't seem too long before they arrived back home. To Jane's surprise, Sir John dropped them off and went to the office. "Back at three o'clock, Jane. Have everything ready." Jane just acknowledged him.

They entered, and Mrs Brown greeted them. She had made a cold buffet.

"Thank you, Mrs Brown. We will be leaving about three o'clock." Lucy and Jane went into the dining room to have something to eat.

At precisely three, Sir John arrived and said, "Ready."

Jane nodded. "Come on, Lucy," she said, and they set off for Ditton Thames. Upon arrival, Daisy was waiting for them and helped them with their baggage. She made them a cup of tea. After a while, Jane said, "I think I will go and freshen up." Lucy was already in her room. Sir John didn't even look up.

* * *

Later, Jane came downstairs. Daisy and Mollie had made a light dinner. Sir John was in his study. He rang up Max to tell him he was at Ditton Thames.

"Any news? asked Sir John.

The voice said, "Yes, things are moving nicely. Watch this page!"

"There is one more assignment for you," said Sir John. "Meet me near the railway bridge tomorrow about one o'clock." Max said OK.

Jane called Sir John's study his retreat. If only she knew what really went on with clandestine meetings with this Max fellow, she would be mortified.

Lucy was already downstairs. "Is everything all right with you and Granddad now?" she asked her grandmother.

Lady Jane replied, "Yes. Fine."

Lucy went into the dining room to have something more to eat. She then said she was tired and went up to her room. The atmosphere was not what Jane had expected. She switched the TV on, poured herself a drink, and sat to watch a film. After a while, she was bored, and she decided to read her book. She poured herself another drink.

When she woke up, the telly was still on. It took her a while to come around, and then she remembered she was home at the Harrows. It brought a smile to her face. She went upstairs, and for a while she was contented.

The only disappointment for Lucy was that Ben wasn't around. He had stayed on at Oxford. He was now over twenty and becoming a young man. Jane felt for Lucy. She knew how much Ben meant to her.

"Lucy," she said, "life is full of disappointments. It's how you overcome them that's important," said her grandma.

Lucy just looked and said nothing. She was becoming a young lady now. She loved uni and had many friends. She and Laurie, Olivia, and Cate would get up to all sorts of things. They loved going to the movies and then on to McDonald's when they could. Lucy worked hard at her studies, especially art class. Her ambition was to become an interior designer.

Regardless of the fact that Ben was not around, Lucy enjoyed herself with her grandma, and her aunts when they came to visit. For Jane, it was like old times. She was happy – for the time being, at least.

* * *

It was almost time for Lucy to return to uni. She wanted to go back a week sooner to stay with Auntie Eve and Uncle Matt. They said they would take her back to Bath.

Eve was perturbed. She could see her mother was deteriorating. Jane's zest for life was disappearing. It concerned Eve so much that she mentioned it to her father, who said he wasn't aware of anything, which made Eve even more anxious. Eve knew her father could be difficult at times. She noticed it much more now that she worked alongside him.

When they arrived at Holland Park, Lucy went straight to her bedroom. An hour later, she came downstairs. Matt was in the lounge watching TV, and Eve was in the study. Lucy knocked and entered.

"Can I have a word, Auntie Eve?"

"Yes, of course, Lucy."

Lucy looked at Eve and then said, "Will you be truthful with me if I ask you a question."

Eve now was put on her guard. She had a premonition of what Lucy was going to ask her.

Lucy hesitated and then said, "I know you may think I am paranoid, but I need to know the truth."

"What is that, Lucy?" said Eve, knowing what was coming,

"Is Auntie Jo my mother?"

Eve replied, "Yes she is, Lucy."

Tears started falling from Lucy's face. She looked at Eve and asked, "Why didn't anybody tell me? I just knew there was something. When Grandma and Granddad talked about her, they would start to argue. Grandma would get very upset. All I want to know is why did she leave me and not take me to America with her?"

Eve went into her desk drawer. Matt walked in, and Eve said, "Not now, Matt." He could see Lucy was upset, and he left them together.

Eve pulled out a pile of letters and said, "I knew this day would come, Lucy. If it is any consolation to you, your mother loves you very much. I want you to have all of these and read them." Eve gave Lucy cuttings from various newspapers. Lucy took them away without saying another word.

As Lucy went out of range of hearing, Eve rang Ruth and told her everything. Ruth was relieved.

"I'm glad it's out in the open. They should have told her years ago."

Eve said, "Mother and Father will hit the roof!"

Eve went into the lounge and poured herself a stiff drink. "Matt," she said, "do you think you could hold the fort for a couple of days at work? I need to be with Lucy."

"No problem. Why, what's up?"

Eve set about telling him everything about Joanne. Matt listened intently and said, "Your family have more skeletons in the cupboard than a cemetery."

Eve replied, "Oh, I don't think so," and laughed.

Eve also mentioned her mother to Matt. It was then that Matt told her about what had gone on in Tuscany. Eve couldn't believe it. She and Ruth used to speculate about their mother having an affair, but the reality of it all was there for everyone to see.

"How do you know all this?" asked Eve.

"Ruth told me that your father and mother were thinking of getting a divorce – that your mother had met up with this Angelo chap again on the last holiday, in fact."

"You didn't think to tell me!" Eve was furious.

"Just a minute, Eve," Matt said. "I was told in confidence. Besides, you were in hospital fighting for your life. When you came out, Ruth advised me to leave it while you got stronger."

Eve went quiet and thought to herself, *So his name is Angelo.* She remembered the paintings in the art studio. It was too much of a coincidence to dismiss it.

For the next couple of days, Lucy was very quiet. Eve left her alone to evaluate things for herself. Then suddenly Lucy asked Eve, "Can I write to Jo?"

Eve smiled at her. "Of course you can write to Joanne. But Lucy, she is not 'Jo,' she is your mother."

Lucy said, "Only in name. She is Jo to me. I see you and Grandma as my mother."

Eve went over to Lucy, hugged her, and said, "And you are my daughter to me. What do you intend to do about Grandma?"

Lucy replied, "We carry on the same as before. I just want to correspond with Jo, that's all. I have read the letters. I can see it was the best thing to do at the time. I would never hurt Grandma. I love her too much."

Lucy soon got back into the swing of things at uni. She was always happy when she was with her school friends, as they were all the same age. She loved her family dearly but realised that they were all getting older. She started to write to Jo but asked Jo not to mention anything to Grandma about writing to her. Lucy said that it would be easier all round.

CHAPTER FIFTEEN

Jane decided to go into town. She was wandering aimlessly around, not looking at anything, when she was tapped on the shoulder, which made her jump. She turned around, and it was Marjorie Winters.

"Good heavens, Jane, what's wrong? This isn't you, letting yourself go like this. You look dreadful."

Jane started to blubber. Marjorie took her to a discreet corner of the store. Finally, Jane composed herself, and then they went into the café area in Harrods and ordered coffee. Jane told Marjorie absolutely everything. Marjorie was shocked.

"Why don't you just leave him?" she asked.

Jane started to cry again. "Do you really think John would let me just leave him? I think not, Marjorie. Truth is, it's a bloody mess."

She went on, "I have never mentioned this to anyone, but after the awful accident, Joanne gave us hell. We did all we could do under the circumstances. Then we received a phone call to say Joanne was fit enough to leave. We assumed she would want to come home to the Harrows, as we had been looking after her daughter, Lucy, who was nearly six at the time. But Joanne didn't come to us. She took off without a by-your-leave, and we were left picking up the pieces once more. John was furious and said, 'That's it. She has made her bed. Let her lie in it.'"

Jane continued, "I had never seen him that angry. It was one shock after another. I wanted to come and see you, but I felt so guilty about Joanne surviving and your Maggie and Racheal not making it – and with the outburst at the Masonic Ball from Elizabeth, it was just the last straw. I approached John about getting in touch with you both again, but he said it wouldn't help. Then time moved on and it became more difficult."

Marjorie put her arm around Jane and said, "The past is the past. Get over it, Jane. When you get back to London, you can start socialising with me and my friends."

Jane interrupted her. "I am already back in London. We only go to the Harrows when John is with me. He keeps me on a tight rein these days. I can't go anywhere without him."

"You leave John Kershaw to me," Marjorie said in an emphatic voice. "Now tell me about you granddaughter."

Jane set about telling Marjorie about Lucy and the girls. Marjorie looked at her and said, "What about Joanne?"

"We've lost touch. She is in New York. Eve knows more than me," Jane answered.

Marjorie was so annoyed with her. "You stupid, stupid woman. How could you? I suggest you find out where Joanne is and make it up."

By this time, Jane was sobbing uncontrollably. In between sobs, she said, "It's not me. John will never forgive Joanne for what she has done to the family. He can't understand why I miss Joanne, because I have the girls and Lucy."

"Right," said Marjorie. "I will pick you up Monday. Get spruced up. I will introduce you to the book club at eleven in the morning."

Jane hesitated. "I don't know what John will say."

"You leave John to me. Just be ready."

Jane felt much better now that Marjorie was in charge. She was always the stronger of the two.

They made their way out of Harrods. Marjorie took Jane's arm and said, "You're coming home with me. You can't go back looking like that. He'll know that you've been upset about something."

When they arrived at Notting Hill, they entered the house, and Marjorie said, "Look who I found wandering around Harrods."

Charles looked up and said, "Jane, how lovely to see you! It's been a long time."

"Too long," Jane replied.

Marjorie gave him the eye, and he said, "If you'll excuse me, Jane, I'm off to the club." He pecked Marjorie on the cheek and left.

"You go and freshen up, Jane," said Marjorie.

By the time Jane came back, Marjorie had made tea and sandwiches. She filled Jane in on what had gone on in their lives. Peter was now married, and they had two lovely granddaughters. Marjorie showed Jane photos of Jessica and Holly. They lived in the Cotswolds. Peter was a civil engineer. He had kept in touch with Tommy Ashurst for a while after the accident.

"Elizabeth is only a shadow of the woman she once was," said Marjorie. "She has never gotten over the loss of Racheal, and with Robert dying suddenly, it's gotten to be all too much for her. She still blames Charles for some reason for Racheal's death, which Charles denies all the time. I just think she needs to blame someone. Tommy left home as soon as he could. I believe he is somewhere in the states."

Marjorie got up and said, "Excuse me, Jane." She went into the lobby and telephoned John Kershaw.

"Hello, Sir John here."

"Marjorie Winters here, John. Jane's with me. I'll drop her off later."

"That's OK, Marjorie. I'll come and pick her up."

"No you won't, John. There's no need. I'll see Jane gets home. What's the rush? We have a lot of catching up to do."

John went quiet and then said OK. He wasn't happy about it, but he let it go.

Marjorie put the phone down and said to herself, *That's put you in your place. You have always been a bully boy just like Charles when you don't get your own way.*

It was seven o'clock by the time Jane reached home. Marjorie went inside with her and said, "Hello, John. It's been too long since we saw you and Jane. You must come for dinner, no excuses. Charles was upset that you didn't get in touch with us after the funeral service."

For once, John was shocked and speechless.

When Marjorie arrived home, Charles was in. "What was that all about?"

Marjorie filled him in, leaving some things out.

Charles looked at Marjorie and asked, "Did you remind him?"

"No. I thought you would be subtler than me."

Charles laughed. He knew John Kershaw from old and knew the man was no pushover.

* * *

The next day, Marjorie picked Jane up as arranged. She was amazed at the transformation. "Wow, Jane, you look wonderful. How did it go after I left?"

"Surprisingly well. I don't know what you said, but it worked."

They went off to the book club, where Jane was more congenial than Marjorie. She was in her element. Of course, it helped when Marjorie introduced her as her oldest and dearest friend, Lady Jane Kershaw. Jane just smiled at Marjorie and said to herself, *Now we are even.*

Everyone wanted to sit near them. The book being discussed was called *The New Beginning*, which seemed particularly appropriate to Jane.

After that, Sir John relented somewhat towards his wife. He realised that he had been an utter bastard towards her. He never apologised, but he would now and again ask her how her day had gone and vice versa.

It wasn't too long before they began getting invites from people they didn't even know. Jane rang Marjorie up and told her, "Whatever you said, Marjorie, it has worked. We are inundated with invites."

"It's not me, Jane. You are in the *Tatler.*"

Jane was speechless.

Marjorie asked, "Are we still on for tonight?"

"I think so. John hasn't said anything to me one way or the other."

Marjorie interrupted her. "Jane, I've told you time and time again. Just tell him that he's going."

"I'm not bold like you, Marge. I wish I was. Hopefully, we will see you tonight." Jane said goodbye and immediately went out to buy a copy of the *Tatler.*

* * *

Meanwhile, Eve had had strong words with Ruth about her mother and father wanting to divorce. Ruth was full of apologies, saying she thought it was for the best. She had intended to tell Eve, but with work and other commitments, she had completely forgotten. Anyhow, their parents seemed to have patched things up again.

"I'm not too sure about that, Ruth." Eve then told her sister about Angelo being their mother's lover. "Our speculation was right all along." Eve went on to tell Ruth how she thought Mother was despondent. When she asked Father what was wrong, he never said a word.

Ruth interrupted her. "Eve, Mother can't be that despondent. I'm looking at her and father in the *Tatler* with Charles and Marjorie Winters. I think you are worrying needlessly. I have to go now. See you soon." And with that, Ruth put the phone down.

Eve was taken aback and decided to ring her mother. Mrs Brown answered the telephone. "Is Mother there?" asked Eve.

Jane came to the phone. "Eve," she said. "Lovely to hear from you. It's been ages."

"I know. Father is keeping me busy, and now I know why. He's keeping busy socialising with the Winters."

Her mother laughed. Eve was overjoyed. *There was no need to worry after all*, she thought.

* * *

A couple of weeks later, Sir John received a call from Charles Winters to tell him that Elizabeth Ashurst has been found dead. John was saddened by the news. He had always liked Elizabeth – more than Marjorie. "Do we know when the funeral is?"

Charles replied, "Not too sure, John. The coroner has been informed. It was suicide."

John was really upset now, and he felt guilty. "Will you keep me informed? I suppose they must wait till they have an autopsy and get in touch with Tommy."

119

Sir John rang home to let Jane know, but of course she knew already. News travels fast when it is bad.

The funeral of Elizabeth was a sombre one. Some of the old girls attended from Hadlington's. Elizabeth had a simple service and was buried with Racheal and Robert in the churchyard at Ditton Thames.

After the service, Tommy came up to Marjorie and Jane. Marjorie comforted Tommy; she felt sorry for him. The Ashurst household wasn't a happy one after Racheal died. Robert and Elizabeth had been convinced it wasn't an accident, but people thought it was the grief and guilt because Racheal was driving. Now Marjorie was having doubts also. She and Elizabeth knew of the rumours surrounding Charles's mother's suicide.

"What will you do now, Tommy?" asked Jane.

"Not sure. I must try and sort the bloody mess left for me to clear up first."

Marjorie got hold of him. "You can you stay with us if you want to," she said, "and if we can help you in any way, we will. It's the least we can do."

Tommy's eyes filled up with emotion. Of course, unknown to Tommy at the time, Charles and Marjorie Winters as well as Sir John had their reasons for helping Tommy out. Charles offered to assist Tommy with the solicitors and other legal requirements.

Jane had put a buffet on for the old girls at the Harrows. It was like a school reunion. The former chums all started reminiscing about the old days and wondered what happened to some of their classmates, each giving an answer if they knew anything about one of them.

Then someone mentioned Suzanne Emmott. "She was one of your pals, Jane."

Jane had to think. "You mean 'Motty'?"

Everyone started to laugh. They all had nicknames at school.

"I don't know what happened to her," said Jane. "She just disappeared. Of course, there was a lot of speculation at the time that she was pregnant. She left Hadlington's under a cloud, that's all

I know. She was Marjorie's friend more than mine, as they were in the class above me."

Just then, Charles and John entered the lounge. Charles asked, "What are you girls taking about?"

Jane said, "Suzanne Emmott. Charles, didn't you go out with her at one time?"

Charles pretended he didn't know her. He gazed over at Marjorie and John momentarily.

"You remember her," Jane persisted. "You must do."

Charles replied, "Yes, now I come to think about it. I went out with her briefly. She had loads of fellows after her. I couldn't keep count!" Everyone laughed, except Jane. She never thought of Suzanne as being a fly-by-night – more like her and Marjorie, albeit from a poorer background. Suzanne had won a scholarship to Hadlington's, as Jane recalled.

Tommy came over to Jane and said, "Can I have a word, Mrs Kershaw?" He didn't realise that she was titled. He hesitated and then said, "I have seen your Joanne a few times in New York. In fact, she has put me up a few times when I have been waiting for a new assignment."

Lady Jane's heart leapt. She had so much to ask him, but before she could say anything, Charles came over. Tommy swiftly stuffed an envelope into Jane's hand and smiled.

"We'd better get going, Tommy," said Charles. "Tommy is staying with us till his affairs are sorted out. You'll have plenty of time to catch up."

By the time everyone had left, Jane was exhausted. She looked at the mess and thought, *To hell with it*. The caterers would clean up most of it anyway. Cigarette smoke still lingered in the lounge, something Jane loathed. She opened the French windows to freshen the air.

John came in and said it was good of Charles and Marjorie to look after Tommy. "It must be terrible to lose one's parents so young and in those circumstances. He was telling me he now works freelance for the New York *Herald* as a correspondent and can be in any part of the world to cover a story. It all sounds very exciting."

Jane wasn't really listening. She wanted to read the letter from Joanne.

"Drink, Jane?" asked John, jolting her from her thoughts.

"Yes, please," she replied. Then, right out the blue, Jane asked John a question. "Do you remember Suzanne Emmott who went out with Charles? I thought they were an item at one time."

"What of it?" asked John.

Jane replied, "Well, I know she left Hadlington's under a cloud. I just wondered if you knew why?"

"I do recall something. I believe she was gang-raped by a bunch of boys from that council estate near Hadlington's. They never found the culprits. You know how it is on those estates. They look out for one another. That's all I know."

Jane left it at that, and John was relieved. Of course, he knew exactly what had gone on, and so did Marjorie Winters and Charles. It was secret only they shared.

"I think I'll go up now and change into something more suitable," said Jane. She couldn't wait any longer to read the letter.

Hi Mum,

I sincerely hope you are keeping well. Shame about Tommy's mum. He was telling me what a terrible time he had after Racheal died, that he couldn't get away quick enough once he graduated. I am assuming you are reading this letter. Lots to tell. Firstly, do you remember a Suzanne Emmott from school? Well, she recognised me, and asked me if you were my mother. She remembered Father also, and the Harrows. To cut a long story short, she gave me a job.

Suzanne owns a fashion house haute couture, with emphasis on one-off designs. She was kind enough to give me six months probation, as I had no experience at all in fashion design and what it all meant and how much work was involved to create a garment. You will be pleased to know that I stuck at it and now have my own clientele, I think of you all the time and miss you very much and especially Lucy, who will be it uni now, I suspect. Would love you to write back and let me know how everyone is getting on and especially Lucy. Send photos if you can.

Love always, Joanne.

Joanne, of course, couldn't mention the fact that she and Lucy were corresponding with each other. Jane had no idea, and they wanted to keep it that way.

By the time, Jane had read the letter, tears were flowing like a tap. She vowed then and there to heal the rift. Jane thought how strange it was that they had only just been talking about Suzanne, and right out of the blue, she popped up in New York. *I must ask Joanne if she is married and has any children. Best keep this to myself for the time being,* Jane said to herself.

CHAPTER SIXTEEN

Ruth and Robert were getting on famously. They had bought themselves a lovely house quite near to Eve's place. They would meet up with Matt and Eve occasionally when Eve decided to throw a dinner party. Sometimes Ruth and Robert had to take a rain check if their timetables clashed.

Though their personal life was going well, Robert was becoming restless in his career. He knew going into a private clinic was the way forward, if he was given the opportunity. Ruth, however, was happy doing what she did. She thought it more challenging.

A chance meeting with an old friend gave Robert the opportunity he wanted. He was enthusiastic about it, but Ruth was more cautious. She had already turned down such an opportunity once.

Robert said, "Just meet up with him, Ruth. He's no fly-by-night. Honest. You'll like him."

Reluctantly, Ruth agreed to meet up with this mate of Robert's. The chance came about a month later. Robert introduced his friend as Dr James Slater.

"I have heard so much about you," he said to Ruth. "How did you manage to catch him?"

Ruth replied, "That's easy. He caught me instead."

That lightened the conversation somewhat. After they had eaten, James outlined what he proposed to do. He explained that he was a general practitioner dealing with minor everyday illnesses, unless something more serious was diagnosed. He was doing very nicely, but he wanted to expand his practice to accommodate other services that he could offer to his patients – for a fee, of course. He was looking for doctors with specific experience in orthopaedics and paediatrics to join his team. His premises were quite near to Harley Street, and he was hoping one day to move onto Harley Street itself.

"I have known Robert since med school," James went on, "and thought of him instantly. I am able to offer you both a good salary – not quite as much as you are probably receiving at present, but nevertheless good enough, I think. If we expand the way I want to, your working day would be considerably shorter."

Ruth took it all in her stride, not saying yes or no. She needed to investigate further. As with all propositions, there were certain loopholes. Her father had taught her that. The meeting ended very genially, with each side promising to get in touch at a later date.

When they arrived home, Robert said, "What do you think?"

Ruth replied, "We need time to study everything before we commit ourselves. It sounds good on paper, but let's do a thorough check before we reach a decision."

Robert could see where Ruth was coming from and agreed.

* * *

Several weeks went by, and Robert met up again with James Slater. He was waiting for a response from Robert as to whether they were in or out.

Robert said, "I need to talk to Ruth first before we take it any further."

When Robert arrived home, he said to Ruth, "I met up with James this afternoon. He's waiting for a decision."

Ruth looked at him. She had more things to think about at this moment in time, she told him.

"What's wrong?" Robert asked, concerned.

Ruth blurted out, "I think I'm pregnant!"

Robert was overjoyed by the news, but Ruth wasn't all that enthusiastic.

"You'll get used to the idea, Ruth," said Robert.

"I'm not too sure yet. It could be something else. Let's wait and see before we tell the whole world." Ruth was always the cautious one.

"There is one thing for sure," she added. "The private practice is out for me. You can go ahead if you wish, but just make sure it's not a scam, friend or no friend."

It turned out Ruth was indeed pregnant, but her celebration was muted. She was thinking of Eve and her situation. She decided to have a word with her mother, who of course was delighted by the news, even though Ruth was on the verge of 40.

"What's troubling you, Ruth? Your age?" asked Jane.

Ruth replied, "No, Mum. What will Eve think, knowing she can't have any?"

"If I know Eve, she will be delighted for you. Besides, she sees more of Lucy these days than we do. Lucy is just a bundle of energy. She tires us out."

* * *

The whole family was overjoyed when Ruth gave birth to a little boy. She named him Andrew John.

Lucy was thrilled and said, "I have a cousin! Yippee!" Everyone laughed.

Eve came over to her mother and said, "Any more news from Jo?"

"Not a word," her mother replied.

* * *

Joanne had been extremely busy with her clients; her list was increasing all the time. Suzanne noticed this and decided that Joanne should not take on any more clients for the time being. As it was, Jo was working flat out. The show was in four months' time, and she hadn't even started on her own collection, which now had Joanne's own label sown inside the garment.

Suzanne was a canny businesswoman, and she saw the potential of letting Jo have her own designs and label. After all, Jo was her top designer now. Discussions were to take place after the show to offer Jo a stake in the business. This, of course, was unknown to Joanne.

"Have you written to your mother yet about the fashion show?" asked Suzanne.

"I haven't had time," was Jo's reply.

"You must make time, Joanne. Family is important. I suggest you take the day off tomorrow, get some rest, and write to your mother. You have to learn to prioritise yourself. I'll make sure everything runs smoothly here."

Joanne protested, but Suzanne was adamant. Reluctantly, Jo agreed.

"I need you to be fit and healthy," said Suzanne. "You have only got four months to get everything ready."

Joanne wrote to her mother first thing, but from there, the morning went by very slowly. She wasn't used to having time on her hands, and that was the way she liked it. Jo decided to go to Fifth Avenue and window-shop to look at the top designer clothes, such as Gucci, Yves Saint Lauren, and Versace – the high end of fashion design.

Suddenly, Joanne saw Suzanne Emmott coming out of Chanel, another famous label. *What is she up to?* Jo said to herself. She decided to follow Suzanne, who then went into the Gucci shop next. Jo tried to see what was going on.

Suzanne was greeted by another lady, and they went into the back of the store. This put Joanne on her guard. It bothered her. After all, the fashion industry was a very competitive business. Some might even say it was cutthroat.

Jo couldn't sleep that night thinking about how Suzanne may have betrayed her. She then had the thought of creating a special designer label with the name Lucy and sewing it into the garment in a hidden place, to avoid any confusion as to who owned what design.

* * *

A month went by. Jo received a phone call from Suzanne, asking her to come to Suzanne's office. Jo was hesitant and on her guard, knowing what she had witnessed on Fifth Avenue that day.

Jo knocked. "Enter," came Suzanne's commanding voice. Jo entered with trepidation.

"Ah, Joanne. I would like you to meet my dearest and oldest friend, Grace Dawson. We started out together, and she is now the top designer for Gucci. I asked her to come along and look at some of your designs. She is most impressed."

Jo was taken aback. "Well, thank you."

Suzanne carried on, "Grace agrees with me that you're ready to put you own label on your designs, in time for the fashion show in the spring."

Jo was delighted. All her fears subsided, and now she felt guilty for not trusting Suzanne. They had a long chat between them. Suzanne asked for coffee to be brought in. After a lot of informal chit-chat, Grace excused herself. She had another appointment to go to.

"Don't go, Joanne. I need to discuss something else with you."

Jo listened to what Suzanne had to say and was dumbstruck. It took a while for it to sink in. She just went over to Suzanne, hugged her, and said, "Thank you. It is what I have always dreamed of. I won't let you down."

* * *

Lady Jane was delighted to received the letter Joanne had written, although she waited to read it until John was not about.

Hi Mum,

Hope you are OK. Thanks a bundle for the pictures of Lucy. I can't believe she is so tall and is making a lovely girl thanks to you both. You say she wants to be an interior designer, how interesting, and is in her final year. How time flies. It doesn't seem that long ago that she was five. Sorry to hear about Eve losing her baby, and delighted for Ruth, a boy, wow! Father will be pleased.

I have some good news to tell you. I have my own label. My designs are known as Lucy. I have several A-list clientele, and for the first time I will be showing off my designs in next year's spring fashion show here in New York. I would just love you and Dad to come over with Lucy if that's possible.

Do you remember me telling you about Suzanne Emmott from your school? Well, she reads the *Tatler* so she is well informed about what you and Dad get up to, which of course she tells me about. So you had better be careful, and by the way, she never talks about her private life. I haven't a clue if she has family or not. I must respect her privacy, Mum. It is the right thing to do.

Tommy Ashurst has been staying with me. He looked dreadful, Mum. I felt so sorry for him when he told me how it was after Racheal had died. His mother and father thought there was some sort of conspiracy going on between the Emmott family and the Winters. He never found out what. I guess he'll never know now.

You know, Mum, I really didn't want to leave home or the family and especially Lucy, but I couldn't bear thinking about Maggie and Racheal dying. I just knew had to get away. Then when you said come home and live with you, I couldn't cope with it. I know I was horrible with you both, but it was the only way out I could see at the time to get away from everything and everyone, and to battle my own demons. It broke my heart to leave you all and especially Lucy.

Write soon let me know if you can come over to New York, I will send you the invites a.s.a.p.

* * *

Sir John was meeting up with Max once more. He waited for him by his car. Max worked for an organisation that helped people make certain problems go away – for a price, of course. The organisation was very influential and powerful, and one thing you didn't do was cross them.

Sir John and a few of his associates, if you could call them that, had used Max on numerous occasions. Now he gave Max another envelope. "That should cover it. Let me know when it's done."

Max said nothing. He simply got out of the car and headed towards the railway station. Sir John watched him disappear and then drove off.

Sir John had always thought Max was a strange guy and very dangerous. It was the way the man used to look at him. It made John feel uneasy. Max had a massive scar down one side of his face, which he had covered up with a beard. From afar, it wasn't that noticeable.

When John arrived home, Jane was waiting anxiously.

John asked, "What is it?"

Jane gave him the letter. At first, he didn't want to read it, but Jane said, "Please read it, John. It's gone on long enough. I think we should bury the hatchet for Lucy's sake. We are living on borrowed time. We won't last forever. She needs her mother now."

John read the letter and said nothing. He looked at Jane and went into to his study. Jane was really upset. She rang Marjorie and arranged to meet up with her when she returned to London. What Jane didn't know was that John was more perturbed about what Tommy had said about a conspiracy. *Surely not*, thought John. *He wouldn't be so stupid, would he?* It really did disturb him.

* * *

It was the weekend, and Matt had decided to pop home and see Eve. He only had six months more to do, and then hopefully he would have his law degree. He was reading the morning paper when he noticed a public announcement. It said that Hunter and Owen solicitors had been struck off by the Law Society and would no longer be able to practise law.

He shouted, "Eve, Eve!"

Eve came running in. "Whatever is the matter?"

"Read this!" said Matt.

"Well, I never. Serves them jolly well right," Eve replied.

There was no explanation as why they had been struck off. Eve was just glad they had got their just rewards.

The rest of the day, Matt and Eve just chatted about things in general. Then right out of the blue, Eve realised something and said, "You know, Matt, I'm of the opinion that my father may have had something to do with the demise of Hunter and Owen."

"How so?" asked Matt. "I remember you telling me the Law Society were after them for misconduct."

Eve had forgotten all about that. "Yes, but Matt, I hear rumours about another company, William and Thomson Asset Strippers. They also are under investigation. and they were associates of Hunter and Owen."

"I think you're barking up the wrong tree there," said Matt.

Eve wasn't too sure. Her intuition was telling her something else.

CHAPTER SEVENTEEN

Jane waited patiently for John to go to the office. She wanted to show Marjorie the letter and tell her John's reaction. Finally John left, and Jane immediately telephoned Marjorie. The phone rang and rang. *Pick it up, Marge*, she was saying to herself, but no one answered.

Jane decided to write Joanne a more in-depth letter this time. She was taking Marge's advice about being more positive. She set pen to paper and sent Joanne a lovely letter, with more photos of Lucy and a couple of Eve's and Matt's wedding, as well as couple of Ruth and Robert with baby Andrew. She also mentioned getting back in touch with Maggie Winters after all this time, and that Eve was now working with her father. Ruth was now a consultant at Great Ormond Street children's hospital as well as Robert. Lastly, Jane gave Jo every single detail about Lucy and how she would be sitting her finals sometime in April or May.

Lady Jane asked Mrs Brown for tea to be brought into the lounge. When the telephone rang, it startled her. She went to pick it up.

"Jane, I will be home late tonight," said John. "I'm off to the club; I have some business to attend to. Don't wait up. I might stay over."

Jane just said OK and put the phone down. Mrs Brown came in with the tea.

"Thank you, Mrs Brown," Jane said and smiled at her. Then the phone started to ring again. Mrs Brown answered and then said, "It's for you, Lady Jane." She handed over the phone.

Jane put her hand over the mouthpiece and said, "Before you go, Mrs Brown, will you ask Jenny to post this letter for me?" Mrs Brown just nodded.

Marjorie said, "Is anyone there?"

"Hi, Marge," Jane said. "What's up?"

"Jane, do you fancy playing bridge at the Willmotts' tonight? Charles has another engagement."

"Second best, am I?" They both laughed.

Jane said she would love to. "What time?"

"I'll pick you up at seven," said Marjorie.

Jane and Marjorie had a smashing night at the Willmotts'. Of course, it was a feather in their caps that Lady Jane had attended. Jane and Marjorie were just bemused by it all, with all the fussing they did. Jane was as gracious as ever.

Eventually it was time to leave. "Thank God for that. Let's get out of here," said Lady Jane. When they arrived at Jane's house, she said, "Come inside, Marjorie, and have a drink. I need to talk to you about something."

They both went inside, and Jane poured them a whisky. She showed Marge the letter from Joanne. After Marjorie had read it, she was shocked at what she had read about Tommy Ashurst and what he had said, and also about Suzanne Emmott, but she kept herself composed. Looking at Jane, she said, "You must go, Jane. You can see Joanne is hurting."

"I know," Jane said with tears in her eyes. Then she said, "I took your advice and have written back to Joanne telling her we would love to come, but John is adamant that he won't go." Her tears started flowing again.

Marjorie was furious. *This has gone on long enough, you bastard*, she said to herself. To Jane, she said, "I'm sure he'll come around, and if he doesn't, I will go with you."

Jane put her arms around Marge and said, "You are truly a wonderful friend to have."

* * *

Meanwhile, at the club, Sir John was beckoned by Judge Maxwell. "There you are, my boy! I've been wondering when you would show up."

Sir John said, "What is it, Judge?"

"I would like you to meet an associate of mine from the states. This is Jake Johnson. He's like a son to me," the judge said with deep affection.

Sir John acknowledged Jake and shook his hand. "Any friend of Henry is a friend of mine."

Jake just smiled and said nothing.

Judge Maxwell carried on, with a smile that said it all. "Do you remember asking about Hunter and Owen?"

Sir John pretended to be vague and rubbed his chin. "Yes, I do remember, now that you mention it. Did anything come of it with the Law Society?"

The judge replied, "Yes, indeed it did, my boy. They lost their license to practise law, but it's going around the circles that several companies are being investigated by the police. They think a conspiracy is going on.

"Wow," said Sir John. Secretly, though, this news worried him.

The judge carried on. "That's not all. Owen was found hanged this morning by his wife in his garage."

"I'm sorry to hear that, Judge. What a way to go."

John showed remorse, although deep inside he was elated. *Nobody messes with my family*, he said to himself. Sir John sat a while longer with the judge and his guest, who said nothing but took it all in. Sir John was hoping to glean any more info he could.

When Sir John retired to his room, he telephoned Max and said, "Do it now. The sooner the better. The heat is on." He put the phone down.

* * *

Meanwhile, Marjorie told Charles everything that was written in Jo's letter to Jane. She wanted to know if there was any truth in what Tommy had told Joanne. Charles was shocked – in more ways than one.

"Marjorie, on my mother's grave, it is pure speculation," he assured her. "The Ashursts needed to blame somebody. After all, if you remember, Racheal had only just learnt to drive. You don't really think I had something to do with it?" said Charles in an indignant way.

Marjorie wasn't so sure. She had often wondered how Charles had managed to stay clear of the law, knowing what he got up to.

"If I thought you caused the deaths of my Maggie and Racheal, plus those boys, Charles, I would never forgive you – and I would go straight to the police, do you hear me?"

By this time, Marjorie was crying.

Charles went over to her. "Would I kill my own daughter? You are being totally irrational, Marjorie. I had nothing at all do with the accident. You have got to believe me."

Charles got hold of Marjorie again and comforted her, and then he said, "Now tell me about John. What is he up to now?" Marjorie told him. "What do you propose to do?" asked Charles.

"I think it is about time we give Sir John Kershaw a sharp reminder of his transgressions over the years, don't you, Charles?"

Charles hesitated, and said, "It would be better coming from you rather than me. After all, Margie, John can be ruthless when he wants to be, as we all know."

So can you, Charlie Winters, Marjorie said to herself.

It was agreed that Marjorie would put Sir John in his place, once and for all. If there was no joy, then Charles would handle the situation.

* * *

A couple of weeks had passed, and John had not relented over Joanne. Marjorie decided that enough was enough. She went over one evening unannounced. Sir John opened the door and said in surprise, "Marjorie! What brings you here this time of night?"

Marjorie replied, "You! In your study. I want a word."

"Who is it, John?" called out Jane from the lounge.

"It's for me, Jane. I'll go to the study," he said sheepishly.

Deep down, John was furious. When they were safely in the study, he turned around to Marjorie and said, "Who the bloody hell do you think you are, telling me what to do?"

Marjorie was taken aback. He was extremely angry. *No wonder Jane's frightened of him*, she said to herself. She kept her composure and said to him, "I have come to remind you that you have no right to treat Jane like you do. She wants go to see Joanne, and you should go with her."

John glared at her. "I think you should leave."

"Not till I've had my say – and by the way, Jane knows nothing about this. I remember everything about you, John Kershaw, and Charles and me for that matter – what you both have got up to over the years – and don't you forget it, or I will tell Jane everything, do you hear me? Everything."

* * *

Jane was totally unaware of what had just gone on. She was too absorbed in watching a film. After about fifteen minutes, John joined her.

"Drink, Jane?" he asked. He had to ask twice, and finally he went over to her. It made her jump. "Drink, Jane?" he asked again. She nodded, still watching the film. He gave Jane the drink, and then he sat down mulling over what Marjorie had said. He was still extremely angry and said to himself, *I'll get you, Marjorie Winters, if it's the last thing I do.*

After the so-called showdown with Sir John, Marjorie could see a marked improvement in his attitude towards Jane – so much so that he said he would travel over to the States with her and visit Joanne. He didn't think he was up to going to the fashion show, but he would meet up with Joanne at some point. Jane was grateful for that.

"What changed your mind?" Jane asked.

"I had a change of heart, that's all."

Jane went over and kissed him and said, "Thank you."

It was a couple of weeks before Christmas. Jane sent Joanne a notelet:

Coming over for the fashion show. Lucy will be not being coming over; she has her finals. We are staying for a couple of months. Can't wait to see you. Send the invites to the London address.

Lots of Love

Mum

* * *

They had a wonderful Christmas. Everyone came down to the Harrows, and for once, the Kershaws were happy ... well, as happy as they would ever be. Jane was in her element. She held baby Andrew all the time. John was smitten with him. Eve, Ruth, and Lucy chatted happily, while Matt, Robert, and John just talked about work.

Daisy came in and went to Sir John. "You have a telephone call. It's urgent."

Sir John excused himself. He picked up the phone and a voice said, "It's done – and the other, you'll read about." Sir John went to join the others with a satisfied smirk on his face.

Ruth stood up and said, "I have an announcement to make. Or should I say *we?*"

Everyone laughed. Her mother looked at her, and when their eyes met, all at once Jane knew and smiled back.

"I am pregnant again," said Ruth. "Three months, to be precise."

Eve was the first to congratulate her. "Well done, Ruth."

Lucy hugged her, and then of course her mother and father. Robert just put his arm around her. They were happy, and everyone could see they were madly in love with each other.

"This calls for toast," her father said. All raised their glasses. "To Robert and Ruth!"

Ruth said to her mother, "Are you excited about seeing Joanne?"

Lucy glanced at Eve, and their eyes met momentarily.

Her mother answered, "I can't wait to get there – and your dad is also looking forward to seeing Joanne again."

He just said, "We have also booked a sightseeing tour."

"Where are you staying?" asked Ruth.

Her father replied, "Two weeks at the Waldorf, and then an apartment for the rest of the holiday. Joanne has fixed it up for us."

Again, Lucy and Eve looked across at one another. This didn't go unnoticed by Ruth or her mother.

CHAPTER EIGHTEEN

After their Christmas visit with Eve's family, Matt and Eve went to visit Matt's parents for a few days. Matt was really excited. It had been a while since he had seen his parents, with all his studying.

They had a lovely time. On the last afternoon of their visit, however, Matt's mum, Gwyneth, said something that shocked them, especially Eve.

"Do you remember, Matt, that lad your grandmother used to talk about going out with rich American and English women? Angelo was his name."

Matt just nodded and quickly glanced over at Eve.

"Well," she went on, "they found him dead. Apparently he had been missing for a few days. He had gone over a ravine on his scooter. Turns out he had a puncture and lost control. You know how fast they drive down the mountainside. They are like madmen. The police said it was accidental death."

"How do you know this?" asked Matt.

His mother replied, "Your Auntie Dell told me."

Matt didn't know what to say. Eve broke the uneasy silence. "Drink, anyone?"

"Me, please," said Matt's dad.

Not long after, they said their goodbyes to Matt's parents. Eve hugged her mother-in-law warmly and waved till they were out of sight.

When they were finally alone, Matt turned to Eve and said, "Wow."

"When do you intend going back to Oxford?" Eve asked.

"Why? What do you have in mind?" asked Matt.

"I'm thinking of going back to the Harrows. Ruth and Robert will still be there. They are staying till the New Year."

Matt said, "Fine. I'll get my things sorted. You ring them and let them know."

By the time they arrived back at the Harrows, it was night-time. Jane greeted them. "Come on, you two," said Jane. "You must be starving. Cook's left something for you."

Eve shivered. It was a cold damp night.

"Here, drink this," her father said.

Eve just looked at him and said nothing. She was in shock. Was her intuition right? There were too many coincidences for Eve to comprehend.

Matt came over and put his arm around Eve; her mother and Ruth noticed but said nothing. Jane knew Eve would say something in her own time, if there was something on her mind. She was like her father for that.

* * *

The next day, when Eve finally arrived downstairs, she ordered a light breakfast and then went into the lounge where her mother was. Eve went over to her mother and said, right out of the blue, which was uncharacteristic of Eve, "What about Lucy? Why is she not going to America with you?"

Her mother looked shocked and replied, "You know perfectly well. Lucy has her finals in May, so it's impossible to take her this time, but I'm sure she will be able to visit Joanne as often as she wants to later."

Eve hesitated and then said, "When are you going to tell Lucy about Joanne being her mother?"

Again, Jane looked at Eve, this time face to face. "Why don't you tell me what's really going on in your mind? Just come out and say it."

Eve replied, "I'm sorry, Mother. I don't know how to tell you this, and it raises all sorts of questions for me that I need to know answers to." But just as Eve was about to tell her mother everything, the conversation was interrupted by Daisy entering the room.

"Eve, your breakfast is ready," she said.

Eve looked at her mother and went into the dining room to have her breakfast. Lady Jane just sat there in a meaningful way, not knowing what to expect. Jane knew she had secrets. Had Eve finally twigged after all these years, or had John said something just to be spiteful?

Eve never got the opportunity to tell her mother about Angelo. Lady Jane was constantly kept busy with Robert and Ruth and the baby, plus she was at Lucy's beck and call. Lady Jane kept glancing over at Eve and vice versa.

Now it was time for everyone to leave, although Lucy was staying at Grandma's for a few more days. The weather was beginning to move in. Ruth and Eve embraced their mother tenderly and gently and kissed their father.

Eve then said to her mother, "We'll talk when you get back to London." To John, she said, "Father, stay down a while longer if you wish. I can manage till you get back." In truth, she wanted to do some snooping around his office.

Her father didn't say yes and didn't say no. Eve then turned to Ruth and whispered, "Ring me when you can. It's important. I have something to tell you."

Then Eve hugged Lucy and said, "Hopefully I'll see you soon."

Ruth gently kissed Lucy and said, "Good luck with your finals," probably thinking, *I'm glad it's not me.*

* * *

The weather did close in, and they had the fiercest snowfall they'd had in years. Sir John was irritable; he had things to do. What made matters worse was that the telephone line was down.

Lucy and Grandma made the most of it while Sir John stayed glued to the TV, trying to see how long the snow would last and, more importantly, to watch the news. He was grumpy. Jane ignored him.

She went into the snug room and started to play the piano. For Jane, it had always been her escape from reality, along with her painting. She would daydream and go into some form of trance.

Sir John interrupted her to say, "Jane, I'm off upstairs. Goodnight."

It was three days before they could venture outside. Lucy kept herself busy with a design for the stables. Her granddad helped her. Deep down, he was very proud of Lucy. He had a feeling that they might need planning permission, but he said nothing.

Jane kept herself busy with various jobs around the house. Then the snow cleared. That meant they could leave for London.

The doorbell rang, and Daisy came into the lounge. "It's for you, Lucy."

Lucy was puzzled as to who it could be. There, standing in the hallway, was Ben. She flung her arms around him, and he hugged her.

"I've missed you terribly," he said in an American accent.

Jane came to see what the commotion was, and she was thrilled to bits for Lucy.

"Hello, Ben. Nice to see you," said Sir John.

"Likewise," Ben answered.

They stood there for a time, and then Lady Jane said, "Please come in, Ben. I'm sure you and Lucy have lots of catching up to do."

Lucy took him to the stables to show him what she had in mind. She showed him the drawings. He couldn't get a word in edgeways.

Lucy stopped to take a breather, and then the bombshell came. Ben looked at her and said, "Lucy, I will be living in America for the foreseeable future. I have been offered a post as a tutor at Yale University. It was an offer I just couldn't refuse. On top of that, I ... I'm getting married. I am sorry I gave you the impression that we would be an item one day."

The truth was – he had a gun at his head. His only option was to marry the girl, or else her father would inform Yale University of his transgression, which Ben couldn't allow or afford to happen. He had reluctantly agreed to marry her, but first he wanted a paternity test to be carried out. Truth be known, he didn't really like the girl.

She was a loud brash Texan who slept around. Ben wasn't even sure that he was the father.

But Becky's father had threatened Ben and said, in a loud Texas drawl, "If my Becky says you are the father, then that's good enough for me."

After that, Ben had no choice. There was no way out. And there was no way he could explain all that to Lucy. All he could do was walk away. He really was upset about the whole damn mess.

Lucy let out a scream. Lady Jane came running out, with John not far behind. Lucy saw her grandma and granddad, ran past them, and went up to her bedroom. Lady Jane went to make her way towards the stairs, but Sir John stopped her.

"Leave her, Jane. She'll tell us when she is ready."

An hour had gone by when Sir John said, "We have to get going, Jane."

Lucy was still in her bedroom. Lady Jane went upstairs and said, "Lucy, we have to go back to London now. Please come down. We are waiting to go."

Lucy opened the door and went downstairs red-eyed. The tears had dried on her face. Jane's heart sank; she looked at her granddaughter and grabbed hold of her, and Lucy burst out crying again. Eventually Lucy told them what had happened. Sir John couldn't bear to see Lucy so upset.

They set off back to London in a sombre mood. The next day, Lady Jane decided to ring up Ben's mother to see why Ben had decided to live in America. The news came as a shock to Jane. His mother was distressed about it as well. They both had always thought Ben and Lucy would get married at some point. Lady Jane thanked her and put the phone down.

* * *

Sir John and Lady Jane only had a month to go before they set off to New York to see Joanne. Jane rang Eve and Ruth to tell them what had gone on. Eve was very upset; she loved Lucy to bits and thought it was just too much for Lucy to take in, especially as she had her exams coming up. Ruth was more philosophical about it.

"I shouldn't worry, Mother," she said. "Lucy is a sensible girl."

Lady Jane was now torn about leaving the country. She didn't want to leave Lucy alone.

Sir John said, "We are going, and that's that. Lucy will sort herself out when she is ready."

All thoughts of what Eve wanted to say to Jane had now been forgotten.

CHAPTER NINETEEN

Sir John and Lady Jane had been in New York a week and were invited by Suzanne Emmott for dinner at the Waldorf with Joanne for seven thirty, although both Suzanne and Joanne were extremely busy with the spring show. It was now only three weeks off.

Suzanne mentioned the Winters to Joanne. Joanne replied, "Wait until after the show, and then you can tell Mother."

Joanne greeted her parents warmly and then introduced Suzanne. "Mother you know, and this is my father."

"Please to meet you," said Suzanne. "John, isn't it?"

Sir John just nodded.

The evening was going very well when suddenly a voice said, "Hello, Lady Kershaw." It was Ben.

Sir John wanted to thump him right there and then. Lady Jane withered him. Ben blushed and said he was sorry about the whole bloody thing. "I had no choice," he told them. "I had a gun put to my head."

Lady Jane was about to say something when she heard a shriek. "Come on, Ben. Daddy's waiting." A young woman grabbed Ben's arm and then looked Lady Jane up and down, as if to say, *Who the hell are you?*

Joanne whispered to Suzanne, "Wait for the fireworks."

Lady Jane then said in a tone that everyone knew, "Excuse me! I didn't ask you to join our conversation, did I? I suggest you go back to where you came from, and your daddy too, whoever he might be. Ask him to teach you some manners."

Ben just smiled at them as if to say *thank you*.

"Come on, Ben," said the girl. "Who does she think she is?"

As they walked away, Ben said, "You senseless, senseless woman. They are friends of mine from England, and for your information, if you can take it in with that little pea you have for a brain, they are Sir John and Lady Kershaw."

Joanne burst out laughing. "That put her in her place, Mother."

They all laughed. Everyone in the dining room could see and hear what had gone on. They all had disdainful looks on their faces as they stared toward the table where the Texans were sitting.

The head waiter came over and asked, "Is everything all right, Sir John?"

Lady Jane said, "Your clientele isn't what it used to be, Carlo," and deliberately looked over at the Texans' table.

When the waiter had left, Joanne asked, "Who is the chap?"

"It's Ben Johnson," Lady Jane replied. "He used to live in the village next to us."

Joanne said, "He's the Ben Johnson that Lucy is fond of. What is he doing with that awful woman?"

Lady Jane was taken aback. "How do you know about Ben?"

"Evie and I keep in touch now and again," Joanne lied quickly.

Soon it was time to leave. Suzanne invited them to the fashion house. Sir John said immediately, "Not for me. You go, Jane, if you want to. I can keep myself occupied."

The truth of the matter was that he needed to speak to Max again. The list was getting even longer, but Sir John had made up his mind that when all the tasks were done, he would resign from the brotherhood once and for all.

* * *

The next day, Lady Jane met up with Joanne, and they travelled to the fashion house together. It was as though they had never been estranged. It brought a warm feeling to Jane. She started to stare at Joanne.

"Stop it, Mother. You're staring."

"I'm sorry, my darling. I am so happy that we are together again, and I was thinking what a beautiful young woman you have become." Joanne blushed.

When Suzanne arrived, she greeted Jane warmly. "Thank you, Joanne," she said. "Your mother and I have some catching up to do."

Joanne was miffed. She wanted her mother to be with her. However, Joanne went back to her office. She had made six gowns and leisure outfits for the show. She had to write out a brief description of each garment for Suzanne, who needed it for opening night.

Suzanne showed Jane to her office, and then said, "Now tell me, Jane, all about the old girls meeting up at Lizzie Ashurst's funeral."

Jane set about telling her everything. Suzanne remembered everyone.

Jane then said, "Everyone wondered what had happened to you. There was a lot of speculation at the time, I remember."

Suzanne dithered and then told her story. "I was going out with this boy – a pal of your John's, as a matter of fact. It was in my final year; it was the graduation party. I had made myself a fantastic gown and felt a million dollars in it. He picked me up – ever such a gentleman, I thought. After the dance, he took me to his house. I was chuffed to bits to think a girl like me could be mixing with a well-to-do family like his.

"He gave me a drink which made feel very dizzy. Looking back, I think they must have drugged me. We were so naïve in those days, Jane. I remember the boy took me into the library to meet his father, and then he excused himself to go to the bathroom. It was then that his father raped me, again and again. I was terrified.

"After my ordeal, the boy dumped me on his father's orders. I think the boy was as terrified as I was. I was wandering around in a complete daze. I didn't even know where I was. By the time I managed to get home, I was distraught and in a terrible state. No one would believe me at first about this so-called affluent family. Luckily for me, the boy's mother did believe me.

"Anyhow, to cut a long story short, I became pregnant and was made to get rid of the baby. My mother and father were paid off. I was heartbroken at the time. You know how it was in those days, Jane. Girls didn't have a choice – not like today. My father was also offered a job in New York, which he took along with the payoff."

Jane then asked, "And who was the father of this boyfriend of yours?"

Suzanne looked at her and said, "I have never revealed his name to anyone, but I tell you this: I will one day, and the whole world will know. He was a pal of your husband at the time, I recall, but you weren't dating John when this happened to me."

Jane was shocked. Suzanne just nodded.

"What happened to the lad's mother?"

"I believe she committed suicide. I suppose she couldn't live with herself. I believe the boy was dating another girl by this time, from another wealthy family. But mark my words, Jane – sins of the father."

When Jane arrived at Joanne's office – still shell-shocked at what she had just heard and wondering who it could be, her mind working overtime – Joanne's face lit up. Jane looked around at the designs, some on dummies, some hung up.

"My, Joanne," she said, "you are very talented indeed! These are beautiful gowns."

"Coffee, Mother?" asked Jo.

"Don't mind if I do," her mother replied. "I don't suppose your father and I will see much of you till the show is over?"

Joanne replied, "It's doubtful. I'll have more time after the show. Anyhow, you have booked a tour for yourselves, haven't you?"

Lady Jane replied, "Yes. Your father booked it. I haven't the faintest idea where we are going." They both laughed. Jane embraced her daughter and said goodbye.

* * *

By the time Jane arrived back at the Waldorf, Sir John was in the lounge having afternoon tea. To Jane's surprise, he was chatting with

Ben Johnson. As Jane appeared, they both stood up. "No formalities here, please," she told them.

"Ben was explaining everything to me, Jane," John carried on. "It seems the girl likes the boys, if you get my drift."

Jane's eyebrows raised. "I think I understand perfectly well what you are implying, John, and what you are saying," she said in a sarcastic tone, which Sir John choose to ignore.

"Well, thank you, my boy," said Sir John to Ben. "I'm glad you put us in the picture. Think about what I proposed, will you?"

Ben nodded and bid them farewell.

"What was all that about?" asked Jane.

"Later, Jane. I'll tell you later. I have an appointment at four. Will you see to the itinerary for the trip tomorrow? Here's the card. Give them a ring." He handed Jane the card and left.

After an exasperating half hour or so, Jane finally had all the information she needed. They were to be picked up at the hotel for 8 a.m. prompt. Jane then ordered dinner. She was not too pleased with John leaving her alone.

Jane decided to ring Eve. She looked at her watch and decided the timing was OK. The phone rang for some time. *Oh, bother*, thought Jane. She was about to put the phone down when finally there was an answer.

"Hello, Matt here."

"Is Eve there Matt?"

"Just a minute."

Eve's voice came on the line. "Hello, Mother. This is a nice surprise. Are you enjoying yourselves?"

Jane set about telling Eve all that had gone on – about meeting up with Joanne and Suzanne, an old school chum, and also about meeting up with Ben. She gave Eve all the lowdown on that. "Don't tell Lucy, Eve. Your father has had a chat with Ben. Not sure what it is about as yet. And by the way, why didn't you tell me that you and Lucy keep in touch with Joanne?"

Eve hesitated. "I had to tell her, Mother. Lucy kept hearing you and father arguing about Joanne, and she wanted to know. After all, she is 22 years of age, and with her finals coming up, I thought she had enough to deal with. I begged you to tell her."

Jane said nothing and put the phone down. She stayed in her room and tried to relax. She was mulling over what Suzanne had told her.

When John finally came home, Jane looked at her watch. It was ten o'clock. "I thought you had left Eve in charge of the office now?" she said.

"I have," John told her. "This was an out-of-hours meeting with one of my fellow Freemasons. I'm sorry it lasted so long." He poured himself a drink. "Did you manage to get the details?"

Jane gave him her notes. "Wow!" he said. "Looking at this, we won't have much time to ourselves."

Jane agreed and said, "Well, I'm off. See you in the morning."

John poured himself another drink and then sat and pondered on his meeting with Max. He opened his little black notebook and started to cross names out. He then retired to his room.

* * *

The next morning, they were ready for their sightseeing tour. The first day was in New York, and then they would be travelling on to Connecticut, Rhode Island, Boston, and the Great Lakes, with a day's rest here and there. Finally, they would return to New York.

Before the trip began, Sir John had a word with the tour guide. He gave the man a $100 bill and said, "No formalities here. We are just John and Jane Kershaw from London."

The guide took the money and said, "I'll see to that, sir."

Despite some of the accommodations and eateries they had to endure, John and Jane did enjoy the trip. It was fascinating, with all the history that went with it. Unfortunately, there was never enough time to fully digest what they had seen before they were whisked off to go somewhere else. By the end of the tour, they were both jaded.

Jane said to herself, *We are getting too old for this kind of thing. Never again.* John kept waltzing off and leaving her for a couple of hours, to Jane's annoyance. He said he needed to get away from the incessant bragging; it was getting on his nerves. Truth was, he was meeting up with his man. Max gave John a cutout of a newspaper and said, "Nothing to do with me, John. The brief story read:

Marjorie Winters, the wife of prominent businessman Mr Charles Winters, O.B.E., M.B.E., was tragically killed in a car accident on the A40. No other cars were involved. The police said it was an accident waiting to happen.

Sir John had a wry smile on his face and thought, *You bastard, Charles, how could you! Your own wife*. Sir John then handed Max another wad of cash and said, "I am hoping this is the last, but take your time with this one. It is very special to me personally. It needs a great deal of planning for both our sakes." Max took the envelope and disappeared.

* * *

Eve rang Ruth to tell her that Mother knew about Lucy writing to Joanne.

"What did she say?" asked Ruth.

"Nothing really. I think she was too shocked. She just put the phone down."

"Did you mention Marjorie Winters and this fellow Angelo?" Ruth asked.

Eve replied, "No. I thought I would leave it till they got home. Have to go now. Matt is waiting for me. Kids all right and Robert?"

Ruth replied, "Yes, fine." The phone went dead. *Gosh, you are getting like Father*, Ruth said to herself.

* * *

The fashion show was imminent. Jane was excited. John said he wouldn't go, but Jane said, "You must go. It would please Joanne

151

immensely, and besides, it's for Lucy's sake also. After all, she is Lucy's mother." Sir John reluctantly agreed to go.

On the opening night of the fashion show, Jane was in her element. All these famous people! There film stars and fashion critics from all the major magazines – *Vogue,* and many more.

Suzanne Emmott gave a short résumé of the designers and the theme of the show. Then the show opened in earnest. The audience began to clap in approval at what they saw. Jane was totally absorbed by it all. Sir John was bored out of his mind, but to Jane, it was something she had never experienced before.

When the interval came, Suzanne came to Jane and took her around the back to see Joanne. Jane went over to Joanne and, even though she was busy, embraced her and whispered, "Darling, thank you for inviting us. It is something I will always cherish."

Joanne was emotional. It wasn't often she let her emotions get the better of her, but she was crying. Jane grabbed hold of her and said, "I love you, Joanne, and always have done. Please come home to us and Lucy. We have missed you so much."

The show was a resounding success. Suzanne introduced Joanne to the audience, and everyone was clapping, whistling, or standing up in admiration of Joanne's fashion designs. She had finally made it. Joanne was embarrassed, but Suzanne said, "Look over there. Even the fashion critics are clapping. You should be very proud of yourself. I know your mother and father are." Joanne glanced over at them and saw that they too were standing up and clapping. Joanne choked with emotion again. It was just too much for her to take in. She headed back to the dressing rooms.

Suzanne had put on a reception at the Marriot Central Park for a few distinguished guests. Jane couldn't get over all the A-list people who had come to the reception. Joanne introduced her to some of them. Sir John, by this time, was getting fed up. It was going up to two in the morning, and he wanted to leave and retire for the night, Jane wanted to stay, and a row ensued.

Joanne came over to them and said, "You go, Mum and Dad. I'll ring sometime tomorrow, and we can catch up then."

Sir John kissed Joanne on the cheek and whispered, "I am so proud of you, and I am sorry we waited so long to patch up our differences."

Joanne just hugged him and said, "So am I. After all these years, perhaps we can make up for lost time now."

A lump came to Sir John's throat. For what it was worth, he had missed Joanne terribly, but he wouldn't admit it to anyone, not even to Jane. Joanne had hurt him so much.

* * *

Sir John and Lady Jane had had a wonderful time in New York, but now it was time to leave. Jane grabbed Joanne and said, "Come home, please. Come back to us. Set up your own fashion house in London. Call it Lucy's. Please think about it and look after Lucy. We are not getting any younger. Your father isn't 100 per cent fit these days."

Joanne felt guilt creeping over her. Tears filled her eyes. "Tell Eve I love her," she said, "and hopefully I will meet Matt one day. Tell Ruth I am really happy for her and her new family. Tell Lucy her I love her dearly. But it is the wrong time right now. I have made a name for myself. Tell Lucy my designs have a hidden label in them with her name sewn inside them, which is my brand name, and that I am always thinking of her. Tell her to keep writing to me."

CHAPTER TWENTY

It was a relative short journey from New York to London. By the time they reached home, Sir John and Lady Jane were absolutely bushed. They dumped everything in the hallway and retired to bed. It was well into the morning when Jane was wakened by noises. She half opened her eyes to see what time it was. She managed to find her gown and proceeded downstairs, where she found Eve looking pensive.

"What is it, darling?" asked Jane.

Eve burst into tears. "Mother it's terrible news. While you were away, Marjorie Winters was involved in a car crash. The police were satisfied that it was an accident; something to do with the brakes. The car was faulty. There was an inquest, and Charles Winters said he blamed himself for not putting the car into a service, which was due. He had arranged it for the following week."

"When did the accident occur?" Lady Jane asked.

"When you were in New York," replied Eve.

Lady Jane then said to Eve, "You know, Eve, Marjorie loathed Charlie Winters at times, especially when she found something out about him and his father being involved in some scandal many years ago. If I recall, it was something do with a rape." Suddenly the penny dropped, and she realized it was Suzanne Emmott.

Jane calmed herself and carried on. "It was all hushed up at the time. Charlie's mother committed suicide through the shame of it all. Marjorie by this time had married Charlie, so it was too late for her to do anything about it. She had to try to forget the whole nasty episode. Marjorie told me this in confidence. You are the first to know. I am relying on you not mention it to anyone."

Eve said, "Can you cope with another shock?"

Her mother looked at her in expectation. "What is it? Not you and Matt?"

"No, nothing to do with the family. Well, in a sort of a way ..."

Her mother was now very wary. "Out with it, Eve."

Eve gave a sigh. "You remember that man Angelo, the one with the studio in Tuscany that you had an affair with?"

Jane was shocked to hear what Eve had said. "What makes you so sure I had an affair with him?" said Jane in an uncompromising tone.

"Mother, Ruth and I have always thought you had someone else, so don't play the innocent with me."

"What of it?" her mother asked.

Eve blurted out, "He's dead, Mother. Angelo is dead." She waited for a reaction.

Jane feigned a laugh. "You and Ruth have it all wrong. We were just friends and business partners, that's all. I'm sorry to hear he has passed away. Now if you'll excuse me, Eve, I must ring Charles up with our condolences."

When Jane went into her bedroom, she just couldn't believe her beloved Angelo was dead. Deep inside, she was broken-hearted, and part of her died with him.

For Eve, there were so many unanswered questions. First, there was the demise of Hunter and Owen, with Owen committing suicide and Hunter vanishing. Add to that the arson attack on Williams and Thomson, and a few more nagging incidents that had gone on in the boardroom. When her father came across someone who questioned his authority, disagreed with him, or irritated him, you would never see that person again.

Eve was becoming increasingly distrustful of her father. She wanted out of the business altogether, but how could she manage it without her father becoming suspicious? She didn't know. After a long and intensive search of his office, Eve had found nothing incriminating about her father except for a couple of missing files, which didn't seem to be significant at the time.

* * *

Sir John had arranged to meet up with Max one more time to see if everything had been done. It was now getting too dangerous for them both, especially as Charles had finally gotten rid of Marjorie. What a heartless swine he was, thought Sir John.

He waited patiently for Max to arrive. He was beginning to get apprehensive, but then Max finally showed up.

"Well, you took your bloody time," Sir John snapped. He then asked if everything had been tied up. "No paperwork, Max, or we are both dead meat."

Max said everything was in order. No one would be able to trace anything back to Sir John or to him. Then Max pulled out a gun.

John looked at him and said, "Don't be such a bloody fool, Max. There's no need for that. We can ride the storm out like we've always done."

Max just looked at John and said, "I have my orders, John. I'm afraid, you cannot talk you way out of it this time, old chap. You are a ticking time bomb waiting to go off. Now drive!"

They arrived at some wasteland on the east side of the city. Max said, "This is it, John. End of the road, I'm afraid. Sorry it has come to this, but it's an order from the brothers."

John just looked at Max and smiled, and then he said, "They won't get away with it, Max. The truth will come at some stage. Tell Charlie."

Just as he said it, there was a shot. Sir John hadn't noticed Charles Winters creeping up on him till it was too late. Charles had held a gun to John's temple and shot him at point-blank range while John was distracted.

So long, old buddy, said Charles to himself. To Max, he said, "Get rid of the body. Make sure it can't be found. Dump the car somewhere."

Max nodded. Charles walked casually over to his car and drove away. He drove to the embankment and tossed the gun into the Thames. He stayed there and watched it slowly sink.

When Charles arrived home, he telephoned someone. "Hello," a voice said.

"It's done," he replied. The phone just went dead.

* * *

Jane was becoming increasingly anxious as to where John could be. It was nearly midnight. She thought that he must be staying over at the club, so she decided to retire to bed.

The next morning, Jane was disturbed by a knock on the door. She hastily put her gown on and opened the door to find Mrs Brown.

"I'm sorry to disturb you, Lady Jane," she said, "but there are two police officers downstairs wishing to speak with you."

Inside, Jane crumbled. *Please, God, no*, she said to herself. She went downstairs, numb with fear, and found an inspector and a constable waiting for her.

The inspector said, "Can we talk in private?"

Jane took him into the study.

The inspector hesitated and then said, "I am sorry to inform you that your husband, Sir John Kershaw, was found dead in the early hours of this morning. He was found at a disused warehouse that was ready to be demolished. Workmen found him. He had been shot." He then asked, "Is there any reason why your husband would be in such an area? Was he meeting someone?"

Jane just sat motionless. She didn't even hear him speak to her. She was trembling all over. She was in shock.

"Is there anyone we can ring for you?" the officer asked.

Jane just nodded.

The inspector said to the constable, "Go and have a word with this Mrs Brown."

The constable nodded. When he came back into the room, he said, "Her daughter is coming over."

When Eve arrived, Mrs Brown quickly directed her to the study. When Jane saw her daughter, she burst into tears.

"We may need to interview your mother at some stage," the inspector said to Jane.

"Just telephone first, will you? Mother is in no fit state at present."

The police left, and Eve poured her mother a large whisky. Meanwhile, Mrs Brown telephoned Ruth, and then she went into the study.

"Do you mind if I get off now, Eve?"

Eve replied, "Not at all, Mrs Brown. I should leave it a few days. We can manage till then."

Ruth came running in, took one look at her mother, and said, "Eve, she is in shock. Ask Dr Walker to come around. She will be able to give Mother something."

Eve rang the doctor up. Dr Walker arrived a little later and gave Lady Jane a sedative. She turned to Ruth and said, "Your mother needs complete rest. I'll be around sometime tomorrow." Ruth thanked her and showed her to the door.

Ruth then said, "Shall we let Lucy know?"

Eve sat and thought. "I think she sits her last exam today. I'll give the university a ring. Once the press gets hold of this, they'll have a field day. There will be all sorts of assumptions and speculations going around. But we must to let Joanne know right away."

* * *

The verdict at the inquest was death by person or persons unknown. It was put on the police files as an unsolved murder. Sir John's body was released for burial. It was a very low-key funeral, which was what the family wanted. Only a few people were invited, Charles Winters being one of them.

"If there is anything, Jane, you will let me know, won't you?" said Charles.

Jane said, "Of course I will. And Charles, keep in touch, won't you?"

Charles then said, "I'm thinking of moving over to the Riviera and living there. It has all been too much for me, Jane, with Marjorie and now John. I need to get away. Peter is well taken care of. I will keep in touch." He kissed Jane gently on the forehead.

Eve came over. "What did he want?"

Jane looked at her, surprised by her aggressive manner. "Eve, that's very ungracious of you. You know he has just lost Marjorie, and now your father. They had been friends since prep days. He needs to get away and start afresh, that's all."

Eve never said another word. Deep down, she was beginning to wonder about Charlie Winters. Whenever there was trouble, he was always somewhere in the background.

* * *

It was time for the will to be read. They went into the study, and the solicitor greeted Jane.

"Hello, Martin. Nice to see you."

"It's never easy, Jane, for anyone at time like this," he said.

He proceeded to read the will. Jane was stunned to learn that John had essentially written her out of it. Eve put her arm around her mother. When the reading was done, Jane excused herself and went upstairs. Eve, Ruth, and Joanne – who had returned for the funeral – just stared at one another. Lucy had gone upstairs to see Grandma.

She knocked on the door and said, "Can I come in, Grandma?" She entered the bedroom, went over to her grandma, and said, "The Harrows will always be yours, Grandma. You can live there with me forever if you want to."

Jane hugged the girl and said, "Thank you."

It turned out that Lucy had been left the Harrows. The villa had been sold many years earlier. Eve was left with controlling shares of the company – in fact, she was the major shareholder – while Ruth and Joanne held 25 per cent of the company between them. Each daughter had received a substantial amount of money, with a trust fund set for Lucy till she reached 25. Jane was left with a small legacy.

After the initial shock, Jane was quite rational about it all. In some ways, she was relieved that a burden had been lifted from her shoulders as lady of the manor, so to speak. The press, of course, had a field day when the will was finally published.

The girls had a joint meeting with their solicitor to see if they could do anything to help their mother out. He said that she had been well provided for, and then he explained to them, "Your father thought it would be better for your mother this way, because of inheritance tax and other taxes incurred, which your mother would have been liable for. He decided to leave everything to you girls many years ago."

Joanne had to go back to the States. Suzanne had now given her a partnership in the fashion house. Jo asked Lucy to come with her, but Lucy told her, "I am very happy living here with Grandma and Auntie Eve, and besides, I have great plans for the Harrows."

Joanne said her goodbyes to everyone and left for New York. Eve came up to Lucy, put her hands on Lucy's shoulders, and asked, "All right?"

Lucy replied, "Fine, Auntie Eve."

Ruth came up to Eve and asked, "Please tell me what's going on, Eve. I can't get my head around it all."

Eve replied, "Not now, Ruth. Someday, perhaps."

Ruth looked at Eve and thought, *Now who's being enigmatic.*

CHAPTER TWENTY-ONE

Max travelled to Texas to carry out another assignment, this time for the fixer – and it was also John Kershaw's last request, so to speak. The fixer thought it was the right and proper thing to do to honour the contract. Charlie Winters too felt an obligation towards John Kershaw – as it was Charlie, of course, who shot John, and who had also arranged with Max to eliminate Marjorie so he could inherit her fortune. Not that Charles needed her money; he just wanted out of the marriage. She was getting too nosey and asking too many questions.

Max waited for Chuck Grayson in his study while going through all his paperwork. There was some interesting reading. Suddenly, he heard a voice drawling, "Goodnight, baby." Shortly after, Grayson entered his study.

"What the hell!" he exclaimed at the sight of Max sitting comfortably at his desk. "Who the hell are you?"

"I'm the one who has a gun to your head," said Max amiably.

The Texan hadn't a clue what Max was talking about. When Max pulled a gun out, Chuck went to his desk drawer for his own gun, but it wasn't there.

"Is this what you are looking for?" asked Max, dangling the weapon from his free hand.

By this time, Chuck was perspiring. Beads of sweat were running down his face. He started mopping his brow and said, "What do you want?"

Max said, "My nephew wants out of this so-called marriage with your daughter, Becky. If you value your life, you'll get them a quickie divorce in Vegas, pronto, or I'll be back. Do you understand?"

By this time, Chuck was shaking from head to toe.

"I'll be watching you," Max said. As he left, he repeated, "I'll be watching you!"

The next day, Chuck rang up his daughter. "Baby, I need you home now. Bring that so-called husband with you."

"But Daddy, I haven't seen him for at least two years. I don't know where he is." Ben had left when he found out she'd faked her pregnancy, and by then she was bored with him.

"Well, f—in' find him, or I'll cut you out of the will. Now get your ass down here as quick as you can. Do you hear me?"

Unknown to Chuck Grayson, Max was listening in on the conversation.

* * *

Becky was stunned. She didn't even know where to start. One thing was for sure: she sobered up very quickly. Becky searched for three days. She was frantic by this time. Then a mate of hers said, "Hi, Rebecca. You're looking for Ben Johnson, I believe."

Becky said, "Where is he?"

The lad said, "What's it worth to you? A hundred dollars?"

What the hell, she said to herself and gave him the money.

Becky went to the address on the note. It was in a terrible part of town. Ben had dropped out and was just taking students on now and again when he was strapped for cash.

"Geez, Ben, you've let yourself go," she said when she found him.

He looked at her and asked, "What do you want?"

"We have been summoned to the ranch. Daddy wants a word with you."

"Go to hell," Ben answered. "You whore, you've ruined my f—in' life. Leave me alone."

Becky said, "Daddy insists he wants to talk to you."

Ben asked, "What's it worth?"

"I don't f—in' know, do I, you moron," Becky replied. Finally, she rung her daddy up and said, "He won't come."

"Is he there? Put him on the phone," her father said.

Ben reluctantly took the phone.

"Ben, my boy," said Chuck. "I realise what a terrible mistake it was with you and Becky. I want to make it up to you."

"How much?" asked Ben.

Chuck contemplated, "Three thousand dollars."

"Make it five, and I'll meet up with you," Ben replied.

"Not here – in Vegas. I'll pay for the tickets. You and Becky pick up the tickets at the airport. Make sure Becky comes with you. Put her on your back if you have to."

Ben handed Becky the phone. She listened and started protesting. A heated argument ensued. Then she finally said, "OK. If that's what you want, Daddy, we will be there."

Becky turned to Ben and said, "Get whatever you have together and stay with me overnight. We leave first thing in the morning."

Ben didn't have that many possessions. Most of his belongings and valuables were in storage. Becky found some old clothes some poor sod had left behind when she was fed up with him. Ben cleaned himself up and came out of the bathroom looking totally different. Becky looked at him and thought he was a really a good-looking guy, but much older than she remembered.

The next morning, they were at the airport collecting their tickets to fly to Vegas. Ben was wondering what the hell this was all about, and so was Becky.

When they arrived, a limousine was waiting to take them to a judge to get a quickie divorce. Ben looked at Becky in surprise.

"Don't look at me! I'm as shocked as you are," she said.

When they arrived, her father was waiting. "We're here. What is this all about, Daddy?"

He didn't answer. They entered, and the judge was waiting for them. All they needed to do was sign on the bottom line, and they would be divorced. Witnesses had been provided.

Ben couldn't believe it. Chuck then gave Ben an envelope and a ticket for a return flight to Connecticut. Becky started to protest, but she was taken by the arm by her father. Chuck Grayson never let his daughter out of his sight. Becky was getting cheesed off with it. She wanted to leave.

* * *

One night, Chuck said to Becky, "We have guests coming tonight, so behave yourself, do you hear me?"

Becky was introduced to Peter Winters and Jake Johnson. The night was cordial enough. The boys went into the den to discuss matters with her father. The fact was, he was in deep shit. He had run up a colossal bill with his gambling. He was given two weeks to pay up or else. By the time the meeting was over, Becky was as drunk as a newt. She was on the veranda when Jake Johnson appeared. He said in his Yankee drawl, "Can I get you another?"

"Sure, why not," replied Becky.

They sat and chatted. Becky told him how her father kept her on the ranch now, and she wished he was dead.

Jake said, "Sometime wishes do come true, don't they?"

Becky just stared at him and said nothing.

Just then Peter Winters came out. "Is it always this hot here?" he asked.

Becky replied, "This is nothing compared to daytime." Then she asked, "How long are you staying?"

"We leave tomorrow," answered Peter. "We had a good chat with your father, and our business is concluded."

"You talk weird," said Becky.

They all laughed.

* * *

Three weeks later, Chuck was out riding on his ranch to inspect the fencing for his cattle. Someone had rung up to say some fencing was down by the creek. His charge hand wanted to do the job, but Chuck said he would go. He would enjoy the ride.

Chuck had ridden a few miles when he noticed someone waving at him. He was standing near a station wagon. Chuck went over and said, "Howdy, stranger. What can I do fer yah?"

The guy said, "I think I've hit a rock or something."

Chuck went over to see. He bent down and then he heard a click. When he turned around, the stranger said, "This is the offer you couldn't refuse."

He pulled the trigger. You could hear the gunshot for miles around. The stranger tied Chuck's horse to the station wagon and slowly took off. It was several days before they found Chuck's body. It had been badly mauled by a mountain lion.

* * *

Ben thought it was ten Christmases all rolled into one. He knew what he had to do, and he wasted no time in putting his house in order. A couple of weeks after his liberation, he was travelling back to England with all his belongings already packed and sent over to his mother's. His father had died some time before. The plane touched down at Heathrow, and Ben hired a car to take him home to see his mother. She was overjoyed to see him.

"Ben, is it really you?" she said, crying. "I thought I would never see you again."

Ben looked at his mother. She was so frail, and he felt so guilty. "I'm so sorry, Mother, for putting you through all this, but I am here to stay now." He kissed her gently on the cheek. His only thought now was of Lucy.

He said to his mother, "How is Lucy?"

His mother replied, "Why don't you go and see for yourself?"

He was off like a shot, When he arrived, he could see Lucy telling some workers what to do. He laughed to himself, *That's Lucy, same old bossy boots.*

He got out of the car and walked towards her. Her grandma watched through the window, her heart full of joy for Lucy. Mrs Johnson had rung to tell her Ben was home.

Lucy could sense something or someone behind her. Ben crept up and said, "Hello trouble."

She looked around, and when she saw Ben, she let out a scream. All the workmen stopped what they were doing. He grabbed hold of her and said, "I'm here to stay. Will you marry me?"

"Oh, yes. Yes!" Lucy replied. All the workmen started clapping.

Jane came out, and she, too, was looking much older. Ben realised how much time he had wasted wallowing in self-pity. He aimed to make the most of his life from now on.

Lady Jane invited Ben inside. "Mollie," she called out (Daisy had retired), "get some champers out. This calls for a celebration." When they all had glasses, Lady Jane gave a toast: "To the happy couple!"

* * *

After that, Ben and Lucy were inseparable. They had a lot of catching up to do. The stable's living quarters weren't quite ready. Ben told Lucy everything about Becky – how he had been duped into marrying her and that the marriage was dissolved. Lucy never said anything to Ben; it didn't matter to her. He was here now, and that was all she cared about.

Lucy wanted Ben to move in with her. Ben said no – he wanted to stay with his mother till he got himself sorted. It wasn't what Lucy wanted to hear, but she said OK.

Jane rang up Eve to tell her the news. Eve was overjoyed. "I'll try to come down this weekend," she said. Jane left Ruth a message and thought about ringing Joanne, but she thought better of it till she had spoken to Lucy.

Ben was never away from the Harrows. He helped Lucy with her decorating – under orders, of course. He was waiting for a reply from Oxford University. He had applied for a posting there for the new semester in September.

* * *

The whole gang descended on the Harrows one weekend. Jane was put out by it. Ben was introduced to Eve and Matt, and then Ruth and Robert, who still had not gotten married, much to the disgust of her mother. Ruth's children, Andrew and Olivia, were running around everywhere.

Lady Jane went up to her room to lie down. The weather was very humid. In fact, it had been a very hot summer.

Rob and Matt put on a barbie. You could smell the burgers across the courtyard. "Ready, everyone! Come on before it gets cold," they called out.

They all eagerly made their way for eats … except for Jane. Eve noticed that her mother wasn't around, and she went upstairs. Jane appeared to be fast asleep.

"Come on, Mother. The burgers are ready," Eve called out.

Jane didn't move. Eve touched her, and then she ran down for Ruth. "Quick, come quick, it's Mother!" she cried.

Ruth went up with Eve to their mother's bedroom and confirmed with Eve had feared: their mother was dead. Tears trickled down Eve's face.

"Mother was a good age, Eve," said Ruth. "No one lasts forever. She's had a good innings. Be grateful for that."

Ruth telephoned the police and the hospital. Matt and Rob made their way back to London.

CHAPTER TWENTY-TWO

There was an inquest, which found that Lady Jane Kershaw had died from natural causes – which, of course, Ruth could have told them from the start. She was buried with John in the local churchyard at Ditton Thames, with only a few guests at the funeral. The family held a small reception at a local restaurant.

It had been a tiring day. Everyone just wanted to get back to the Harrows. Ben and his mother joined them. They had a few drinks, and then the girls started to reminisce. Joanne had managed to get home for the funeral and was thrilled to see Ben and Lucy so happy – and of course, her sisters. Jo promised she would come over for the wedding and asked Lucy if she could make her wedding dress. Lucy was thrilled to bits.

Matt noticed Eve sitting on her own. "Penny for your thoughts, Eve," he said gently.

She looked up and smiled. "I was thinking how things turn out. It took Mother's death to bring Joanne back into the fold, and Lucy is deliriously happy. You can see that they are so much alike when they are together."

"No regrets, Eve, that you have lost Lucy?"

Eve looked at Matt and said, "I haven't lost Lucy, Matt. She will always come to us for advice when she needs it."

Matt kissed her. "Come on. Let's get back."

* * *

Jo stayed on for another week. One night, Eve went over to Joanne and asked, "What happened to Suzanne?"

Joanne said, "She passed away a couple of years ago and left the business to me. She also left me something else."

Eve looked at her with curiosity, but Jo said, "Not now, Eve. When I come over for Lucy's first fitting, I will bring the file with me."

"It all sounds very mysterious, Jo."

"It is, Eve! Wait till you read it!" Jo left it at that.

Ruth and Robert as well as Matt and Eve had to return to London. They hugged Jo and told her to come back soon. Jo, with tears in her eyes, said goodbye to them. She had only a couple of days left, and she wanted to spend it with her daughter. There was a lot of catching up to do.

Ben received a letter from Oxford telling him that there might be an opening for him and that an interview had been arranged on 12 August at 10 a.m.

All too soon, it was time for Jo to leave. She had Lucy's measurements, and with the technology available to them, it would be easy to keep in touch. Jo said she would send some drawings to Lucy via email.

Ben looked at Lucy. She was so happy to be with her mother.

Lucy had tears in her eyes as she watched the plane take off for New York. Ben hugged her and said, "She'll be back soon." They called to visit Matt and Eve, but they were both still at work, so Lucy and Ben dropped in to see Ruth and Robert, who now had a private practise on Harley Street. Ruth was delighted to see them. Andrew and Olivia were at school. Ruth said, "I have a twenty-minute gap. Coffee please, Kate."

They entered Ruth's office. "Gosh, Ruth," said Lucy. "I have never been here before. It's lovely." They sat down on a sofa. Lucy went on, "We have just said goodbye to Mother at Heathrow. We called to see Matt and Eve, but they were out."

Ruth said, "Eve is very busy at the moment, selling the American arm of the business. She wants to retire."

Lucy was shocked to hear this. "Why?"

"I don't know, Lucy," said Ruth. "You had better ask Eve."

They stayed with Ruth till her next patient arrived.

Ben and Lucy then decided to paint the town. They went to the Ritz, where the doorman said, "Good evening," and tipped his cap. Ben just looked at Lucy.

"I've been here with Grandma loads of times, Ben."

"You have, have you? My, get you," Ben said in a sarcastic way.

The restaurant manager came to them and asked, "Have you booked your table?" Then he recognised Lucy and said, "Good evening, Miss Lucy. Follow me," and took them to a table.

Ben was agog. "Wow, Lu," he said.

Lucy smiled and said, "It's nothing. You'll get used to it."

* * *

Eve was extremely busy with the possible buyout of the holdings the company owned in America. She just wanted to keep the UK business for now. It would mean less work for her and Matt, and a more an attractive offer when they decided to sell the UK company.

Eve's idea was to gradually reduce her workload and leave the day-to-day running of the business to those around her. Eve had already appointed a new chairman and the most trusted and loyal employees to run the company.

* * *

Lucy's big day finally came, She looked beautiful. Her dress was something else – no frills, just a lovely white satin figure-hugging dress. It suited Lucy with her slender figure. Lucy's three friends from uni came. The sisters were all emotional.

Tommy had come over with Joanne, to Eve's surprise. "How long have you two been an item?" she asked her sister.

Joanne said, "We're just muckers, that's all."

Eve said, "Well, you could have fooled me, the way he's looking at you," and walked away.

Joanne looked over at Tommy. He winked, and she went over to join him.

"OK, Tommy," she said.

He nodded, and then asked, "When are you going to tell your sisters?"

"Not just yet. I'll wait till Eve and Matt are at our place." She went on, "I've been thinking. Would it be possible for you take some time out and help investigate the paperwork with us? These initials might mean something to Eve or Ruth," Jo asked Tommy.

"I might be on an assignment by then," Tommy replied.

* * *

Before Eve and Matt's vacation, they had to sort out Jane's personal letters and documents. Eve set about clearing out her mother's bedroom at the London house and came across a safe. It was locked. Eve eventually found the key, opened the safe, and took out its contents. There was a large envelope and letter addressed to Eve.

She called Matt, and he entered the bedroom. Eve showed him the safe and the contents. Matt read the letter, and it was very disturbing, to say the least. There was also a little black notebook with dates and initials written down. Eve decided to take the contents home so she and Matt could go over them properly and take in what they had read.

* * *

An announcement came over the speakers: "The plane now landing is the nine forty-five from Heathrow." Jo was very excited, and she eagerly waited for the passengers to appear.

"There they are, Tommy!" She rushed over to them and flung her arms around Eve. Tommy greeted Matt, and they just watched as the two girls babbled on. Matt and Tommy went for their luggage. It took an hour to arrive at Joanne's place; she now lived in Manhattan. Eve was fascinated with it all. She and Matt had never really had the time to travel abroad.

Jo had ordered a meal in for them. She knew travelling could be tiring, and Eve was getting on a bit now. After a while, Eve came out of her bedroom fully refreshed. Eve and Matt had decided not to say anything to Joanne just yet; they wanted to try to decipher some of the cryptic notes themselves.

"How's Ruth doing?" asked Joanne.

Eve said, "I had completely forgotten to tell you." Jo looked at her puzzled. Eve carried on, "Ruth and Robert have decided to emigrate to Australia. They got married at a registry office. It was low-key wedding. They didn't want to take the limelight away from Lucy."

Jo was shocked. After that, they had a lovely evening. Jo then said, "I too have some news."

"What's that?" asked Eve, thinking she too might be getting married.

"I have sold the business. Finalised it last week. I want to live in England again."

"What about you, Tommy?" Matt asked.

"It makes no difference to me. I am a freelance investigative journalist."

Eve and Matt hadn't a clue what that meant.

* * *

Joanne and Tommy took Eve and Matt sightseeing. They went everywhere of interest. Tommy even took Matt to see the New York Yankees at Yankee Stadium. Jo took Eve to Macy's and then on to the famous 21 Club.

Eve and Matt only had a couple of weeks to go now, and they were looking forward to getting home. They were bushed. It was then Jo and Tommy decided it was time to show them the papers and newspaper cuttings Suzanne Emmott had left for Jo.

Eve and Matt just looked at one another in incredulity. Tommy started the conversation.

"We have managed to tie a couple of things up, but that's about it. We thought you might have some ideas, as you are closer to the action in London."

Matt said, "We can do better than that. We too have found some information regarding some of these dates and clippings."

Eve went to the bedroom and came out with the little black notebook and the letter from her father.

"Have you read the letter?" asked Tommy.

Eve replied, "Yes, we have."

Tommy started to examine the notebook. He whistled. "This is explosive."

Eve and Jo looked at one another. "What do you mean?" asked Eve.

Tommy was very hesitant. Jo blurted out, "Tell us, Tommy, for heaven's sake. We are all grown-ups here."

"If you want to crack the code, it could prove a very dangerous undertaking." Tommy looked at them and added, "Just so you are sure you know what you are letting yourselves in for. The information in this notebook with certain initials are assignations. I would bet my life on it. The other dates with initials are for assassins to carry out their assignments."

Eve was shocked, and so too were Matt and Jo. Eve exclaimed, "How do you know all this?"

Tommy replied, "I have worked undercover long enough to know how it works. What we must do is tie up the murders with these initials and vice versa. Are you prepared to put your lives in danger?"

Eve was now sorry that she had given Tommy the notebook. Jo was also upset.

Matt spoke first. "Are you able to give us something that checks out?"

Tommy replied, "That's easy. The initials R.A. refer to my father, Robert Ashurst, who died suddenly. E.A. is my mother, Elizabeth Ashurst. who as you know committed suicide."

They all looked at one another. Matt then said, "We need to give this lot of thought, Tommy. You're sure it's not a coincidence?"

Tommy answered, "Definitely not."

Jo suggested that they come over and stay with Eve and Matt if they decided to go ahead with the investigation. One thing was for sure: Tommy was certainly going to investigate, with or without Eve and Matt's approval.

* * *

When their plane landed at Heathrow, Matt and Eve went straight home. It had been a silent flight home, with each of them lost in thought. Eve was already trying to decipher some initials that she had memorised, while Matt was wishing and hoping Eve wouldn't proceed with the investigation. To Matt, it was a matter of self- preservation.

Tommy never read the letter. He said he wanted focus on one thing at a time, and that was to decipher the codes.

* * *

Lucy and Ben arrived home from their honeymoon and went straight to the Harrows. Ben returned to Oxford and came home at the weekends. Lucy kept busy with the refurbishment of the Harrows. The stable was now Lucy's workroom.

One weekend, Eve arrived to see Lucy. She was impressed with the transformation. Some rooms had been knocked down to make a larger room. The snug room had completely gone, and the piano was now in the lounge, upstairs. Lucy had managed to put an extra bedroom with an en suite in, and it was now Ben and Lucy's room. The other two bedrooms were larger and had a Jack and Jill bathroom. To Eve, the house looked much more spacious inside but the same size on the outside. It baffled her.

Eve spent a lovely weekend with Ben and Lucy. She really wanted to tell Lucy that Tommy and her mother were coming over to stay with her in London, but she didn't.

* * *

When Jo and Tommy arrived in London, Eve and Matt greeted them warmly. They made their way to Holland Park, and after dinner, they discussed the notebook. Eve had managed to tie a few things up. Joanne asked Eve if Ruth knew about the notebook. Eve said, "No, we haven't said anything. They are off to Australia in a couple of weeks' time. I have invited them next weekend, and also Lucy and Ben. Matt and I thought it is better we say nothing to Ruth or Lucy." Tommy agreed.

Joanne said, "Unfortunately Tommy has an assignment in the Middle East in three weeks' time, so we are hoping to crack some of the codes before that."

Tommy reiterated what he had said – that it would be a very dangerous undertaking, and did they all know just what they were letting themselves in for? It could even mean leaving London. Matt and Eve hadn't bargained for leaving their lovely home and indeed London. *And what about Lucy?* Eve thought to herself.

Eve didn't commit one way or the other. Jo said she would stay in Manhattan for the time being – till the shit hit the fan, was her expression. Eve wasn't too impressed with her analogy.

The next day, they started in earnest to try to decipher the notes and marry them up with what their father had written in the notebook. They were hoping it would be like a jigsaw puzzle and all slot into place, so it would make sense to them. They intended also to peruse the notes Suzanne had left for Joanne.

* * *

Meanwhile, Lucy had started to take in clients with her new enterprise. She was hoping it would take off. Ben was happy with his tutoring at Oxford, but he missed Lucy, and sometimes he wished he was there with her.

They had been married for twelve months now. Lucy rang Eve up and asked, "Are you and Uncle Matt free this weekend?"

Matt and Eve were still wading through the enormous mound of paperwork and getting nowhere. Eve was cheesed off, so the offer of a visit was music to Eve's ears. She said yes immediately.

Matt wasn't too pleased with what Eve had done. He thought they were finally getting somewhere.

Eve said, "I wish I had your confidence."

The weekend came, and off they went the Harrows. Eve had received a letter from Ruth. She and Robert had settled in Melbourne, and they were loving it. Robert was working in a private clinic, and Ruth was taking a twelve-month sabbatical to acclimatise and help the kids to settle in. "We live so near the beach, Eve. It really is beautiful," Ruth wrote. "When you have the time, please come over and stay with us."

Eve was wishing she could be there right now. She was fed up with the little black book and wanted out. When they reached the Harrows, Lucy came running out to greet them. She made tea, and they chatted about all sorts of things. Then Lucy showed them her workshop and pictures of before and after of various projects she had done for clients. Eve was fascinated.

Ben showed up, saying, "Sorry I'm late. Traffic was dreadful."

Lucy said, "You're here now."

They entered the house. Matt was mesmerised by what Lucy had done to the place.

"I'll show you around later, Uncle Matt," Lucy said before going into the kitchen to check on dinner.

Eve turned to Ben and said, "Has Lucy no domestic help?"

Ben laughed. "Not at weekends. We prefer just us two."

Eve couldn't imagine having no domestic help.

Lucy came in and said, "Dinner's ready." They all trooped into the kitchen for dinner. The talk over dinner was easygoing. Then they went into the lounge.

"Drink, anyone?" asked Ben.

Matt asked, "Have you got a beer?"

"Sure!" Ben said. He poured Matt a beer. "What are you having, Eve?"

"A sherry, please."

"Lucy?"

"Not for me, thanks."

Eve noticed that Lucy and Ben kept looking at one another and smiling. She said, "Come on, you two, what's going on?"

Lucy looked at Ben and said, "I'm pregnant."

Eve jumped up and hugged her. "That's wonderful news, Lucy! Does your mother know?"

"Not just yet. I wanted you and Uncle Matt to be the first."

Matt went over to Ben and shook his hand.

The two couples spent a lovely weekend, but it was now time for Eve and Matt to return to London. As they drove home, Eve said, "Matt, why don't we drop all this deciphering business. I've had enough of it now. Jo and Tommy were supposed to help, but we haven't heard a thing from them. I've a good mind to ring her up and tell her we are done with it all."

Matt turned around to her and said, "Let's carry on till the end of the month, and if we are no further, then we jack it in."

Eve agreed to do that.

Matt switch on the TV, and then he shouted, "Eve, come quick, hurry up!"

Eve came running in. "What is it?"

"There," said Matt,

"Where?" Eve asked.

"On the telly."

Eve looked, and it was Tommy giving a report from the Middle East for CNN News. "Well, I never," she said. After the report had finished, the credentials came up, but it wasn't Tommy Ashurst – it was Michael T. McCready. *How odd*, Eve thought.

CHAPTER TWENTY-THREE

It was nearly the end of the month, Eve was out when the telephone rang. Matt answered, and it was Joanne calling to say she was coming over. They had managed to tie everything up on their end. "How are you and Eve doing?

"Not too good," answered Matt.

"Well, we can cross-reference everything when we get over. Have you heard the news?"

Matt hesitated and then said, "What news?"

Joanne yelled, "I'm going to be a grandma! Isn't it great?"

Matt just said yes, it was great news. He felt a twinge of sadness that Eve would never know the joy of being a mother, or in fact him being a father, or indeed of them being grandparents. It hurt like hell.

When Eve arrived, he was in a melancholy mood.

"What's up?" asked Eve,

"Jo is coming over this weekend," said Matt.

"Is that all? I thought it was something serious," said Eve with a laugh.

* * *

Upon arrival, Jo made her own way to Eve's house. By the time she arrived, she was feeling jaded. Eve welcomed her as sisters do and took her to her bedroom. It was a twofold gesture, really. Eve wanted to show Jo the letter their father had written. It read:

My darling Eve,

I am presuming I have met my maker and have died of natural causes or I have been assassinated by Max and his associates. I leave you with a heavy burden to carry. I need you to expose Max and Charlie Winters, and the fixer who I have never met and only spoke to by phone. Everything you need to know is in the notebook, with dates and initials and times etc. I know you will be able to work things out with that analytical mind of yours. I am aware that you have already been snooping around. Be very careful, Eve. Charlie Winters is no fool. Take down Charlie Winters and his cronies, and Max if you can, and try to identify the fixer. Keep a very watchful eye on them.

I'm sorry it has ended like this. I just want you to know I did it for your mother's sake and the family. I just wanted to protect you all. I got in so deep with Charlie and Max that I couldn't get out. If you do decide to go public with the information, it will ruin the family's name and my reputation. Please find it in your heart to forgive me.

Your loving father.

After Jo had read the letter she said, "The bastard! After what he put me through having to leave Lucy and Mother, well, he can go to hell!"

Eve put her arms around Jo and said, "I don't want to investigate this any more than you do, but surely we can't let Charles Winters and this fellow Max get away with murder. If we do, we are just as bad as they are."

Eve and Jo eventually came downstairs. Matt looked Eve; she smiled at him and shook her head. Matt said, "Drink, anyone?"

Jo said, "Not for me, Matt. I'm teetotal now, but don't let me stop you. Tommy drinks like a fish." She laughed.

Matt went into the kitchen and made Jo a cup of tea. Joanne was amazed. Eve noticed and said, "We have got rid of our live-in domestic now and only have a daily three times a week. Your Lucy got us into the idea."

Jo didn't question it any further. They had to decide and fast whether to get involved or not. One thing was for sure: Tommy wouldn't let it go. He wanted revenge.

By the time Tommy arrived, Eve, Jo, and Matt had made a joint decision not to show the letter to Tommy – or for that matter, to anyone – unless they really needed to. They wanted to protect Ruth and her family and also Lucy. They agreed to help Tommy with the decoding and to work behind the scenes.

Another major factor as far as they were concerned was to ask Tommy to take on the assignment on one proviso: if he found any incriminating evidence about their father, he had to show it to the family first so they could destroy it. They would only help to bring Max, Charles, and any associates to justice. If Tommy agreed, they would pay all of Tommy's expenses.

Tommy thought long and hard about the proposition. In any of his findings, he had always been truthful, and he had never held any information back. He had to be as straight as a die; his type of work depended on it.

Tommy turned around to them all and said, "I have never compromised myself in any investigation that I have undertaken, so I cannot agree on those terms. I'm sorry."

Jo turned to him and asked, "How can we find out anything about Charles Winters without involving my father?"

Tommy just stared at them and said, "Take it or leave it. And besides, have you any idea how much undercover work costs? It can be thousands."

Matt decided to say something. "Look, Tommy, we don't want to compromise you or your reputation in any way, so if you can give us some pointers and point us in the right direction, we'll take it from there."

Tommy thought long and hard and then said, "Look, I have a suggestion. I know a colleague who would be willing to take the job on for a fraction of the cost. He is very good with surveillance and phone-tapping, which is really all you need, and then just collate the information yourselves. I can then read it when I get back from my travels. I will personally see to Charlie Winters in my own way. Matt and Eve, you go to the Riviera and watch him. You can say it's a belated honeymoon or something. Joanne can work with my colleague."

"What about Max?" asked Jo.

"We will find this fellow Max. Have no fear."

Eve, Matt, and Joanne discussed Tommy's proposal, and then Matt said, "OK, we'll do it your way. Can you set it up?"

"Eve, I suggest you sell the London house as soon as possible, and you need to let Ruth know."

"The London house belongs to the company, Tommy, but I will make sure it gets sold. Before we do that, we need to go through it with a fine-tooth comb and make sure there is nothing to incriminate Father." Eve still couldn't get her head around the fact that her father was a criminal. Matt and Jo just looked at one another.

Jo and Eve were not happy about letting Ruth know. They agreed to tell Ruth but not everything, unless they really had to.

Tommy had a couple of weeks before his next job, and he set about fixing everything up with his colleague Joey (if that was his name). He met up with them all at Eve and Matt's place. Tommy had already outlined exactly what they wanted. Eve had made supper for everyone. It was very pleasant, and it helped them to relax. They were briefed by Joey on their tasks and given a timetable to ring in with any information they might have.

When it was time for Joey and Tommy to go, the family wished them luck. Jo showed Tommy to the door and added, "Come back safe."

He kissed her and went on his way.

Jo stayed on a couple more days, and then she went to see Lucy and Ben. The baby was due anytime. Eve and Matt sent their love. They decided to stay in London for a while, as they had a lot to consider about their future and the company's as they embarked on their mission. Eve wrote to Ruth asking for her approval if she decided to sell the company. She said she wanted to retire. Joanne would be no problem.

Matt and Eve went out for dinner at the Ritz – her favourite place to eat – and they had a long chat about their future and where they would like to live. After all, they only had themselves to think about. The chatting went on all evening, and then the decision was made to sell the company. Of course, Eve had to consult her board about her decision.

* * *

Lucy was delighted to see her mother. She had only approximately three weeks before the birth. Ben being in Oxford gave Jo premium time to spend with her daughter. They talked about all sorts of things.

Jo asked what Lucy's plans were for after the baby was born. Lucy hesitated, and Jo noticed. "What is it, Lucy?" her mother asked.

Lucy then said, "Ben has been promoted. He wants me and the baby to live in Oxford with him. He wants to be part of the baby's life and see more of us."

"So what's stopping you?" asked her mother.

"The Harrows has been my home all my life, more or less. I wanted my children to grow up here. And besides, what would Auntie Eve think if I sold it?"

"Oh, Lucy! Eve is only interested in your happiness. You must go to Oxford and live there with Ben. You have your own life now. If I know Eve, she will be happy for you, and so will Auntie Ruth. After all, Ruth has moved over to Australia because she wants the best for her children. At least you are only going to Oxford. We can still visit you. The Harrows is only bricks and mortar. Home is where you make it."

Lucy never said anything.

Jo asked, "Now, where shall we go tomorrow?"

Lucy thought about it and said, "Let's go to Oxford, meet up with Ben, have lunch, and look at some properties."

Jo kissed her and said, "That's my girl."

* * *

Lucy and Joanne spent a lovely few days. Jo was hoping the baby would arrive before she left. Lucy chose a lovely four-bedroom Victorian house. The owners had totally modernised it but had kept some of its unique features. Lucy wasted no time in putting the Harrows up for sale.

Finally, Joanne only had another day before she returned to the States. "Come on," she said. "I'll treat you and Ben for dinner."

Lucy booked an up-and-coming bistro not far from the university. It had an à la carte menu. As they walked in, Ben noticed Becky. He pretended he hadn't seen her, but Becky certainly saw him.

Ben was on pins all night. Joanne thought it was nerves, as Lucy's time was imminent. They ordered their meal, and it was a strained encounter. Joanne could sense there was something wrong with Ben, although Lucy was oblivious to it all. Finally, the meal over, Ben couldn't wait to get outside. Just as he was about to leave, however, he was confronted by Becky.

"Don't I know you?" she asked in her Southern drawl.

Ben sheepishly said, "I don't think so. You must be mistaken."

"I'm sure you were at Yale," Becky replied.

"I was at Yale, but I certainly don't recognise you."

"Oh, well, you must have a double. Come on, Brad," Becky said and left, dragging another unfortunate fellow behind her.

Lucy said, "How odd!"

Joanne never said anything. She just looked Ben straight in the eye. She remembered Becky from the Waldorf. Ben must have his reasons for keeping quiet – and besides, Jo didn't want to alarm Lucy.

The next day, it was time for Jo to go home. She and Lucy were both crying. Jo so much wanted to be with Lucy, but she had other things to attend to. She was torn between helping her daughter and helping Eve and Matt.

Jo contacted Eve and put her in the picture about Lucy being very close to giving birth. She also mentioned Ben and this woman called Becky, which gave Eve a bit of a jolt, but she couldn't think why.

Eve said, "You must stay with Lucy. Matt and I have important matters to see to before we can go to the South of France. It may well take a couple of months before we can start in earnest."

Jo didn't hesitate. She cancelled her flight and stayed on till after the baby was born.

CHAPTER TWENTY-FOUR

Joey had everything in place. He was just waiting for Tommy to give the go-ahead. Eve wasted no time in informing the board of directors that she was putting the business up for sale. She told them, "We can either put the shares into the public domain or sell them as a private limited company."

It took the better part of six months to sell the company, plus the London house. Eve and Matt kept their property in Holland Park.

Lucy gave birth to a little boy and named him Matthew John, to Eve's delight. Jo and Tommy came over for the christening. Ruth couldn't make it – Robert wasn't well enough to travel – but she sent a lovely card and present.

Eve hadn't seen Lucy's house in Oxford and was looking forward to it. The house was overlooking the river. It was a lovely setting, and so peaceful.

Tommy and Jo, along with Matt and Eve, compared notes. Tommy said, "We can now start in earnest. I have had a word with CNN. They are happy for me to investigate, if they get the exclusive."

"What does that mean?" asked Matt,

Tommy answered, "CNN will fund my expenses."

Lucy came over and asked, in a jovial way, "What are you lot talking about, a conspiracy?"

Eve said, "Wouldn't you like to know."

Jo said, "Come on, you lot, and mix in. We can talk later after the christening."

The four of them left Oxford to carry out their mission. Jo had mentioned to Lucy that she wouldn't be available for a couple of months – she was off with Tommy on one of his assignments – and not to worry.

As Eve and Jo turned around to wave to Ben and Lucy, there was a certain trepidation about what they were letting themselves in for. Eve said, "I have written to Ruth to tell her that Matt and I will be on our travels for a couple of months and not to worry, and I will ring her when I can."

* * *

Meanwhile, there was trauma in the Waddell household, unknown to Eve or Jo. Robert was recovering from a serious operation. He'd had to have his left lung removed, as a tumour had been found. Robert was finding it difficult, and his doctor suggested convalescence in a rest home out of the city for six weeks. He would arrange everything, if Robert and Ruth agreed.

"I'll let you know," said Ruth. "I need to have a word with Rob first."

"I understand. Let me know as soon as possible," said the doctor.

Ruth went back into the Roberts's bedroom. She was worried sick about him. "Robert," she said, "we need to talk."

He opened his eyes, and Ruth set about explaining what the doctor had suggested. Robert became agitated and started gesturing to Ruth. She couldn't make out what he was trying to say. Then he pointed to a pen. Ruth immediately gave him the pen and paper. It took a while for Robert to write, but eventually he put his hand out.

Ruth took the paper off him. It read: "Please, Ruth, no rest home for me."

Ruth nodded and immediately rang up Eve, but there was no answer. She tried again later. Ruth was getting exasperated, but Robert was persistent. He wrote, "Just keep trying."

* * *

Eve and Matt were now in situ on the French Riviera, watching Charles Winters' comings and goings. They filmed him from a distance. Eve, in disguise, tried to get the names of his guests. Matt had grown a designer beard, which was the latest fad. On one of their assignments, they saw Peter Winters with another man.

"Are you sure that's Peter Winters, Eve?" asked Matt.

Eve replied, "I'm almost sure it's him. It's been a long time. I'm sure Mother told me he lived somewhere near Oxford and was a civil engineer. I'd love to know who the other man with him is."

"You don't suppose that could be our mystery man Max? I'll go over and try to find out. You stay here and keep filming if you can."

"Be careful, Matt," said Eve.

Matt watched the men from a distance. It was getting dark by now, and Charles Winters made a move to leave. Peter and the mystery man – Matt was just going to call him Max for now – said goodbye. Charles made his way outside. Peter nodded to Max, and Max followed Charles. This intrigued Matt.

Suddenly, Peter came out and started walking the other way. Matt was wishing Tommy was with him. He decided to follow Max. Max caught up with Charles, put his arm around him, and shot him. Matt was horrified; he stayed well hidden. Max dragged Charles, propped him against the sidewalk, and poured a bottle over him. He then made his way back towards Matt.

Matt was panic-stricken. He didn't know what to do. Suddenly, Max veered into an alleyway. Matt watched, holding his breath, as Max threw what Matt thought was the gun into a dumpster. Matt froze; he was definitely in a quandary. He made his exit as quietly as he could and scarpered quickly away. His heart was pounding. Once he was well out of sight of Max, he made his way back to Eve.

Eve was waiting patiently, but she was starting to get anxious. Then she saw Matt. He beckoned her to come over, and she made her way over to him. They went and sat at the bar in the hotel. Matt told Eve everything he had seen, and she was shocked.

"Where is this alleyway? How far is it?" she asked.

Matt just stared at her.

Eve carried on, "Let's see if we can find the gun! It will have fingerprints on it."

Matt said, "Definitely not. It is too dangerous."

"Come on," Eve prodded him. "This our chance to get some real evidence." She made her way outside, determined to go with or without him.

Matt reluctantly followed. When they reached the alleyway, they ventured down it. Matt saw a couple of dumpsters. "He must have chucked it in one of these," he said.

Eve just looked at him as if to say, *Well, I'm not climbing in.*

Matt dithered, and then he jumped in. It wasn't the most pleasant thing Matt had ever done – wading through people's unwanted rubbish. There was nothing in the first dumpster, so it had to be the second. By this time, Matt was not amused. He stank to high heaven. Eventually, however, he said "Eureka!" and held up what looked like a gun, wrapped in a dirty cloth.

When they reached their apartment, Matt went straight into the bathroom. He scrubbed himself from head to toe several times. Finally, he came out, and Eve made him a stiff drink. He downed it in one go. Then he went over to the cloth and unwrapped it. There it was: a small gun, but nevertheless lethal. Matt gently wrapped it again and put it in a safe place.

They sat and ate supper. Matt then showed Eve his notes and photos. Matt said, "I think this one is Teddy Richardson, also known as Toby, the son of a notorious gang leader in Soho and very dangerous."

Eve looked at Matt and asked, "How do you know all this?"

"I forgot you only read the *Times*," he said and laughed. Matt could see Eve was perturbed by this. "Don't worry, Eve, we'll show everything to Tommy when he arrives. He can take it from there. I think we should head back to London."

Eve decided to ring Ruth. It was eleven thirty at night, which worked out to morning in Melbourne. She rang the number with fingers crossed that it was the right one. It rang and rang, and then someone said "Hello" in an Aussie accent.

"Is Ruth there? It's Eve."

"Hi, Auntie Eve, it's Olivia. I'll get Mum."

Eve felt uneasy for some reason.

Finally Ruth came on the line. "Hello, Eve. Bad news, I'm afraid. Robert has had to have a lung removed. The doctors found a tumour, and it was malignant. Rob is having radium and chemotherapy now."

Eve went cold and then said, "What's the prognosis?"

"We don't know yet. Early days," replied Ruth.

"Shall I come over?" asked Eve.

"Best leave it a tad longer. Will keep you up to date. I have to go now, Eve."

Eve hurriedly gave Ruth a telephone number to ring day or night. She was dumbstruck and in a state. She just sat there motionless.

Matt came in and said, "Guess who I have just seen through the window heading this way?"

When Eve didn't answer, Matt went over to her and repeated himself.

Eve blurted out, "Robert is dying of cancer!"

Matt tried to console her. He made her a cup of tea and said, "All right now?"

Eve just nodded.

There was a knock on the door, which alarmed Eve. "Don't worry, it's Tommy," Matt assured her and opened the door. Matt whispered something into Tommy's ear.

"Shall I come back later?" asked Tommy.

Matt shook his head and said, "It's fine." Tommy could see Eve was upset.

"You'll have to excuse me, Tommy," Eve said and made her way to the bedroom.

Matt explained what Ruth had said about Robert being very poorly. Tommy didn't say anything; he was too focused on Charles Winters. He pulled out a file and showed it to Matt. Matt was awestruck; he couldn't get his head around it. It was a conspiracy. Matt showed Tommy the pictures he had taken and also the gun, and he told Tommy what he had witnessed.

Tommy just looked at him and said, "I don't think you should stay here any longer, Matt. It's too dangerous for you both. Joey and I can take over. I advise you to go over to the States. Joanne is already there."

"I doubt Eve will go. She'll want to go over to Australia to see Ruth, if I know her."

"Well, you do what you think is best, but in that case, do not get in touch with Joanne till all this is over."

"I can't do that. Eve would never forgive me," said Matt.

Tommy sat and thought. He used his mobile and rang Joanne. While it was ringing, he asked Matt to go get Eve. When he brought her back to the room, Tommy gave her the mobile.

"Joanne? It's Eve. I have some bad news." She went on to tell Joanne about Robert's prognosis.

"What are you going to do?" asked Jo.

"I'm going over there. Sod the bloody investigation," said Eve.

"I'll come too," Jo replied. "Put Tommy on."

Eve gave Tommy the phone. A row ensued. Tommy went outside, and Matt and Eve just looked at one another. Tommy came back and said, "Jo is adamant that she wants to go with you." Tommy was furious. He handed the phone back to Eve.

Joanne said to her sister, "We'll meet up at the Hilton in Melbourne in a few days. Ask Tommy to buy you a mobile, so we can keep in touch." Eve had never even thought about owning a mobile, never mind using one.

By this time, Tommy was quite irate. Matt took Tommy to one side and said, "Look here, Tommy. I know it's important for you to get this story out, but we are real people here, and Eve is hurting. So is Joanne. So I suggest you stop your antagonism and accept that they are going to see their sister in Melbourne."

Tommy calmed down somewhat and went over to Eve. "Sorry, Eve," he said. "This has taken the best part of fifteen months, and we are on the verge of exposing these bastards. The longer we stay here, the more dangerous it becomes. You and Jo do what you have to do; you'll probably be safer there anyway. I'll get you a mobile and explain how it works."

* * *

A couple of days later, Eve was on her way to Australia, not knowing what to expect. She tried to rest but couldn't. She had a fretful sleep for most of the journey. She was about to settle down when she had to change planes in Singapore.

Her mobile rang. It took two or three minutes for Eve to register it was hers. "Hello?"

"Jo here, Eve. I'm in the departure lounge waiting to get the flight to Melbourne. Where are you?"

"I have just arrived and am still in the terminal, on my way to gate number ten, I think."

"Good. I'll see you there shortly."

When the sisters arrived in Melbourne, they headed for the Hilton exhausted. Eve said, "I hadn't bargained for such a long journey. I don't think I will be doing this again."

Jo just said, "You and me both."

Eve went to rest and fell into a deep sleep. Joanne left her there. She didn't feel too bad, considering it was a longer journey for Jo from America.

* * *

Meanwhile, back on the French Riviera, the birds had flown. Tommy was seething.

"All this bloody hard work down the f—in' drain."

"What do we do now?" asked Matt.

"Go home. Back to square one," said Tommy. "You make your own arrangements, Matt. It's best we are not seen together."

Tommy took all the notes, photos, and gun from Matt. He knew a chap on the police force in New York and would ask for a favour. The man worked in forensics, and Tommy knew he would help for a price.

* * *

Matt had been home a month when the phone rang. It was Eve.

"Lovely to hear from you, Eve. How's things?"

"Robert died this morning," she told him.

Matt didn't know what to say.

Eve then said, "We are staying for the funeral and expect to be back in London by the weekend. I'll ring you before we set off. Love you." Then she put the phone down.

Matt had been working on the notebook. In fact, that was all he had done since he got back to the UK. He had made a breakthrough and was rather pleased with himself.

The doorbell rang, and Matt went to answer it. It was Tommy, clean-shaven now. They entered the lounge.

Tommy said to Matt, "Joanne has rung me to say she is coming to London with Eve. I've been summoned to go to Iraq in a couple of days' time to cover the war."

He carried on, "I want to leave all these with you if I can. Look after them till I get back. Put this somewhere safe." It was the gun, a thick file, and loads of paperwork. "Make sure they're safe, Matt. Tell Joanne I'll marry her when I get back."

Matt couldn't speak. His head was spinning. Everything was happening too quickly for him to digest. Tommy was like a whirlwind, and then suddenly, he was gone.

* * *

Finally, the sisters arrived at Heathrow. Jo's thoughts were now of Lucy and her grandson. Eve was hoping Matt was waiting for them. As they approached the airport arrival lounge, Eve could see Matt. He waved, and his face was beaming. Eve just smiled at him. Jo was too preoccupied with arranging to see Lucy to notice.

Chapter Twenty-Five

When they arrived home, Matt made them a cuppa while Eve went to freshen up. Matt was itching to tell them everything that had gone on. Eve just wanted to relax.

"Can't it wait till tomorrow?" she asked. "I'm bushed. It's a hell of a way. Never again."

Matt was deflated but just said OK.

When Joanne arrived downstairs, Matt said, "I have a message for you from Tommy."

Matt hesitated. Jo looked at him, and Matt said, "Tommy said he will marry you when he gets back."

Jo said, "Is that all? He's always saying that," and never batted an eyelid.

They had a peaceful night. Eve and Jo retired early. Matt was chuffed that Eve was back. He had missed her so much.

Jo rang Lucy up and said, "Hi, Lucy. It's Mum."

"Where the hell have you been?" Lucy cried. "I have been worried sick about you."

"It's a long story, Lucy. I will tell you when I come to see you this weekend."

"Good. I've got some news too, but it can wait till then."

By the time Jo left for Oxford, Eve had acclimatised and was feeling more like herself. She was saddened, of course, about Robert, but she realised that life goes on.

Matt asked Eve, "What will Ruth do now?"

"I'm not sure. She needs to sort things out for herself and her children. Andrew is in med school, and Olivia has just finished a secretarial course. She hopes to be a reporter. I think Ruth's life is with her children. She still has her private practice, but I tell you this, Matt. If Ruth decides to return home, Jo and I must tell her absolutely everything."

"I have something to show you, Eve," said Matt.

Matt produced all the paperwork that Tommy had left, plus the gun. Eve wasn't too happy about having a gun in the house. Matt carried on and showed Eve the notebook and what he had managed to decode and match up with events that had already happened. Eve was amazed.

Matt went on to tell her that Tommy was now in Iraq and didn't know when he would be back. "He wants the three of us to carry on, with help from Joey."

Eve was fascinated by all the paperwork and set about putting everything in date order. Matt showed Eve what Tommy had managed to decipher.

Eve said, "I knew all along that Hunter and Owen and Williams and Thomson's were all tied up in this somehow."

Matt and Eve finally cracked most of the code. The can of worms was ready to be opened. Eve wondered if they were doing the right thing going public. It could have terrible repercussions for everyone, including Lucy and her family. Eve was very apprehensive about going any further with the investigation. They decided to wait for Tommy to arrive back in London before going any further.

* * *

Jo finally arrived in Oxford and made her way to Lucy's house. As she approached, she could see someone watching the house. As Jo got closer, she recognised the woman but not the man.

"I recognise you from the Waldorf in New York," said Jo. "You came over to our table when Ben Johnson was taking to us. It's Becky, isn't it?"

Becky answered, "It is."

"What are you doing out here? In Oxford?" asked Jo.

"I just want to ask Ben about my father." Becky's eyes filled up.

"Can I help in any way?" asked Jo.

"I just need to speak to Ben, but he has refused to have anything to do with me."

Jo said, "Follow me." They found a tearoom not far from where Lucy and Ben lived. They ordered coffee, and Jo then said, "Now tell me from the beginning what's this all about and how does your father come into it."

Becky set about telling Jo everything about Ben being married to her, that she had made up a story up about being pregnant, and that she only fancied him because of his English accent. It was a mistake from day one.

"One day I get a call from Daddy telling me he wants me and Ben to be in Vegas," Becky went on. "I argued with him, but he was adamant. I detected a certain fear in his voice, and I couldn't understand why after all these years he suddenly wanted me to divorce Ben. I didn't even know where Ben was. We separated as soon as he realized there was no baby; he wanted a divorce, but I refused. I wasn't a nice person in those days. I've had a lot of growing up to do."

You and me both, thought Jo.

"We did get divorced," Becky went on. "Ben returned to England, and I stayed on at the ranch being an absolute bitch to my father and everyone around me. My father refused to let me return to New York; he wanted me to take over the business, which meant nothing to me at the time. However, some guys called round to see my father – one was named Jake and the other Peter. They seemed nice enough. In fact, I got along well with them both. My father was never the same after that, though. He wouldn't tell me what it was all about."

She continued, "About three weeks later, my father was out riding looking at fencing or something, He never returned. I was frantic. We called the state police. Eventually, his body was found. He had been mauled by a mountain lion. The thought of it shook me to the marrow. An autopsy was ordered, and it turned out my father had been shot. It's haunted me ever since as to whether Ben ordered a hit man."

Jo laughed. "You must be joking, Becky. Ben is purely an academic. It wouldn't even enter his head." Then it dawned on Jo that she knew someone whose head it would indeed enter. She went quiet. Finally, she said, "Look, come back to the house with me. I'm sure if Ben can help in any way, he will. You both have regrets, like we all do."

Jo put her arms around her and saw that Becky was crying. "Come on, girl. Texans are stronger than that, aren't they?"

Becky laughed. "That's more like it," said Jo. "And who's the fella?"

"This is Brad. We cohabit. It's a long story."

They all trundled off to Lucy's. Jo was a little apprehensive and was hoping she was doing the right thing. Jo felt a kindred spirit in Becky and thought she needed people to help her with her pursuit. Of course, Jo also wanted to protect her father's memory and the family name.

She rang the bell. Lucy came bouncing to the door, opened it, and said, "What do *you* want" in a nasty tone.

Jo said, "Not here, Lucy. You need to hear this for your sake and Ben's."

Jo pushed past Lucy and beckoned both of them to follow. Lucy was really annoyed. Jo looked at Lucy and could see she was angry.

"Lucy, you need to listen to what Becky has to say. Please don't interrupt her. This isn't easy for Becky."

After Becky had told Lucy everything, Lucy just stared in disbelief. She then cried out, "And you think somehow Ben is involved?"

Becky said, "No. I just don't know. I need answers, and I thought if we could talk about what happened, it might shed some light on why my father was found murdered. I haven't come here to upset you or Ben. I want justice for my father. I have limitless resources, and I will stop at nothing to catch the perpetrator or perpetrators and bring them to justice."

When Becky had finished, Lucy said, "Ben will be home shortly, but he will not be too pleased to see you. I think it would be better if my mother and I had a word with him first. Where are you staying?"

"The Old Bank," Becky said. She gave Lucy a card. "Please ask him to meet me. I know I'm clutching at straws here, but I need answers."

When Becky left for the hotel, Lucy turned around to her mother and said, "You put me on the spot there, Mother. Why?"

Jo was in turmoil and changed the subject. "When is the baby due?"

Lucy gave her a look.

"Lucy, I really can't tell you anything. Please don't ask. All I know is, it is imperative that Ben talks to Becky. I can only say it's for the honour of the family."

Lucy just glared at her mother and went into the kitchen.

Suddenly, Ben arrived with Matthew. Jo was delighted. "My," she said to her grandson, "you are getting to be a big boy. Do you remember me?"

Matthew replied, "You are my grandma from America."

Jo said, "I have brought you something." It was a New York Yankees cap and baseball bat.

Matthew threw his arms around his grandma and said, "How did you know?"

"A little bird told me," replied Jo.

Matthew was thrilled to bits and went into his room. He was now 10 years of age and looked so much like Ben.

Lucy came out of the kitchen and said, "Dinner's ready."

They all trundled into the kitchen. It was mainly catching up on what had gone on. Jo told Lucy about Auntie Ruth, and that she and Auntie Eve were with Ruth when Uncle Robert died. She also mentioned that Auntie Eve was very upset about it; she and Ruth were very close. Jo mentioned to Lucy that she had made her mind up to return to England and live in Oxford so she could be near them.

Lucy was overjoyed to hear this, and so was Ben. Matthew just took it all in his stride.

"When do you expect to settle here?" asked Lucy.

"As soon as possible, but first I have to return to the States and sell my property over there. Now tell me," she asked again, "when is the baby due?" She could see that Lucy was pregnant again and realised that this is what Lucy had wanted to tell her.

"Not till Easter. We have only just found out."

"Have you told Auntie Eve?" asked Jo.

Lucy said, "No, you are the first. I'll let Auntie Eve know after my first check-up."

Jo said, "I will definitely be here for the baby. I promise." She then said, "Have you had a word with Ben yet?"

Lucy glared at her mother. "Not yet!"

"What's this?" Ben said with a laugh. "Secrets already? I shall have to watch you two."

They just smiled at one another.

After dinner, Jo went to see Mathew in his bedroom, but before she left the room, she glanced over to Lucy and tilted her head as if to say, *Tell him now*. Lucy was quite agitated with her mother. Ben, of course, was quite oblivious to all this. Jo was right: he was a typical academic.

Lucy decided to bite the bullet. Jo could hear a heated argument going on downstairs. Matthew looked at his grandma with concern.

"I'm sure it's nothing, Matthew," Jo assured him. "A storm in a teacup, I shouldn't wonder."

Mathew shrugged his shoulders and carried on showing Grandma his football cards. Jo really wanted to be downstairs, but she thought better of it.

After a lengthy and heated discussion, Ben capitulated and said, "Where is the bitch staying?"

Lucy was shocked. "Ben, there is no need for that sort of language, if you don't mind."

Finally, with a lot of coercion from Lucy and Jo, Ben agreed to meet up with Becky.

Jo said, "It's for the best, Ben. It will clear the air once and for all. All she wants is justice for her father. You can understand that, can't you?"

Ben made no comment. The atmosphere was not what Lucy was used to. She was very angry with her mother.

Lucy arranged to meet Becky at the Old Bank at seven thirty. Jo was to look after Matthew. She wanted to be there but Lucy was adamant that they go alone.

Jo said, "Let me know how it goes, won't you?"

This put Lucy on guard. "Why are you so interested in what goes on, Mother?"

Jo was on her guard and replied, "I'm just being nosey, I suppose," and left it at that.

Matthew and his grandma played games all night. Jo's mind was somewhere else for most of the time. Matthew had to keep prompting her.

Suddenly, there was a commotion. Matthew went to see. He beamed and turned to his grandma, saying, "It's Mum and Dad and some people!"

Jo went to look, and you could see the relief on her face.

CHAPTER TWENTY-SIX

Tommy was still in Iraq. He was finding his reporting dangerous – more so than at any other time. He had to be very careful. There were insurgents everywhere. With Iraqis just wanting to make a fast buck, the biggest worry was betrayal. It was no secret that atrocities were carried out on both sides, with much of the news coverage at the time not being what you would call entirely accurate.

Tommy was fatigued. He had been there for six months and wanted out. He just couldn't see an end to it all. He made up his mind to resign as a war correspondent with CNN so he could concentrate on his conspiracy theory closer to home. With reluctance, CNN let him go pursue his investigation into the criminal syndicate actives in the UK and Europe and the USA, and to find out more about the reasons behind the murders and turmoil in the criminal world.

On his return to the US, Tommy was shocked to see that the house in Rhode Island had been sold. He had tried to get hold of Jo on many occasion with no joy. The owners of the property gave Tommy a letter, which he took with him. He opened it a little later in a nearby bar. It read:

> Tommy, hope you are reading this. I have moved over to the UK and have settled in a village near Oxford to be near Lucy and Ben. I need you to come over to this address when you can. I have found out some significant pieces of information that may help us in quest for the truth.

I know Matt and Eve have some very important evidence too. We are all worried about you. For the moment, we are all sitting tight. Matt and Eve are still living in London. By the way, Robert died. Ruth has now decided to return to the UK. Her children are well settled in Australia. She is coming over to visit us and will be staying with Eve and of course will visit Oxford. Ruth is staying for twelve months. We are all very excited, and yes, I will marry you, if you promise to settle down and live with me in Oxford.

Love Jo

Tommy wasted no time. He made his way to the New York office and had a word with his boss. Tommy outlined his proposal and asked if the offer still stood for exclusive rights to the story. His boss said, "It'll have to go upstairs again, Tommy. We have a new management structure here now."

"What the bloody hell is that?" asked Tommy. "Don't ask, I doubt they know!"

The boss said, with a smirk on his face, "Come and see me in a couple of days. Get cleaned up and rest. You look shocking."

Tommy went to his apartment, cleaned himself up, and rested. He started to go over things in his head. By the time Tommy woke up, it was eleven thirty at night. He quickly changed and went out for a bite to eat. That was one of the good things about New York – nothing ever seemed to close, day or night.

He went into the Irish Bar and ordered a meal. The girl came over. "Burger and fries," Tommy said. The waitress just nodded.

A little later, he ordered a beer. He was looking at his notes when he noticed a guy. It took him a while to remember where he had seen him, and then it dawned on him: it was Peter Winters. He walked past Tommy, and Tommy just carried on eating. He was itching to see who Peter was meeting up with.

The waitress came over with the burger and fries and the beer. When he had finished, he beckoned the waitress. When she arrived, he asked for the little boys' room,

She said, "Over there, through that door."

Tommy thanked her and said he'd have another beer, then he headed towards the boys' room. He pulled his cap down over his face and had his mobile at the ready, just in case he could get a snapshot. He glanced over but could only see Peter Winters. When he came back, he was shocked to see Tommy Two-Fingers passing him. No one knew why everyone called him that, as he had all his digits intact, but there was one thing for sure: he was an extremely dangerous man who, if you had any sense, you wouldn't get involved with ever.

There was no doubt in Tommy's mind that the Mafia was involved in this whole mystery in some way or another, which put the wind up Tommy. His only thought now was to protect Jo and her sisters. He finished his beer and kept his head low, not daring to look up.

As he got up to leave, a man brushed past him. Tommy said, "Watch it, mate."

The man looked straight at Tommy. It was Max. Tommy made his way to the door and then scarpered away quickly. By the time he got back to his apartment, he was breathless.

This put a new emphasis on his investigation. He couldn't leave until he had exhausted all leads in New York, at least. He did, however, write to Jo, telling her that he was still on the case and would only make a flying visit, incognito.

* * *

Eve and Matt were waiting patiently for Ruth to arrive. The flight had been delayed due to bad weather. When the plane finally landed, all the passengers, including Ruth, were practically brain dead. Eventually the passengers came into view. When Eve saw her, Ruth was nearly motionless.

Matt took her luggage, and Eve put her arms around her sister. Tears were flowing. When they had finally consoled themselves, they made their way to Eve and Matt's place. Matt had made tea for them all, with some snacks – nothing too heavy. Matt enjoyed cooking. Eve was happy to let him do it. She never needed to unless she wanted to, which wasn't very often.

For the next couple of days, Ruth rested. She and Eve just relaxed and talked about all sorts of things. Matt was still waiting to hear from Tommy, and he was getting anxious about it.

Eve tried to pacify him. "He'll be here when he can. Don't fret."

"What's all this, Eve?" Ruth said in an Aussie twang that Eve thought was funny. Her English accent had gone completely. It bemused Eve.

Matt said, "Don't you think Ruth should know now?"

"I'm waiting for Jo to arrive, Matt," said Eve. She wasn't too pleased with him. "I'll give her a ring." Eve went to the telephone.

Eve returned and said, "Jo is on her way. She will be here in an hour or so."

Ruth went upstairs and brought photos down of Olivia's wedding and Andrew's graduation. "My, Ruth, you have two beautiful children. Any sign of grandchildren?" asked Eve.

"Not just yet. They are just settling into married life."

Suddenly, there was a commotion. Jo had arrived with Lucy and her newborn baby girl, who she had called Jane, after her grandma. Eve was overjoyed to see them, and Matt also. Jo greeted Ruth warmly. They sat and chatted all afternoon, catching up and showing each other photos. Matt was bored and decided to go out and have a pint somewhere. The girls took no notice of him – except Eve, who waved in a nonchalant way to Matt.

Ruth and Lucy were chatting. Ruth giving Jane the once-over. While this was going on, Eve asked Jo why she had brought Lucy. "I had no choice," Jo said. "She wanted to come and see you and Ruth. How could I say no? Anyhow, she will be leaving at four. She has ordered a taxi to take her to the station."

"Have you and Matt said anything?" asked Jo.

Eve replied, "Not yet. We were waiting for you."

Ruth came in and said, "What are you two whispering about?"

Eve blushed and said, "Wouldn't you like to know."

Lucy said goodbye to her two aunts and asked them if they would be coming over to Oxford to see Ben and Matthew.

Ruth replied, "Of course! I have made arrangements to stay with your mother for three months, so there will be plenty of time to meet up with you and your family."

Lucy then said, to Eve and Jo's amazement, "When you do, I want to know everything that is going between you all – Auntie Ruth excepted, of course. This cloak-and-dagger stuff has gone on long enough!"

Eve looked at Jo. Jo looked at Lucy and said, "I haven't the faintest idea what you are talking about."

"You know damn well what I am talking about," said Lucy, looking straight at her Auntie Eve.

"I should hurry, Lucy. You'll miss your train," said her mother. "We'll talk later. Now is not the time."

With one last glare at the both of them, Lucy left to catch her train.

Ruth looked questioningly at her sisters. Eve said, "Leave it, Ruth, for now. Cup of tea, anyone?"

Ruth said, "I could do with a stiff drink after all that." She looked at Jo.

Jo said, "Don't mind me, Ruth. Have a drink. I'm teetotal."

Matt arrived and said, "Hi, everyone. I'm back."

"I can see that, Matt," said Eve. She gestured for him to follow her into the kitchen so she could tell him what had just happened.

Matt said nothing. He got on with making dinner, which bemused both Ruth and Jo. Matt didn't care what they thought.

After dinner, the time had come to let Ruth know everything about what they had found out, and that Tommy Ashurst was in New York at this very moment investigating. They were waiting to hear from him so they could tie things up once and for all.

Ruth was awestruck. "How do you know all this?" she asked.

Matt went upstairs and brought down two boxes with files in them. Eve said to Ruth, "If you read these, Ruth, there is no turning back. Do you understand?"

Ruth acknowledged Eve, but went ahead. She was fascinated by it all. It took most of the night to show Ruth everything. The final piece of the jigsaw they decided to leave to the next day, when they were all rested. They all said goodnight and retired upstairs. Matt and Eve stayed down a while clearing up and replacing the files in the boxes.

The next morning, it was time to show Ruth and Jo the pièce de résistance. Eve and Matt waited a while after breakfast. The daily had arrived, and they said, "Can you leave the lounge today please, Mrs Redfern, and just concentrate on the rest of the house? We do not want to be disturbed." Mrs Redfern just nodded and said nothing.

Ruth groaned. "Do we have to? I haven't digested last night's lot yet."

Eve looked at Matt and Jo. She was disappointed but said, "What would you like to do, Ruth?"

"Let's go to Harrods and Oxford Street, then on to Annabel's, if it's still there."

So the girls agreed to do that. Matt said, "I'm not going around with three women. One's bad enough. I'll meet up with the boys later and have a few beers."

"Make sure it is a *few* beers, Matt. We have no spare bedrooms. I don't want my sisters to get a fright," Eve laughed. Matt threw a cushion at her.

CHAPTER TWENTY-SEVEN

The three sisters set off to go into town. To Ruth, it was still a trendy place to be. Melbourne was OK, but it didn't have that buzz feeling you get in London.

They had a ball. When it got to be four o'clock, Eve suggested the Ritz instead of Annabel's, simply because of the time. As they arrived, the doorman came to meet them.

"Good evening, ladies," he said with a tip of his cap. Ruth thought, *Some traditions keep going, even in these days of anything goes.*

They entered, and the head waiter came to meet them. Eve said, "Table for three, please."

"Do you have a reservation, Madame?"

Eve replied, "I'm afraid not." *That's a pity*, thought Eve.

As they were about to leave, the manager came up to them. It was Henry. "Miss Eve, Miss Ruth, and I believe you might be Miss Joanne, table for three, is it?"

Eve said, "Please, Henry, if it no inconvenience."

Henry showed them to a table, gave them a menu, and went over to the wine waiter. Then he came back to them and said, "I cannot let my favourite girls not have a table. You and your family have always been extremely generous and always found time to chat with me about my family over the years. I am only too pleased to find you a table."

Eve blushed and said, "Thank you. What a lovely thing to say, Henry."

Ruth said, "I see the Kershaw name still works in some circles."

Eve just smiled and looked at Jo. *Not for long*, thought Jo.

They had a fantastic dinner. Eve thrust a £50 note into Henry's hand and said, "Thank you very much. It's appreciated. It's not that often we get together these days." Henry just smiled at Eve.

As they stepped outside the Ritz, there was a flash and then another one. It was one of those freelance photographers. *Bloody nuisance*, said Eve to herself.

They hailed a taxi to Holland Park. The traffic was heavy. It took ages to arrive home. When they entered, Matt was still out. Eve poured herself and Ruth a drink. Jo went upstairs to change – and then came running back down.

"He's here! He's here!" Jo said.

"Who's here?" asked Ruth.

"Tommy Ashurst!"

Ruth just looked at Jo as if to say, *Who the hell is Tommy Ashurst?*

"It's long story, Ruth. I'll fill you in later," Jo said to Ruth.

"Are Tommy and Jo an item?" Ruth asked Eve.

"To be honest, I haven't a clue," replied Eve.

Jo looked at Eve. Then Ruth said, "OK what's on your minds? You might as well tell me. My inquisitive nature is killing me."

Eve was about to tell Ruth about everything but the letter when Matt and Tommy entered the room. Eve was delighted to see Tommy. He could explain everything to Ruth now.

Jo flung her arms around Tommy and said, "About bloody time. Are you ready to stop globetrotting and settle down with me?"

Tommy replied, "I will, baby, when all this is out of the way. I promise."

Matt said that it was too late to discuss things now tonight and suggested they take it up in the morning when everyone was fresh. They all agreed except Ruth. She wanted to know now.

Eve looked at Jo, who said, "OK, Ruth if that's what you want. We will tell you what we know. But just so you know, there is no turning back!"

Ruth then said, "All right, then, I'll wait till tomorrow. I might as well get some shut-eye. But before I do, can I give the kids a ring, Eve?"

Eve replied, "Of course you can, anytime, Ruth. You don't need to ask."

Everyone except Ruth retired upstairs lost in thought on the task ahead and, more importantly, where they would go from here. They had got to the point of no return if they all decided to go ahead.

* * *

The next morning, Matt and Eve, along with Jo and Tommy, were up very early setting their stall out. Matt and Eve had put the information they had in date order, and they had listed every relevant detail, plus the codes which they had managed to decipher, except for one or two initials – to Eve's annoyance. Tommy did the same with his information.

Jo knew she had to mention what Becky Grayson had told her at some point, but she didn't want to muddy the waters.

Eve made coffee and toast for everyone while they waited for Ruth to surface.

"Gee her along, will you?" said Tommy in a tetchy way.

Eve just withered him. Of course, he didn't notice. He was too focused on the job at hand.

Ruth finally arrived. Eve went over and greeted her. "Breakfast is on the table," she said. "Help yourself."

Ruth poured herself a coffee and came into the lounge.

Tommy stood up and began, "Ruth, I am aware that you are not privy to what is going on now and what is going to be discussed, but I ask you please, no questions till after we have all the information in front of us, so to speak."

To Matt, Eve, and Jo, he said, "Since our last meeting, I have discovered that Peter Winters and this Max fellow are working in conjunction with Tommy-Two-Fingers and the Mafia."

The girls at this point started laughing and looked at one another. Tommy was annoyed with them. "This is no laughing matter," he snapped. "You must take this very seriously. Lives could be in danger here."

In a very stern voice, he carried on. "I have proof." He showed them photos he had taken on his phone. "That's all I have now. I needed to get away fast. This is a brief visit, so we need to discuss whether you want to continue. You know my thoughts on the matter." He added, "There is one thing for sure: we have come across the illuminati. How the Mafia fits into all this, I don't know yet. I know I keep repeating myself, but these are very dangerous people we are dealing with, and how far it stretches is anyone's guess."

The three sisters just looked at one another. They really had no idea what Tommy was talking about.

Ruth was itching to get answers. She said to Jo, "Can I ask questions now?"

Jo replied, "Not just yet, Ruth. You haven't got the full picture."

Ruth just stared at Jo, which obviously, Jo noticed.

"Ruth," she said, "just listen to what Matt and Eve have to say."

Ruth's mind was in a tiswas. She dealt in facts, not innuendos. She decided to listen and say nothing till after the meeting.

Matt stood up. "Just to put Ruth in the picture, we came across a little black notebook when clearing the London house, with a letter addressed to Eve. At this moment in time, the letter is irrelevant. However, we showed Tommy the notebook with certain initials written down, and he immediately recognised two sets initials – that being his father and mother – showing in the black book as being crossed out. Upon further investigation by Eve and myself, we think we have cracked the codes, with one or two exceptions.

Matt then began to explain the codes in the book. "R.A. and E.A we know."

Ruth whispered, "Who they are, Jo?"

Jo replied, "Tommy's parents, Robert and Elizabeth Ashurst." Ruth was agitated; however, again she decided to listen.

Matt went on, "S.E. is Suzanne Emmott, who was badly raped by Charles Winters' father, and Charles Jr helped to cover up, along with someone else, who at this moment we haven't found out.

"R.M. is Roland Matthews of Matthews Iron Works. He committed suicide because of his dealings with a prostitute.

209

"W.T. is William Tatum of Tatum Electrical Engineers. He was found in a compromising situation with rent boys and was shot by people or persons unknown.

"S.T. is Samuel Turner of Turner Sheet-Metal Works. He disappeared, having embezzled the company, which went into bankruptcy.

"H.M. is John Henry Morgan of Morgan Steel Works. He retired and sold the business. We don't know if he is still living or dead."

"Can we stop for a break, Matt?" asked Ruth. "I need to take all this in."

Matt agreed, although much to his annoyance. He was just getting in his stride.

Jo helped to make coffee with Eve. "Wow, Eve, you and Matt have certainly worked hard at this end," said Jo.

"You haven't heard the best yet, Jo. Let's say it is the pièce de résistance."

They re-entered the lounge.

Matt was itching to carry on. Tommy nodded at him. He, too, was fascinated.

Matt stood up again. "As you can see, the initials in this book are there for a reason. The next three are recent." He carried on.

"H.O. is for Hunter and Owen Solicitors, who were struck off by the Law Society, with Owen committing suicide. To this day, Hunter has disappeared without a trace.

"W.T. is Williams and Thomson Asset Strippers. Their premises were burnt down. Arson was suspected. To this day, no one has found Williams or Thomson.

"M.W. is Marjorie Winters, the wife of Charles Winters. Again, we suspect her car was tampered with. We both assume that she was about to blow the whistle about Charles's activities.

"J.K., we presume, is John Kershaw, who was murdered by whoever.

"M. is for Max the fixer. We presume this is the hired assassin at this point.

"C.G.? We have no idea at this present time.

"J.H.M., we have no idea.

"J.B. RHM has only a telephone number. We tried it, but the line is dead. If we are correct, *RHM* means right-hand man.

"I also witnessed Peter Winters, along with this Max fellow, meeting up with Peter's father, Charles Winters, in the casino. I watched and waited; Eve was in the background. I ventured over nearer to the casino. I watched for about half an hour or so, and then they all made their way outside. Peter said goodbye to his father.

"Charles and Max walked about a few hundred yards. Max then looked around and took Charles into an alleyway. By this time, Charles was protesting. I gently approached and saw Max shoot Charles Winters. He took his wallet and watch, and then produced what I think was whisky and poured it over Charles, and then he casually walked away. I was shocked to the core and scarpered as quickly as I could back to Eve.

"We then went back to where Charles Winters was lying. Everyone thought he was drunk and just passed by. Carefully, we approached the alleyway, Eve keeping a look out. I trawled through two dumpsters and found this." Matt unwrapped the cloth and showed them the gun. Everyone gasped in horror. Matt covered the gun and gave it to Tommy.

"We know that Max met up with Peter Winters and this chap Toby Richardson," said Tommy, "whose father is the head of a syndicate that operates in the Soho area and deals in drugs, prostitution, illegal gambling, and many more illegal activities. This is only the tip of the iceberg."

Tommy asked if anyone had any questions.

Jo answered, "Yes, I do. Well, it's not a question, really."

Jo looked over at Tommy. He was agitated. Jo carried on, "Those initials, C.G. I think it is Chuck Grayson of Grayson Oil and Petroleum. He was found murdered, shot in the head. They still haven't found the person responsible."

They all stared at Jo

"How do you know this?" asked Matt.

"It's a long story, and it may be relevant to what we are working on."

Jo then set about telling them about Becky and Ben. Eve gasped at this, which distracted Jo. She finished by telling them that Becky was in England. She had wanted to meet up with Ben to see if he had any inkling as to why her father was murdered, which of course he didn't. "However, she is here for another week, so I was hoping we could all meet up with her."

Tommy interrupted everyone's thoughts. "This might be the opportunity we have been waiting for," he said. "This may very well open doors for us. Jo, can you fix a meet with Becky? I would like to have a chat with her."

"I can do better than that, Tommy." Jo gave him Becky's business card. "Ring her yourself."

Tommy went all quiet and into himself. Ruth looked at Jo, who just shrugged her shoulders. All at once, Tommy said, "Right. This is what we'll do. Matt, you and Eve try to figure out, if you can, the other missing initials. I will meet up with this Becky. I will leave the gun with you for now. Keep it safe. I have had the ballistics and fingerprinting carried out on the gun, which I have a report on.

"What I am thinking," he continued, "is that the same gun that shot Charles Winters might have been used on Chuck Grayson. If that is the case, it means we can go to the FBI and ask them to start an investigation into Grayson's murder, which of course would include Special Branch over here at some stage, I'm sure. If the bullet matches, then we are home and dry."

Eve blurted out, "Does that mean we can go back to normal?"

Tommy replied, "With a little bit of luck, yes."

Matt was elated. "I will try to see what I can come up with on the initials."

Eve opened a bottle of whisky to celebrate. Everyone said cheers and savoured the moment – except for Jo.

Tommy went outside to ring up Becky Grayson.

"Hello, Becky Grayson here."

Tommy said, "Hi, Becky. A mutual friend of ours, Joanne Kershaw, mentioned, that you might need help with your father's murder. Is it possible to meet up with you as soon as possible? I am only in London for a day or so."

Becky went quiet and then said to herself, *What the hell.* She arranged to meet Tommy in London at the Savoy, as she too would be leaving in a couple of days.

Tommy went back into the lounge and said, "I have fixed up a meeting with Becky. Hopefully it will be useful. You won't see me after tomorrow. I will keep in touch when I can."

Jo went over and said, "So soon, Tommy? I was hoping you could have seen Lucy and the children."

"When it's all over, Jo, I will."

Jo excused herself and went with Tommy upstairs. They had a lot of catching up to do.

Eve looked at Ruth and said, "Penny for your thoughts."

Ruth said, "I don't know where to begin. I thought this would be a mundane trip, just going down memory lane. What I have just witnessed is like a Jimmy Cagney movie."

Eve laughed and said, "You know us Kershaws don't do normal. Another drink?"

CHAPTER TWENTY-EIGHT

After goodbyes were said to Tommy, Jo returned to Oxford. Ruth and Eve decided to go out. Ruth wanted to visit Ormond Street, so off they went. As they were passing by a newsagent, Ruth noticed the *OK Magazine.*

Ruth said, "Gosh, Eve, it's ages since I bought one of these. The Aussie ones aren't quite the same."

Eve just tutted at her and muttered, "A load of nonsense, if you ask me."

Ruth said, "Hell's bells, we're all in the magazine. Look!" The photo showed all the three of them leaving the Ritz, with the caption, "The Kershaw girls back in town" with all their names.

Eve wasn't happy about this and said, "For goodness sake, Ruth, don't show Matt or Tommy."

The two sisters had a great time walking around town and remembering their old haunts – some still there, others not. Eve thought it was time for home. She hailed a taxi and said, "Holland Park, please." It wasn't too long before they reached home.

Matt was waiting for them, looking rather pensive. "What is it, Matt?" asked Eve.

"I went to my local, having a quiet drink, and this guy came up to me and said, 'Tell McCready to lay off if he knows what's good for him.' I asked him, 'Why are you telling me this? Who is McCready?' He said, 'I've seen you chatting with him a couple of times.'"

Matt went on, "I told him, 'Just a minute. I don't know him. He's just a chap who comes in every so often, that's all I know. So piss off and leave me alone. Go and talk to the other guys in here; they might know who this guy is.' I tell you, Eve, it put the fear of God in me. I sincerely hope he believed me."

"Did he follow you here?" asked Eve.

"I don't think so. He did go over talking to the other guys. I waited until he had gone."

This was something that none of them had thought about. It perturbed Eve.

"Obviously, Tommy's rattled somebody's cage," said Eve.

"I'm beginning to wonder if I have done the right thing coming over here. I think I will go back as soon as I can," said Ruth. She was really unnerved by it all.

Eve put an arm around her. "I'll give Jo a ring. We'll leave for Oxford tomorrow. You can stay there; you'll be safe, and I will come down every so often, if that makes you feel easier. I am so sorry, Ruth. We didn't really want you to know about all this."

Ruth looked at her and said nothing.

When Matt and Eve retired for the night, they discussed their situation. They didn't know whether to sell the house or rent it out. They really loved the house, so they were hoping to let it, and then move to Oxford and rent there if they found something suitable. Matt said he would start the ball rolling while Eve was with Ruth and Jo, and he would keep in touch. Eve just smiled at him. She was heartbroken inside. This was their home that they had shared for the better part of thirty-odd years. All her memories were here, and she didn't want to leave or sell.

The next morning, Matt said goodbye to Eve and Ruth. "Enjoy Oxford. See you soon."

* * *

It took a couple of hours to reach Oxford. Jo was waiting patiently. She had a lovely cottage near the river, with a waterwheel. Ruth fell in love with it. It was secluded; you wouldn't even know that a cottage was there. Ruth felt much safer now. Matt was to bring the remainder of Ruth's belongings at the weekend. Eve told Jo everything, and Jo too felt uneasy.

"I'll be glad when this bloody lot is over. I wish I had never embarked on such a dangerous task," said Jo. She went into the kitchen and made them tea and sandwiches. They chatted for the rest of the day. Eve kept thinking of Matt and praying he would be safe. He was her life. If anything happened to him, she would never forgive herself.

* **

Matt, for his part, was busy sussing out estate agents and generally getting organised. If he went out, it would be in shabby clothes that he had bought from a charity shop. He grew a beard and looked unkempt. Most of his business was over the telephone.

Eve stayed down for a week before she returned to London. She had been busy looking at places to live, and she had one or two ideas that she needed to put to Matt.

When Eve arrived home, she was shocked to see Matt in such a state. He whispered, "Boy, have I missed you."

Eve said, "Obviously."

Matt laughed. "This my undercover mode," and he gave her a wink.

Eve stayed just over a week, and then she went back to Oxford, having shown Matt some of the prospective houses to look at. She was to stay with Jo and Ruth. The girls finally settled down and had the most wonderful time reminiscing, laughing, and joking. It was good for them – a kind of therapy. After all, they never really had a chance to talk to one another – not like this, not the three of them together.

They were just about to go out when the phone rang. It was Matt.

"Be down this Friday about 4 p.m. See you then."

CHAPTER TWENTY-NINE

Tommy arrived in Dallas, Texas, to find Becky Grayson waiting for him. As they drove, she told him, "Everyone thinks that you are my second cousin on my mother's side, and your name is Michael McCready from Donegal."

He saw a sign for Grayson's Ranch, and after about another two miles, they finally arrived, The ranch was huge. Becky got out, as did Tommy. A ranch hand tipped his cap to Becky, which she ignored. The house was huge, with sheepskins all over the place, an extra-large open fire, and umpteen leather chairs and settees. They entered the kitchen, and a little Chinese man came into view and bowed his head. Tommy was taking all this in. *Gosh, they treat her like royalty,* he said to himself.

Becky turned to Tommy and said, "Ling will show you the guest room. Dinner's at eight. See you then."

Tommy watched as Becky went into her office. His first impression was that it wasn't really a house, but an exceedingly large bungalow. He entered his bedroom. Ling gestured with a slight bow, and Tommy felt obliged to do the same. He perused the place, and then he went to shower. Suddenly he heard a knock on the door. It was Becky.

"Can I come in?" she asked.

"Just a minute," replied Tommy. He hastily dressed and opened the door.

Becky entered and said, "Sorry to bother you, but I thought you might need these." She handed Tommy the police and forensic reports, as well as photos of the scene with footprints and tyre prints, plus a couple of fingerprints which the local police said they couldn't match up to anything in their files.

"How did you manage to get hold of this lot?" asked Tommy.

"With a great deal of money. You can get anything with money, Tommy. The price is always right for somebody," Becky said in a sarcastic voice.

* * *

The next day, Becky took him to the crime scene. There was nothing significant that Tommy could see.

"How far is the nearest town?" asked Tommy.

Becky replied, "About 25 miles." She went on, "We searched for the horse, but we never found him. He was a beautiful black stallion named Tigger, after his father. I don't know if everyone was upset about the death of my father or the horse." She had a wry smile on her face.

When they returned, Becky said, "I have a lot of work to do today, so if you will excuse me, I'll see you at dinner."

Over dinner, Becky put a proposition to him, which he listened intently to. She finished with, "Think about it and let me know so I can set everything up."

Tommy just nodded at what Becky had proposed. It was very tempting indeed.

* * *

Matt and Eve found a lovely country cottage to rent in Abingdon – not far from Jo and Lucy and not too far from London via train. Time was now moving on. The sisters were even closer than before. Lucy's children were growing up fast; Matthew was now attending grammar school, and Jane was at primary school. Ben had been promoted and was now head of a department.

Ruth went back to Australia to be with her children, but she stayed in touch as much as possible. In a way, everyone was just getting along with their own lives. For Matt, Eve, and Jo, all thoughts of a conspiracy were put on hold.

The days for Matt and Eve were idyllic. They would sometimes go to their local, and Matt always liked a pint or two. Eve would have either wine or sherry, depending on what mood she was in. They joined in the pub quiz every week, and Matt played darts. Eve was fascinated to find that Matt was quite good.

"How did you learn to play darts?" asked Eve.

"Misspent youth, Eve," replied Matt.

* * *

Jo was becoming more and more anxious about Tommy; she wondered if she would ever see him again. Nothing had been heard from him for absolutely ages, and she was starting to believe he had been killed in one of his assignments to the Middle East or somewhere else in the world where there was a war or conflict going on. All thoughts of sussing out the last two initials was put on hold.

One afternoon, Eve rang Jo to ask if she and Matt could come over and stay for a couple of days. "Have you heard anything from Tommy?" Eve asked.

"Not a sausage. It looks like we will never solve the little black book," Jo replied.

"Well, that's not a bad thing," said Eve. She added, "I haven't heard from Ruth either."

"I suppose no news is good news," said Jo.

When Matt and Eve arrived at Jo's, she greeted him warmly and made them all coffee. Eve had brought her mail, and when she went to open it, there was a letter from Australia. Eve opened that one first, albeit with some hesitation. After all, they were all getting older, and there was always the possibility of bad news.

She started to read the letter and suddenly let out a scream. It made Matt jump, and he nearly spit his coffee. "Ruth is coming back to England!" Eve exclaimed. "Andrew has been offered a post at Papworth Heart Hospital in Cambridge." The letter continued:

I will sell up here and be over in about six months I should think. Olivia hasn't made her mind up yet. She is living in Sydney and works freelance for the Sydney Herald. She is happy for me to come over. It breaks my heart to leave her, but she has her life to lead with James. I don't want to put any pressure on her.

Will get in touch when everything is finalised.

Love to everyone.

* * *

Back in Texas, Tommy was getting tired of Becky. He wanted to get back to his investigation, which Becky said she would help fund, with a big fat bonus if brought the murderer to justice. He was hampered by her. She always wanted to be with him, and he was sorry he had gotten entangled with her – in more ways than one. She had a possessive nature due to the fact that her family was mega-rich, and she was spoilt rotten.

Things came to a head one weekend. He got his things together and bit the bullet, telling Becky that he needed to get back to New York to carry on with his investigation from there, and he would keep in touch. He put it to her that she would be in grave danger if she travelled with him and said he had to sleep rough sometimes and worked all kinds of silly hours. It just wouldn't be practical. She would be extra baggage that he could do without at this moment in time. Becky was furious; she went ballistic.

He tried to calm her down, saying, "Listen to me! Do you want me to find your father's killer or not?"

Becky nodded.

"Then let me do it my way. I can't do anymore here. I need to be back in New York. I must collate all my information, and I need to be on my own to do this. It has nothing to do with you."

Becky just looked at him and said nothing.

* * *

It took Tommy a week to get organised. Becky drove him to the train station. He said goodbye and added, "Remember, keep a low profile, Becky, until this is all over."

Becky kissed him and said, "Keep safe and come back, won't you?"

Tommy said he would, although he had no intention of meeting up with Becky ever again. His thoughts were now fixed on the job at hand. He had wasted six months staying with Becky, although it did help him to compile a dossier with all the information he had. Now he needed to get back to Jo and her sisters to see if they had managed to glean any more information from the notebook.

Tommy arrived in Dallas and laid up for a couple of days. After a few days of taking stock of everything, he made his way to the airport destined for New York. Tommy arrived in New York late afternoon and went to his apartment. He had to push himself in. He picked up the pile of pamphlets and mail, tossed it on the table, and went to shower. After cleaning himself up, he wondered whether to get rid of the fungus on his face but decided against it for the time being.

Tommy started to read his mail. There were a couple of letters from England and a couple from CNN. Tommy opened his letter from CNN; it said that he had got the go-ahead to continue with his investigation and could he call into the office when available to go over contracts and sign. Tommy was pleased. He didn't remove his beard, as everyone knew him as Michael T. McCready.

With the contracts signed, Tommy was now able to relax. He had given them his work so far. They would go over it with their legal department and from there would eventually produce a documentary. As Tommy looked out of the plane to London, he noticed he was flying over the channel. *Not long now*, he thought to himself. He read Jo's letter again:

Hi Tommy,

Hope you are safe. I am now in situ in Oxford, near
Lucy and family. Eve has put her house up for rental
and hopes to move over to the Cotswolds and rent
something there. Ruth has returned to Australia.
Please find below my new address.

Love you

Jo

He had a wry smile on his face. Suddenly, there was an
announcement: "Please fasten your seat belts. We are about to land."
Tommy was getting excited. He longed to be in England for good,
and he swore when it was all over he would settle down with Jo for
a quiet life.

As Tommy was walking through the arrival lounge, he noticed
Max with another fellow. Tommy quickly took a couple of photos. He
was intrigued by this and decided to follow them if he could. They
caught the commuter train into the city. The two men were unaware
of being watched, as they were engrossed in conversation.

Tommy trailed them to a hotel near Euston Station. He hovered
around for a while and then went into a scruffy-looking café across
from the hotel. He ordered a coffee and sat surveying who came in
and out. Suddenly, the two men appeared minus suitcases.

Tommy watched them till they were out of sight, and then he
went over to the hotel – a dingy sort of place – and asked for Max.
The man said, "You've just missed him."

Tommy asked, "Was there another man with him? I can't
remember his name. And what room number were they in?" He
slipped the guy a £20 note. The man gestured for another note, and
Tommy complied.

The man went out and turned the register book around for Tommy
to look at. Tommy took pictures of the names registered, and then

he turned it back again. He then proceeded up the stairs. As he was walking up, he looked at the photos. It was room 102 he was looking for. When he found it, he glanced around and picked the lock.

Tommy looked around again and entered. He searched the case for clues and took more photos of passports, papers, names, addresses, and a map of London with various markings, which he jotted down. He left everything as it was and went down the stairs to the basement to find another way out, but he couldn't. He had to gingerly go back up the stairs and wait while the chap was engrossed in serving another customer. When the opportunity came, he quickly dashed out.

He was making his way to go left when he saw Max and this other guy coming towards him. He pretended he was a drunkard bum and banged into one of them. Max glared at Tommy; Tommy kept his head down and started to mumble and stumble.

"Leave him, Jake. He's out of his trolley; he's not worth it. The judge will be waiting for us," said Max.

Tommy was about to leave for Oxford when the man called Jake came out of the hotel with his suitcase and headed for Euston Station. Tommy followed in him. Jake caught the tube back into the city and headed towards London Tower. Soon he reached his destination; it was the Tower Hotel on the embankment.

Tommy was in a quandary now. Did he enter with his beard, or did he shave it off and look respectable? He decided just to hang around and wait a while longer. He was rewarded by seeing Peter Winters arriving with Max and another chap. Tommy took more pictures. They were all chatting and must have felt safe from prying eyes. Finally they too entered the hotel.

That did it for Tommy. He couldn't go in clean-shaven now. He entered, proceeded to the bar, and glanced around. There were six of them sitting together in a huddle. Tommy didn't know the other one with Peter Winters. He recognized Max, Toby Richardson, and Jake Johnson, and also Tommy-Two-Fingers, but who was the sixth one? It frustrated Tommy that he couldn't get any pictures of them all together. It was too risky. He just had to sit and watch and try to be patient.

A waitress came up to him and asked, "Can I get you anything, sir?" He ordered a club soda and whisky and a bar snack.

Tommy hung around for an hour. He ordered another club soda and whisky. He was extremely agitated by this time. It was annoying him to be so near yet so far, but he couldn't chance Peter Winters recognising him.

Just then, a party of women came in – probably a hen night or something – and sat close to Peter Winters and his mates. The girls were all pissed and very loud. They were taking pictures of themselves, and it distracted the men. They were laughing and looking at one another.

Tommy seized his moment. He went to a vantage point and started to take pictures, as many as he could. He was happy now. He finished his drink and bolted.

Tommy went to a Travelodge and booked in for the night. The next morning, after breakfast, he went to an Internet café and sent the pictures along with Jo's address to a friend who worked for the FBI. Then he headed straight to the station to travel to Oxford. He bought a first-class ticket. When the train set off, Tommy went to the bathroom and came back clean-shaven. He felt much safer now, and he looked forward to seeing Jo and her sisters again.

* * *

It didn't take long to reach Oxford. Tommy hailed a taxi and showed the driver the address. In ten minutes, the driver pulled up.

"Here we are, sir. Just turn left there and walk for about fifteen minutes. You'll come to the address. It's easier than me taking you the long way around."

Tommy gave him a tip and followed the driver's instructions. As Tommy approached, he could see why it was call Rosewood Cottage: it was surrounded by roses, rambling roses. It was an idyllic situation, and it took Tommy some time to find how you got into the place. The cottage was backways to front.

Finally, he knocked on the door. Jo opened it and flung her arms around him. "Where the hell have you been? We have all been worried sick about you. We thought you dead."

"I'm here now, and boy, am I hungry. I could eat a horse."

"Will steak do?" asked Jo.

"That'll do nicely," Tommy replied.

They chatted most of the night, catching up on what the girls were up to, and Lucy too. Finally, Tommy yawned and said, "I'm bushed. I could sleep a week."

Jo made the bed up in the spare room so Tommy wouldn't be disturbed. Lucy and the children were coming over to visit the next day, and she wanted Tommy to rest up before he saw everyone. Quite honestly, to Jo's eyes, he looked dreadful.

Tommy spent near a week recuperating and getting his house in order. He had to go back into London for two or three days. He had contacts that he needed to get in touch with and a special contact who would do almost anything for a price. He gathered all the photos and other paperwork and set off. Jo wanted to go with him, but he refused, saying it was too dangerous for them to be seen together.

* * *

Meanwhile, at Eve's, a postcard popped through the door. It was from Ruth. It was a picture of Singapore, and it read:

Hope everyone is OK. We leave 17 September. We should arrive by the 20th. See you then. Love Ruth & Andrew

Eve wasted no time in ringing Jo to tell her the news.

"I too have news," said Jo. "Tommy's back. He arrived a couple of days ago. I'll fill you in when I see you."

Eve set about preparing the spare bedroom for Ruth and Andrew. Matt was busy as usual in the kitchen. Eve said, "Tommy's back."

Matt groaned. "I do hope we are not going on with all this cloak-and-dagger stuff again. We haven't even tried to find the last two initials."

"But I do have some good news," Eve told him. "Ruth and Andrew arrive 20 September, so we can look forward to that at least."

It was all getting too much for Matt and Eve now. They just wanted a quiet life, mixing with friends when they wanted to, having the odd lunch out, and going to the quiz night, which they still enjoyed. Eve had made her mind up to tell Tommy that they weren't interested now. Too much time had passed. They would rather let sleeping dogs lie.

* * *

Eve was awakened by the telephone. She gathered her thoughts. It was only 6 a.m.

"Hello," she said quietly.

"Hi, Eve. I'm outside your place. I hope it's your place. It took some finding."

Eve jumped out of bed, ran downstairs, opened the door, and lo and behold, there stood Ruth with Andrew. They hugged and laughed.

"Come in! You must be exhausted."

"It wasn't too bad," said Ruth. "We travelled business class. At least you get a decent night's sleep." She turned to her son. "Andrew, do you remember Auntie Eve?"

"Vaguely," answered Andrew in an Aussie accent, which bemused Eve.

CHAPTER THIRTY

Jed Butler was having his beard trimmed at his local salon. While he waited, he picked up a couple of magazines. One was on motor racing, and the other was *Hello*. He started to flick though the *Hello* magazine and came across a picture. It said, "The Kershaw sisters" followed by a short paragraph underneath saying who was who. When Jed was called by the hairdresser, he stuffed the magazine into his pocket. His vendetta against Ruth was stronger than ever. He blamed her for all his woes and for leading him into a life of debauchery and crime.

Toby arrived to pick Jed up, and Jed showed him the picture. Toby was furious; he needed Jed to be focused on the task at hand. He didn't want Jed to go off on a wild goose chase after this Kershaw woman. That wasn't the only thing, though. Toby was jealous. He and Jed were an item, and Toby wanted this woman out of Jed's life forever.

He gave Jed an ultimatum: "Wait while everything is finalised, and then you can do what you want. But take care: if my dad thinks you are going AWOL, then it might be you who gets it first, if you catch my drift." Jed agreed to wait while the deal was done.

Toby had to attend a meeting with his dad at the Paradise Club in Soho. It turned out that Toby's father was not happy about his son going with a fella. His dad couldn't understand it – in fact, it nauseated him to even think about it. He never wanted to see Jed unless he had a job for Jed to do, and he definitely didn't want the man anywhere near his private residence.

Toby was his son, so he had to turn a blind eye to it for the moment. But Toby's father loathed Jed, and when all this business was over, he intended to do something about it. Toby's dad outlined the details to Toby before Jake Johnson arrived. Toby was gobsmacked and said to himself, *Wow, this is big time.*

What Dave and Toby didn't realise was that Jed Butler was the fixer and worked for the illuminati. He had a file on every one of Dave Richardson's associates connected to the Richardson dynasty, including his son Toby. It transpired that the Richardsons had the opportunity to join up with other criminal organisations who were in nearly every strategic city in the world. It would be known as Omega Trading Inc., registered in Switzerland, and it would tackle anything illegal – for a price, of course. That price was paid by greedy bankers and merchants.

For a fast buck or big business, the Richardsons and others like them would get certain jobs to undertake on behalf of the fraternity. "You as individuals will carry on as you have always done before with your illegal activities, such as gambling, prostitution, and so on," Jake Johnson explained. "We do not want to get involved with the everyday running of a club. This organisation is too big for that, and we will only take on very profitable assignments where there is a handsome profit to be made. Where the money ends up, no one will know. There has to be a great deal of trust for those involved. Any disputes will be dealt with on a hierarchy structure."

He continued, "Each group will be provided with a bank account. Money will be wired to Switzerland. Anyone who defaults, no matter what their circumstances are, will be dealt with severely. Do you follow what I am saying?"

Jake added, "I must point out that this is not the Mafia or the Russian Mafia, or any other criminal organisation. We are not on anyone's radar, and that's how we like it."

Jake then stood up and said, "You have twenty-four hours to decide in or out. You will be given a telephone number and a code name." The meeting was over. Jake shook everyone's hand and left.

Dave Richardson looked at his son. "What do you think?"

Toby answered, "Are you sure you want to get mixed up in this? It sounds good on paper, but if we can't deliver, we are up a creek without a paddle."

His father acknowledged that and said, "I know, Son, that's why I have to really think about it. I have your mother and sister to protect, plus my properties. Twenty-four hours is not a long time to get my house in order."

It was mid-afternoon by this time. Richardson rang his solicitor up.

"Scott and Sons Solicitors. How can I help you?" a voice said.

"Dave Richardson here. Is James in?"

"Just a minute, sir," a girl said.

"James Scott here. Nice to hear from you, Dave. How can I help?"

Dave asked if he could see James urgently – today, if possible.

"I'm rather busy now," James replied. "Can you pop in about six thirty this evening?"

"That'll do fine," said Richardson.

Richardson just wanted to make sure he had everything tied up in his wife's and daughter's names. There was no way Omega Trading was getting any of his personal wealth.

Toby went to meet up with Jed. They had a lovely apartment overlooking the Thames. Jed wasn't in when Toby arrived, much to his disappointment. He wanted to go out and celebrate. Unknown to Toby, Jed was meeting with Jake Johnson and the judge.

Jake said to Jed, "As soon as we acquire all the necessary deeds and paperwork and bank statements, we can start to eliminate the unsuccessful ones."

Jed hesitated. "What is it?" asked Jake.

"Do you mean eliminate Toby?"

"Everyone, Jed," said Jake.

Jed then said, "He owns this apartment, and I like living here. Besides, he's arranged for me to have plastic surgery on my scar."

"Sorry, Jed. He's like the rest – just collateral damage. Make sure you get your surgery done before it happens. The sooner, the better. It will take a few weeks to set up everything anyhow – and if you want the apartment, it's yours. I might even use it for my headquarters from time to time, if you don't mind sharing, that is."

This suited Jed. No one knew he worked solely for the organisation, and he knew it would be up to him to carry out any assassinations. Really, no one was safe – not even Peter Winters or Judge Henry Maxwell, who was the one who set the whole thing up in the first place. An associate of many years introduced Judge Maxwell to Chow Ling in Hong Kong. It intrigued the judge, and the thought of sorting out the chafe from the wheat gave him a lift. He felt the judicial system in the UK was totally inadequate and never fitted the punishment to the crime.

* * *

Ruth had been in the UK for six months now. She and her sisters were having a great time catching up with old school chums and past work colleagues. Those who were still working at the hospital of course remembered Robert and were sorry to hear of his death.

Ruth introduced her son, Andrew. Her old work colleagues couldn't get over how much like his father he was.

Ruth took him to the old house in St John's Wood. To Ruth, nothing had changed. Then they went on to Holland Park. Nothing much had changed there either.

Finally, they went to the Savoy, her father's favourite restaurant. They were shown their table. Ruth never noticed someone watching her. It was Jed. He just sat staring at her.

Toby distracted him. "Ready, Jed?"

Jed was dying to go over and speak to her, but Toby was waiting patiently for him. On the way out, Jed deliberately bumped into Ruth's table.

"Sorry," he said.

There was no reaction from Ruth. She just said, "Fine," and carried on talking to Andrew.

Jed was seething. *She never recognised me*, he said to himself.

Of course, Ruth did recognise Jed. In fact, it put the fear of God in her at the chance he would say anything to her, especially in front of Andrew.

With Jed gone, Ruth and Andrew had a lovely meal and made tracks to go home. Ruth was hoping Jed wouldn't be around. She surveyed the area as much as she could, and then she said to herself, *He's gone. Thank God.*

They hailed a taxi to Paddington station. Ruth was relieved when she arrived at Eve's. Matt welcomed them.

Ruth was now living in Cambridge near to Andrew, but they were spending a few days with Eve and Matt. Ruth just lazed around, while Andrew was getting on famously with his uncle Matt. It was quiz night at the local pub, so they all trudged along. They had a great night, and they won the quiz. They were duly paid £40 pound as winners. Eve gave half to Ruth and said, with a wry smile, "Don't spend it all at once."

* * *

Meanwhile, Tommy was itching to get back to the investigation. He and Jo had tied up a lot of loose ends. Tommy was waiting for his friend in the FBI to contact him.

"Do you think Matt and Eve will want get involved again with what I have found out?" he asked Jo.

Jo said she didn't know. "You'll have to ask them. Remember, Tommy, they are much older now."

Tommy sat and pondered. Then he said, "Can you set up a meeting with them, either here or at their place? I need to get things rolling again."

Jo said she would, but not this weekend. "Tommy, Ruth and Andrew are staying with them."

* * *

A week went by, and then Tommy received an envelope from the States. He couldn't wait to open it, and he tipped the contents out onto the table. There was a letter:

Hi Tommy,

You have definitely hit on something. There is a lot
of activity going on here. At first we thought it was
the usual turf wars that go on now and again, but the
snouts say it is not the Mafia or the Russian Mafia,
and that the Mafia wants to know just who is behind
this other criminal syndicate trying to muscle in on
their territory. But up to now, no one knows anything.
They fixed up a meeting with the Russians to find out
if they knew who was causing all this havoc in their
own backyards, both here in New York, in Jersey, and
in Chicago. We are also getting reports from Vegas
and Miami. The Russians don't have a clue. There was
a lot of mistrust between the Mafia and the Russians.
It's a case of watch this space.

One glimmer of hope: our sources say these people
have a tattoo on their arms with the sign alpha, which
doesn't ring any bells here. Now we are presuming that
it is the new group that has been set up to take over
the Mafia's and the Russians' business and strongholds.
Please find the photos you sent us. No joy yet, I'm
afraid, as to who the fifth man is. Keep in touch. Mike.

This gave Tommy the impetus to get things going again, but first
he needed the help of the three sisters and Matt.

Tommy wasted no time in ringing up Matt. He asked, "Do you
want to help me carry on with the investigation?"

Matt hesitated. He knows exactly what Eve would say, but he told
Tommy, "I'm not too sure what Eve or Ruth will say. Can we think
about it and get back to you tomorrow, Tommy?"

Tommy replied, "I need to know tomorrow at the latest, or Jo
and I will carry on without you till we have all the answers." Then
he put the phone down.

Jo had heard everything Tommy had said to Matt, but she didn't say a word about Tommy's ultimatum. She knew where Tommy was coming from. He had spent three years of his life working on this investigation, and he wanted to put an end to it once for all.

* * *

Eve asked, "What did have to Tommy say?"

Matt replied, "He wants to know if we are willing to carry on with the investigation – one final push, as he put it. I said that we needed time to seriously think about it. Tommy is adamant that he and Jo will carry with or without us."

Matt carried on, "To be honest, Eve, I think it is too much for us now. It's been three years or more."

Eve looked at him and said, "If we don't help Tommy, my father's name might get mentioned in the process of the investigation, and that is something I don't want to see happen. Our family name has to be protected at all cost!" Eve said an emphatic voice.

Matt said no more on the subject. He was resigned to helping Eve and her sisters, even if it meant one or all of them getting killed.

* * *

A couple of days later, they were all at Jo's – the three sisters, Tommy, and Matt.

Tommy stood up and began his presentation. "I have it on good authority that some sort of takeover is going on in the criminal world – not by the Mafia or the Russians, from all accounts. The FBI are baffled as to who this new group is. So are Interpol and the British, French, and German intelligence services. I only managed get the identities of five of them who are involved. The sixth one, I don't know."

Tommy named the five: "They are Peter Winters, Max, Jed Butler – we think he is the assassin here in Soho – Dave Richardson, and his son, Toby."

Ruth eyes raised at Jed's name, which Tommy noticed.

He carried on, "Also, Tommy-Two-Fingers from New York, a gangster involved with the Mafia connections who would do just about anything but has never been caught with his hands dirty. According to my friends in the FBI, the people involved have a logo tattooed on their arm.

Tommy showed them the picture. Eve was about to speak, but Tommy said, "Questions after, Eve, please. We need to work on this man and try to find out his identity."

Tommy then said, "I think our task is nearly over. I must go back over to the States and put the story together, and then my job is done. Can I count on you for one last effort?"

"If you put it like that, Tommy, we'll help in any way we can," said Matt. "But the lead must come from you. I don't want to put any of us in danger. We are not really used to this sort of thing, as you know."

Tommy answered, "I will be here till it's done and dusted. Eve, you wanted to say something?"

"Yes, two things really. I think the tattoo is the alpha sign, meaning the first. The second thing is, I think in one of the pictures is the eminent Judge Henry Maxwell, a friend of my father. He is a member of Boodles, the gentleman's club in London that my father was involved with. Father always went to him when he needed advice on family matters. Well, that's what I thought at the time," Eve explained.

Tommy then said, "The first of what, though?"

Ruth suggested, "It could mean a new order, or first order."

Tommy was amazed that Ruth, the one who said very little, might just have come up with the answer. "Good thinking, Ruth, that must be it. 'The New Order' – I like it. We'll use it as our code word. Now Ruth, you raised your eyebrows at Jed Butler's name."

"Oh, it was nothing. I used to know a lad called Jed, that's all." Ruth blushed, which didn't go unnoticed by her sisters.

Matt went out to the car and brought back all the stuff they had. Tommy suggested they go through everything again and separate out what they knew, and then concentrate on the snippets of information they didn't know or were not sure about. "We'll split up into groups,"

Tommy proposed. "Matt and I will look for positive leads. Jo, Eve, Ruth, if you notice anything, stockpile it for me and Matt."

Jo went into the kitchen to make sandwiches and coffee. Eve followed her. Ruth hovered.

"Coming, Ruth?" said Eve.

"In a minute," Ruth replied.

Tommy was outside smoking. Ruth went to have a word with him. "Those things will kill you," she said.

"Something will kill me one day, Ruth," said Tommy. "I just hope it's not now." He laughed.

"Can I have a word in private?" asked Ruth.

"Sure," replied Tommy.

Ruth hesitated and set about telling him all the sordid details of Jed Butler. To this day, it was loathsome for her to even think about it. She told Tommy that she had some personal things of Jed's that she had left with Eve to look after. Chances are, he had came around to pick them up. "To be honest, I don't know if he did or didn't," she said. "The fact is, Tommy, I do not want Jo to know that I was compromised. Only my father and Eve knew, as I couldn't live in the flat anymore. I'll see if Eve kept the box. She may very well have gotten rid of it with moving, and to be honest, I had forgotten all about it till you mentioned Jed's name."

"What are you two talking about? Your coffee getting cold," cried Jo.

* * *

The gang had worked on the information they had for weeks, and finally they could see some daylight. Tommy's friend had sent him more information. Mike said they had heard on the grapevine that Chow Ling, who ran a criminal syndicate in Hong Kong, was hiring certain people with "specialist skills, shall we say. What you came up with, Tommy, for the tattoos is brilliant. First Order or the New Order? Oh, and by the way, the French and German police forces are seeing more activity going on, with suspicious deaths, which again leaves a question mark. Nothing from the Brits yet. We'll keep plugging at our end. Keep up the good work."

Tommy suggested that he and Matt go back into London and watch Jed Butler, Toby Richardson, and this Jake Johnson. "We'll stay somewhere near the Paradise Club. If you girls somehow find where Peter Winters lives in Oxford, that'll be great. By the way, Ruth, did you ask Eve about the box?"

"Crumbs, I forgot. Sorry, Tommy."

"What's this about a box?" asked Eve.

"Do you still have that box I left just in case Jed came to your place at Holland Park to pick it up, when I left to go abroad with Robert?" said Ruth.

"Yes, I think so. I'll dig it out tomorrow. Matt can give it to Tommy. It might be useful – who knows? I didn't know you rubbed shoulders with the criminal underworld, Ruth. You kept that quiet." Then Eve laughed, and so did the others.

Ruth was furious with Eve. "There was no need for that sort of comment, especially from you, Eve. It doesn't become you." She spoke in a tone that the other two sisters knew only too well, as it reminded Eve and Jo of their mother.

* * *

That night, they all got spruced up and went into Oxford to celebrate – except Jo. She felt guilty at not visiting Lucy.

They chose the Old Bank, as it had a good reputation. It was nice for them to just relax and enjoy themselves. The meal was superb, and the wine was to everyone's taste.

They were about to leave when Peter Winters came in. Tommy swiftly went outside. Matt, Eve, and Ruth also kept a low profile. When they got outside, Tommy was nowhere to be seen; in fact, he was in the car park taking pictures of registration numbers. There were about a dozen cars parked.

When Tommy finally appeared, he was surprised to see Jo. "Lucy wants you all around for coffee," she said.

Really, it was the furthest thing from their minds. Before they made their way to Lucy's, Tommy asked Matt, "Can you go back in? Peter Winters doesn't know you. Try to get some pictures."

Matt was mortified at the thought. He wavered.

Eve said, "I'll go in." She quickly took Tommy's phone and re-entered the hotel.

They waited in the car for Eve. She seemed to take ages, and they were getting anxious. Then suddenly she appeared. Jo waved and gestured through the car window to come over. Eve quietly strolled over and got in.

"Hope these will do, Tommy," she said and handed him his phone back.

* * *

Lucy was overjoyed to see them. She hugged her Auntie Eve and Ruth. "Where have you all been? I feel like the neglected orphan. You have not been around to visit for ages," said Lucy.

Eve said, "We'll make it up to you and Ben once we have helped Tommy. I promise."

Jo withered Eve, but Eve took no notice.

Ruth just said, "Sorry, Lucy. I have been busy with the move to Cambridge. This is only a flying visit. Once I settle in, you are welcome to stay with me and Robert anytime. That goes for Ben and the kids too, of course."

Lucy hugged her and said, "We'll do just that when Ben is off at term time."

They spent a lovely time at Lucy's, but soon it was time to leave.

* * *

Tommy and Jo arrived to pick Matt up – and of course the cardboard box, which after a lot of searching for in the loft was found. Eve vowed after this lot was over she would declutter. They all left for the station. Jo and Eve watched as the train slowly moved out.

"What shall we do now?" asked Jo.

"Fancy driving over to Cambridge this afternoon and staying with Ruth overnight if she'll have me after the dressing down I got?" Eve suggested.

They both laughed. Jo said, "Why not? It will be fun. But Eve, no talk of the little black book. I want a complete break for at least three days. Tommy has driven me potty. He is paranoid about everything. It's enough to send me to drink."

Eve asked Jo if she ever had the urge to drink again.

Jo replied, "At the beginning, it was hard work, but I kept focussed on the fact that I was still alive and my friends weren't, and then there was Lucy. I had terrible lonely nights and days and often thought of ending it all, but something inside kept me going. I can't really explain it to anyone, but here I am."

Eve said, "We are all very proud of what you have achieved, and I know Lucy is too."

CHAPTER THIRTY-ONE

The sisters drove over to Cambridge to stay with Ruth and Andrew. They had a lovely time. They all got on well together in spite of the age difference, which was something rather unusual. Ruth was to travel back with Eve and Joanne. Tommy had left them instructions whilst he and Matt where in London.

With heavy hearts, the sisters made their way back to Oxford to carry on with the investigation. None of them had a clue what they were looking for. Eve wanted to be dropped off at her home, just in case Matt had left any messages. She said she would drive over to Jo's the next day, where Ruth would be staying as well.

As she watched her sisters drive away, Eve had a sudden premonition that things were not quite right. She entered the house with a certain trepidation. Everything seemed in order. She checked all the windows and doors. She checked the bathroom and opened every wardrobe in the bedrooms. Nothing seemed to have been disturbed. *Now who's being paranoid*, she said to herself.

She made a coffee and went to see if there were any messages. Then she noticed something. It was a small thing, really, something one would never have thought about under normal circumstances: the telephone was not in its place. The dust that had gathered in the last few days showed signs of movement, minute as it might be. It was Eve's analytical mind that brought it to her attention.

She picked the phone up, and there was the usual dialling tone. She listened for a while, and noticed that there was a click every now and again. This put the fear of God in her. She immediately grabbed her mobile, but something told her to go outside, which she did. She had watched too many movies and seen it all before – although of course, only as fiction.

Eve rang Matt up. It took ages for him to answer, and he sounded half dead. "Hello, who is it?" he said in a low voice.

"It's Eve. Is Tommy there with you?"

"No, he is in another bedroom."

"Can you wake him? It's very important. Get him to ring my mobile."

By this time, Eve was feeling very vulnerable. She went back inside for a coat, but when her mobile started to ring, she hurriedly went outside.

"Tommy here. What's up?"

Eve explained the situation to Tommy. He advised her to put the TV on loud or the radio. "Do not answer your phone no matter what," he said. "I'll get hold of someone in the morning to help you. Can you also let Jo know as soon as possible? They may have bugged her phone also. In fact, I'll ask him to check all four houses, just to be on the safe side."

Eve was not happy at all. She did what Tommy asked and put the radio on in her bedroom. Maybe the music helped Eve to relax, because she soon fell into a deep sleep.

She was awakened by her mobile. She went into the bathroom and ran the water taps. This she had seen on the movies; whether it worked or not, she didn't know. It was Tommy to tell her that a chap called Nigel Hunter would be down sometime that morning. He gave her a mobile number to ring him on if she needed to.

"Must go now," he said. "You'll be OK with Nigel. He's a good lad, and I trust him implicitly." Then the phone went dead.

Eve made herself breakfast and watched the early news. Later, she had a shower. By now, it was 9 a.m. Eve went outside to ring Jo and explain the events of the night to her. She advised Jo to only use her mobile.

"No need to worry Ruth at this point. I'll be over as soon as I can."

After a couple of hours, the doorbell rang. Eve opened the door.

"Hi! I'm Nigel," said the man. He entered the house, and they went out the back, into the garden. "I needed to ask you one or two things first," he said, "so I can get a better picture."

"Sure," Eve replied.

"Have you noticed anything unusual, such as men in white vans or men working on the telephone lines, men digging up roads, anything like that?"

Eve answered no to them all, and then explained that she had been away for a few days.

"Leave it to me, Eve. Do you have anywhere I can work – a garage or shed or spare room?"

"We have a large garage around the back which we don't use that often. It might be full of junk," replied Eve.

"Can I have a look?"

Eve showed him the garage. "This is perfect. I'll work in here. Can I move a few things to get my van in?"

Eve replied, "Sure. Whatever suits you." She added, "I have to go over to my sister's, if that's OK. There's food in the fridge. Just help yourself," said Eve.

"Are you able to stay there for a day or two?" asked Nigel.

"I don't see why not," replied Eve.

* * *

Eve arrive at Jo's a little after lunch. Jo opened the door and said, "You poor thing, Eve. How are you feeling now?"

"Better, now I am here."

They entered. When Ruth saw her sister, she said, "Hi, Eve. Are you OK?"

Eve put her finger to her mouth.

Jo said, "It's OK here, Eve. Nigel has checked everything out. We have no bugs here, thank goodness. Nigel has set up a device so he can watch what is going on around the house and block any kind of phone tapping. It's great, isn't it? Just like the gangster movies." Jo laughed.

Eve was not at all amused. She said, "I'm not cut out for this kind of thing. It's all too much for me. I want out. I'm sorry, but I can't do this anymore. I'll have to leave it to you two." She started to cry. "I never realised how lonely the house was till I was on my own. I felt so vulnerable with Matt not there. I was so frightened."

Jo put her arm around Eve and comforted her, while Ruth went to make tea. When Ruth came back, she said, "Eve is right. It is too much for her. I suggest Eve stays here with you, Jo, and just works on the paperwork." Jo agreed.

The telephone rang. It was Matt for Eve. "Hi, baby. Is everything all right? Tommy told me everything. I tried home, and Nigel said you were at Jo's."

Eve said she was fine but had made a decision not to carry on with the investigation. She would help with the paperwork and only that. "And I want you here with me, Matt, safe," she said. By this time, she was crying inconsolably. This upset Matt no end, but it put him in a dilemma. "I'll see what I can do, Eve. You stay with Jo. I'll ring again when I can. Love you."

"Drink your tea, Eve," said Ruth in a commanding voice. She went to her doctor's bag and took out two tablets. "Eve, I want you to take these."

"What are they?" Eve asked.

"They will help you to calm down and rest, so take them now," she said, again in a commanding voice.

It took half an hour before the tablets started to work. Ruth suggested Eve lie down and helped her up the stairs into the upstairs bedroom. Eve kicked her shoes off and lay on the bed. Ruth covered her with a blanket and closed the door gently.

When Ruth went back downstairs, Nigel was there. "I found a device in her land telephone but nothing else. I have secured the line for her, and as with you, I have set up a surveillance device. It really shook your sister up. When I arrived, she was white."

Jo asked, "So our houses are now safe?"

"As safe as I can make them," replied Nigel. He gave Jo Eve's door key and went on his way.

Ruth looked at Jo. "Eve's right, Jo," she said. "It is too much for her. I didn't like the look of her when she came in. When she's up for it, I need to give her a good check-up."

The girls didn't feel like doing anything. They just wiled the afternoon away and watched a film on the telly. Eventually, Eve came downstairs to join them. Ruth thought she looked much better. Jo made some sandwiches and coffee. Nothing was done that day.

CHAPTER THIRTY-TWO

Meanwhile, back in the States, things were coming to a head, with more killings. The Russians were suspected, as it fitted their profile. Mike and his men finally made a breakthrough: one of the men found had a tattoo of the alpha sign. Forensics took fingerprints, DNA, and photos of the dead man and sent the information to the various undercover operators in the US, along with copies to London and Paris Interpol, and then copies to Hong Kong.

Mike sent all the information he had to Tommy, who was still staking out the Paradise Club in London with Matt. Tommy was happier than he'd been for a very long time. Now they would get some answers. Tommy and Matt were still trying to identify the fifth man properly (even though Eve had told them it was Judge Maxwell). And where did Max fit into the picture? *Another enigma,* thought Tommy.

They had watched the Paradise Club for days. Matt was feeling fatigued, and he was worried about Eve. Tommy decided to bite the bullet.

"Look, why don't we go into the Paradise Club tomorrow and have a few beers, play the tables, and take it from there?" said Tommy.

Matt was apprehensive. "I'm not too sure I'm cut out for this, Tommy. I don't know the first thing about cards, roulette, and whatever else goes on."

Tommy realised then that Matt was out of his depth and had had enough. "I'll tell you what, Matt. You help me for the next couple of days, and if you still want to call it quits, it's OK with me. I am almost finished here anyway." Matt agreed.

For the next couple of days, they played the tables. Tommy kept an eye on Matt, telling him what to do. For someone who didn't know how to play roulette, he wasn't doing badly. At least he was in profit; Tommy wasn't.

Tommy suddenly nudged Matt and quietly said, "Over there."

Matt cautiously looked over. Tommy went to the gent and bumped into him. "Sorry, mate!" Tommy said in a cockney accent. The guy just withered him and moved on.

Tommy said to another guy, "Who was that? Not very friendly, is he?"

A bloke said, "You don't want to get tangled with them, mate, or you're dead meat. He's Jimmy Malloy from the States – a friend of Jake Johnson and the Richardsons who own the Paradise Club." Then he whispered, "Mafia."

"Thanks, buddy, I'll keep well away from him!" said Tommy. He went over to Matt and whispered, "Go to the bar and order a couple of beers." Matt obliged.

Tommy strolled over, clocking everything with his mobile camera and videoing as much as he could. His main target was to try to get pictures of the top table, with bodyguards on both sides. People were going up and showing a pass or something, and then sitting down. It looked as though they were signing something.

Tommy was itching to get nearer, but he couldn't risk blowing his cover. He was hoping his camera would be good enough to do the job. He meandered towards the end of the bar to talk to a couple of guys – in cockney, of course.

"What's all that about?" he said, gesturing with his head towards the top table.

One guy said, "Shh! They'll hear you!"

Tommy slipped the guy £20. The guy replied, "Give me a couple of minutes, and then meet me in the gents. Tommy should have been more cautious; he was not thinking straight at all. He was usually more careful, but not this time.

He whispered to Matt, "Pretend you're not with me. When I go into the gents, wait for me where we said we would meet up if we get separated."

Matt just gave him a slight nod, not looking anywhere really. His eyes were transfixed, looking straight ahead.

Tommy said, "See ya then" to the barman, who never even looked at him – except to say to Matt, "Weren't you with that guy?"

Matt replied, "He was with me. We just had a couple of beers together, that's all. He's off somewhere else. I'm quite happy here." The barman just walked away, not thinking too much about it, and went to serve another customer.

Matt hung around for another half hour or so. He was enjoying his pints. It wasn't that easy these days to have a good few beers, except on a Thursday quiz night at the local. Matt was daydreaming – thinking of Swansea and Mumbles, and how he would like to spend his time there again – when his phone rang.

"Where the hell are you?" said Tommy in an exasperated voice.

"Be with you in a jiffy," replied Matt. When they met up, Matt asked, "How did it go with that guy?"

"Would you f—in' believe, he thought I wanted to do a job on him?" Tommy was embarrassed.

Matt laughed.

"It was no laughing matter, I can tell you," snapped Tommy. "I scarpered out the back door as quick as I could." By this time, even Tommy was laughing. "Serves me right, I suppose, giving £20 and then going to the gents."

It wasn't too long before they reached their hotel. Tommy said, "Meet you at seven thirty at the George for a bite to eat." Then Tommy went off in another direction.

By this time, Matt was feeling rather dopey. The beer was having an effect on him. He opened his bedroom door only to find the place had been turned over. This jolted Matt into reality. He hurriedly went outside to ring up Tommy, but Tommy's phone was switched off.

Matt was in a tiswas. *They must be watching us*, thought Matt. He wondered about his phone, but it had been with him all the time.

There was no paperwork or anything else in the room other than his clothes. Matt couldn't think; he went back up to his room and surveyed everything. Nothing appeared to have been taken. Trouble was, Matt was not focusing very well with the beers he had drunk. He decided to shower, but first he locked the door and checked the windows. Like Eve, he was unnerved.

After his shower, he went downstairs, ordered a coffee, and sat in the lounge till Tommy arrived. Matt was nodding off when he was disturbed by the waiter.

"Finished, sir?"

Matt just nodded to him. *Where the hell can Tommy be?* Matt said to himself. He then made a momentous decision: he decided to check out and go to another hotel. He went upstairs to pack, went to the reception to pay his bill, and then went into the restaurant and ordered a meal. He checked his watch. It was 7.45 p.m.

Matt was really jumpy by this time. He was in a quandary as to what to do. *I have to let Tommy know some way or another,* he said to himself. It got to eight thirty, and by this time Matt had finished. He decided to leave. Just as he was just stepping outside, he noticed Tommy in the background and made his way over.

Tommy went around a corner. Matt followed him. Tommy was loitering, looking through shop windows. Matt went up to him but kept his distance. Matt told him what had happened and what he had done.

Tommy was shocked to hear this. "Someone's got it in for you and Eve, that's all I can think of. You and Eve had better get your thinking caps on and find out who it is. You are of no use to me now, Matt. Might as well go home – and make sure you are not followed. Let me check your phone," Tommy said.

Matt gave Tommy his phone, saying, "It's been with me all the time. How could someone tamper with it?"

Tommy said, "Quite easily, if they wanted to." He gave Matt the phone back and said, "It's OK. Eve is with Jo, so go there. Do not go home under any circumstances."

Matt caught the 9 p.m. train back to Oxford and stayed the night there. He decided to ring Eve in the morning to pick him up. As he gazed out of the train window, he caught a glimpse of someone – he thought it was Max. Matt was horrified; he was really scared now. He stayed very watchful but never saw Max again.

Then he realised that Max had a beard and started to relax. His mind was playing havoc with him. *But what if he has shaved his beard off?* he said to himself. He took out his notebook and began to sketch Max with a beard or without. By this time, his brain was dead. He stuffed his notebook away and waited till he arrived. He booked into the Old Bank. *At least I'll have a good night's sleep and a good hearty breakfast in the morning*, he thought.

The next day, Matt was fully refreshed. Surprisingly he had managed to sleep. He showered and thought to himself, *I need a shave*; then he thought, *I'll leave it for now*, and went downstairs for breakfast.

To his horror, as he entered the dining room, he saw Max with Peter Winters. Fortunately, they were too busy to notice Matt. He fidgeted to get his mobile out.

The waiter asked, "Morning, sir, what'll it be?"

Matt jumped at the unexpected interruption, but managed to reply, "Full English and coffee, please."

"Right you are, sir," said the waiter, who then returned to the kitchen. Matt tried to video, but he was not as proficient as Tommy. He had to try to act normal. Luckily, he had picked up the *Times* newspaper from reception, so he pretended to read it.

The waiter came back, saying, "Here you are, sir." Matt just nodded. He was too preoccupied with what was going on.

All at once, the men got up from the table and walked over to where Matt was sitting. He transfixed himself on his breakfast, not daring to look up. They walked straight past him. He heard one say, "Till the fifteenth, then," as they passed by.

By this time, Matt was trembling. *Calm down, Matt. They're gone*, he said to himself.

* * *

Matt couldn't get to meet up with Eve quickly enough. He checked out of the hotel and told her where to meet him. It wasn't too long before they arrived at Jo's. Matt was very watchful. It unnerved Eve.

"Are you going to tell me what the hell is going on?" she asked in a voice that Matt knew only too well.

He said, "Not here, Eve. Inside. Then I'll tell you."

Jo greeted him with, "Hi, Matt, everything OK?"

Matt didn't answer. Eve shook her head at Jo.

"I'll make coffee," said Jo.

Matt just sat there motionless. Eve was worried sick. She went into the kitchen.

"I've never seen him like this, Jo, in all the years we've have been together," she said. "Something must have happened. And where the bloody hell is Tommy?"

Jo said, "I'll ring Ruth and tell her how he is. You go back and sit with him." Jo kept trying Ruth, but she wasn't in. *I thought she had retired now*, thought Jo, hanging up the phone.

At the same moment, the phone rang. It was Tommy. Jo took the phone out into the garden.

"What the hell has happened, Tommy?" she asked heatedly. "Matt has hardly said a word since he arrived."

Tommy told Jo everything – about Matt's room being searched and seeing Max and another Mafia guy as well as Peter Winters at the Paradise Club. "Matt had one or two beers too many, if you ask me. I left him there and arranged to meet up with him for supper."

Jo was furious with him. "Why the hell did you leave him there? Tommy, he is not like your mates. He's just an ordinary English guy who has no idea what sort of world you live in. I can tell you this, something has happened to him. He's hardly said a word to me or Eve. I think you had better get back here, and fast!" Jo was raging.

Tommy came straight back at her and said, "I can't come back. I'm in the last throes of wrapping this up. Matt must deal with it himself." Tommy put the phone down.

Jo was seething. *He can go to hell now. There's no way I'll have him here again. You've made your bed for the last time here, Tommy Ashurst.*

He can bugger off to bloody Texas with that Becky Grayson. He talked enough about her when he was here, she said to herself.

Jo entered the lounge. Matt was fast asleep.

Eve looked at Jo and asked, "What has happened to him? Does Tommy know?"

"Tommy hasn't a clue. I think it is all too much for Matt, Eve. Is it really worth all this sacrifice for the sake of the family name? I think not. Look at him. He may never be the same again."

Eve burst into tears. "I curse my father for bringing this onto our doorstep. It is not worth it, Jo. You are so right. I will tell Tommy we're through."

"We won't be seeing Tommy here again if I can help it," said Jo. "Help me to get his things together. He only used this place as a bolthole. He never had any intention of settling down here with me. For what it's worth, Eve, he can go to hell. He had no right to expect Matt to do undercover work like he does."

The phone rang. It was Ruth. Jo explained the situation.

"Can you bring him up to Cambridge?" Ruth asked. "I'm helping out at our local surgery. Say about one thirty tomorrow afternoon?"

Jo agreed to do just that. She thanked Ruth and then went to have a word with Eve. Matt started to stir. He still looked bewildered, as if to say, *Where am I?*

Eve spoke to him. Matt looked at her and started crying like a baby. Eve was shocked.

Jo said to her, "Let him cry. Let him get it out of his system."

* * *

An hour had passed. Matt was beginning to focus on where he was and how he had gotten there. He saw two anxious faces looking at him. He smiled and said, "Thank God I'm here."

"But Matt," said Eve, "you have been here most of the day."

Then it all came flooding back to him. He told Eve and Jo everything, including how he thought he'd caught a glimpse of Max on the train. "But I think my mind might have been playing tricks," he said. "I want out, Eve. Nothing is worth this. I just want peace and quiet. I want to go and live in Mumbles where no one knows where to find us."

Eve hugged Matt and then said, "We'll do that. We'll give notice at the cottage and rent in Mumbles, if that is what you want. We will let people think we are moving abroad. But first, we have to see Ruth in Cambridge. She wants to examine both of us for some reason."

The rest of that day was taken up with planning where they would live. Mark's parents had passed away long since. Matt fancied Langland, but Eve fancied Port Eynan. Anyhow, they would keep their decision to themselves until they had seen Ruth.

The outcome of Ruth's examination was that Matt must have been fatigued and had had an anxiety attack. Eve's prognosis, however, was more serious. Ruth had detected a heart problem which needed a full and extensive examination. Ruth made an appointment for Eve to see a specialist. It came as a shock to Eve. She knew she had been slowing down but had put it to age. Matt was also concerned about the news.

CHAPTER THIRTY-THREE

A few weeks had gone by. Matt and Eve's plans for moving had been put on hold, as Eve had a blockage in the left ventricle of her heart, which meant surgery. Jo and Lucy were very concerned. Ruth assured them that the procedure was straightforward these days, and so long as Eve took it easy from now on, who knows? The operation was set up for the end of the month. Meanwhile, Eve had to rest.

On one visit, Ruth and Eve, along with Matt, went into a coffee house. Ruth was just starting to explain the procedure to Eve, to put her at ease, when they were confronted by Jed Butler. Matt immediately concluded that this was who he had seen on the train.

"Hello, Ruth," Jed said in a friendly voice. "It's been a long time since I saw you," he added with a smile on his face.

Ruth was speechless. Her heart sank.

"I'm waiting to meet up with an old acquaintance of mine from the States," Jed went on. "Ah, there he is. Have to go now." Then he said, "You must be Eve and Matt! Nice to meet you at last face to face. I'm so pleased I've met you all together."

Before stepping away, Jed added, in a lowered voice, "I just want to tell you as a friend, Ruth – and please don't take this personally – the whisper is that there is fatwa on the Kershaw family. I really shouldn't be telling you this, Ruth, but it's for old time's sake. Be seeing you around, hopefully."

Jed walked away with a smirk on his face. He muttered to himself, *Now we're even.* Then he walked out with his friend.

Matt, Eve, and Ruth hadn't a clue what he was talking about, but it put the fear of God in them. This was not what Ruth had in mind to keep Eve calm; in fact, it had the opposite effect. She telephoned Andrew to arrange an immediate bed for Eve at the clinic. *At least Eve will be safe*, Ruth thought to herself.

The next morning, Eve was in situ in the clinic. Her operation was brought forward at Ruth's request. Andrew was not happy about it, but he asked his colleagues to change their calendars, which they kindly did at great inconvenience to them. Matt stayed with Eve.

Meanwhile, Ruth went to see Jo and told her what had gone on. "Do you know what a fatwa is?"

Jo said she had no idea, so she looked it up on Google. "Oh my God!" Jo yelled.

"What is it?" cried Ruth.

Jo looked at Ruth and said, "It's a death threat!"

They sat there in silence. Ruth then said, "What does it mean? Are we going to be murdered?"

"That's what it looks like," answered Jo.

"Well I, for one, am not going to sit around and let it happen," Ruth said in a steely voice.

That startled Jo. "What do you propose to do, Ruth?"

Ruth replied, in a defiant voice, "Beat them to it."

"You mean kill this Max guy?" Jo wasn't too pleased to hear what Ruth had suggested.

"Precisely, and you are going to help me. You have Lucy and her family to protect, and I have Andrew and Olivia, so I suggest we set our stall out. We'll keep Matt and Eve out of this. It will be better for us this way. I'll do my homework and let you know. In the meantime, if you can get hold of Tommy and tell him about Jed, he too might have some idea as to how we can handle it."

Jo just nodded at Ruth, only half believing what she had heard.

* * *

Tommy was in New York, having clandestine meetings with his friend and confidant, Mike, from the FBI. He had finished his report and handed it over to CCN News. They would work on it to produce a documentary but wait for Tommy's final report, with full credits going to Michael T. McCready, investigative journalist.

To Mike, Tommy gave a dossier with names and assailants in various counties around the world. He had tied them to one organisation: the New Order, or the Alpha movement, or whatever name they had chosen.

Tommy asked Mike to give him a couple of weeks, as he had one or two loose ends to tie up to complete the whole picture. "There are a couple of things still nagging me," he said to Mike. "First is this chap Jed Butler, and secondly this chap called Max, who seems to float in and out of the picture." Tommy thought that was fishy. "In the meantime," he said, "you can send out this report to various contacts you have in law enforcement here in the States and Europe. They might be able to help."

Tommy gave Mike a list and asked him if he could get things Tommy needed. "It will help me with the last piece of the jigsaw."

Mike saw no problem in accommodating Tommy with what he wanted. "When do you need this lot for?" asked Mike.

"As soon as possible," replied Tommy.

"You do realise, Tommy, that you will be a hunted man after all this comes out."

"That's what I want to talk to you about." Tommy told Mike what he had in mind.

"Give me a couple of days. Meet same place on Tuesday, same time," Mike said.

Tommy felt great relief that it was finally over. His thoughts now were of Jo and her sisters, although he knew it would take some convincing to persuade Jo that he was really sorry for what had happened to Matt. He knew Jo had said she wouldn't have anything to do with him. However, he was ready to brace the tirade of abuse he would get from her. He smiled to himself. He had a genuine soft spot for Jo.

* * *

Eve's operation was a success, and she was to leave hospital in the next day or so. Ruth advised Matt to take her away for a couple of weeks, preferably somewhere warm. Matt said he would try, but Eve was adamant that she wanted to go home.

Ruth is not too pleased to hear this. It took a lot of persuasion, but Eve finally agreed to go off on vacation. She chose Madrid, Spain. Matt was pleased. Eve attended to the arrangements. The hospital loaned her a wheelchair just in case she needed it. Ruth and Jo watched as they flew off to Spain, each relieved Eve was out of the way.

"Right," said Ruth. "We will set our stall out now and follow Jed Butler. I know his old haunts, and if he hasn't changed his persuasion, he will still visit them."

Jo didn't quite follow, but left it.

"We will need to find a cheap hotel somewhere," Ruth went on. "It might take a month. Who knows? We will need to change our appearance – pretend we're hookers or something."

Jo burst out laughing. "Where the bloody hell is this all coming from?" Ruth was the one who never cottoned on to anything.

"I watch movies too, you know," Ruth snapped, annoyed at Jo for interrupting her. "Eve's away for a month, so the time is perfect. Are you with me, Jo?" asked Ruth.

Jo answered, "Yes, let's get the bastard."

First, though, Jo travelled over to Lucy's and spent a week with her. They had a lovely time together, doing what mothers and daughters do all over the world: shopping. It was while they were on a shopping spree that they noticed Becky Grayson. Lucy was about to give her a shout when Jo put a hand on her arm and shook her head. Lucy looked bewildered.

"Leave her, Lucy. She is probably with someone. I wouldn't like to intrude," said Jo. She had clocked Becky meeting up with a guy and though it was the one Ruth had mentioned. Jo took her mobile out.

"What are you doing?" asked Lucy.

"Taking a picture of you, if that is all right?" But really, Jo was taking a picture of the man Becky was with.

Lucy shrugged her shoulders and then started posing in all sorts of queer ways. Jo was in tucks. Silly sod Lucy smiled, and they moved on.

That evening, Jo telephoned Ruth to tell her that she saw Becky Grayson and was sure she was with her friend Jed.

"Who is Becky Grayson?" asked Ruth.

"Don't you remember, the Texan who asked Tommy to help her?" Ruth vaguely remembered. "Why, what's so intriguing?"

"It's a long story. I'll tell you sometime," said Jo.

She forwarded the pictures to Ruth and then went back into the lounge. She told Lucy that she would be returning home the following day. She mentioned that she would not be around for at least a month but would keep in touch.

"You're being mysterious again, Mother," said Lucy.

"Not at all. Your Auntie Ruth and I are going to clean Auntie Eve's house up for when she returns home, and you know how large that house is." Jo laughed, and Lucy joined her.

Jo got a ping on her phone. She opened it, and it was a text. "Don't know who this guy is, Jo. See you in two weeks." Ruth didn't recognise him because he had a beard and Jed didn't, although she thought she might have seen him with Jed at some point. She just couldn't figure out where.

* * *

By the time Jo got back home, she was feeling jaded. The nights were beginning to draw in now, and it felt a bit chilly. She lit the fire, made herself a coffee, and dozed off – only to be startled awake by a tapping on the window. She nervously went to the window and saw that it was Tommy.

"What the hell do you want? I told you to stay away!" said Jo.

Tommy begged Jo to let him in and listen to what he had to say. First of all, he told her that he had not been entirely honest with her regarding

256

Becky Grayson – but whatever he did, it was only in the name of getting a story. He told her that he had finished his investigation and things were afoot to start arresting people. He said he only came to see her to warn her and her sisters of what was about to happen and to be vigilant. He now had to go back to the States for the final piece to the jigsaw.

Tommy then told her of his plan, stressing that she must not divulge it to anyone, not even her sisters. Finally, he mentioned that he had been nominated for a top award for his journalism.

"Good. Bully for you, Tommy. Forget the minnows along the way so long as you get your story," Jo said in an angry voice.

Tommy ignored her and carried on. "Now, don't forget, the FBI and other law enforcement officers will be synchronised to raid simultaneously. I need you to be safe."

Jo was stunned by what she heard. "Ruth and I have an assignment of our own, Tommy." She told him of the fatwa. Tommy was amazed to hear this.

"Who told you that?" he asked.

"That Jed Butler fellow. Apparently, he knows Ruth from way back."

"And you believed him?" said Tommy.

"We didn't know what it was till we googled it. Of course we believe him!" said Jo emphatically.

Tommy shook his head and said, "Believe me, Jo, if there was a fatwa on you or your sisters, you would be dead now. He was just trying to put the frighteners on you all for some reason. Ruth must have upset him in some way or other. She must have found out he's as queer as a ten-bob note, if you get my drift."

Jo shook her head. Tommy looked surprised that, after the lifestyle she once led, he had to spell it out to her. She was gobsmacked and wondered how Ruth fitted into all this.

After a couple of days, Tommy was ready to go back to the States. "Remember, Jo, no matter what happens, be brave and trust me," Tommy said as he walked out the door.

Jo was in turmoil. She rang Ruth and said, "The sooner the better. I hope you have a good plan for this, Ruth, or it will be curtains for all of us."

CHAPTER THIRTY-FOUR

Jo met up with Ruth in Soho. They had booked themselves into a dingy hotel which was in a right old state. They had left all their possessions at home – rings money, credit cards, all of it. They just had money and handbags with make-up in them. They had left their good clothes in one of the station lockers. Their hair was dyed, and they dressed like a couple of has-beens.

When they signed the register, the guy never asked for any identification or information. He just handed them the keys.

When they entered the room, Ruth was immediately nauseous. She tried to open a window, and after a great deal of force by both, it opened.

"We are not sleeping on these beds," Ruth said. She lifted the two mattresses off the beds and placed them near the window.

Jo just watched. She had lived rough before, so she could hack it.

"I'll be back in a jiffy, Jo," said Ruth.

While Ruth was gone, Jo set about checking everything. The bathroom was no cleaner, but it was adequate. They could set about cleaning it themselves. Jo went downstairs and said in a Northern accent, "Any sheets?"

He went to get fresh sheets and said, "Fiver each."

Jo came out with a load of abuse.

"Take it or leave it; I don't give a shit," he said.

Jo gave him a tenner, muttering under her breath, and went back upstairs to wait for Ruth.

When Ruth entered the hotel, the man on reception said, "Absolutely no food in here!"

Ruth told him it wasn't food; it was something she had picked up from a charity shop. He just ignored her and went into the back to watch the telly.

Ruth arrived at the bedroom fully laden. "I got this lot from a charity shop. They should be all right. I had to go to a few till I found two." She tossed Jo a sleeping bag.

Jo showed Ruth the sheets and said, "I had to pay a tenner for these. I should have waited."

* * *

The next day, they set off in earnest clocking all of Jed's movements. They observed him all week at the Paradise Club. It was one of his favourite places, which Jo knew about from Tommy. The other was a hotel where they thought he might be staying. They also followed him to a luxury apartment block facing the Thames. He often came out with another guy. Sometimes they would walk to a pub. Other times, to the Paradise Club.

Ruth and Jo couldn't go into the Paradise Club; it would be too risky. They would have to choose the hotel or the apartment – whichever was the easiest. One thing was for sure: they had their work cut out for them.

They went back to the hotel and weighed up the situation. It was decided that they would pay what they owed and leave. They went to the reception; a woman was working there this time.

"Yeah, what do you want?" she said in a husky voice.

"How much do we owe you?" asked Ruth.

"Err, let me see," said the woman. "Fifty quid should do it. Don't forget to bring the sheets back," she yelled.

As they left, Ruth said, "Thank God! I never thought I would stay in a dingy dirty smelly place like that."

Jo just laughed.

They reached the station and emptied their lockers, went to the ladies, and came out respectable women once more. They booked into a four-star hotel near Kings Cross station and were shown to a twin-bedded room. It was in pristine condition, which Ruth was pleased about. She surveyed the bathroom, and again, it was to her liking.

Jo was amused by all this. Ruth hadn't noticed Jo; she was too preoccupied as to how they were going to fix this Max once and for all. She had no idea that Max was in fact Jed Butler.

* * *

Meanwhile, Eve and Matt had returned home. Eve rang the cleaner up to say they were in situ and could she please do a double shift the next day. The cleaner said she would come early.

"I'll leave the key in the usual place," Eve said, "just in case we are not up and about. Give me a knock, will you, if that's the case? I need to have a chat with you."

The cleaner said that was fine.

Eve lit the fire.

"Shall I put the heating on?" asked Matt.

"If you wish," Eve replied.

Matt got distracted and went up to unpack. Then he rang Ruth up to let her know they were back and to talk about Eve's health.

Andrew answered, "Mother is not here. She is with Auntie Jo in London for a few days."

"I see," replied Matt. They had an informal chit-chat and then said goodbye to one another.

Matt rang Lucy up. "Hi, Lucy, Uncle Matt here. We are home. Any idea where your mum is staying?"

"Haven't a clue, Uncle Matt. She and Auntie Ruth are being very mysterious again."

"OK, it's just to let them know Eve is well. The trip did her good. Come over if you can and stay. She would love to see you," said Matt.

"I'll see what I can do," replied Lucy.

Matt went into the lounge. It was lovely and warm. Matt made a light meal, and then they just relaxed in front of the log fire. Eve was feeling tired from their journey, so Matt helped her upstairs. She retired to her bedroom.

"Shall I put the heating on now and warm your room?" asked Matt.

Eve replied no; she was OK. "And besides," she said, "I never have my radiator on in my bedroom."

Matt went downstairs, poured himself a beer, and sat near the fireside. He was feeling cold. He went to turn the central heating on, and then he carried on with his drink. He had another drink, and by this time, he too was feeling sleepy. He thought it must be the fire.

* * *

The following day, the cleaner arrived. She went into the lounge and saw Matt still in the armchair. She went to wake him and felt instantly that he was dead. Shocked as she was, she went upstairs to Eve's bedroom and knocked on the door. There was no answer. She ventured over to Eve's bed with a sense of dread.

"Mrs Emerson, are you awake?" She repeated, "Mrs Emerson, are you awake?"

Eve stirred and looked at her vacantly. Then she closed her eyes. It was then that the cleaner realised what might have happened and opened Eve's windows and closed her door. She then rang for an ambulance. She opened all the windows and doors downstairs and went outside till the ambulance arrived.

Matt was pronounced dead. Eve was barely breathing, and they rushed her to Nuffield Manor Hospital. One of the paramedics asked the cleaner to stay and wait for the police to arrive.

Eve was rushed into accident and emergency. By this time, she was drifting in and out of consciousness. The doctors took blood tests and gave her oxygen to stabilise her.

Lucy arrived at Eve's about eleven that morning only to find the police there. She went into sheer panic and entered the house. An officer came to her and said, "Can you go outside, miss? I'll be along shortly." Lucy waited anxiously.

Finally, the officer came out to her and asked who she was. Lucy explained that she was their niece.

"Are there any other relatives?" he asked her.

By this time, Lucy was in a panic. "Yes, she has two sisters, but they are in London for a few days, and I'm afraid I cannot get hold of them," Lucy answered. "Can you tell me what's going on?"

The officer was reluctant to give her any answers until a full investigation had been carried out. He was waiting for forensics to arrive. The report had signalled a red alert for the National Crime Agency.

"Your aunt and uncle are in Nuffield Manor Hospital. That's all I know," he said.

Lucy was off like a rocket, tears flowing from her face. She immediately went to Nuffield Hospital.

* * *

Meanwhile, Ruth and Jo took it in turns to watch the hotel. It was on one of these surveillances that Jo realised something fishy was going on here. She went into the hotel and asked for Max. She told the receptionist she couldn't remember the man's last name.

The receptionist was reluctant to divulge any information and asked, "Why do you want to know?"

Jo replied, "Well, me and my friend had a night with him at the Paradise Club, and he left this on the seat when he went to meet up with another guy and left. I think his name was Jed Butler – but not too sure of that last name."

The receptionist whispered, "Room 301 – that is Jed Butler's room. He has permanent residency here. I'll see if he is in."

The receptionist talked on the phone for several minutes and then returned. "You can go up. Third floor."

Jo thanked her profusely and entered the lift with a little apprehension. Ruth had briefed Jo on what to do if she got the chance. She looked for room 301. The door was slightly opened. Jo hesitantly entered.

"It's you! I thought it might be Ruth – but then, Ruth wouldn't have the balls. What do you want?" Jed said in a threatening voice.

Jo said, "I was inquisitive to know if Max was really Jed Butler."

"Well, aren't you the clever little irritation," he said with a wry smile on his face. "What shall I do with you now? You know you won't leave here alive, don't you? And I suppose Ruth is in the background somewhere."

"How do you know it is Ruth who's with me and not Eve?"

"Because your snooping sister Eve and her husband are dead!" Jed took great delight in telling Jo this.

Jo reeled from the news, but she kept to her plan. "Well, at least let's have a drink, if it's going to be my last. I haven't had a drink for years since the accident."

Jed said to Jo, "I know all about your accident. You don't think it was accidental, do you? It was planned by Charlie Winters. He wanted to shut the Ashursts up once and for all, as Elizabeth was about to blow the whistle on Charlie's involvement with a rape. Oh, and by the way, your father was no innocent bystander."

"Why are you telling me all this?" asked Jo.

"Because this will be your last drink."

Jed handed her a whisky. Jo hesitantly took a sip and hoped it wouldn't lead her to drinking again. Suddenly she saw her opportunity, as Jed went into the other room to use the telephone. Jo suspected he might be ringing Peter Winters.

He came back and said, "Drink up, Jo."

"Join me, Jed, in a toast. I've got to hand it to you, Jed," said Jo. "You outfoxed everyone with your charade. Tell me, why portray yourself as Max?"

Jed saw no reason not to tell Jo. After all, she wouldn't live long enough to tell anyone about the organised syndicate that was to run every crime syndicate in the world under one umbrella. It would be known as the New Order. "It was my job to see the gangsters in Soho towed the line, so I pretended to be someone else to protect myself."

"Bottoms up, Jed," said Jo.

Jo waited it seemed an age, and then suddenly Jed slumped. He looked at Jo and said, "Touché." Then he murmured, "You're too late. The new order has already begun."

Jo picked up the whisky glasses and took them with her. She carefully opened the door and then went down the stairs, hoping she would be able to leave without anyone noticing her. As luck would have it, a party of tourists had just arrived, so Jo removed her disguise, stuffed it into her bag, and walked out. As she did, she noticed Peter Winters walking towards the hotel with two other guys.

Jo turned around and walked the other way, catching up with a man she didn't even know and putting her arm around him. He looked startled.

"Oh, I'm so sorry! I thought you were my boyfriend. Please accept my apologies."

The man, to his credit, thought it was amusing. As they turned the corner, Jo again apologised and headed for her hotel.

* * *

"Where the hell have you been?" Ruth yelled.

Jo explained that she would tell Ruth later about what had happened – when they were safe. For now, they needed to get out of London as quickly as possible.

"We'll split up," said Jo. "Meet you at Kings Cross. You book us out of the hotel."

Ruth did exactly what Jo said. She was pleased to be going home. They caught the train to Oxford, and Jo told her sister every single detail.

Ruth was shocked, especially to hear what Jed had said about Eve and Matt. They both switched their mobiles on and looked at one another – the missed calls were numerous.

Jo rang Lucy. "Hi, Lucy. It's Mum."

"Where the hell have you and Auntie Ruth been? All hell has broken loose here. We've been frantic." Lucy told Jo about Auntie Eve and Uncle Max. "It's been horrendous. Why didn't you ring? Auntie Eve is here with me and Ben."

"I'm sorry, Lucy. We couldn't get a signal. We were in Switzerland relaxing in the Alps." That was all Jo could think of. She looked at Ruth, who just nodded in total shock.

As the train rattled along, Jo opened the carriage window and threw the two glasses from Jed's room out. When they reached the station, Jo tossed some clothes into a bin. Ruth kept her clothes to dispose of later.

By the time they reached Lucy's, they were worn out. Jo rang the bell, and Ben answered. He looked at them both and said nothing.

Jo turned to Ruth and said, "We're in for it now." Sure enough, Lucy was most indignant with her mum and Auntie Ruth. They both just sat there quietly and took it.

Finally, Ruth interrupted her. "Lucy, don't you think we would have gotten in touch with you if we could have? We can only apologise profusely, but remember this: Eve is our sister, and we are in shock to hear what's gone on with her and Matt. I think you have said enough on the subject. Now, if you don't mind, we would like to see Eve."

Lucy said, "Second door on the right."

They both trudged upstairs, not knowing what to expect. Eve was sitting in an armchair.

Ruth said, "Hello, Eve. Sorry that we weren't here. We can only apologise and hope you can forgive us. We were on a mission – that's all we can say at the moment."

Eve didn't say a word.

Ruth went over to her and said, "Eve, it's Ruth."

Eve looked at her and started to cry. "Oh, Ruth, it's terrible what happened to me and Matt." Eve started to tell them what went on. Ruth and Jo were shocked.

"But you are all right, Eve? No side effects?" asked Ruth.

Eve replied, "Not as far as I know."

Jo then said, "Can you take another shock, Eve?"

Eve looked at them both and said, "What have you two been up to?"

They set out and told Eve absolutely everything, including nearly bumping into Peter Winters. "We are hoping the police will arrest him under suspicion of Jed's murder."

Eve was upset, hearing about her father. She vaguely remembered her mother telling her something about Charles Winters and his father. She was really shocked to hear about the car accident planned by Charles Winters.

Ruth asked Eve what she planned to do now.

Eve replied, "I am planning a funeral." Jo's eyebrows raised. "Yes, Jo, there will be a funeral. Well, a cremation, to be precise. I have been waiting for you two to show up. I knew you were both up to something."

* * *

The day of the funeral was a sombre one. Lucy was distraught; Ben comforted her. Eve, Jo, and Ruth kept a low profile on the chance that they were being watched. In the background were armed police from the Met, plus a cameraman filming everything. After the service, it was to be family only, with a post-funeral reception at the Old Bank. A plain-clothes policeman came up to Eve and said, "You are doing very well. Keep it up."

Eve gave him a wry smile. Ruth noticed. "Who was that man you have just spoken to?" she asked.

Eve replied, "A work colleague of Matt's."

After the funeral, Eve said goodbye to her sisters. "Keep in touch, Ruth, won't you?" she said. "Don't forget what I told you."

"I won't. I promise," replied Ruth.

Lucy was sobbing. "When I'm ready for visitors, Lucy, you'll be the first to know," Eve told her.

Lucy hugged Eve so tightly she could hardly breathe. Eve then turned to Jo and said, "You get Tommy back here. You've both wasted too much time."

Jo kissed her and said, "If I ever see him again." Jo too had secrets.

Eve set off to settle back in Holland Park. That is where her heart was. With Matt gone, she needed familiar surroundings.

CHAPTER THIRTY-FIVE

Meanwhile, in Texas, Tommy was hedging his bets. He was in constant contact with Mike. As soon as he got the go-ahead to move in for the kill, so to speak, Tommy would drop the bombshell to Becky about what he had found out. Becky was beginning to get restless. Tommy had already been there for well over a month. He said he was finalising his report for CNN. Becky didn't know that Tommy had already filed it.

"Just a few more pages and then it's done," said Tommy.

"About time," said Becky. She was not the most patient person he had ever met.

Tommy rang Mike and said, "I can't string her along any longer. She is getting suspicious."

"We move in tomorrow," said Mike. "I'll text you."

Tommy said, "Till tomorrow, then."

* * *

The next morning, Tommy was up with the larks. He packed all his gear and waited for the signal from Mike. He was on edge. He went outside to light a cigarette, and he could see Becky in the distance taking to someone. They were deep in conversation.

All at once, they made their way to the house. Tommy was definitely feeling on edge by now. Luckily he still had his beard, because he suddenly recognised Peter Winters.

Just then, he got the text from Mike. It simply said, "Now!"

Tommy gave a big sigh and composed himself.

Becky and Peter entered. "This is Michael McCready, the guy I told you about," said Becky.

"Heard a lot about you, McCready," said Peter, looking him straight in the eye.

"What's up?" asked Tommy.

"Oh, nothing. You just remind me of someone from years back," said Peter.

"Have you finished your report now, Michael?" asked Becky. Tommy could see the fear in her eyes.

"I sure have, but before I give it to you, why didn't you tell me, Becky, that it was Peter Winters who had your father killed and that he was in cahoots with Max – or is it Jed?"

Peter said, "Well, you might as well know. You won't be telling anyone."

Tommy said, "It turns out, Becky, that your father was having serious financial difficulties. He borrowed money from the syndicate. When he couldn't keep up with the exorbitant payments, Max was ordered to eliminate him."

Peter added, "My father had also made a promise to eliminate Chuck Grayson for John Kershaw, who wanted Grayson out of the way – something to do with a chap called Ben. So you see, Michael – or should I really call you Tommy Ashurst, like the old days?"

Tommy was taken aback. For once, he didn't know what to say. He was praying Mike was getting all this on tape.

Becky, by this time, was yelling at Peter. "You bastard! I'll kill you for this!"

"Shut up, you spoilt brat. I want to hear what Tommy knows first."

Tommy said, "With pleasure." He started telling Peter what he knew about the multiple deaths that had been going in the States and Europe, mainly small-time crooks, to frighten the big-time crooks into submitting to the organisation's demands.

Peter was agog. "Go on with your fantasy," he told Tommy.

Tommy carried on, "It's no fantasy. You are part of an organisation known as the First Order, or New Order, under the direction of

Chow Ling and Sami Lee in Hong Kong. Your headquarters are in Switzerland. Shall I go on?" asked Tommy.

"No, I think I've heard enough," said Peter.

Becky interrupted and pulled out a gun. "You bastard! It was you who killed my father!" Tears were falling from her face. She was distraught.

Peter waved her away. "I've heard enough of this cock-and-bull story." He also pulled a gun and aimed it at Tommy.

"Do you think killing me will stop the investigation?" said Tommy coolly, but really, he was petrified.

Suddenly, the door burst open. "FBI! Lay down your weapons!"

Becky went to shoot Peter. She aimed, and the gun went off.

Tommy stood there motionless as Becky stumbled to the floor. Peter Winters just smiled at Tommy and then slumped to the floor himself. Becky had been shot in the crossfire and killed. Unknown to Peter, law enforcement officers throughout the States and Europe had coordinated to simultaneously arrest as many suspects as possible who they knew had connections with this new criminal syndicate.

Mike entered.

"You took your bloody time!" said Tommy. "I thought it was curtains for me."

Mike got a call. "Fantastic!" Looking at Tommy, he said, "That was Hong Kong. Chow Ling and Sami Lee have been shot by persons unknown."

"That's a pity; we won't know who the rest are now," said Tommy. Then Tommy asked, "What about the Switzerland connection?"

"No joy there, I'm afraid. The Swiss are being obstructive," replied Mike.

It turned out that Judge Henry Maxwell had taken an overdose, and Dave and Toby Richardson had also been found murdered by person or persons unknown.

Tommy-Two-Fingers was now in a high-security prison along with Jake Johnson. Unknown to the authorities, there were always ways and means to keep in touch with the outside world and get things done – for a price, of course.

* * *

A month later, Michael McCready was indeed given an award for the best investigative journalistic documentary. The Pulitzer Prize was awarded to him. Tommy went up to receive his award, but as he was about to leave the stage, a man came up and shot Tommy at point-blank range. Tommy fell to the ground. The police pounced on the man, and in the confusion that followed, the man was shot. Tommy, in shock, was taken away to a private room.

Mike entered the private room, which was heavily guarded. "It's all set up for you, Tommy."

Tommy removed his bulletproof vest. He turned to Mike, shook his hand, and then looked him straight in the eye and said to him, "It never ends, Mike."

Tommy left for the UK.

* * *

Eve had settled in nicely back at her London home. Ruth visited her as often as she could. Ruth didn't want to raise any suspicion as to why she kept popping to London to Eve's. When Ruth arrived, she would proceed to give Matt a full medical; he had become a paranoid wreck.

The truth was that Matt somehow managed to survive his ordeal, but he was so frightened that only feigning his death and keeping him hidden could give him any peace.

Eve had hoped that living back in London might help him forget, but Matt never ventured out. The trauma of it all was now having an effect on Eve too, which Ruth was very concerned about.

* * *

Jo, of course, was upset about Tommy getting shot. She received a lot of sympathy off her sisters and Lucy. Sometimes Jo felt like a fraud, but it soon passed.

One day, Ruth popped over to see Jo, saying, "I have some good news and bad news. Which do you want first?"

"The bad news," said Jo.

"The bad news is, I'm leaving Cambridge and going to London to be near Eve. I've seen a lovely three-bedroom house. I wondered if you'd fancy coming and living there with me?"

"What is the good news?" Jo asked.

"Olivia is coming back to live in the UK. She has married a teacher, and he has got a job in Bristol, I think. Isn't that wonderful news?" said Ruth.

Jo hesitated. "I can't leave Lucy and the grandchildren, Ruth. Thanks for the lovely offer, but we must do what is best for us all now as we get older."

Ruth was disappointed to hear this, considering what had happened to Tommy, but she understood Jo's position with Lucy and her grandchildren.

"When do you expect to leave?" asked Jo

"After Christmas, I should think." Ruth so much wanted to ask Jo to come and visit Eve with her so Jo could see Matt. Ruth didn't like having secrets, but she had made a promise to Eve never to tell anyone about Matt still being alive. Eve said people would not understand.

Ruth had to accept it was Jo's life, and she had missed so much of Lucy's upbringing that she probably wanted to make up for lost time.

* * *

Tommy finally arrived at Heathrow and made his way to Jo's. He arrived late in the afternoon. Jo was out, so he rang her.

"Hello?" said Jo.

"Where's my hero's welcome?" Tommy asked.

"Is it really you?" Jo screamed. "I'll be home in a jiffy."

Tommy hovered around, lit a cigarette, and waited. He wasn't too happy about being outside. He went around to the garden to sit and wait for her. Suddenly, he heard a car. He went to have a look, and it was two men dressed in black suits. Tommy panicked and hid in the bushes.

The men knocked on the door and tried the handle. The door was locked. They went around the back, checked the garage, looked at one another, and then drove away. It unnerved Tommy. This whole episode had made him a nervous wreck.

Jo arrived, and Tommy shouted, "In the garden."

Jo asked him, "What on earth are you doing in the garden?"

Tommy told her about the two men.

"Oh, those they are my bodyguards. They are from Special Branch. They have been assigned to us – except Lucy, of course. It is something to do with a guy called Mike. It's something he fixed up for us from the States. Anyhow, how do you feel after being dead?" Jo asked. Then she said, "Boy, have I got a story for you, Tommy Ashurst. You'll never believe this. It's straight out of a movie."

They both laughed.

"Not just yet, Jo," said Tommy. "My head is spinning as it is."

* * *

It was a month off Christmas. Eve had the usual invite from Lucy. Of all of them, Eve always thought that Lucy was the caring one. Of course, Eve was delighted to go, and she asked Lucy to set a place for a friend of hers to join them.

Eve rang Ruth and asked, "Have you got your invite from Lucy? I have asked her to set an extra place. I think it's time they knew," said Eve.

"Are you sure, Eve? It may upset them all that they were deceived. I wish you'd wait till after Christmas," said Ruth.

Ruth then told Eve that her daughter would not be arriving till after the new year now. "Her husband has already arrived here to takes up his posting at Bristol Cathedral school in the new year. I have spoken to him once or twice. He seems all right. I have yet to meet him. I am so excited at thought of Olivia being here with us."

Suddenly, Ruth realised how insensitive she was being. "I'm sorry, Eve. Does that sound very selfish of me?"

"Not at all, Ruth," said Eve. "I understand perfectly."

"Anyhow, Eve, I found a lovely three-bedroom mews house. Cost me an arm and a leg, but it is quaint – much larger inside than out, if that makes sense. Hopefully you'll see it yourself soon.

* * *

Jo got a telephone call from Lucy. "You are coming for Christmas, aren't you?"

"Would I miss it, Lucy? But I have an extra guest, if that's OK," said Jo.

"What? Another one? At this rate, you'll all be eating on the floor."

"Why, who else is coming?" asked Jo.

"Auntie Eve is bringing a friend too," replied Lucy.

"Really, Lucy? Eve has always been melodramatic," said Jo.

"Oh, and you're not? So who are you bringing?" said Lucy.

"Wait and see," Jo answered.

Ruth was disappointed about Olivia not arriving for Christmas, but she had to accept it. Andrew had had a girlfriend for years, but it was a funny relationship, thought Ruth. They each had their own apartments and would stay over now and again, but never any mention of marriage.

* * *

Jo told Tommy about the Christmas arrangements. "Do you think they are ready for the shock?"

"They have to be. You can't very well live in a cupboard all your life," said Jo.

A similar conversation was going on at Eve's place.

"Will they be ready to accept me?" asked Matt. "It will be a great shock to them after all this time, Eve."

"They'll get over it, Matt. They'll have to," said Eve.

Later that evening, Eve was in a thoughtful mood. She looked at Matt and said, "I think you may be right, Matt. We should leave it till after Christmas, and invite them to our place. Ruth could come first when she moves into her new place, and then Jo, and then Lucy and Ben and the children."

Matt got fidgety. "I don't know, Eve. I prefer no one knowing. I feel safer that way."

Eve looked at him. She blamed herself for what she had done for the sake of the family name. In her head, she despaired at what it had done to Matt. She wished she could turn the clock back. She had put herself and everyone in danger – including Tommy losing his life. She felt so guilty.

CHAPTER THIRTY-SIX

Christmas arrived. Lucy was her usually bossy self. Ruth had arrived, and they were waiting for Eve and Jo. Ruth was getting restless.

Lucy noticed and said, "They'll be here. Don't worry, Auntie. They might have been delayed."

The doorbell rang, and it was Eve by herself.

"I thought you were bringing someone with you?" said Lucy.

"Yes, I'm sorry, Lucy. That is why I am late. They couldn't make it."

Ben gave Eve a glass of sherry. Ruth went over to sit with Eve and said, "I'm glad you've changed your mind. Two shocks in one day would be just too much."

"Why, what is it?"

Ruth whispered to Eve, "It's about Tommy."

Eve gasped at the news. "Gosh, how is Lucy going to react to that?"

At that moment, Jo and Tommy were standing at the door. "Ready, Tommy?" she asked. "Don't worry. I have already briefed Ruth and Lucy. It's Eve I'm worried about, what with Matt and all."

They entered. Lucy greeted her mother, and Tommy likewise greeted Ben and the children, who were quite grown up now. Ruth greeted Tommy warmly, and then Jo looked at Eve and started to cry.

"I wanted to tell you so many times, Eve, but the FBI planned all this charade to keep Tommy safe. It hurts to think Matt died for us all."

Eve grabbed hold of Jo and said, "Please, it was our choice to do what we did, so no recriminations. Let's just enjoy our Christmas together as a family."

"Did I ever tell you, Auntie Eve, how much I love you?" asked Lucy.

"Quite often, Lucy," said Eve, and tears tricked down her face. "I'm sorry," she said, "the emotion is just too much for me."

Eve had indeed become very emotional now – whether it was her age or all that had gone on, no one quite knew.

Eve walked out the door, and Jo followed her. "Come on, Eve. We didn't mean to upset you. I couldn't very well keep Tommy hidden forever, could I?"

After all the tension and emotion had subsided, it turned out to be a smashing Christmas Day. Eve was staying with Lucy along with Ruth for a couple of days. They arranged to see Jo and Tommy after Boxing Day. The evening was cordial, and then Lucy said she was off to bed.

Eve said immediately, "We'll come up too."

"No need on our account," said Lucy. "Just switch the lights out when you are ready."

Now that they were alone, Ruth asked Eve why she had changed her mind about bringing Matt. Eve explained to Ruth that she and Matt had done a dummy run and gone into their local to have a pint.

"Ruth, it was terrible," said Eve. "Suddenly, Matt went into a trauma. He just couldn't move. He was so paranoid that he was going to be killed. It took me all my time to calm him down. People kept staring at us. I finally managed to get him home. It was then I realised that I had lost him a long time ago. He would never be the same again. I have made a huge decision, Ruth." Eve told Ruth what she had decided.

Ruth just nodded and said it was for the best. Then they both retired upstairs to bed.

* * *

The next morning, Eve was feeling much better. All that pent up feeling she'd had was gone. At least she now knew what she had to do. There was no mention of Matt by anyone. They spent a lovely quiet day with Lucy and her family. Ruth received a call from Andrew to say he was going to pop down with Carol, his girlfriend. Ruth was delighted.

Jo rang to see if they were definitely coming down to see her. Eve said, "Of course we are. Why the urgency, Jo?"

"I just needed to know, that's all," said Jo. "Roast beef OK?"

"It'll be fine, Jo. See you tomorrow."

When it was time to leave, Lucy hugged them and said, "Don't leave it too long next time, or I will be up in London to drag you up here."

They reached Jo's and entered to find a lovely log fire burning. Eve always thought Jo's cottage was inviting.

After dinner, Tommy said, "I have something to show you both which I think will complete the whole picture of the task we undertook. Although I would have loved to have given you all the credit for some of this documentary, I hope you understand that I couldn't. It would have been too dangerous for you. As it was, we had collateral damage with Matt's death and nearly my own. Please watch this, and no questions till after you have watched it. The documentary is a reconstruction of what went on in the investigation.

Tommy had left no stone unturned in the investigation. His report was conclusive in one respect, but this was an account from Tommy's perspective and not the three sisters'.

Eve, Ruth, and Jo were glued to the TV, taking it all in. It did give them the fuller picture. Had they had a crystal ball, none of the sisters would have taken this on, especially Eve, as she was the one who had sacrificed dearly.

When it was over, Eve apologised to her sisters for being so pig-headed. "Knowing what I know now," she said, "I would never had put you all in danger like this. I am utterly sorry for any heartbreak I have caused." She start to cry inconsolably.

Ruth went to comfort her. Jo was shocked, and Tommy too. They both looked at one another.

Ruth gave Eve two tablets to take and said, "Jo, take Eve upstairs to lie down, will you?"

Jo, in total bewilderment, did what Ruth asked.

Tommy looked at Ruth in a quizzing sort of way. He then said, "If I had thought it would have caused so much pain to Eve, I would never have shown you the damned CD. I thought you would be pleased with the outcome of what you all helped me to achieve."

Ruth went over to Tommy and whispered, "It's not the CD, Tommy. I'll explain when Jo gets back."

When Jo returned, Ruth said, "I think you both need an explanation as to why Eve reacted like she did." Ruth carried on telling Jo and Tommy about Matt and what the police suggested they should do. Now, after two years of sheer hell, Eve had decided to put Matt into a private clinic. "He is a manic depressive and won't step out the door unless Eve is with him," said Ruth. "He imagines all sorts of people are out to kill him. He has these delusions. Eve's at her wits' end."

Jo was really upset and asked, "Why didn't she tell me?"

Ruth replied, "She did want to tell you, Jo, but then she heard about Tommy being killed. She thought you had enough on your plate."

Jo said, "All these lies and secrets we have all had. It would had paid us to be truthful with each other. We could have avoided all this and helped Eve in her plight."

Ruth just nodded in agreement.

Tommy poured them all a drink. Ruth was surprised to see Jo having a whisky. Jo said she just had an occasional one now. "Jed Butler told me the car accident was arranged by Charlie Winters – and that he didn't know Elizabeth Ashurst had lent her car to Racheal that night. It was Elizabeth Charles wanted to get rid of. She was becoming a nuisance, and she knew something about a rape that my father was involved with also. All those years of guilt I suffered, blaming myself for letting Racheal drive when I knew she was out of her trolley with the drugs."

Eve came down after a couple of hours and apologised for her outburst.

"No need to explain, Eve. Ruth has told us everything. I'm only sorry you didn't tell me. I could have helped," said Jo.

Tommy made some beef sandwiches. He gave Eve a large sherry and poured them all another drink. Jo said, "I have something else to tell you, Eve, if you are up to it."

Eve just nodded and wondered what was in store for her now.

"Eve," Jo began, "you tell me if you want me to stop, do you hear me? But it will help me to clear the air to get this off my chest. You may not like what you hear, Eve, but it must be said once and for all."

Eve remained motionless and said nothing.

Jo told Eve what Jed had said about her father bring in the thick of it. "He reminded me of the car accident, which was no accident. Upon hearing this, I went ape, Eve. Ruth had given me a tablet to put into Jed's drink, if I or Ruth had the chance. It was really intended to be in a bar rather than the hotel. Anyhow, Eve, I murdered Jed, whose alias was Max, just in case you had forgotten with all that's gone on with Matt."

Eve got up and put her arm around Jo. She said, "Ruth and I have always loved you, Jo. We may not have agreed with your lifestyle, but nevertheless, we loved you dearly and only wanted the best for you."

By this time, it was Jo who was crying. Tommy went out for a smoke. He couldn't cope with all the sisters' emotions.

It was now time to leave. Ruth was driving Eve back to London and staying for a couple of days to help her get Matt into the best clinic they could find. Ruth had done her homework and was well informed on the clinics they were to visit. Ruth had also planned to meet up with Olivia later in Bristol and stay two or three days, which she was looking forward to very much.

When they arrived at the house, it was in complete darkness, which perturbed Eve and Ruth to some extent. They entered with trepidation, and their fears were well-founded. Matt was lying on the floor. Ruth looked at Eve and said, "He is dead, Eve."

Eve was distraught. "This is all too much for me, Ruth. I can't cope any longer." Ruth had to give her another couple of tablets to calm her down. Ruth picked the phone up, but there was no dialling tone. Ruth went to investigate and found that Matt had cut the wires. Ruth immediately drew her own conclusion that Matt had indeed committed suicide.

Ruth was in a dilemma. Should she tell Eve or not? Then she remembered what Jo had said: no more secrets from one another.

Ruth went over to Eve and touched her shoulder. Eve jumped. "Eve I think you should know ..." she began.

Eve looked at Ruth and said no need. "It was suicide, wasn't it?"

Ruth just nodded. Eve got up to ring someone.

"The lines have been cut. You'll have to use your mobile," said Ruth.

Eve went into another room and came back with a notebook. She perused it and then started to dial a number. "Chief Inspector Bradley, please." Eve calmly told the inspector what had happened.

"Be with you as soon as possible," said the inspector. "For what it's worth, Eve, it is for the best. It was what Matt had wanted to do for a long time. He had your interests at heart."

Ruth had made them a coffee. Eve looked at Ruth and explained to her that they could not hold another funeral. This one must be incognito. "Inspector Bradley will see to it for me."

"I see," said Ruth.

"After all, I have already buried Matt, haven't I?" Tears flowed from her face again. Ruth embraced her. *Thank God I brought her home*, Ruth thought.

* * *

After the formalities were over, Eve decided to stay on in the house. Ruth wanted Eve to live with her till she was emotionally stronger, but Eve assured Ruth that she was fine. "I did all my crying three years ago for Matt. There's nothing left now, Ruth."

Ruth rang Olivia up to say she had been delayed, and she stayed with Eve for a couple more weeks. Finally, she left for Bristol.

"Keep in touch, Ruth," said Eve. "Tell me when you are to leave Cambridge and live in the Mews. Promise me."

Ruth said, "I promise."

It was lovely for Ruth to be with Olivia again after all these years. It was as though they had never been parted. They were inseparable, and with Ruth about to become a grandma for the first time, it put another emphasis on her life.

CHAPTER THIRTY-SEVEN

Eve received a phone call from Ruth. "Hi, Eve. I'm calling for two reasons. Olivia's had a little girl, and they are naming her Eve after you. Isn't that wonderful? I hope you'll be OK for the christening. The other thing is – this chap Inspector Jonathan Bradley is trying to get hold of you. I have his number if you have lost the number you have."

Eve replied, "I still have his number, Ruth. Tell Olivia well done, and tell her I'm overjoyed at her baby being called Eve. I will definitely visit her."

Eve was intrigued as to why Inspector Bradley needed to get in touch with her. Eve dialled the number.

"Chief Inspector Jonathan Bradley's office."

"Can I speak to the chief inspector? It is Mrs Eve Emerson."

When the chief inspector came on the line, he said, "Eve, so glad you have rung. I have some good news to tell you."

Eve listened and was flabbergasted by what he had to say.

"I would like you to call into the London office," he concluded. "We don't want any publicity, do we?" the chief inspector said.

Eve said she would let him know soonest. She immediately rang Ruth up and then Jo and asked whether they could meet up with her in London. Jo immediately said yes. Ruth said she would let Eve know as soon as she could.

Jo was delighted and told Tommy. "Apparently, we must keep it under wraps for now," Eve said.

* * *

The news of this lifted Eve's spirits. Even more, it rejuvenated her. Ruth and Jo were as excited as Eve. They still couldn't believe it. They stayed at the Marriot. It had been decided that rather than the three of them showing up at the office, he would meet with them in their room.

"I'll open the door. I know what he looks like," said Eve. The other two just looked at one another as if to say, *She's never got over it.*

"Come in, Inspector," said Eve.

"This is my secretary, Alice," said the inspector. After the niceties were over, the inspector gave them a brief speech and then handed them their certificates. It was the Good Citizens award for helping the police with capturing known criminals. They just stared at one another, speechless.

"I just have one more duty to perform, and then I'll be on my way. Eve, I would like to present this to you. It is the George Cross for Matt's bravery and putting his life in danger in the name of justice." He handed Eve the medal.

Eve broke down in floods of tears again. Her sisters comforted her. The inspector bid them good day and left. Eve looked at her sisters and kept shaking her head.

Finally she said, "Matt didn't die in vain after all."

Eve gradually composed herself. Ruth wanted Eve to go back with Jo and see Lucy and Tommy. "I think it is time for Lucy to know everything that has gone on in the past," said Jo. "We owe her that much at least. She knows we have all been up to something. I have been accosted by her on many occasions."

* * *

It was now nearing Christmas once more. Eve planned to stay with Lucy and Ben in Oxford till after Christmas.

They had a wonderful holiday. The whole family had come to see Auntie Eve. Lucy was stepping over bodies. Ben was amused by it all. Everyone was laughing and joking and catching up on what everyone was doing. Ruth was in her element with baby Eve.

Then, right out of the blue, Lucy said, "Ben and I have an announcement to make."

Everyone just stared at one another.

"We have asked Auntie Eve to live with us, and she has agreed to do so. When the alterations are finished, she will move in with us. Auntie Eve will have her own two-bedded flat downstairs, and we will live upstairs."

Everyone was so pleased that Eve had agreed to live with Lucy and Ben.

Tommy said, "That is the wisest thing you have done."

Jo came up and hugged her, and so did Ruth. They were all relieved that Eve would not be on her own.

After Christmas Day, Jo and Tommy picked Eve up to spend a few days with them. Jo thanked Eve for helping Ben and Lucy out financially with the renovations to the property.

"Who else would I leave my money to?" asked Eve. "You and Ruth certainly don't need it, so it may as well be put to good use now when she needs it. But don't tell her that. I want her to think she has to pay me back."

Jo embraced Eve and then said, "I am so glad you have decided to live with them. I have always known that Lucy sees you as her surrogate mother because you were always there for her in her formative years. You and Ruth have truly been wonderful sisters to me over the years and supported me, even when I was a pain in the neck."

Tommy yelled, "And you still are!" Both sisters laughed.

* * *

New Year's Eve was pandemonium in the Johnson household. Lucy and Ben were striding over bodies – they were everywhere. Matthew and Jane had arrived with their partners unexpectedly. By the time everyone had left, the place was in a tiswas. Eve started to tidy up.

"Leave it, Auntie Eve. Ben and I will do that in the morning."

Ruth was staying with Lucy and Ben, while Olivia and James were staying at a hotel in Oxford. Andrew and his girlfriend,

Carol, had been invited to an all-night New Year's Eve party somewhere near the university, so they weren't expected to be seen for some time.

It was lovely to see Olivia and James. They looked so happy with baby Eve. Also, Eve noticed how deeply Ruth was wrapped up with her family and only now realised how much Ruth must have missed her children coming back to England. It also made Eve realise how much Ruth must have been hurting after Robert's death.

Ruth went over to Eve and said, "Penny for your thoughts, Eve."

The clock started to strike twelve midnight. Everyone counted down the chimes. They all wished each other a happy New Year, each with his or her own expectations. Jo and Tommy were planning a round-the-world trip. Ruth was looking forward to Olivia and James moving nearer to London; James having secured a new posting, they expected to be in situ for Easter. Eve was looking forward to her new granny flat, as she called it, and Ben and Lucy were preparing to start the renovations in the new year. Everything seemed to be on the up.

The sisters decided not to tell Lucy anything of their secret mission to clear the Kershaw name. They did, however, leave her an envelope with the CD in it. It was agreed that whoever was the last to leave, so to speak, would make sure Lucy received it. The sisters hoped they would finally be able to put the past behind them once and for all, and they looked forward to a happy future together.

* * *

Little did they know that the organisation was not dead and buried, as everyone had thought. Indeed, it was thriving. Their names were still in someone's little black book somewhere – you could bet their lives on it. One day, someone would try to eliminate them, if Mother Nature didn't take them first.

The CIA was watching the illuminati activities very closely indeed and monitoring every move, but it was impossible to pinpoint just who was behind this resurrection – or had they been there all the time, lying dormant? No one knew, of course, and so it goes on.

The resurgence of the New Order was worrying for the authorities, but fortunately for the three sisters, there was no mention whatsoever in any of the files on record of their involvement in the last investigation. Only Michael McCready was mentioned as an investigative journalist who liaised with the CIA and an agent called Mike Oldfield. McCready, of course, had been killed.

The head of counter-intelligence in the UK arranged a meeting with the CIA and other agencies throughout Europe to get a clearer picture of their past and present activities. It was agreed by all to monitor and report. In the meantime, a review of the old files would be necessary so they could collate all the information and get a clearer picture.

It took six months or so for that picture to take shape. The CIA reported that in all major cities, there had been a significant rise in homicides within the criminal fraternity, including various premises being torched – gambling joints, sleazy hotels where prostitutes hung out, nightclubs, and strip joints. All were under siege, but no one would say who was behind it.

In France – in fact, across most of Europe – the same problem was evident. The little guys were being squeezed out for the big organisations taking over, with ruthless consequences if they didn't toe the line. Likewise, in America, all major cities were targeted. The UK reported exactly what the others had said, except the authorities in the UK had heard a name being brandished about: the Alpha Trading Company Inc., which was registered in Hong Kong. The owner or front man was a Chinese man called Sami Lee.

There was very little information on Sami Lee or indeed the Trading Company. The only clue was that Sami Lee had once been Chow Ling's right-hand man. He was supposedly killed along with Peter Winters in the US.

It was agreed that a special task force would be formed to try to discover what information they could and to locate this other chap called Tommy-Two-Fingers. He apparently had escaped high-security prison in the States. How he managed that, no one knew. It would be an ongoing operation.

There were so many unanswered questions. Was this Alpha Trading Company the same as the Omega Trading Company? It begins again!

The End

Printed in the United States
By Bookmasters